Gallows Wood

Louisa Scarr studied Psychology at the University of Southampton and has lived in and around the city ever since. She works as a freelance copywriter and editor, and when she's not writing, she can be found pounding the streets in running shoes or swimming in muddy lakes.

LOUISA SCARR

GALLOWS WOOD

CANELOCRIME

First published in the United Kingdom in 2024 by

Canelo
Unit 9, 5th Floor
Cargo Works, 1-2 Hatfields
London SE1 9PG
United Kingdom

Print ISBN 978 1 80436 651 6
Ebook ISBN 978 1 80436 652 3

Cover design by Dan Mogford

Look for more great books at www.canelo.co

Printed and bound in Great Britain by Clays Ltd, Elcograf S.p.A.

1

In memory of my mum, who would have loved this book.

Janet de Lange

January 1951–May 2023

'The two most important days in your life: the day you are born, and the day you find out why.'

Mark Twain, 1835–1910

Prologue

The ground is uneven, her breathing heavy. Her foot catches on a stray root; she nearly falls, but rights herself in time. Keeps running. Her muscles ache. She ignores the niggle in her knee, the tiredness in her thighs. Something drives her on.

The sun is high and beats down hard on her scalp. Her trainers are old, her T-shirt slick with sweat as she counts the thuds of her feet. Her mouth is dry. She longs for water but won't allow herself to stop. Not yet. Another hundred metres, another mile. Then, maybe.

The dog is having no such trouble. He's built for this: strong, muscular legs, infinite energy. He's relentless. Out of the corner of her eye she sees his sharp white teeth, the slick of his saliva. Her hair sticks to her face; she pushes it out of her eyes with a shaking hand.

Out here, she's his rival. A pathetic excuse, one he can beat with ease. As if sensing her failings, the dog slows – giving her a chance to catch her breath – and his attention locks on a point in the distance.

He's spotted something. A rabbit. Peaceful, head raised, ears alert at the sound of their approach. The dog pauses, his mouth closes for a moment in concentration, and then he's off. She feels the tug of her waist belt as he pulls. The rabbit disappears into the foliage in seconds, but the dog carries on, catching another scent. His tail is high, his nose low to the ground as he weaves first one way then the next, gathering each smell and savouring it as he charges down the path.

She sees the water before the dog does. A gently flowing river, sunshine dappling across its surface. He pulls up abruptly, then looks backwards, tongue lolling.

'Okay, okay,' she says. She leans down and unclips her belt from his harness. 'Go on then.'

The dog doesn't need to be told twice. He leaps without hesitation, all feet off the ground until he hits the water with a splash. She laughs – the sound feels strange, but welcome. She envies his complete abandonment as he jumps around, lapping eagerly. He runs out, then back in again, loops of the river, his joy clear. She debates joining him – the cool water is inviting – but holds back. She's more restrained. More anxious. There's a lot she can learn from her dog.

She makes the most of the opportunity to catch her breath and takes pleasure in the view of the countryside around her. Fields of tall grass and buttercups, the footpath they've just trodden winding up the centre. White flowers bloom in the hawthorn, the verge full of golden celandine and vicious nettles. The sky is powder blue and endless, clouds few and far between. She takes a deep lungful of air. The tension fades. It's been months, years since she felt normal.

The dog has had his fill of the river, and after a few final laps, he climbs out and shakes. Droplets of water fly through the air but she makes no attempt to move, the shower a respite rather than a bother. She's filthy from the run, a sprinkle of river water isn't going to make much difference. She calls him to heel and reclips the harness. He gazes up at her, fur soaked, panting. He looks like he's smiling.

'Is that better? Shall we go?'

She checks her watch. Two miles covered, another two back. The dog has had refreshment, but she's still desperate for a drink. She turns and they head for home, the dog once again in front, hauling her forward.

The run home is easier. The promise of water and a sit-down in the garden. The thud of her feet lulls her, the repetitive action, the quiet of the landscape. There's no one else here. She's alone. No expectation. No job. Even her thoughts are silenced by the unrelenting effort of the physical.

She turns into her road, and everything changes in an instant. Shafts of light dazzle off the abrupt yellow and blue of the police car; two officers in black stand in her front garden. They watch as she approaches, their faces devoid of emotion.

She slows to a walk, commands the dog to heel. She opens the gate. The police officer in front is a large man, sweating in the heat. His hand goes to his waist, the other to the radio on his shoulder.

'Lucy Halliday?' the cop says. She nods. 'PC Mumford, Hampshire Police.'

As if she didn't know.

His colleague steps forward. The cuffs are already out, ready to go.

'Place your hands over your head and lace your fingers together.'

She tries to remain calm. She fails. 'Could you tell me what this is about?' she asks, her voice shaking.

The cop starts talking, reciting the familiar caution. The other officer moves behind her and tugs her hands to the base of her back, fastening the metal tight against her skin. She feels sticky sweat on her body; a cold nose nuzzles her leg.

'Moss...' she says.

'We'll take care of your dog.'

The cop looks embarrassed, maybe even sympathetic. But they have their orders. The dog is unclipped; he whines quietly as he's led away. She worries about him – he needs water, he needs his kennel. He needs her.

But the dog will be fine. Moss will be well looked after. She's not so sure about herself. For twelve months Moss has been her comfort. Her safety blanket. Someone to talk to when she can't sleep, reassurance when she feels alone. He's saved her. But there's nothing the dog can do now.

The officer has paused. 'Do you understand?' he asks.

'I… No… I haven't…'

The cop's empathy wanes.

'You know the drill, mate. Don't make this harder than it needs to be. Do you understand?'

She looks up and meets his gaze. She's been in his shoes. Held the handcuffs; read the caution. Arrested more people than she can remember.

But she's never been this side of the fence.

She understands it now. The barely concealed hostility behind the impenetrable stare. No police officer wants to arrest one of their own. He resents being here; he resents her. In his eyes, she's under suspicion, has potentially broken the law. Abused the position of trust they swear to uphold.

She does as she's told. She forgets her aching muscles, her dry mouth. She bows her head.

'Yes, I understand,' she replies.

But nothing could be further from the truth.

Part One

Six Days Earlier

Monday

Chapter One

Beeping slices through her consciousness like a razor. She lifts her head, gropes for her phone. Holds it up to her ear. Mumbles a greeting.

'PC Lucy Halliday? You're needed.'

The woman at the other end relays the information, but Lucy's barely taking it in. Her brain's foggy, body heavy, still enmeshed in the web of sleep. She puts the phone down, then rolls over onto her back and, for the first time, fully opens her eyes.

The world is muted, the sun barely up. She squints at the clock: just gone half-five. No wonder she feels like shit. She must have got three hours' sleep, dropping off after two.

She sighs deeply, then swings her legs out of bed, padding to the shower. The jets provide some relief; she stays there longer than she should, given the urgency of the call. She dresses quickly in yesterday's uniform, licking her finger to wipe at a smudge of something on her trousers. Mud, chocolate? She's not sure. She brushes her hair and ties it back, still wet, in a tight French plait. She pads downstairs in her bare feet. No clean socks here.

She heads out of the kitchen door to the kennel. Inside, the dog looks up from the entrance to his bed box, his dark brown eyes curious.

'I know. Don't blame me.'

He gets up, stretching, his hind legs almost touching the floor, then trots outside to the garden, nails clicking on the concrete. She leaves him to it, boils the kettle, spoons instant coffee into last night's mug. All the others are filthy, piled up in the sink. She sniffs the milk; she'll have it black.

She carries her drink out into the garden and waits, her bare feet growing numb while the dog does his ablutions. She's come to learn the ways of this small black cocker spaniel and knows that these things can't be rushed. The dog sniffs and circles, then finally decides on a place on the thinning grass.

Lucy sips the hot coffee slowly. It's going to be a nice day: still cool, but the sky is clear, the sun starting to cast a dim glow across her tiny lawn. It's no more than a patch of grass. Simple, unloved – and the house is the same. She can't call it home. It's the place she's living in while… While what? What is she waiting for? This is it now. The house full of packing boxes. The job she barely makes it through, hour by hour. The life she lives alone.

The dog ambles up to her and she crouches down, running her hand through his soft black fur. He rests his head against her, looking up beseechingly, but she isn't fooled. It's not love; he wants his breakfast.

She obliges, going inside and pouring kibble into his bowl, then opening the fridge for herself. There's an old crust in a plastic bag, so she puts it in the toaster; once that's done, she gets a pair of socks off the drying rack where they've been for weeks. She puts her shoes on and gathers her bag. The toast pops. She smears it with peanut butter, then holds it in her mouth while she locks up the house and ushers the dog out to the car and into the boot.

The new neighbours are grumpy about having a cop car on the street, even though it's not a proper one, not a patrol car. The unmarked blue Mondeo sits in stark contrast on the driveway alongside her personal vehicle, a rusty VW estate.

Anyone would think they'd be pleased. The best burglar deterrent there is. But no. They regard her with suspicion. This lone woman who never speaks to them, never smiles. Whom they hear up all hours of the night.

She climbs into the front, resting the toast on the dash while she plugs the co-ordinates into the sat nav. She heads out. Five miles west. To Gallows Wood, in the New Forest.

It seems she's not the only one who's been deployed at this time in the morning. She's waved through the outer cordon by a uniform, and stops next to a patrol car and a Ford Focus she recognises. She frowns. If Fran is here, why do they need Moss? She dusts crumbs off her trousers, then gets the dog out of the back, clipping his harness to the lead. She gives Moss her saved toast crusts; he snaffles them in a second then pulls, eager to work.

Together they walk towards the activity. Towards the blue-and-white tape, the crackle of radios, the chatter of conversation. People mill around; it feels like they're waiting. Not for her, surely? She gets barely a cursory glance as she arrives. She spots a familiar face on the far side and heads over.

Dr Francesca Rosetti is head to toe in her white suit, boots on her feet, gloves on hands, although the hood and mask are down as she talks to a colleague. She sees Lucy and waves from her side of the inner cordon.

'I hoped I'd see you,' Fran says with a smile. 'I heard them mention the dog unit.'

Lucy glances around, confused. 'Present and correct and ready to go. Aren't we, Moss?' The dog looks up and gets a rumple of the ears for his efforts. 'But I'm not sure why you need me. You already have a dead body?'

Fran's attention is diverted before she can answer. The noise of the crime scene stills. Conversation halts. Eyes turn as a man makes his way down the path.

He's in a suit and tie. Smart, clean. He looks out of place in the mud and the mulch of the forest, an aberration in a world where everyone is either in protective gear or uniform. There's a man by his side, talking – Lucy recognises the bumbling manner, the half-untucked shirt: DS Harry Blake, a career cop with the Major Crime Investigation Team. The new guy has his head tilted, listening as they stride towards the cordon. His authority is clear.

'Who's this?' Lucy hisses to Fran.

'He's new. Ellis.'

First name or second? Lucy wonders, but before she has a chance to ask, he's standing in front of them. He nods to Fran.

'Thank you for coming, Dr Rosetti.'

'Of course. But there's not much I can tell you. Until PC Halliday here does her job.'

The man looks at Lucy for the first time. He's tall, over six-foot, slim, with deep-set eyes and dark, almost dirty-looking blond hair. He holds out his hand.

'DI Jack Ellis. You're the dog man.' He falters, a tiny slip of the mask. 'Dog handler.' His gaze flickers to the spaniel and back up again.

She shakes his hand. It's warm and soft. 'PC Lucy Halliday. And this is Moss.'

He doesn't acknowledge the dog. Strange. Cops know to ask permission before petting a working dog, but after introductions most look forward to giving the spaniel a bit of fuss. Not Ellis, it seems.

'And you're cadaver-trained?'

'Moss is.' Her attempt at humour falls flat. 'We prefer "victim recovery" nowadays. Better PR.' He says nothing so she points into the woodland. 'I assume you already have a body? I'm not sure what good we'll be.'

Ellis looks beyond her, into the cordon.

'You've photographed it?' he asks Fran. 'Captured the scene?' She nods. 'Bring it here.'

Lucy waits, even more puzzled. Something small is brought their way. Held carefully, in black polythene.

The bag is opened and directed towards them by the technician.

Lucy's mouth falls open. Now she understands. Visible bone, edges splintered, no doubt chewed away. The remaining skin is grey and mottled; the flesh dark red, blood congealed. It's curled in on itself, as if it was an animal, crawling off to die.

Lucy stares at it. She feels Ellis watching her and meets his gaze, no reaction showing on his face.

'All we have is a hand,' he says, his tone dispassionate. 'We need you to find the rest.'

Chapter Two

It's what he's been trained for. What he loves. Ever since he was a year old, Moss has been assessed, rewarded, encouraged, guided. Everything to do this job.

Lucy glances down to the dog. His nose is quivering, looking up at the source of the familiar scent of decayed flesh and blood he's trained to find.

Next to her, DI Ellis is bending down to the hand, scrutinising it carefully. 'What can you tell me so far?' he directs to Fran.

'It's been out here a few days. Judging by the size, adult male, although don't quote me on it.' Fran uses a gloved finger to poke at the jagged edges of the wrist. 'Tooth marks, I'm assuming from a fox or even a domestic cat. Chewed it off, then dragged it away to consume.'

'Found this morning by a dog walker.'

Lucy turns slowly at the familiar voice. Harry Blake is next to her, notebook in hand; she suppresses the urge to step away.

'What time?' Ellis asks.

'Half-four. The dog picked it up and carried it back to the path. Lucky for us, he didn't eat it.'

'That's early for a dog walk.'

'His owner works shifts, down at the docks. We've made him late.'

Ellis nods, suspicion averted. 'So it was originally further in?' He looks past them, into the undergrowth. 'Begin your search there,' he adds, without looking at Lucy. *I'll begin my search where I deem fit*, she thinks, but stays quiet, casting a disbelieving glance to Fran as Ellis walks away without further comment. Fran raises her eyebrows in response.

Blake is still standing next to them. Lucy turns to him with a glare.

'Can I help you?' she snaps when he doesn't move.

'It's nice to see you again,' he says. 'I'm sorry about…'

'Yeah, so am I.'

Lucy's jaw clenches. Her hands grip the dog lead like a vice.

'I was thinking, if you ever fancy—'

'Your boss is waiting,' Fran interrupts, gesturing to Ellis, who's standing at some distance, watching the exchange. Blake scuttles away.

'Wanker,' Fran mutters when he's out of earshot. 'Still got a thing for you, then.'

'I nearly get fired and that arsehole gets promoted,' Lucy growls. She crouches down to the dog, who's sitting patiently by her side. She strokes his head. 'What of it, Moss?' she asks. His ears go up, he stops panting, recognising that the fun is about to start. 'Are you ready?'

All eyes are on Lucy as she and Moss head to the edge of the woodland, to the path where the missing limb was found. Aware of how the smell coming from the dismembered body part might interfere with the search, she moves away from the group, directing Moss into the trees. He strains on his harness, his tail raised, his nose forward. He looks back to her, waiting. She assesses the area – it's open, free from danger, so she unclips his lead. She gives the command, and they go.

He's fast. Lucy keeps as close as she can, directing him, 'Look, look,' but for the most part she lets Moss work. The dog will always be quicker than the human, but the spaniel has more to do. Her purpose is to focus the search, but for now she follows his guidance, letting him roam. They make their way deeper into the forest. The undergrowth is no match for a small spaniel, but Lucy finds herself scratched and tripped, hurrying around bushes and brambles, trying to keep the dog in sight. Occasionally, Moss pauses, sniffing for the scent, and then he's off again, head weaving in search of his quarry.

The radio crackles on her shoulder; she ignores it. She knows they're eager, but the dog needs time. Conditions are right: damp with dew, gentle breeze, long grass. If it's there, if the wind speed and direction is on their side, and if the dog doesn't tire, they'll find it. And if not, she's learned that that's not her fault – and it's certainly not Moss's.

She can feel they're circling back. The noise of the road and the crime scene return in her periphery as they continue through the wood. The brambles have lessened, the ground becoming more hospitable, but Lucy's aware they've been out for a while. Maybe they need to put together a proper plan to methodically comb through the woodland. An open-area search is good for speed – if it works.

She's contemplating turning around, when the dog abruptly stops. His nose goes up, nostrils quivering. Every inch of him is poised. She recognises the signs; he has a scent. Her body tenses in response. But it could be a false positive. Out here, dead animals are common.

She encourages the dog forward. He heads off again, darting this way and that, his body language different, all senses on alert. Until he stops. Absolutely still. His nose pointing to a patch of ground.

She slams the brakes on. He's found something.

Lucy's heart beats hard. This is what they're here for. It's happened a hundred times before, but it never gets any easier.

Lucy takes a step forward. She doesn't want to call it in until she's sure. She bends down and pulls back a branch. A scrap of checked shirt, blue and green. She clears away more leaves – a torso is revealed, and a leg. Tattered jeans, rendered brown from the elements.

She can't tear her eyes away. Moss is still completely motion-less and she signals her praise with a quick, 'Yes!' then pulls a ball on a rope out of her pocket. He snatches it eagerly, chomping happily. He knows his job is done. Someone else's is beginning.

She reaches for the radio on her shoulder.

'X-ray Delta, twenty-nine. Got a find. Need you to come to scene.'

'You have him?'

'Most of him,' she replies, and checks off her co-ordinates, relaying them down the radio.

She's about to call the dog away, when something tugs on the corner of her consciousness. A flicker of recognition. That shirt.

She pauses. She needs to go. Step away now, she shouldn't contaminate the scene further. But this could be it. The answer to the question that's haunted her for years. That ruined her life. Her career.

She takes another step. She moves the foliage away from the body. From the face. His face. It's definitely a man, eaten away by animals, leaving white bone, flaps of skin, features almost unrecognisable.

Almost unrecognisable.

Her heart thumps in her ears. Her breathing quickens. Her vision blurs. And as her muscles turn to mush, the last thing she hears is Fran's voice: 'It's not him, Lucy. It's not him.'

Chapter Three

Detective Inspector Jack Ellis watches the scene from afar, calmly observing the panicked reaction from the dog handler as she's led away, the spaniel at her heels.

He notices a change in focus. Towards him. More than the usual deference to the senior investigating officer at the beginning of a case – this is the stir of curiosity. A whisper of speculation and the hope of gossip. The new guy, brought in at a moment's notice. Jack knows the announcement only went out on Friday, so there was little time for people to google, to find out about him. And what they could discover online would be sparse.

A quick ascent up the ranks. High-profile murders, solved fast. Nothing about his personal life. Nothing about his childhood. How he likes it. They won't dig further; there's nothing to find.

He walks over to the body. The air has stilled; he can smell it now. That mixture of gone-off meat and sour dread. A stirring of the subconscious that makes the hairs prickle at the back of his neck, goosebumps rise on his arms. Even now, after all this time.

He glances to the dog handler; she's loading the spaniel into the boot of her estate, head bent. The pathologist is walking back towards him, white suit in hand.

'She's fine,' Dr Rosetti says when she's next to him. She hands him the coverall; he takes it with a nod of thanks.

'She must have seen hundreds of dead bodies,' Jack mutters.

'She has. It's just… this one.' The pathologist shakes her head. 'You don't need to worry.'

'I'm not,' he replies. 'Shall we?'

He gestures towards the body. He suits up and follows her, treading carefully over the brambles and foliage. He gestures back to his new DS.

'Get this under cordon. Fast. I want this area controlled.'

Blake nods and hurries off, eager to please.

Rosetti has crouched next to the body; he joins her, looking over her shoulder. She's staring down into what used to be the man's face while the SOCO snaps photographs, capturing the scene before the corpse is taken away.

'Considerable animal activity, as you'd expect.' She points to his arm, and the missing hand. 'I'll confirm a match when I get to the mortuary, but I can't imagine it came from anyone else.'

'Time of death?'

'Not long ago. Entomology will confirm for sure, but you have larvae here. Rigor's gone, body's flaccid. Temp's cold, we have decolourisation but no putrefaction. First estimate, he's been here more than thirty-six hours, but less than a week.'

'Cause of death?'

'Nothing obvious. Can't tell until I get back.'

'But a category one?'

A death involving a suspected offence. She looks up at him, patronising. 'Yes. Until we know more.' She works her way down the body, checking his pockets. 'Nothing.'

'Damn it.' Identifying the victim was one job Jack could do without. But he doesn't think it'll take long. Despite the deterioration of his appearance, the man looks like someone who would be noticed if they went missing. Someone loved. The shirt and jeans are filthy but in good nick, his hair cut short. Only a few days' worth of stubble. He mentally notes the first course of action: missing persons, hopefully a match from DNA or prints. Notify next of kin. Then work out how he ended up here.

He glances around. Was he killed *in situ*, or somewhere else? Difficult place for a body dump. There's no easy path, no way you could bring a car down. A man like this would be heavy. Jack backs away, retracing his steps. No. This guy would have had to have walked here, at least part of the way, under his own steam.

He turns back to the scene.

'Check his feet,' he barks. Running shoes, hiking boots, trainers — it would give them some indication of the man's purpose. 'What's he got on his feet?'

The doctor turns sharply at his tone, but directs her team's attention accordingly. A SOCO photographs, then clears the leaves and dirt from the lower extremities. Bare feet are revealed, intact from being partially buried.

He watches as Rosetti shifts her position, then appraises the soles of his feet. 'Scratches, abrasions, bruises,' she comments. 'Would have been slow progress across this terrain. Painful.'

Based on the injuries, Jack assumes his shoes were removed prior to walking out here. To what end? So he couldn't run? Nobody would walk barefoot through a forest willingly — unless he was on drugs?

'Do a full tox screen,' he directs back.

He receives another glare from the doctor. 'You do your job, DI Ellis. I'll do mine.'

He takes the hint and leaves Rosetti to it. In the distance he sees a white van arrive. More SOCOs and hopefully an experienced crime scene manager. A pang of loss — at his old place he knew the team, he could trust them to do their jobs. Here there is no such certainty. Until he knows more, he needs to be on it, twenty-four seven. Keeping a watchful eye. He looks at his DS: Harry Blake chats with a uniform at the edge of the cordon, seemingly without a care in the world. He sighs. He doesn't even have a decent second-in-command.

He takes a long breath in. It will come. He's done it many times before; he can do it again. But he knows from experience: he's not going to make any friends in the process.

Chapter Four

The shock when she saw the body, the realisation that it wasn't him. She's still shaking, hours later.

She'd gone home, written up her paperwork from the sofa, the dog sleeping upside-down beside her. Every part of him – from his nose to the tip of his tail – is the perfect pairing of ridiculousness with comfort: hind legs splayed, belly exposed, jowls flapping. If only Lucy could be as relaxed.

Her normal day as a handler is made up of either slow-time taskings or urgent deployments to crime scenes to search for bodies or blood. And around that – driving out on patrol, depending on the intelligence briefings for the area, plus dog care and training. And paperwork. Never forget the paperwork.

She hasn't had any call-outs for the rest of the day, to her relief. Seeing that man there, the upset had been visceral, taking over her whole body. And it's only now, in the quiet of the empty house, that she realises how numb she's been for so long.

Moss hears it before she does. The dog's ears go up and he stands to attention immediately, his paws resting on the edge of the sofa. Then the quiet knock on the door. She pulls herself up and walks through to the hallway, Moss jumping in front of her.

She opens it tentatively. Fran smiles.

'I wanted to check on you.'

'I'm fine.' Lucy welcomes her in and Fran steps over the threshold, bending down to say hello to Moss.

Lucy notices her taking in the packing boxes, the piles of unopened post by the front door. The mess on the kitchen counter from last night. 'Clearly,' Fran comments.

Lucy ignores her sarcasm. She heads to the fridge and takes out a bottle of wine, twisting the cap off and pouring herself a glass. 'Do you want one?'

'You're drinking again?'

'One glass, Fran.'

'As long as it doesn't turn into a bottle.'

'Do you want it or not?'

'I'm driving.' Fran pauses. 'Okay, then. Make it small.'

Lucy reaches into a packing box and takes a glass out, pulling the paper off then dusting it quickly with a tea towel. She fills it halfway and hands it to Fran.

They walk together into the living room. Lucy collapses on the sofa, pulling her feet under her. Moss jumps up, curling his body against her legs.

'Remember when you first got him,' Fran says, joining them.

'No dogs in the house.' Lucy strokes his head affectionately. 'Didn't last long, did it, Moss?'

Moss opens an eye, then goes back to sleep with a grunt.

'What would Sergeant Andrews say?' Fran mocks.

'"Separate entrance to the garden,"' Lucy parrots, doing a good approximation of her skipper's Birmingham accent. '"Police dogs should not go to the kennel via the house. He is not a pet." But he's so soft and fluffy,' she finishes, caressing Moss's silky ears as Fran laughs.

Lucy's always had dogs in her life. Growing up, her family had a trio of rescue mutts and they soon became her loyal companions. She spent all her free time with them, trained them. Instinctive, responding to their cues, soothing their neuroses, helping to cure hers. Those dogs were her friends, when supplies of the human variety were short. When her parents were too wrapped up in their own divorce to worry about their daughter. Life was simple where dogs were concerned. Loyalty was unconditional, love unlimited – important for a loner, a friendless little girl who didn't mind getting muddy and had no interest in dolls or princesses.

Her bond with those mongrels grew a burgeoning desire to work around animals. This was the perfect job for her – not that anyone else thought so. She knew there were grumblings when she was first appointed, sixteen months ago now – there are only so many places in the dog unit and competition is fierce. Many felt she shouldn't have got one of them. But strings were pulled, favours called in. This is a good thing, she was told. At the time, it didn't feel like that.

Moss came to Lucy as a one-year-old. A young spaniel who howled at night, who never slept, hardly did what he was told. He ran laps of the garden, left scars on her arms with his razor-sharp teeth. Houdinied the kennel, chewed everything, had no respect for her. But he grew, and she soon realised that he was smart and learned quickly if she put in the time.

Thirteen weeks of initial training school were followed by another eight with Moss on bodies and blood. Refresher courses to fit around earlies, lates, night shifts. She's earned her place now, and here she is. For better or for worse.

She realises she's been quiet for a while, her fingers buried in his soft fur. She takes reassurance in his warmth and temporary calm, in the small twitches and yelps as he dreams.

Lucy looks across to Fran, her friend waiting for the inevitable question.

'Who is it?' Lucy asks.

'It's not him. Same colour shirt, that's all.'

'I know. But who is it?'

'Unclear. The new DI's on it. I get the feeling it won't take long. He seems to know what he's doing. Bit of a dick, but efficient.'

'What do you know about him?'

Fran shrugs. 'Not much. I asked around and nobody's sure. Came from the Met, most recently. Made a name for himself in Ops doing something in Covert Policing, so the gossip goes.'

'And now he's here. In MCIT. Seems a strange decision.'

Fran grins. 'Bit of a looker, though.'

'If you like that sort of thing.'

'Tall, handsome. Intelligent. Well dressed.'

'Arrogant. Rude.'

'Aren't they all.' Fran pauses. 'And how are you doing?' Fran continues but, before Lucy can reply, she quickly adds: 'And don't say fine, because you're clearly not. Look at this place. How long have you been here? Six months? And all you've unpacked is one wine glass, one plate, one saucepan. And they're dirty in the sink. Have you even cleaned? There's dog hair everywhere.'

Lucy stays quiet. There's no excuse. At least not one Fran will accept.

'You have to stop with the theories. You have to move on.'

'I am moving on. I moved house, didn't I?' She sips her wine. One glass, Lucy tells herself. One.

'Only because the bank made you.'

'I know—'

'He left you, Lucy. He walked out.'

'Christ, Fran. Don't hold back.'

Fran gives her a stern look. 'I'm saying this because I love you. It's been nearly two years. Nico's gone.'

'You never liked him.'

'I didn't say that.'

'You didn't have to.'

Fran sighs. 'When you met him, he was living out of his van. You were looking for stability, and he was the opposite of that. He was always one of those guys who could up and leave at any second.'

'So why did he stick with me?' Lucy challenges. 'Why marry me?'

'Because he loved you. And the wedding was spur of the moment, even you have to admit that. You never had children, because Nico was always putting it off. He was terrified of commitment.' She pauses in the well-worn argument. 'And where's his van? Where's his laptop? You know they've never found them.'

'Stolen. Broken up for parts. Who knows? He left his clothes,' Lucy adds desperately. 'Everything else he owned. His phone. He always...' Her voice trails off. She hardly dares to articulate the thought that has been plaguing her all day. She clears her throat, takes another sip of her wine. 'He always intended to come back.'

She risks a glance at Fran. Her friend's staring at her, her frustration clear. 'We've been over this, Lucy,' she says slowly. 'You can't still think—'

'That he's dead, yes. That someone killed him.'

'But why?'

'He was working on a new investigation, just before he...' Knowing Fran's views, Lucy hardly dares to say it. '...disappeared. He was obsessed, buried in it. It was big.'

'But that doesn't mean—'

'Nothing else makes sense,' Lucy interrupts. 'That dead body. I know that's not him,' she adds quickly. 'But maybe...'

'Maybe, what?'

'How did he die? The John Doe?' Fran shakes her head slowly. 'You must have done the post-mortem? You always do them straight away.'

'I can't tell you. You know that.'

'Please. If you don't give me the details, I'll only go and look it up on the system and get into more trouble.'

Fran sighs. 'Fuck's sake, Lucy. But I haven't told you this, right?'

'Right.'

Fran gets up and fetches her bag from the kitchen. She takes her laptop out then logs onto the Record Management System, pulling up the report. She turns it around to show Lucy.

Lucy studies the photograph – the body laid out on the slab. Naked now, washed, a large gash evident across the skull.

'Blunt force trauma to the head,' Fran begins. 'Multiple abrasions to the feet, ankles and wrists.' She pulls up another shot, dark red bruises clear against the pale mottled skin. 'Suggesting he was bound for a short amount of time, then made to walk barefoot into the woods.' She pauses. Lucy knows she's holding something back.

'He was a big guy. Hard to subdue,' Lucy prompts.

Fran accepts defeat. 'Evidence of opiates in his bloodstream, and injection points on his forearms and groin. I've sent hair away to be analysed, to see how long he's had them in his system.'

'Drugs?'

'Lucy…'

'So he might have been held for a while.'

'Not that long. Stomach was empty but he was well nourished, only mildly dehydrated.'

'But he was restrained?'

'Lucy, this is not related to Nico. Your husband is not locked in a basement somewhere. He's fucked off and is living his best life in the South of France ·or something.'

'I have his passport!'

'He knew people. He got another one. And he's probably under a fake name before you say anything else, because I know you checked that at the time.' The exasperation is clear on Fran's face. 'Let it go, please,' she pleads. 'Finding Nico will not magically make your life better, but this…' Fran gently caresses the dog's head. 'This might. Get on with your life. Make the most of it. Not everyone gets a second chance.'

Fran finishes the last of her wine and sets her glass down on the table. 'I've got to go. Don't do anything stupid. Please?'

'Okay.'

'Promise me?'

'I promise,' Lucy agrees reluctantly.

Fran nods, satisfied, then pulls herself to her feet. Lucy waits, and after the slam of the front door, she gets up and fetches her own laptop. She clicks onto the RMS and enters the same login and password she just watched Fran use. And, unable to stop herself, she starts to read.

Tuesday

Chapter Five

The early start brings grumbles and bleary eyes, but this is murder. Jack can't see the problem.

He's been up since six. Showered, dressed – shirt and tie. He'd watched the birds in the garden out of his kitchen window, mug of tea in hand, enjoying the sight of the starlings dropping seeds to the ground, where fat pigeons waited; the blue tits fluttered with the sparrows. He'd even had time to refill the feeder.

He's been in the incident room since seven. Like the offices in many nicks around the country, it's a mass of paper and mouldy coffee cups, buzzing fluorescent lights and stained cheap carpet tiles. He sees DS Blake and scowls. He fits his surroundings: unshaven, shirt unbuttoned at the neck. The man's a mess.

Jack stands in front of the group. Four in total, including him. Not the level of resource he's used to, but it's early days. He knows nothing about them, these disparate people he needs to mould into a team. Forge trust, understanding, co-operation. Efficiency and hard work. That's what they need to solve a murder. Without that – without *them* – he's nothing.

Behind him, a whiteboard is already covered in his small, neat handwriting, outlining the crime scene, the cause of death – everything they've gathered in the twenty-four hours since the body was found. He waits patiently for the chatter to calm. This is it – the beginning of a murder investigation.

'We have two main priorities,' he says once he has their attention. 'Tracking down who this man was, and finding out everything about these woods and how he got there. Witnesses, CCTV, ANPR. I want a fingertip search of the full hundred-metre radius around that body. I want his shoes. I want to know which way he came in, who was with him.'

A hand goes up. A young woman, dark hair. She smiles.

'Yes, er...'

'DC Amrit Gill, boss.'

She's new. Started the week before him. Inexperienced, but keen – he has to give her that. 'What's your question, Amrit?'

'We're assuming there was someone with him?'

'For the moment. Our victim was hit around the back of the head with a blunt object. Something that caved his skull in so substantially that the pathologist says he would have sustained immediate catastrophic brain injury. So yes, I'm assuming he didn't do that to himself. Have you read the post-mortem report?'

'No, I—'

'Read it.'

Titters of piss-take from the group. The detective next to Amrit nudges her on the arm; she pulls a face back.

'All of you. And on that subject, I want the murder weapon. Dr Rosetti says there's a good chance of comparing it to the remaining mess of his skull, so get on to the SOCOs and make sure they find it. Plus, everything else. Footwear marks, cigarette butts. If it's there, I want it in an evidence bag and catalogued.' He feels the ripple of discontent. 'None of you have worked with me before, so this might come as a shock. I expect nothing but 100 per cent commitment while you work this case. No corners cut. No paperwork or procedure ignored. I expect you to turn up on time, ready to go. Not chatting in the kitchen. Not waiting for your computer to boot up. Ready to go. Dressed well, shirts ironed.' He notices Blake lick a finger and wipe at the coffee stain down his front. 'DS Blake?' The

27

man looks up, his mouth half-open. 'You're on point for ID'ing our vic. Review all outstanding mispers, speak to the Missing Persons Unit at the NCA. I'm assuming you've already been in contact with the mortuary to get his DNA and prints?'

Blake nods. 'No direct match.'

'So, he's not in the system. Let's make sure that doesn't slow us down. You have your lines of inquiry – keep going. I expect you all to hand in your daily progress reports at seventeen hundred hours without fail. And come to me straight away if you get a lead.' He pauses. 'Let's get this done.'

The team slowly move away. Heads down, paper being shuffled – it's hardly a hotbed of motivation. He hears the beginnings of conversations, mutterings of his name.

'And who's in charge of getting that stick out of his arse?' he catches, a barely concealed whisper, followed by a snigger. He doesn't catch the perpetrator, but would put money on it being Blake.

Jack turns back to the board. He straightens his tie, smooths down his shirt. He knows his style is abrupt. But any other manner feels wrong. Like he's pulled on someone else's shoes. Still, it never gets easier, the sting of mockery, the isolation of being on the outside. At least he's in charge, the one calling the shots.

'DI Ellis?'

A voice distracts him and he turns. There's a woman there. In dirty uniform, smudges of mud down her leg. Dark hair with a heavy fringe, dark eyes. A twitch of recognition but for a moment he struggles to place her.

'PC Halliday, boss.'

The dog handler. The one that made such a fuss yesterday. She looks uncomfortable, shifting from foot to foot. She has a file in her hand and looks more of a state today than she did before, if that is even possible.

'How can I help?' he replies.

She points to the board. 'The man. Your victim. Have you identified him?'

'Not yet.'

'He was held captive, yes. Abducted?'

Jack stares at her. He doesn't answer the question. 'I struggle to see what this has to do with you?'

'I don't think he was the only one. I think there are other victims. I've been keeping a file. Other men that have gone missing. That have died.'

She hands him the folder. He opens it cautiously, going through the pages. They're printouts from the local newspaper – some tatty and old, some crisp and new. Men of the same age, similar descriptions. Pertinent phrases have been highlighted with a jagged yellow pen. Drug overdose, family man, odd behaviour. Missing, beloved son, presumed dead. He scans the dates. All over the past few years.

'How long have you been doing this? We have no evidence to suggest these men are connected.'

'For a while.' She moves on quickly, before he can ask his next, obvious, question. *Why?* 'But it's a line of inquiry you're exploring?' she continues. 'He was drugged, he was restrained—'

'How do you know that he was drugged?'

'Was there any evidence on his clothing as to where he may have been held? Have you asked the lab to check for foreign DNA, fibres, trace in his hair—'

'I do not need you to tell me how to run my investigation, PC Halliday.'

His voice is raised, and the room stills, people turning, interested in what's going on. He leans down to the woman.

'Leave. Now.'

Her face has turned pink. She blinks a few times, then points back to the file.

'Please,' she says quietly. 'Just look.'

She turns and leaves, but slowly, confidently. Her shoulders back. Holding on to a last shred of dignity. 'Get to work,' Jack directs to the room, and faces snap back to their screens.

He half-closes the file, when something snags. Like the newspaper articles, it's a printout. He recognises it from the police system – a duplicate of a misper report, a standard form issued by the investigating PC when someone's reported missing. He looks at the name: Nicolas Halliday. Profession: journalist. Reported missing October 2021 by his wife, Lucy Halliday. And her profession: detective inspector. MCIT. Hants Police.

He squints at it for a moment. What the hell? This woman – this scruffy, pale, mess of a woman – used to do his job?

He frowns, then heads out of the incident room. Up the stairs, along the corridor. Following a route he last took for his interview, barely a month ago. He pauses outside, then taps gently on the door of his detective chief inspector's office.

DCI Emily Kane looks up from her desk. She's a smart woman, Jack liked her way of thinking from the moment they met. Her office is decorated with accolades, certificates denoting her extensive training, her achievements. She's older than Jack – by a few years, he'd guess – and wears her hair in its natural grey, twisted up this morning into a bun.

'DI Ellis. Jack. Come in, come in.' She points to the chair in front of her desk, and he sits down. 'How's it going? Sorry I wasn't there to greet you on your first day, but the case came out of nowhere. I trust you're finding your way around?'

'Yes, thank you, ma'am. I'm used to hitting the ground running.'

That's an understatement. But each command has been the same. A chance to make his mark, to prove himself. And move on, before anyone gets too close.

'And the case? I read your initial report last night. It's a murder?'

'Looks that way. We'll have something concrete soon.'

She waves his promise away with a warm smile. 'I have no doubt. How can I help?'

30

He frowns. He fingers the file in his hand, glancing down at it for a moment. 'Is there something I should know? About the person who did this job before me?'

DCI Kane's eyes narrow. 'Plenty of people did this job before you. Do you have someone in mind, Jack?'

She's not stupid. Jack knows hiding something from his DCI is pointless. 'DI Halliday. Now PC. I met her yesterday – she was the dog handler at the scene. Found the body. And now she comes to me with this.'

He hands the file across. She takes it and opens it to the first page, reading it quickly, before closing it and placing her hands flat on the desk.

'She brought this to you today?'

'Just now.'

'I see,' she says. She thinks for a moment. 'DI Ellis, can I trust you to be discreet?'

'Of course.'

She sighs. 'Not that this isn't common knowledge already,' she mutters, almost to herself. She looks back to him. 'Lucy was one of my best DIs. Smart, insightful, diligent. I hoped she would go a long way, maybe even be a successor to my job. But we all have our weaknesses, and Lucy Halliday's husband was hers. There were rumours. That Nico Halliday was getting his information too close to home. Lucy denied it, but there were similarities between the facts Nico knew about certain cases and details he could have only got from the police.'

'She was feeding him information?'

Kane shrugs. 'Unwittingly, or otherwise – we couldn't prove whether he was stealing it. Either way, Professional Standards never had a chance to investigate properly before he went missing. Disappeared, never to be seen again.'

'She said in the misper report that he was abducted.'

'Pah.' She makes a noise of derision, a puff of air. 'Nico was a shit. He left her, pure and simple. I heard rumours that she'd had an affair, that sort of thing, but whatever she did, it was all

31

downhill from there. She was on suspension already, we tried to get occupational health involved. PSD had to intervene.'

'Why wasn't she dismissed?'

'I felt sorry for her. She's not the first woman screwed over by a man. I pulled some strings. Heard there was a vacancy on the dog unit. She'd been turned down at the beginning of her career – I made sure she got it this time.'

'That's—'

'Unusual, yes. For a DI to move to a job of that sort. But there was no way I wanted her frontline on response and patrol. Her mental health was… dubious. This was as good as it was going to get, and she agreed. I thought it would be temporary, but…' She sighs. 'That was nearly eighteen months ago.'

'And now she's interfering in my case.'

'She's obviously got a bee in her bonnet. I'll talk to her—'

'I don't want her—'

'I'll talk to her,' she interrupts sharply. She gives him a hard look. 'I'd have thought you would be more understanding about people's pasts.' She pauses. Looks him right in the eye. 'Given your history, DI *Ellis*.'

His breath hitches in his throat. He swallows. 'Message understood, ma'am.'

She nods with satisfaction. 'I'll need to go out to the press soon,' she says, looking back to her computer. 'Let me know as soon as you have an ID and have informed next of kin.'

He nods and backs out of her office. His heart is beating hard; he wipes his sweaty hands on his trousers. As far as he goes, as much as he runs, someone always finds out.

Someone always knows.

Chapter Six

He hasn't listened. He doesn't fucking care. Lucy drives home, her hands shaking. The way he looked at her. Like she was nothing.

She lets herself into the house, goes outside to the kennel. Moss comes up to her immediately, his entire rear end wagging in time with his tail. She drops to the floor and lets the dog sit in her lap. Curling his body into hers, the same as he's done since he was a puppy. She lowers her face to the top of his head and breathes in his familiar smell.

'You believe me. Don't you, Moss? You'd find him.'

And with those words, she stops, her hand paused, resting in the dog's fur. She gets to her feet and heads through to the stack of packing boxes, Moss following, his ears raised in interest. She pushes them around until she finds the pile she's looking for and opens each in turn. She knows she has one. From the days when she and Nico would go walking in the New Forest, setting off across the network of footpaths, rucksacks on their backs.

Sure enough, here it is. Buried among the cookbooks and the police manuals and the true-crime biographies. A map of the local area.

She stands up and opens it out, spreading it across the dining table. The wood where the body was found lies to the west and takes up nearly the whole of the left-hand side. The size of a small town in the middle of the expanse of the New Forest. Lyndhurst to the west, Brockenhurst and Lymington to the south, her own house in Marchwood to the east; the New Forest is a huge area – covering 219 square miles.

33

But people are habitual. They like patterns and places they know. The killer used Gallows Wood as a dump site once. What's to say they haven't used it before? Lucy knows the crime scene won't stretch that far; nobody will know if she's out there.

She takes a pencil, checks the co-ordinates, then plots where the body was found. She draws a circle around it, guessing at the standard hundred-metre perimeter Ellis would have set up. Then she finds a ruler and divides the rest of the woodland into a grid. Small squares. Each one half a mile across.

She stares at it. It's a lot. But not impossible.

She takes a photograph of the first part of the grid on her phone. She looks down to the dog. He's staring up at her, expectantly. Waiting.

Back to the map. Last chance to do the right thing – to leave Ellis to do his job. To get on with hers. Maybe even make a start on unpacking. Do what Fran said: start over.

But her eyes catch on a photograph left on the side. Her and Nico, at a party, maybe six months before her life imploded. They're drunk, grinning. His dark hair is long and rumpled, his face unshaven. Her arm is around his waist; he's leaning into her, planting a kiss on her cheek. The scratch of his stubble, the taste of beer on his lips. The smell of his skin. As raw and real as if it were yesterday.

They were in love. Despite their problems, despite what she did, they would have sorted it out. He didn't leave her.

She calls her supervising officer, leaves a message, pretends to be ill. She likes Sergeant Andrews; she doesn't enjoy lying to him, but needs must.

She picks up the lead and harness. Grabs her backpack.

The dog wags his tail, hopefully.

'Come on, Moss,' she says. 'Let's go.'

Chapter Seven

While there is no direct match on the database for the DNA of the dead man, it turns out there is a partial. To a serving police officer, at this very nick.

'PC Vincent Carter,' Blake explains as they drive towards his house. 'Career copper, now working in custody.'

Online searches for Carter resulted in a son: a strapping thirty-three-year-old with short, neat hair and a broad, beguiling smile. From what Jack's seen of the man, he looks a likely fit, but there's no sign of him on missing persons, and his father has been turning up for shifts as normal all week.

Jack has left DC Gill back at the nick, requesting David Carter's bank records, contacting his GP. Pulling together a comprehensive profile of the victim. And now they're here. To notify next of kin.

They pull up outside a semi-detached house. Bright foxgloves and marigolds line the flowerbeds but the lawn is overgrown, daisies and dandelions starting to take over. The curtains are shut, even though it's nearly midday.

'Have you done one of these before?' Jack asks Blake, who nods.

'A few.'

'You take the lead. And for crying out loud, straighten your tie.'

Blake puffs out his chest as he gets out of the car and does as he's told, pulling his tie up properly and fastening his top button. Jack's not confident that Blake's experience is as extensive as he's claiming, but he wants to be the observer. Watching to see how this man reacts to the news of his son's death.

Blake rings the bell; they wait. After a moment they hear shuffling footsteps and the door opens. A man stands there in an old dressing gown and slippers. His sparse white hair seems dirty and unkempt, his skin grey – like it would fade to dust should it come into contact with the bright sun outside.

He squints in the unexpected light. His gaze moves from Blake to Jack, and then to the unmarked police car outside his house. Instantly, his face falls.

Blake clears his throat. 'PC Carter, I'm—'

'I know who you are. You're Harry Blake. From MCIT.' Wet, blinking eyes shift to Jack. 'And you're the new guy. Ellis.' He takes a few steps back. 'You'd better come in.'

He knows they're not there for anything good. He moves out of the way so the two detectives can walk through, but before he shuts the door, his gaze shifts and he scans the street outside.

The hallway is dark and smells of fried food. Carter leads them through to the back of the house, to a kitchen displaying more evidence of the man's poor diet. A large frying pan and spatula on the hob, stacks of dirty plates piled up by the sink.

Carter stumbles to the kettle, pushes it under the tap and turns it on.

'You'll be wanting something to drink,' he says. He opens a cupboard and takes out three mugs, pushing a pile of newspapers out of the way and placing them on the counter. But then he pauses. His shoulders collapse in and his back hunches. He puts his head in his hands for a moment.

'PC Carter—'

'Vince, please.' The man turns to face them again. 'Let's get this over with. Why are you here?'

Blake glances nervously to Jack. He's clearly not up to the job and Jack takes over. 'I'm sorry to say we found a body in Gallows Wood yesterday morning,' Jack begins. 'And we believe it's your son, David.'

36

'How did he die?'

There's no disbelief or confusion. None of the shock that Jack would have expected.

'Blunt force trauma to the head. David was murdered.'

The old man wobbles; Blake jumps forward and guides him down into one of the kitchen chairs. He puts his head in his hands and sobs, his shoulders shaking.

'Is there anyone who can be here for you?' Jack asks, softly.

'No, no. David was an only child. His mum died a few years ago. All we had was each other.'

'Were you close?'

The man nods. 'We'd speak a few times a week. That's more than most sons and their fathers.'

The kettle clicks off, and Jack gestures to Blake to make a cup of tea. Blake starts fussing with cupboards and spoons; Jack picks up a chair and positions it close to Vince, sitting down.

'I'm sorry for your loss.'

Vince sniffs. He raises his head and Jack passes him a tissue out of the packet he's brought for this purpose. Vince takes one, dabbing at his eyes and blowing his nose loudly.

'I know this must be impossibly hard, but would you mind answering a few questions?'

'There's nothing I can tell you.'

'Just—'

'I can't help.'

'Any little detail would be useful, if you don't mind. Please.'

Blake places tea in front of the old man. It's in a mug that says *Best Dad Ever!* on the side. Carter eyes it warily; it's unsubtle on Blake's part, but whether deliberate or not, it seems to work. Blake gives him a small encouraging nod and Vince looks back to Jack.

'What do you want to know?'

'When was the last time you saw David?' Jack asks.

'Two, maybe three weeks ago.'

'Did you try and meet up often?'

'As much as we could. David has – had,' he amends with a sniff, 'a busy job. He was a deputy headteacher, at St John's primary in town.'

'And as far as you knew, he'd been going to work?'

'Yes.'

'Has David's school phoned you? It must be rare for a deputy head not to show in the middle of term.'

'You'd have to ask them.'

'Does David have a family, or a significant other?'

'He has a girlfriend.' He frowns, staring at the mug. 'Joanna. I don't know her last name. They've been together about a year. They work at the same school.'

'Has she called you?'

'No. I've only met her once.'

Jack frowns. 'It's just… We don't have any report of David going missing, and we know he'd been gone for at least three days.'

Vince looks up quickly. 'I didn't know. I assumed he was okay. Until you knocked on my door.'

Blake's been standing next to the kitchen counter, and now he interjects, 'But you didn't seem surprised to see us.'

'No, I—' Vincent blinks a few times. 'I saw the reports on the news. And I thought…'

'If you didn't know your son was missing,' Blake continues, 'why would you assume that body was his?'

Jack turns and glares; Blake folds his arms aggressively across his chest.

'Did David ever have any issues with his mental health?' Jack asks quickly, recognising the anger blooming on the old man's face and changing the subject.

'His mental health – what do you mean?' Vince stares at Blake a moment longer, then shifts his gaze back to Jack. 'He didn't kill himself.'

It sounds more like a statement than a question, but Jack answers anyway. 'No, we don't believe he did. But we're looking for an explanation as to why he might have been in that forest. Had he been to Gallows Wood before?'

'Not as far as I know. He didn't kill himself,' the old man repeats.

'Do you have access to David's house?'

'I have a spare key.'

'Would you mind if we went around and had a look? Otherwise, we'll need to break in, and that's the last thing we want to do at a time like this.' Jack's tone is soft and soothing, as if trying to calm a baited animal.

Vincent nods and pulls himself up slowly. He hobbles to a drawer on the far side, giving Blake a wide berth, then opens it and scrabbles inside. After a moment he hands Jack a Yale key with a red fob.

'Please…' he begins. His face falls. 'Try not to make a mess.'

'We'll be careful. I promise. And I'm sorry, but we'll need you to come in and identify the body.'

He nods again. 'I know the drill.'

'Why didn't you report him as missing?' Blake tries again.

'I told you. I didn't know. How could I?'

'Will you give us access to your phone records so we can check your calls?'

'No. I won't.' The man's tone is sharper now, more guarded. 'Listen, do I need my fed rep here? I feel like I'm under suspicion. Do you know what you're doing, lad?' he directs to Jack. 'First you say he killed himself, and now you think I did it?'

'No, no, it's nothing like that.' Jack backtracks quickly. 'We know it wasn't suicide. We're simply trying to get a picture of his life.'

'Well, it wasn't me. Check my shifts at the nick. Probably the easiest alibi ever established. I've been at work all week. Earlies, then on lates both Saturday and Sunday night. You'll see there was no way I killed my son.' His voice breaks at the last word, and he puts his face back into his hands. Jack knows they're not going to get any more from him today. Especially with Blake there.

He gestures to Blake and the two of them go to leave. But Jack pauses in the doorway, glancing back. To the messy room, the man quietly sobbing at his table.

'We'll do everything we can to find out what happened to David,' Jack says. The man looks up, his eyes wet, his face haggard. 'We'll find your son's killer.'

Vince nods, but before he lowers his head back to his hands, another look crosses his face.

Jack frowns, struggling to place it. Because if he didn't know better, if it wasn't so incongruous, he could have sworn he saw fear.

Chapter Eight

Lucy stops, still, in the middle of the woodland. In front of her a deer has paused, its ears high, watching her and Moss. It's so close that Lucy can see the white spotted markings on the brown fur across its back, the quiver of its nostrils as it appraises the dog and the human. And then, in a split second, it's off, leaping high through the brambles, disappearing into the grey haze of the evening.

Lucy wishes she had the same grace. Her hands and legs are covered in scratches, dirt spattered up her trousers and arms. There's a saying in dog handling – if you don't go home covered in mud and bruises you haven't pushed hard enough. She's certainly pushed today.

She glances at her watch, calling Moss and commanding the dog to a sit. Moss waits, panting, turning to watch her as she rests her hands on her knees to get her breath back. It's been hours. And she's covered – what? – almost no ground at all. She's a fool if she thinks she can do this by herself.

The light is fading; shadows take on new meaning now Lucy is out in the woods. Apart from the deer, she is alone. Her only company has been Moss, and an errant terrier who barked frantically before running away at the sound of its owner, their shout faint in the distance. This is the place where someone was murdered. There could be someone out here, ready to kill.

Even before this week, these woods held infamy within police folklore. A place where so-called 'survival training' had taken place, hazing new probationers. Rumours of pranks gone wrong; an ambulance called. It had gone silent since, but the ghosts remain.

She bends down and takes comfort in Moss's warm fur, in that biscuity dog smell. He's damp, having been in and out of a few streams along the way for refreshment. She debates her next move. Her stomach is rumbling; she can't remember the last time she ate. And although Moss shows no signs of flagging, she knows the spaniel must be hungry too.

Her phone rings in her pocket. Nervously, she pulls it out, expecting her boss or even Fran demanding an explanation for her absence. But it's a different number, one she recognises. She answers.

'Lucy, do you have news?'

'No, Cal, I'm sorry. I was phoning to ask you the same question.'

'It's... When I heard your message asking me to call...' There's a long, slow sigh at the other end of the phone. 'I hoped, that's all.'

'You've heard nothing?'

Calvin Watson had been Nico's editor at *The Guardian* since the beginning of his career. Nico had been freelance, and Cal had been his most enthusiastic fan, the two of them talking most weeks, exchanging ideas for articles at all hours of the day. If anyone knew where Nico had gone it would have been Cal, but he'd denied all knowledge from the beginning.

'Listen, Lucy, if I knew anything about Nico's whereabouts I would tell you. And – more importantly – I'd be nagging him to write for me. You knew him better than I did. For Nico to go this long without writing anything – it's unthinkable. Even under a different name... His style was distinctive. I'd have seen.' In the background, Lucy can hear the chime of a train announcement, footsteps as Cal starts walking. 'People talk. Journalists are the biggest bunch of gossips you'll ever meet. And no, nothing.'

Cal's cockney tones start breaking up; Lucy glances at her screen. Signal is patchy out here; she's surprised it rang at all.

'I think he's dead, Cal. A body's shown up – not him,' she adds quickly. 'But this man was restrained, drugged.'

'You think it's related to Nico?'

'You always said you thought he'd got into something he shouldn't have. Before he disappeared, he was obsessed. Working on a new story. Barely eating, barely sleeping. You know what he was like.'

'He'd mentioned he had… new… but…' The line distorts. 'Didn't know…' Lucy waits; Cal comes back for a final moment: 'He didn't tell me. I'm sorry, Lucy. I'm heading down to the Tube, I'll speak to you later—'

And he's gone.

Lucy slowly puts the phone away in her pocket, looking out into the quiet of the woodland. Without her supervision, Moss is lying next to her in a pile of leaves, happily chewing on a stick. She frowns and pulls it off him, hurling it with a sudden explosion of frustration into the trees.

But what was she expecting? She'd mentioned her theory before – that Nico was working on something before he died. Cal's always denied all knowledge of what – but he agrees with her. Adding weight to the nagging voice in her head that tells her that Nico isn't coming home. He isn't in the South of France, not down and gritty and working undercover in central London, but dead and buried, maybe even in this patch of forest, merely five miles away from her house.

She stands up. She stretches out her back, then pushes her hands high up to the sky. Above her the branches are shadows against the darkening blue. There's not long until dark, until it will be impossible to continue.

For so long she's known, deep in her heart, that her husband is dead. A gut feeling. No evidence, no proof, and so she's pushed it down, in the face of disbelievers like Fran that want her to *move on, get over it*. But the body in the woods has jerked her free. Given her the boost she needs.

There's no time to waste. He's out here. Somewhere. She commands the dog to heel and, together, they push on.

43

Chapter Nine

By the time Jack looks up from his desk, the incident room is deserted. Every detective has gone home. He rolls his head one way, then the other; the bones crunch satisfyingly in his neck. He vaguely remembers Blake saying goodbye; DC Amrit Gill sticking her head around the door of his office, telling him her report was in his inbox. He doesn't remember what he said in return.

He's read those reports now, every single word. And they are no closer to finding out what happened to this guy.

Blake had been incandescent after visiting Vincent Carter that morning.

'He's bloody lying. Contradicting himself right, left and centre,' Blake had commented, putting on a pair of aviator sunglasses and climbing into the driving seat. 'Did you hear him? They speak every other day, yet he didn't know anything was wrong. He doesn't report him missing, yet he knows exactly why we're there when we walk up to his door.'

Jack had to agree, even if he hadn't liked Blake's methods. Chewing the poor guy out in his own kitchen. Instead, he diverted Blake towards the victim's house.

'Now?' From the look on Blake's face, Jack could tell he'd been looking forward to a nice sit-down at the nick, maybe a cool Diet Coke and a cake in his future. Jack took perverse satisfaction in shattering his hopes.

'Now,' he concluded.

In David Carter's home, the devastation had been clear. The key had fitted perfectly in the shiny gold Yale lock, in the glossy red front door. As they donned shoe covers and gloves, and pushed into the living room, Jack instantly knew what had happened to their victim.

The coffee table had been turned over; a bottle of wine lay on its side, a stain arching in a foreboding shadow of red across the carpet. A glass was smashed, light catching on the shards as they jabbed viciously to the ceiling. Muddy footprints criss-crossed in a perfect choreography of violence, starting at the door and heading out of Jack's eyeline to the right.

Blake called forensics as Jack peered through. The struggle continued towards the back of the house, chairs ransacked, pictures awry. How do you abduct a six-foot-tall man? Subdue him in the living room of his own home, carry him out the back?

But he hadn't been killed there, just kidnapped. Why? Jack ponders the question now. Why abduct a man, then force him to walk to his death? David Carter had obviously been needed for something, but what?

The forest holds no answers. No CCTV, no ANPR or traffic cameras for miles around. Frequent footfall from dog walkers and families, but not in that area. No witnesses. The lab is quiet, nothing so far on the victim's clothing except mud and dirt. They need direction, they tell him. We can't search every scrap of fabric for foreign DNA. You don't have the budget.

First thing tomorrow, they're meeting with the headteacher at David Carter's primary school. The conversation over the phone with the receptionist had ended at a catch-22 – she wouldn't give any personal details until Jack could verify he was a detective; he didn't want to share anything confidential with someone unknown.

But he had managed to ascertain that 'Joanna' was currently at a teaching conference in Paris and wouldn't be back until later tonight. So she's still in the dark about her boyfriend, a fact Jack's not proud of. He hopes someone doesn't let it slip before he's had a chance to go along tomorrow.

His desk phone rings; he answers it.

'She wants to see you,' a woman says. He knows who she means. He looks back to his screen for one last time, hoping evidence will pop up and solve the case. He clicks his laptop shut with disgust.

He passes Kane's disgruntled PA leaving, bag and coat in hand, as he heads up the stairs. He pauses in the doorway. Kane is talking on the phone but looks up, waving him in with a flick of two fingers. He sits, rucksack at his feet. She puts the phone down without a goodbye then looks at him.

'So, what's your working theory?' she begins, without a greeting.

'I've sent—'

'Not your summary. I've read that. Not that it says anything of help. What am I supposed to tell the baying jackals at the press conference tomorrow?'

'That his name was David Carter and we're investigating his death as suspicious.'

Kane gives him a look. 'And?'

'And can you hold off on the press conference until I've had the chance to notify his girlfriend tomorrow morning?'

'You can tell them yourself. It's about time someone else was in the firing line.'

Jack feels a chill run down his back. 'I have the interview with the school first thing.'

'After that, then.'

'And a murder investigation to run.'

'You won't solve it in that brief half an hour.' She smiles, and Jack gets the impression she's playing with him. A cat taunting a mouse that will soon face certain death. 'Most officers of your rank are desperate to get in the public eye. Why are you so reticent?'

'The press… They don't like me.' It's his Hail Mary, his last chance. *Please don't put me in front of the cameras*, he prays silently.

'What? A young attractive man like yourself?'

'They tend to find me… cold.'

'I can't imagine why.' Kane rolls her eyes. 'Fine. I'll do it. Without you. But you owe me one. Just solve this bloody murder. Before they come after my blood.'

Her eyes tilt back to her computer; he's been dismissed. One day into a murder investigation and already he's feeling the pressure. He picks up his rucksack and quickly heads down to his car, fresh resolve in his mind. They'll interview at the victim's workplace, speak to the girlfriend. Review the detritus they found in the woods, see what's been bagged as evidence. Once they know more about David Carter, maybe something will become clear.

Dusk is settling on the city he now calls home as he leaves the police station. But, curious, instead of heading back for food and bed, he turns his car left towards the New Forest, and the woodland he left barely twenty-four hours before. Streetlights drop away. The roads are dark, quiet.

He drives for half an hour, dropping his speed and obeying the warning signs as he pulls up at the edge of the woodland, tyres crunching on the gravel and mud. He opens the car door and gets out.

The crime scene is on the opposite side of the woods, far away from here. But even so, there won't be many people out now, maybe only a disgruntled scene guard and a few SOCOs doing their last recce of the area. He takes a step, being careful in the dim light. The killer must have known about this place beforehand, but how? Are they a local?

He hasn't seen a single car pass, but now his eyes have adjusted to the darkness, he notices another vehicle on the far side of the road. He makes his way towards it: a dirty old VW estate, with a metal crate in the boot. A dog walker, at this time of night? He squints into the woods. It must be pitch-black in there.

And then a thought occurs to him. He picks up his phone and calls Control.

47

'This is DI Ellis, 3055. I need a PNC check on a licence plate, please.' He reads it out and waits as the operator looks up the information.

'Comes back to a Lucy Halliday, address Marchwood, Southampton.'

He lets out a frustrated sigh. Of course it bloody does. And he knows what she's doing this time of night. He walks back to his car and, climbing in, he resolves that first thing in the morning he'll put a stop to it. Once and for all.

Wednesday

Chapter Ten

Again? Not again, are the first thoughts in Lucy's head that morning. She gropes at her phone, squints at the blank screen. The noise continues; Moss barks from his kennel. It's the doorbell.

She's face down on her bed, on top of the duvet. Her shoes are off, but that's the only concession she made when she got home last night. She gave the dog his dinner, waited, eyes half-closed while he did his thing in the garden, then hauled herself up the stairs to bed. Now, she peels herself up, limbs heavy, and stumbles down the stairs. She feels the ache in her legs from yesterday's exertion and opens the door without thinking.

Had she checked, she would have left it shut. Ellis stands in front of her, hands on hips, glaring.

'What the hell were you doing in Gallows Wood last night?'

'What the hell gives you the right to come to my house? Who do you think you are?'

'I am the SIO in charge of this case. And you are getting in my way.'

Lucy tries to shut the door in his face but he puts his foot in the door jamb, stopping her. 'And how did you get my address?' she challenges. 'There are rules against using the PNC for personal use.'

'This isn't personal use,' he growls. 'I'm stopping someone interfering with an active crime scene.'

'I was nowhere near the crime scene.'

49

'You sure as hell weren't there in an official capacity.'

Lucy debates stamping on his foot, then acknowledges she's in enough trouble as it is. She leaves the door ajar, heading towards the back where Moss is waiting, tail wagging. She pushes the kennel door open; he zooms past to see Ellis.

He's followed her into the house, but now he dithers, the dog between him and the kitchen. Lucy notices his hesitation. She finds it interesting and leaves the two in a standoff.

Ellis pauses, staring at the dog, then uses his shoe to move the spaniel out of the way. Moss is unperturbed and transfers his interest to the open door, dashing out to the front garden.

'You're searching. For your husband?'

That jolts her. Nico. She shouldn't have included the misper report in the research she gave him; she knew it was a mistake. She busies herself with the kettle and her one mug, her face flushing with the suspicion that someone has been talking about her.

'Tea? Coffee?' Lucy asks sweetly.

'No. Thank you. How long have you lived here?' He's taking in the mess, the unwashed dishes, the packing boxes. It rankles, but he's not someone she wants to impress. Who gives a shit about his opinion?

'Six months. Why are you here, DI Ellis?'

'You're interfering in an active investigation—'

'I was walking my dog.'

'When you're *ill*?'

She pauses. He's spoken to her sergeant. If he's reported her, she's in deep shit.

She hears him sigh, and she turns. 'I haven't said anything. I know... I know what this job means to you.'

'You do, do you?' She doesn't like his pity. She can't help being rude, despite the hold he has over her.

He takes a quick breath in. 'Leave my investigation alone.'

'Have you even looked into those other men?'

'One of my detectives has, yes. And there's nothing to show they're connected. One died of natural causes. One's even been found, safe and sound. A man with early onset dementia, who went wandering.' Moss comes back in from the garden and renews his interest in Ellis, tail waggling as he jiggles his way around the detective's legs. 'All signs so far show this is a one-off murder.' Moss jumps up happily, placing two perfect muddy dog prints on Ellis's pristine trousers. 'Call your dog away, will you?'

Lucy can't help a small smile of satisfaction. 'Moss, here.' The dog reluctantly comes to a sit as she pours his food into his bowl. 'What about the opiates in the victim? Was he an addict? A well-known drug user? Any links to organised crime?'

Ellis frowns, swiping the mud off his trousers. 'We're still investigating. And no,' he admits. 'But his father's behaving strangely. And he's a cop.'

Lucy's curiosity is piqued. 'Who?'

Ellis hesitates. 'Vincent Carter.'

'I know Vince. Just moved to custody.' Lucy's surprised. 'He's as straight as an arrow. You think he's hiding something?'

'I don't know. But nothing's adding up yet. This guy was a primary school teacher, no record.' Lucy raises an eyebrow. 'And yet he was found dead, alone, in the woodland.'

'Have you spoken to the school? Anyone lodged a complaint?'

'You're thinking an angry parent did him in?' He catches on to her chain of thought. Maybe David Carter was *too* fond of small children. 'That'll be a fun one to ask,' he finishes grimly.

But her thinking has moved on. 'Were there any signs of sexual assault? Or unusual sexual activity?'

'No, why?'

'Woodland's a prime place to go for dodgy activities. Maybe a bit of dogging. He saw someone he shouldn't have? Got caught up in something that had nothing to do with him.'

'With a vein full of brown?'

Lucy shrugs.

'Did your husband use drugs?'

She's surprised at the blunt volte-face. 'Nico? No. Not in the time we were together. He was a heavy drinker – he was a journalist, there's a stereotype for a reason – but never anything more.'

She's not sure why she's being honest with him. Perhaps it's because, for the first time in a while, someone's showing an interest. Perhaps it helps, talking about Nico.

'You're referring to him in the past tense.'

'He's dead, Ellis.'

'How can you be so sure?'

'He would have never—'

'Left you? People leave. Men leave.'

She feels a flash of anger at his scorn. He's not on her side, after all. 'Are you speaking from experience?' she directs back.

He shuts up then. Something's hit home – his gaze goes down, he sucks his lips in.

She turns away from him, back to the kettle and her morning coffee. After a moment, she hears him sigh. 'Keep away. Please.'

'Whatever you say,' she directs to the kettle. And then she adds, her voice full of sarcasm, 'Sir.'

She pauses, waiting for the click of the front door, then looks back to her empty hallway. Ellis – he's different. In some way she can't put her finger on. The DIs she's encountered in the past, especially after her demotion, have been arrogant, almost mocking once they find out her background. But Ellis? He listens. He seems to care.

And yet.

The fact those other missing men have been accounted for is a setback. She was sure they'd be connected. She hears the rev of Ellis's car engine, listens to it disappear down her street. Then she puts the kettle down, abandoning the coffee.

Decision made, she heads upstairs for a shower.

Chapter Eleven

It annoys Jack that Lucy raised theories he should have considered. Especially when she's a copper not exactly operating at the top of her game. She's not looking after herself. The house is a state, smelling of dog and leftover takeaway. It was clear he'd woken her, that she'd slept in her clothes. But her brain – her detective instincts – is still sharp.

He drives his car slowly away from her house, then comes to a stop down the road. He'll give it ten minutes, to be sure.

While he waits, he pulls up Google and types in *Nico Halliday Journalist*. An impressive number of hits come back. Even a Wikipedia page. He scans a few. It's clear Nico Halliday didn't waste his time on puff pieces; each article is long, complicated, well researched – but his style is simple. He's easy to read. An exposé on an MP taking backhanders from an anti-trans group in exchange for votes against policy. A profile of a junior doctor who died, falling asleep at the wheel after a long shift; critical analysis of the state of the NHS.

He clicks to the Wikipedia page and flicks through it. There's a photograph at the top – dark hair, uncombed, shaggy beard. White, creased, linen shirt. Dark eyes and a supercilious smile. Jack knows the type. Studied English at Oxford, became the editor-in-chief of the *Oxford Blue*. Started a Masters in Legal and Political Theory but left halfway through to travel. A smart guy. The list of his publications is extensive, but it's the section on 'Personal life' Jack's interested in. It's short, but to the point.

Halliday married police detective Lucy Holmes in 2019 in Las Vegas after only knowing her for six months. He went missing in October 2021. His current whereabouts are unknown.

Even Wikipedia is circumspect. But the sentence below is more interesting.

Halliday has been a long-time campaigner against the legalisation of cannabis, stating in 2010, 'It's the beginning of a slippery slope. Kids smoke a bit of pot, then they think, "What's next?"' It is widely reported he was treated for a heroin overdose in 2008 but has never openly admitted a drug addiction or spent any time in rehab.[citation needed]

Interesting. Lucy Halliday hadn't lied, as such, but she must have known.

His attention is diverted from his phone as he notices movement outside Halliday's house. The dog at her heels, she steers him towards her battered VW, the one he saw last night. She encourages him into the crate in the back, shutting the boot decisively.

He sighs. She didn't listen. She's going back out there.

But he can't worry about that now. His phone buzzes, a message from DC Gill, chasing his whereabouts. He's late.

–

The school is bright and breezy, with painted handprints on the wall in the shape of a butterfly. A library full of colourful books takes up the majority of the atrium, doors branching off to classrooms all around. Jack can hear the chatter of happy children in the corridors, conjuring up the unmistakable memory of overcooked cabbage, gravel scraping his knees.

The woman on reception is over-caffeinated and eager as they show their IDs. DC Gill had been waiting in the car park when he drove in, anxiously shifting from foot to foot.

'Sorry I messaged you,' she'd mumbled when he'd greeted her. 'I didn't know—'

'You're good,' he'd said, with his best attempt at a friendly smile. She didn't seem reassured. 'Let's go.'

'Mrs Harrison is busy,' the receptionist says now. 'Registration,' she adds, as if this trumps all objections.

'Fetch her, please,' Jack asks, as politely as he can. The school knew they were coming. He's not sure why they're surprised.

The woman picks up a radio and talks into it. A voice comes back, confirming Mrs Harrison is indeed on her way.

'Can I ask what it's concerning?' the receptionist asks.

Jack almost smiles at her unsubtle attempt to get ahead of the gossip.

'As I said last night,' he replies pointedly. 'It's confidential.'

Mrs Harrison arrives quickly, resplendent in a bright red school jumper and PE shorts, an impressive set of sturdy thighs poking out of the bottom. She shows them into her office, and the three of them sit around the table.

She places a notebook in front of her, lays a pen neatly over the top.

'How can I help?' she asks.

'We're here about David Carter,' Jack begins. He gestures to Amrit, poised ready with her MG11 form. 'Do you mind if we take notes?'

Mrs Harrison looks to Amrit and smiles. 'No, of course.'

'Thank you. Were you aware he was missing?'

'Missing? Yes. I suppose so. It was unusual when he didn't turn up last Monday. David's never sick, always diligent at phoning in. He's only ever been off work for a week before this. When his mum died a few years ago.' Her eyes narrow. 'What part of the police did you say you're from?'

'MCIT. Major Crime.'

Mrs Harrison takes a long breath in. 'So… does that mean…?'

'Yes, I'm sorry. David's dead. His body was found on Monday morning.'

'His...' Her hand clamps over her mouth. 'We never thought... I...' Jack waits while she takes a few shuddering breaths in. 'When he didn't turn up for work, we phoned his emergency contact, and he... He said...'

'Who's his emergency contact?' Jack interrupts.

'His dad. I think he's... Yes. He's a copper too. He's done a few career talks for us in the past. But he said that David was off sick and not to worry.'

Jack feels Amrit's stare; he doesn't have to look at his colleague to know what she's thinking.

'Did he give any more detail? What was wrong with David?'

'He said he had a sickness bug and he'd be back as soon as possible. Oh, no,' she gasps. 'Joanna. She doesn't know, does she? She only got back last night. She'll be devastated.'

'That was my next question. We believe she works here?'

'Yes. Miss Travis. His girlfriend. They've been together about a year. They met here. She's...' The headteacher glances through the glass door to the children on the other side, now lining up, ready for assembly. 'She teaches Year 2,' she finishes. 'I'll fetch her. Shall I?'

'Yes. Please.'

Mrs Harrison gets up and leaves, shutting the door behind her.

'He lied,' Amrit hisses. 'He told you he had no idea his son was missing. He definitely knows something.'

'Let's not jump to conclusions.'

'Where else are we jumping? This woman called him. He lied to her, said his son was fine when he wasn't. He was lying dead in—'

Amrit stops abruptly as the door opens and Mrs Harrison walks back in, a pale woman next to her. Joanna is blonde and pretty and wholesome-looking, in the way that many primary-school teachers are.

She sits down. Her big blue eyes are wide. 'What's going on?' she says, glancing from Mrs Harrison to the detectives and back again. 'Is this about David?'

'Jo – he's dead,' the headteacher blurts out.

'What? How?' She looks to Jack for confirmation.

'I'm sorry, Miss Travis—'

'But his dad said—'

'How did he die?' the headteacher interrupts. Next to her, Joanna has started crying, gulping sobs from deep within her chest. DC Gill places her hand gently on her arm and passes her a tissue. Mrs Harrison continues: 'When you said he was dead, I assumed it was because he was ill, but you're from Major Crime. Detectives from MCIT don't investigate natural deaths.'

'No, we don't. David was found in Gallows Wood in the New Forest on Monday. He'd been dead for a few days. We believe he was murdered.'

'Murdered? David?' Joanna looks up, her cheeks streaked with tears, and Mrs Harrison puts her arm around her.

'I'm sorry to ask this, but do either of you know anyone who would want to hurt David?'

'No!' Joanna protests. 'Everyone loved him.' She looks to Mrs Harrison. 'Tell them!'

'Yes, absolutely. David was a lovely man.'

'Had David ever received any complaints?' Jack asks.

Mrs Harrison blinks. 'What sort of complaints?'

'From parents. Or...'

'Not from the kids, no. David was a wonderful teacher.' Her eyes flash with anger. 'Don't you dare start any rumours like that about him.'

'I'm sorry. I had to ask.'

'But if you're talking about the parents. Then maybe, yes.' She pauses, thinking. 'You'll keep this confidential?'

'This is a murder investigation, Mrs Harrison. If we think it's relevant, we'll have to pursue it.'

'Murder. Right.' She pushes her shoulders back, readying herself to talk. 'There was this boy, last year. Adam something.'

'Cross,' Joanna says softly.

'That's right. Adam Cross. And David thought he wasn't...
That he wasn't being looked after properly. He called the parents
in, or tried, and in the end he had to go to Children's Services.
With my full support, of course.'

'I take it the parents weren't pleased.'

'No, they weren't. Confronted David in the car park one
evening, shouting and screaming. Mr Light, that's our PE
teacher, had to come to his aid, managed to resolve the situation.'

'But you didn't call the police? There's nothing on file.'

'No. As I said, everyone calmed down. And David didn't
want to make matters worse for the family.'

'He was so upset. About that whole thing,' Joanna says. 'He
said all he wanted to do was improve things for Adam, but he
probably made his life worse.'

The headteacher takes her hand and squeezes it. She gives
Joanna a sympathetic look, before turning back to Jack. 'They
moved away, not long after that. I don't know what happened
to Adam.' She says the last sentence almost wistfully. Nothing
good, Jack assumes.

'Would you mind sharing the details?' Jack says. 'I'll dispose
of them if we find it's not pertinent to the investigation.'

'Yes, okay. But please know that David only ever wanted
what was best for the kids. They all adored him.' Her hand flies
to her mouth again. 'Oh, the kids. How will we tell them?'

There's a knock on the door: the receptionist behind the
glass, looking in curiously. Mrs Harrison glares, then mutters a
quick, 'Excuse me,' and leaves, shutting the door behind her.

With the headteacher gone, Jack needs to work quickly. The
one question he's desperate to ask.

'Joanna,' he begins. 'Did David ever do drugs?'

'Drugs?' Her face screws up in confusion. 'No, never. He
barely even drank alcohol.'

'What about prescription medication? Any pain relief?'

'No. Why would David need pain relief?'

That's what Jack would like to know, desperately seeking a reason why that amount of opiate would be in his system. How he ended up dead.

'The New Forest...' Joanna's muttering. 'Why was he out there?'

'Can you think of an explanation?'

'No. Not at all.'

'And when did you last see him?'

She blinks. 'At the weekend. The one before last... 28th of May? We had plans for the Monday night, before I left for France, so when he didn't show up for school, I tried his mobile and it was turned off. Mrs Harrison gave me his dad's number – I know she probably shouldn't have, but I begged – and his dad said he was too sick to speak to me.' She's gabbling now, clearly in shock. 'Been vomiting all night, and... and the other.' She pulls a face; Jack can guess what she means. 'I wanted to see him but his dad said that David had told him no. He didn't want me to catch it and that made sense, because David is nice like that, but then he wouldn't even let me speak to him and every time I phoned, he said that he was sleeping and would call me back, but he didn't...'

Joanna stops, her energy run out. 'I can't believe that that's it. That David's gone.' And she dissolves into tears again, her hands over her face, her body slumped on the table.

Mrs Harrison comes back into the room, a beige file in her hand, and Jack concludes the interview. Someone will have to speak to them again but the bereaved can only take so much; he doesn't want to add to their pain. DC Gill diligently gets them to sign the statements, a hastily scrawled account of what they've told them today, and they both do, their faces pale. Mrs Harrison gives Jack the file; he thanks her.

Jack and Amrit depart, but as they go, he glances back through the window into the headteacher's office. The two of them are sat at the table, Mrs Harrison with her arm around Joanna, heads together, both crying.

That's how he always leaves them – the bereaved, the broken-hearted. Weeping, destroyed. Jack knows they're doing the best they can, but it hurts to walk away.

He wishes he could do more.

Chapter Twelve

'Get him in,' Jack shouts down the phone to Blake the moment they're clear of the school. 'I want Vince Carter in an interview room under caution. Arrest him for wasting police time if you have to, but I want to hear what he has to say for himself. Bloody lying to a police officer.' He hangs up and drives the rest of the way to the nick in a fury.

He stomps into the office. He can't face the team like this, so he takes a moment to calm himself, standing in the empty kitchen. He boils the kettle, methodically loads dirty cups into the dishwasher and puts it on. He gets a clean mug out of the cupboard and drops a teabag inside.

'Oh. Boss, I didn't realise…' Amrit stops short behind him, her own mug in her hand. 'I would have offered to make you one, if I knew…'

'No worries,' he says. He takes her mug from her and rinses it in the sink. She stands, stunned, behind him. 'What are you having?'

'Coffee. Milk, one sugar. Ta.'

'Where were you before this, Amrit?' he asks while the kettle finishes.

'Manchester,' she replies.

'And you have family there?'

'No.'

'Here?'

'No.'

He senses her reluctance and ends his line of questioning. Not everyone wants to talk about the personal stuff at work, he understands that perfectly.

'Could you get everyone together, while I do this?' he asks instead.

'Right, yes. Will do.'

He smiles gently to himself at her surprise; she's probably never been made a drink by an inspector before. But it's helped. The methodical act of making tea has given him time to stop, to breathe. Even asking a few questions to the reticent Amrit was beneficial. He needs to maintain control, especially in front of his officers.

By the time he steps out of the kitchen, the team have shifted chairs forward and are sitting in front of the whiteboard. Faces turn expectantly and look on in astonishment as he hands Amrit her mug.

'Anyone else want one?' he asks. They all shake their heads. 'Let's crack on. Where are we?' The team seem reluctant to talk; paper is shuffled awkwardly. 'Come on. Blake, Vincent Carter? When can we interview?'

Blake frowns. 'Two uniforms went to pick him up, straight after you called, but he's gone, boss.'

'Gone?'

'Up and left. They rang the bell, and when they didn't get an answer, they took the door down. But he's disappeared. As has his car.'

Jack takes a slow sip of his tea to quell his annoyance.

'We've put out an all-ports alert,' Blake continues quickly. 'Notified the duty sergeant on response and patrol, as well as putting a red flag on the PNC. He won't get far. Especially as he's skint. They did a quick search while they were there. Went through his post: overdue notices, right, left and centre. And a massive pile of betting slips. That guy was up to his eyeballs in debt.'

'Good.' He turns his attention to the other DC, Phil Lawrence. 'Background on the victim?'

'Nothing of note.' The DC glances down at his notepad, then bites his lip. He's a young guy, lacking in confidence, but diligent, as far as Jack can tell. 'Everything fits the image painted so far of a good bloke. Attentive boyfriend, devoted teacher. Medical records are clear, no mental health incidents that we know of.'

Blake interrupts. 'His Instagram and Facebook are full of picturesque sunsets, wanky photos of dinners. Loving selfies of him and his girlfriend, even a few with his dad.' Blake pulls a face. 'From all appearances, David Carter is not someone you would expect to find full of smack, dead in a forest with his head bashed in.'

Jack blanches at this description. 'Yes, thank you, Blake. Let's show a bit more respect, shall we?'

'Boss,' Amrit interrupts. 'DCI Kane is going live with the press conference.'

They all pause, as she turns her laptop around, and concentrate on the screen. DCI Kane fills the view, upright and professional in front of the lectern. A blue backdrop behind her shows the logo of Hampshire Police; cameras flash; Kane doesn't blink as she waits for the room to calm. She begins.

'In the early hours of Monday morning, a dead body was found in woodland in the New Forest, to the east of Lyndhurst. This body has now been identified as David Carter, a local primary-school deputy headteacher.' A photograph of Carter appears to the right of the screen. Jack recognises it as the one provided by the school that morning – the victim in a blue shirt and smart tie, clean-shaven. Jack's struck by how normal Carter seems. A paragon of respectability.

'Through our investigation we have established that David Carter went missing on Monday the 29th of May. We are asking anyone who might have seen David in the days between Monday the 29th of May and Monday the 5th of June, or who has any information about his death, to come forward to the incident team by calling 101. All information will be treated with the utmost confidence.'

A banner flashes along the bottom of the screen, with the reference number. It will be shared on social media, as well as across all local news sites. They're going to be bombarded with calls, and few will be helpful.

'Was David Carter murdered?' one reporter asks, straight to the point.

'We are treating his death as suspicious.'

'Do you have any suspects in custody?'

'The investigation is ongoing and I cannot discuss possible leads at this time.'

'Do local residents need to be worried? Is someone killing people in the New Forest?'

Kane gives a tight smile. She is confident and calm, clearly experienced at handling the press. 'We have no reason to believe that David Carter's death is any more than a one-off, unfortunate, occurrence.'

'Who is the SIO on this case?'

'A new detective has been recently appointed to the constabulary. DI Jack Ellis.'

Jack feels his face flush.

'And why isn't he here?'

'Because he's heading up a busy investigation.'

'Are you still searching the woods? Could there be other bodies out there?'

'We have no reason to believe that at this time.'

'But are you searching?'

Kane glances behind her and the press officer leaps forward.

'DCI Kane has finished taking questions. Please direct any additional enquiries to the press office.'

The live stream ends, and Jack breathes a sigh of relief. He knows the reporters will be googling his name, but he won't be the focus of their articles. They have what they suspect is a juicy murder; their priority will be to stir the public into a frenzy about dangerous predators, haunted woodlands, murderers on the loose. But if someone comes forward with information, it will be worth it.

Jack gestures to DC Gill and she shuts down the screen. All eyes turn back to Jack.

'You heard the DCI. Now there's even more reason to make some headway.' Jack puts his hands on his head in annoyance and turns to face the board. He doesn't feel like he's got a grip on the investigation yet. The whole thing is messy: too many lines of inquiry and not enough results.

'What are we missing here?' His eyes scan the neat hand-writing. 'We know Carter was abducted. We know he was found murdered in the woods, made to walk there, barefoot. We know he was kept for days beforehand, and for some reason his father lied to conceal the fact he'd gone missing.' He picks up a pen. 'What don't we know?'

'We don't know where he was held,' Amrit says, and he scribbles. 'We don't know by whom.'

'And we don't know why,' Lawrence suggests.

Jack turns and points the pen at him. 'Theories?'

'Drugs?' Blake says.

'But everything points to him being a nice primary school teacher with no history of narcotics,' Amrit counters, and gets a glare from Blake in return.

'People aren't always as they seem,' Blake replies. 'Maybe a primary school teacher's salary didn't pay the rent?'

'Lawrence,' Jack says. 'Where have you got to with his finances?'

'HSBC sent them over first thing. I can't see anything odd. He earned a decent salary – more than us,' he adds with a grin. 'And he lived within his means.'

'Anything back on his phone or laptop?'

'Digital team said there was a bit of porn, but all heterosexual and all a bit vanilla.'

Jack wonders what counts as vanilla nowadays, and Halliday's dogging theory comes into his mind. He explains it to the team; they stare at him open-mouthed.

'Don't you need a car?' Blake comments.

The conversation deteriorates into a debate about the semantics around dogging, until Jack silences them with a wave of his hand.

'Maybe he was in the woods to meet sexual partners,' Lawrence suggests. 'Of the male variety.'

'Shall we ask the girlfriend, boss?'

'No. No,' Jack repeats more firmly. 'No one is to bother the poor woman with this unless we have any evidence to back it up. Besides, we've seen his house. We can assume he was abducted from there.'

'But maybe there's something in that?' Amrit suggests. 'Maybe he's an innocent bystander? At some point he saw something or someone, and they killed him for it?'

'So, what – or who – did he see?' he asks. 'Why remove his shoes and take him to the woods? Why abduct him and keep him for a few days? Why has his father legged it?'

Amrit goes red and falls silent. 'It's a good thought, though,' he adds encouragingly. 'Look into it. Trace his movements in the days before he was abducted. Speak to his girlfriend about that – nothing else,' he stresses. 'And see what you can find.' Jack writes it on the board. *Innocent bystander? Saw something? Drugs? Sex?*

'Boss,' Blake interjects, 'was Lucy Halliday in yesterday? What did she want?'

'It's not important,' he says dismissively.

But Blake ignores his tone. 'Was it to do with those mispers Amrit was working through? Is she still going on about her husband?' Blake takes Jack's silence as confirmation. 'Told you, Phil. We met him once, didn't we?' Lawrence looks sheepish. 'At the Christmas get-together, year before he left. Quite the life and soul of the party. Got wasted.'

'You think he left her?' Jack can't resist asking.

'Absolutely. All this protestation about him being murdered is denial, if you ask me. He buggered off, pure and simple. That type, you could see it. Bit of a dickhead. She was much too good for him...'

Jack senses the conversation disappearing off at a tangent again and interrupts.

'Okay, thank you, Blake. Enough gossiping for now. Let's get back to the investigation in hand.' He leans over and picks the school's beige file off the table. 'Someone needs to follow up on the parents Carter pissed off by reporting them to social services. Any volunteers?'

DC Lawrence sticks his hand in the air and Jack passes the file across.

'What else?' he pushes.

The whole room is silent. Jack sighs. 'Come on. Give me something.'

As if answering his request, the phone on his desk rings. He answers it.

'DI Ellis? I was told to call you.' Jack narrows his eyes, waiting. 'We have another body.'

'Where?' he asks. He waits for the inevitable confirmation.

'In Gallows Wood.'

Chapter Thirteen

Lucy had been ready to give up. The search was impossible, too extensive, too insane to do alone. Moss had been distracted; she was too tired to focus him properly. But then her foot had caught on a tree stump and she'd fallen painfully in the mud. When she pulled herself to a crouch, there was Moss. Frozen, in a perfect indication.

Her first thought was that he had to be wrong. All she could make out was black plastic – a bin liner, maybe someone fly-tipping. But partly buried, and Moss hadn't moved.

Sergeant Andrews's words popped into her mind. She could see his face, his chapped lips, wind-beaten skin as they trained the dogs just over a year ago.

Always, always, trust your dog.

She reached forward, clearing away some of the mud. The black plastic had ripped, bones poked through. Broken skin, rotting flesh. A human foot.

Surprise and jubilation quickly morphed into fear. Until she looked closer – this wasn't Nico. There was nail varnish on the toes, the foot too small. But it was a dead body, another one, and the thought sobered her up fast.

Through her sixteen years in the police force, Lucy has seen countless dead. Old, withered corpses of the elderly, left alone in their frozen homes. Bloodied teenagers, lost in knife fights. Smashed bones on concrete after a jump from height. Over the years something in her had numbed. To remain competent, a police officer can't respond emotionally to every scene.

But in those early days, she always made sure she took a moment. Later. When the statements had been taken, the relatives informed, she'd sit in the quiet and she would remember that person. She'd cry or, as the years progressed, she'd drink. She doesn't do that anymore. There are too many bodies. Too many dead.

On this particular evening, she releases then rewards Moss, calling it in. She sits cross-legged on a pile of dried leaves, Moss in her lap, and she waits, head down, for the inevitable.

The patrol car arrives fast. Lucy watches as the uniformed officer sets up the cordon, wrapping the blue-and-white tape around the nearby trees, then steps outside the perimeter. He regards her in silence. She lowers her head to her dog's, taking reassurance in his silky fur.

She's hungry and tired, but she knows she has a few hours to go yet. There's a statement to be given, Moss to be fed and watered. And – him.

She hears the commotion before she sees him. Barked questions, loud voices. She can make out a few:

'Is this another body, DI Ellis?'

'Is this a serial killer?'

She looks towards the road. In the distance, she can see the large white vans of the press and TV. Ellis comes striding through the woodland, his face like thunder. She pulls herself to her feet in readiness.

'What did I say?' he shouts before he's even close. 'What did I tell you?'

He stops in front of her, breathing heavily. The PC watches with interest.

'I don't know what you mean,' she says quietly. 'I was walking my dog.'

'Walking your—' He stops, his jaw clenches. He leans forward towards her. 'You're kidding me,' he hisses. 'You were walking your dog? That's what you're going with?'

'Yes. And isn't it lucky that a dog, trained to find the scent of a dead body, happened across another?' She looks up into his

69

eyes. 'Especially when the SIO claimed there was no one else out here?'

'I didn't say there definitely wasn't. I said we didn't have any evidence to support it.'

'Well, now there is. I'm assuming a full grid search of the woodland is in order?'

'I should report you.'

She can't take any more. The dam has broken. Two bodies have been found, and with them the hope and dread that she might finally – *finally* – find the truth of what happened to Nico. Her anger flares, a dangerous cocktail, mixed with grief and exhaustion. Everything she's endured over the last few years – the hope, the worry, the sadness she's kept locked up deep inside. It all comes bursting out now.

'How can you be so fucking callous,' she snaps, not caring about insubordination. 'Have you any idea... Any idea at all how it feels when someone's missing? When the person you love above all else has disappeared. That... space. The uncertainty. Not knowing. It eats you. From the inside.'

She angrily wipes her eyes, then watches as he forces himself to take two long, deep breaths.

'I have some idea, yes,' he mumbles, almost to himself, his focus pulled away into the middle distance.

The two of them stand in a silent impasse, until Moss decides enough is enough and leaps up on Ellis, depositing a nice line of mud on his trousers. Ellis makes a noise, halfway between a sigh and a grunt of annoyance, and takes a step back. His gaze shifts to his feet.

'Get out of my sight,' he mutters. 'And take that bloody dog with you.'

'Doesn't someone need to take my—'

'I'll get a DC to do it later. Or write it yourself, I don't care. Go home, Halliday,' he says wearily.

And with that, he turns and walks slowly back to the small group that have been gathering, watching the exchange with interest.

The triumph she felt at finding the body has faded. He should report her, he's right. And if he does, that's it. No more warnings. No more chances.

No more job.

And if she's not a dog handler, Moss will be reassigned.

Her shoulders drop, tiredness threatens. Her body is heavy and worn. She keeps her head down as she walks quickly to her car, desperate to hide the tears that run, unabated, down her face.

But before she leaves, she hears something that makes it worthwhile: someone's taking her seriously. Confirmation she's so desperately wanted, for all this time.

'Blake?' Ellis calls. She imagines him shouting at his DS, the same furious expression on his otherwise handsome face. 'Call PolSA. Set up a full search.'

Chapter Fourteen

A good PolSA, or police search adviser, is key to running a comprehensive investigation in a situation like this. And Jack's been assured that PC Brian Miller is just that guy. Ex-army, ex-dog handler, he has a thick head of grey hair, pushed underneath a blue cap. Heavy black boots, combat trousers and a tight T-shirt complete the ensemble, with an impressive set of biceps usually seen on men half his age. He greets Jack with a firm handshake.

Miller gets straight to the point. 'You've got 381 hectares of dense forest here, including 27 per cent classified as ancient, so we can't go causing too much of a mess. There are a significant number of protected species, plus two watercourses. It's not going to be the easiest.'

He takes a roll of Ordnance Survey map out of a tube and lays it flat on the wobbly table in front of them. For the first time, Jack can see the full extent of the woodland.

'First body was found here. Second, here. Neither was close to any pathways or easy access routes. We've got dogs coming in from TVP, not to mention our own teams. All the Licensed Search Officers the constabulary can spare.' He leans back on his heels, regarding Jack with a smile befitting a man who doesn't have to make the hard calls. 'Where do you want us to start?'

Jack runs his finger over the map, taking in the body dump-sites, the roads around the outside, the footpaths.

'Let's think about this logically,' he says. 'They must have got here somehow, probably by car or van. And they wouldn't have wanted to park anywhere obvious, where they would have been noticed. You've got villages here and here, the A35 not far away.'

He pauses, squinting at the map.

'What's this?' he asks Miller, pointing to a dotted red line.

Miller perches a pair of wire-framed glasses on his nose and bends down to the map. 'Track, leading to a footpath.'

'You've got one of these not far away from both dump sites. And you couldn't walk a drugged man far. Especially one with no shoes.'

'If you say so.'

'Let's start here.' Jack grabs a pen and decisively draws a ring around the area. 'Use these three points as your jump-off – the two main crime scenes, and this new one near the path.'

'We'll run dogs over each part of the grid first, followed by an LSO. Anything else you want us to look for? Apart from the bodies?'

'Shoes, items of clothing. Anything that looks out of place. Syringes, drug paraphernalia. And a murder weapon. Something that could inflict blunt force trauma.'

Miller looks at him in disbelief. 'We're in a forest, boss. We're surrounded by trees.'

'Trees with blood on them, then.' He looks to Miller and returns his grin. 'Good luck.'

–

It seems they need more than luck. Light fades, dogs tire. A ruck kicks off in the middle of Southampton and they need the teams redeployed. To where they can actually make a difference.

Earlier, Dr Rosetti had arrived to appraise the body. She'd called Jack over to where a rectangle had been marked out, where the undergrowth had been cleared away and initial excavations had begun.

The first layer of mud had been removed, revealing skin like hide, coated with mud. Almost unrecognisable if it hadn't been for the distinctive human form, curled on its side.

'White female,' Rosetti had confirmed. 'Judging from the state of the decomp, she's been here at least a few months.'

'Same COD?'

The doctor's face was grim. 'I can't confirm for sure until we uncover a bit more of her, but the same hallmarks are there.' She pointed to the victim's bare feet, then to a large abrasion running across her forehead. 'Blunt force trauma. Buried naked in the left lateral position, wrapped lightly in plastic bin liners. No deeper than thirty centimetres from the surface. We'll get her out tonight. I'll do the PM tomorrow. Send someone along first thing.'

The heat of the day has receded, and now Jack shivers in his shirt and jacket, wishing for his standard-issue thick Arktis police coat. He stares out into the darkness. A central hub has been set up – tables and floodlights and gazebos. The large map has been pinned to a free-standing board and Jack looks at it now, taking in the details. The areas searched, potential evidence recovered and the space still to go. It looks like an insurmountable task, and seeing it makes him think about Lucy Halliday. She was attempting to do this by herself. Just her and that dog. What chance had she had of finding someone? Had it been luck? Skill? Or something else?

'It's early days, boss,' Miller says, coming up behind him. He picks up a pen, but Jack's hopes are dashed as he puts a big red cross through one of the squares on the grid. 'We'll find something.'

'Do you usually?' Jack asks.

'No.' Miller smiles sympathetically. 'But at least once we've finished, we know for sure.' He gives Jack's arm a friendly punch. 'We're closing up for the night. Back here, zero six hundred hours.'

Jack nods but stays motionless at the board. He hears the barking of the dogs as they're led away; watches the team packing up, keen to get back to their homes. Proximity to death reminding them how lucky they are.

A few unfortunate uniforms will stay out here all night, guarding the scene until the area is released. Because the budget has been spent, the assumption has been made. There are more bodies out there. But how many? It's a hideous thought.

Jack turns away. He needs to get some sleep. Because one thing is clear – there will be no resolution on these murders anytime soon.

Daisy had been sleeping. So deeply that the line between nightmare and waking was blurred. Shadowy figures in her room, rough hands on her arms. Scratchy dark material over her head, muffling sound and turning her own hot breath back onto her face. Darkness. Black. Nothing.

Cold air hits her skin as she is pulled from her bed. Propelled forward, her bare feet hardly touching the ground. Her hands are tugged together, secured tightly in front. Carpet to tiles to concrete. Her toes scuff painfully on the gravel and she cries out. The first noise she's made. Pointless. Nobody comes. Into a car – prostrate on a back seat. Engine noise; gruff, male voices; she is thrown left and right as they take corners at speed, causing her stomach acid to rise.

She hasn't had time to think but now she panics. These people – these men – what do they want with her? She's nineteen, a student. She's done nothing wrong. The car stops; doors open. She is tugged painfully upright then out. She stumbles on wobbly legs; fingers pinch her arms. Grass, glass, gravel underfoot. Her bare feet sting, cut, and she collapses, her legs refusing to go any further. Words are spat, in a language she doesn't understand, and she is lifted off the ground, thrown painfully over a shoulder – nothing more than cargo.

Sound is now dulled, accompanied by an echo. They are inside. Heavy boots on floorboards; she is dumped onto splintered wood. A door closes, a key in the lock.

Daisy has no sense of light and dark, no gradation in the black. Only the cold and the fear, the pain in her shoulders and wrists from her tightly bound hands. She tries to gather her thoughts, work out what she knows, but all she can think is: Why didn't I do more to stop them? Shout, scream, kick, bite? *But it all happened so fast. She was frozen.*

A slamming door jerks her to attention. Shouts, angered words. She cranes her head to listen through the hood.

Two voices, heavily accented. But a tone she recognises – a lighter lilt. Scottish, maybe. Who? They are both shouting. Words overlapping, garbled threats she can't make out.

Do they know she's here?

She has to get away.

Throughout the entire abduction – because that's what this is, isn't it? – she has hardly uttered a squeak. Too stunned. Frozen by the utterly unthinkable. But now she takes a deep gulp of air and starts to scream. Help, *at first.* Please someone help me. *Evolving to a high-pitched shriek as an avalanche of panic eclipses all logical thought.*

Thumping footsteps head towards her. The door opens with force, a loud bang as it hits the wall on the other side.

She jerks her head around, trying to pinpoint the sound. A person, breathing. Where? She listens from inside her hood but can't hear anything except her own frantic heartbeat. She can't see, needs to see. Then the hood is pulled from her head.

A sudden injection of light. She winces, blinking, gasps a lungful of clear, clean oxygen. She's in a windowless room, light blazing in from the door. She starts to shake – fear, panic, helplessness. Vomit-inducing tremors she can't control.

A silhouette fills the entire doorway; he advances towards her. He is broad, with a shaved head and a full beard. She can smell him now. Remembers him from before. Sour sweat, strong aftershave, spicy food.

'You, be quiet,' *he says.* 'No point in screaming.'

'I want to go home,' *she sobs.*

He laughs. 'Soon. Soon it will be over.'

She's confused. But what he says next doesn't leave any room for doubt. 'If you good, we make your death quick.'

'Please—' *she starts.*

But that's as far as she gets. A meaty hand grabs her T-shirt, a rip of fabric as he slams his fist into her face. Her nose explodes in a white-hot blast of pain. Blood suffocates, drips down her throat, fills her mouth.

She gags, spits, and her eyes stream with tears as she slumps in a pool of her own gore.

'You quiet now,' he says.

And the door slams.

Thursday

Chapter Fifteen

Lucy feels something wet and cold in her ear; it moves to caressing her cheek. She opens her eyes, forcing her blurry vision to focus on the sight of Moss's black nose. He steps back, his dark brown eyes watching her. Eager and playful.

She pulls herself up, glances at the clock. It's been twelve hours since she got home, had a long, hot bath, then put herself to bed. Too tired to even lock Moss away properly. She's slept like the dead – a bad analogy, given what she found yesterday.

She picks up her phone, checks the news. But there have been no developments since last night, when it seemed every newspaper in the country reported the new find. Speculation abounds; a press release must be imminent.

But more importantly, nobody has been in touch with her.

While she's been distracted, the dog has taken the opportunity to jump onto the bed. He turns in a quick circle, then settles himself in the middle of the duvet. He half-opens an eye as if to say, *And?*

'Do you want your breakfast, or not?' she challenges. His ears lift, in anticipation. 'Come on, then.'

There is no competition: he jumps off, heading down the stairs to the kitchen, glancing behind him to make sure Lucy is following. She is warier on the stairs, her muscles aching from the day before.

She gives the dog his food, then opens the kitchen door. For a moment she stands there, savouring the sunshine of another beautiful June day.

She makes a cup of coffee and sits on the edge of her patio. A residue of hope lingers. A misplaced faith that she might hear a taxi pull up outside. A message left on her voicemail. Something to show that her husband's alive.

And what would she do if he walked in that door today? Would she greet him with open arms? Or would she shout, tell him to fuck off? Probably the latter, she acknowledges ruefully, but at least she could do *something*. The stillness, the silence, is worse.

Ever since she found the body yesterday, her emotions have leaped around like a spaniel on speed. She'd been right to search. She was redeemed. They're looking now. They'll find him.

But what if they do? She'll be sure: he's dead. But with the relief at that certainty comes the other – that she'll never hear his voice again. Despite this having been her theory from the beginning, it's impossible to reconcile herself to the reality that he will be gone. No more bone-crushing hugs. No more laughter, or the muttering as he worked, the clatter of his keyboard lulling her to sleep late at night.

But at least she'll know.

She hears her mobile ring from inside the house, and she jumps to her feet, cursing herself for leaving it unattended at such a time. But the panic is quickly replaced by dread as she sees the number. She answers it.

'Halliday? You're up, then?'

'Yes, Sarge,' she says, not even bothering to inject an ounce of fake-illness into her voice. Ellis would have reported her by now. This is the invitation to the disciplinary meeting, the formality before her inevitable dismissal.

'Good. Luckily, things are under control, what with that kerfuffle out in the woods, but I need you at the show tomorrow.'

'Sorry, Sarge?'

'The New Forest County Show? Down near Brockenhurst. You're needed, tomorrow, midday.' There's a long pause, Lucy struggling to keep up. Her sergeant sighs. 'Police dog demo. We have Dax on the attack but we need a scent dog. Charlie was going to go, but as you're not allowed in the woods because...' He clears his throat awkwardly. 'Because your husband might be... you know...'

Halliday blinks. Ellis hasn't reported her? She's not—

'Midday. Be there,' her sergeant concludes and hangs up.

She slowly places her phone down on the kitchen table. Moss sits at her feet, looking up, confused.

'You and me both, mate.'

She's in no rush to go to the county show; she's not great at playing nice with members of the public. But she won't complain. She'll do it. Because, somehow, she still has a job. Ellis has kept his mouth shut.

Maybe he's not such a bad guy, after all.

Chapter Sixteen

Normally, Jack would send a DC to observe a post-mortem, but he wants to see close up what happened to this woman. There might be a moment of revelation that he wouldn't get second-hand – maybe then they could make some bloody progress.

He's read all the latest updates from his team; in the woods the search continues. Vincent Carter is still missing, although a cash withdrawal – confirmed by camera footage – from a bank last night in Nottingham shows that he is, at least, alive. DC Gill can't find any dirt on David Carter.

They are completely in the dark.

The body in front of Jack doesn't feel particularly inspiring. Cleared of mud and muck, the woman is laid out on her back, looking more like an Egyptian mummy than a recent murder victim. Her skin is dry and desiccated, shrunk back against bone. Her hair is starting to come away from the scalp. Her mouth is open in a silent scream.

Dr Rosetti has been working for a few hours, Jack quietly watching from the viewing platform at the back of the mortuary. Rosetti takes the protective glasses off and steps away from the body. She gestures for Jack to join her – he pulls a white suit on and does as he's told.

'What do you notice about this woman?'

He's seen more post-mortems in his time than he'd like, but this one's been marginally more pleasant than most.

'She doesn't smell. Only slightly.'

Rosetti nods. 'That ammonia odour – that's the adipocere. This hard brittle shell of fat. Despite the amount of time this body's been in the ground, it's only just reached the primary bloat phase. Barely decomposed. She's relatively well preserved: most of the organs intact and good structural retention of the muscles.'

'Which means?'

'Unlike victim one, this woman wasn't killed in the woods. To get a level of decomp like this, for slight adipocere to form and for desiccation of this sort, she must have been left in a dry, closed room. Somewhere cool, with good airflow. But not for long, as there was little entomological evidence.' She smiles, grimly. 'And we both know how quickly a fly can find a dead body.'

Jack nods. 'An attic or a cupboard?'

'That would work. Concealment favours desiccation. Although without knowing more, it's hard to say how long she was left there before she was buried. An entire body can dry out like this in a matter of days. We've had a relatively mild and dry winter and spring, so that would have helped the adipocere to form and slow the decomposition. The dense woodland where she was buried would have protected the body against temperature fluctuations and direct sun exposure. My guess is somewhere between three to eight months.' She catches Jack's frown. 'Sorry. But I can tell you that the other similarities are present. Ligature marks on both ankles and wrists—' She points to the areas of discolouration, visible even against the dark leathery skin. 'And these marks here, on the anterior aspect of the forearm, would correspond with injection sites.'

'She was drugged?'

'I'm afraid we're too far away from time of death to give any sort of accuracy on her tissues, but I'll submit her hair for testing and we'll get confirmation that way. I've also taken DNA samples, so you should know if an ID pops up soon. And if it doesn't...'

Fran moves around to the left side of the body. Jack follows her; she gestures to the woman's left arm. A huge tattoo covers her shoulder, all the way down to below her elbow. Even through her discoloured skin, Jack can make out the intricate detailing of an octopus, its tentacles trailing around seaweed and fish.

'Unique,' Fran says, and Jack agrees, feeling the judder of apprehension that they have *something*. He starts to speak, but she reads his mind and nods. 'I'll get photographs taken and sent over to you,' the pathologist says. 'And, by the way, victim one, David Carter? The hair follicle analysis came back. No trace of any sort of drug use in his past.'

'Not at all?'

'Nope. Not amphetamines, marijuana, cocaine or any opioid. Not in the last ninety days, at least. Apart from the opiates in his bloodstream, your boy was clean.'

Jack frowns. 'That's consistent with what his girlfriend told us. But still...'

'You were hoping it would shed some light on why he was killed?'

'Yeah.'

'Well, whatever the reason, your cause of death is the same for the new victim.'

'Blunt force trauma?'

'Yes, see here?' She lifts the head up; Jack can see the large gash across her forehead that he noticed at the scene. And another, bigger, on the back of her head. 'That one killed her, although the one at the front was enough to render her unconscious. And by the same murder weapon, or at least something similar.'

She gestures to a side table, far away from the body, where she's been working. A white lump, made out of the plaster powder he's seen at crime scenes for capturing tyre marks. She picks it up.

'I took a cast of victim one's skull. Or, more specifically, the dent left by whatever killed him. As you can see, it's cylindrical, diameter increasing as the injury site progresses.'

Rosetti hands it to him and he runs his finger down the surface. He imagines something smooth, easy to wield.

'A baseball bat?' he suggests.

'That would fit. I believe your latest victim is the same. I need to do some further comparisons but on initial removal of the skin over the scalp, I can see similar indicators. Your victim was drugged, killed, left in an airless room for at least a few days, then carried to the dump site and buried.'

'Why the different MO?'

'You're the murder detective, Ellis. I hang out with the bodies.'

'But your job is essentially the same. You assess the facts, then you come to a theory of their cause of death. What do you see here?'

Fran smiles and tilts her head to one side, appraising him.

'Okay,' she says. 'I'll play.' She pauses for a moment, thinking. 'So, our most recent victim is a small female, no more than sixty kilograms. David Carter was a large bloke. Six feet. And, from memory, there was no vehicular access to the burial site, right?'

'Right.'

'So, let's assume the killer could easily carry the woman, but—'

'But there was no way he could carry a dead six-foot man through the forest.' He meets Fran's eyes. She smiles. 'He refined his method. He kept him alive. Walked him into the woodland drugged, unable to run. Then killed him and buried him there and then.'

Fran nods. 'Don't you have a team for exposition like this?'

'I do. But nobody's been much use except for...' He pauses, about to say Lucy Halliday, then stops himself. 'Thank you for your help,' he says to Fran.

He leaves the mortuary feeling marginally better. Progress. Not much, but something. He phones Amrit back at the nick, telling her to follow up on the DNA results and start looking for tattoo parlours – anywhere that might help to identify their victim.

But what DC Gill says in reply makes the smile freeze on his face, the air still in his lungs. He breaks into a run, sprinting to his car. Brian Miller wants to see him.

He needs to get back to the woods. Now.

Chapter Seventeen

Hours later, Lucy sits in a different kitchen, a glass of red in her hand, her mouth watering. Tantalising smells drift from the oven, yeast and butter in the air as a large plate of garlic bread is put in front of her.

'Dig into that,' Fran says, and Lucy doesn't hesitate to comply.

Fran had phoned at the end of the day, offering dinner, no refusals allowed. Not that Lucy was about to. Fran's cooking is divine. Growing up in an Italian family, Fran is well versed in home-made pasta, pillowy pizza bases and rich tomato sauce. But the menu today is lasagne, and Lucy can't wait.

She feels a nudge on her leg; she pulls off a piece of crust and lowers it under the table to Moss, who gulps it down in a second.

Fran turns at the wrong time. 'Don't waste good food on that mutt,' she says with a smile.

'He's not a mutt, are you, Mossy?'

In response to her silly voice, the dog pushes his way up, resting his paws on her lap. She lowers her face to his fuzzy jowls and gives him a kiss.

'Oi, enough of that. No dogs near the table.' Fran's husband, Mike, comes into the room and Moss's affections are diverted. Mike bends down and gives his ears a ruffle. 'Kids are in bed. But for how long, I don't know.'

He joins Lucy at the table and pours himself a glass of red, then leans back contentedly. 'I swear they know when I'm at my most desperate for them to sleep.'

'Dinner will be ready in five,' Fran says.

'What have I ever done to deserve you?' Mike replies with a grin.

Lucy watches them fondly. They met when Fran was a junior doctor, Mike a pharmacist in the same hospital. As long as Lucy's known them, it's been a treat being in their company. Their easy manner, the way they seem so in love, never a cross word between them. When she remarked on that once to Fran, she had scoffed.

'Oh, we argue,' she replied. 'When I'm backed up with bodies in the mortuary and he's had a long shift at the hospital, believe me, we argue. Especially about whose turn it is to get up for the kids in the night. But we're lucky. We agree on the big stuff. Wanting children, a family. And he enjoys good food, I enjoy cooking it.'

She's so good at it, too. Lucy has no idea how Fran stays so slim, but it's clear the carbs are starting to get the better of Mike. He rests his hands on his portly belly, leaning forward eagerly as Fran puts the bubbling lasagne in the middle of the table. Lucy's stomach rumbles as she is offered a full plate.

'I can't possibly eat that much,' Lucy laughs, but takes it happily.

'See how you get on. It's time you ate a decent meal.'

'I do—'

'Takeaways and late-night bowls of cereal don't count.'

Lucy accepts defeat, then takes the salad that's handed to her, as well as another piece of garlic bread. Moss settles under her chair with a grunt, and they all descend into a reverent hush as they eat.

It's the best meal she's had in weeks, if not months. If not years. The creamy béchamel, rich tomato and beef, layers of pasta just right. Before she knows it, the whole plate has gone. She sits back, her stomach full.

'Fran, you are a goddess.'

'Don't I know it,' Mike says, with a satisfied sigh. He offers Lucy the wine. She shakes her head. 'You could stay?' Mike suggests. 'Spare room's yours.'

'I'd love to, but Moss and I have been roped in for a demo at the county show tomorrow.'

Fran snorts. 'You and the general public? Your sergeant must be desperate.'

'The investigation in the woods has taken all of the available dogs. I'm the only one who can't go near.'

The table falls into silence. Fran stares hard at her wine glass.

'That body. The new one Moss found. She was connected, right?'

Fran screws up her face. Lucy's put her in an impossible position.

'There are differences,' Fran begins warily. 'But yes. I believe they're connected.'

'In what way?'

'Similar needle marks. The same cause of death.'

'She had opiates in her system? Like the other guy?'

Mike looks up sharply. But Fran cuts him off.

'I shouldn't have told you this much. Ellis is on it now. You've done your bit, let him do his.'

'Is he up to the job?'

'From what I've seen, yes. He's a bit…'

'Uptight?'

Fran smiles. 'I would say… closed off. He doesn't give much away. But he asks for opinions, he makes the right assumptions. And he works hard. There's none of this sitting behind a desk while your DCs run around that you usually see with men in charge.'

'And you think Nico's out there? In those woods?' Mike asks.

'Yes, I do. I think he got involved in something he shouldn't have and ended up dead.' Lucy knows that Mike shares the same opinion as Fran, and she feels annoyed at the need to defend her husband again.

The four of them had sat around this table so many times in the past. Nico was a large personality, happy to regale whatever audience would listen with extravagant stories from his adventures. But he was also a reporter, and so he could be quiet and introspective, listening to other people speak and enjoying their tales.

'There's nothing more fascinating than humans,' he once said to her.

Lucy scowled. 'There's nothing more horrific than humans,' she countered.

'That's because you see the worst of them. Take a look from the other side, Luce. And you'll see.'

She wants to. She does. She feels the love in this room – in the display of odd plasticine shapes along the windowsill, in the way Fran is looking at Lucy with motherly concern. In the colourful scribbles proudly stuck to the fridge, muddled among photographs and certificates from school. One catches her eye – a blurry selfie of the three of them grinning, taken one New Year. But Nico was also there at that party. She squints then reaches over and pulls it free from the magnet, opening out the folded edge. Nico comes into view, his face serious, looking sternly at Lucy.

It conjures a memory. Getting home, slammed doors, tears, recrimination. Lucy waking alone; vomit on the bathroom floor.

Nobody moves from the table; she feels Fran's gaze. 'He had too much to drink that night,' Lucy murmurs.

'You never said,' Fran replies. 'What happened? We didn't hear from you for months.'

Lucy closes her eyes for a moment, blocking out the image. She doesn't want to talk about this. Not now. She slowly places the photograph on the table. Face down.

'You know we'll always be here for you,' Fran says. 'No matter what happens.'

Lucy forces a smile. 'I know. And thank you. For dinner. For the amazing lasagne.' She stands up, and Moss jumps to his feet. 'We better go, early start.'

She notices a look pass between the married couple. A subtle scowl and shake of the head from Mike.

'I'll see you out,' Fran says.

Lucy accepts a tight hug from Mike then follows Fran into the hallway, Moss at her heels.

Fran opens the front door, then pauses. Thinking.

'What is it?' Lucy asks.

Fran's forehead is furrowed. 'It's just something Nico asked me. About a fortnight before he disappeared. At the time I didn't give it much thought, and when he went, I kept quiet because... well... I assumed it was something dodgy he'd got into. And you were so convinced he'd got caught up in something, I didn't... I didn't want to add fuel to the fire.'

Lucy frowns. 'What did he ask?'

'He'd got you in so much trouble. You were suspended. Out of control. I wanted you to move on, Lucy. To forget Nico and—'

'What, Fran?' Lucy snaps.

'He wanted to know about opioids. About oxy, fentanyl, morphine, hydrocodone. But also the ones on the street – about heroin.'

'What exactly?'

'He wanted to know whether it was possible to distinguish between them. If there were simple tests that you could carry out on a batch of powder to see what it was and where it might have come from.'

'He wanted to do this?'

Fran shakes her head slowly. 'I don't know. And I told him that, yes, it was possible. But that you'd be the best person to ask. That the labs the police use have the best equipment for that sort of thing. He laughed then. Said he wasn't going to involve you, that he'd probably got you in enough trouble already.'

'He said that? And then what?'

'Then he disappeared.'

Lucy's mind is reeling. That Fran – her best friend – could have kept this from her, all this time. It's unbelievable.

'Why didn't you tell me this before?' she blurts out. 'You should have… You should have told me.'

'I thought about it. But I worried…' Fran winces. 'I worried it would give credence to your theory that he was dead. That he'd dug into something that got him killed, and I was convinced…' She glances back into the kitchen where Lucy can hear Mike loading the dishwasher. '*We* were convinced that he'd just left. He was always so flighty, such a free spirit. I'm sorry. I wanted what was best for you.'

Lucy glares, the betrayal hitting home. 'And what do you think now?'

'I think you might have been right.' Fran reaches out and gently touches Lucy's arm but she pulls away, folding her arms across her chest. 'If that is the case, and this is why, promise me that you'll go through the proper channels. Speak to Ellis, see if he'll help. But don't go out there alone, again, please? I'm worried you'll end up like Nico. Wherever he is.'

Lucy can't bring herself to reply. She always believed Fran was 100 per cent on her side, that her friend was open with her, about anything. But how could she trust her, when she'd been keeping this from her – for years?

Lucy turns away without a word and commands Moss into the boot of her car. But before she climbs in herself, she looks back to the doorway where Mike has joined Fran. They're standing together, arms around each other. Joined in their deceit. Fran lifts her hand in a wave; Lucy ignores it.

She drives off, her right foot hard to the floor. Her mind hums with images of Fran and Mike talking about her, maybe even laughing at her stupidity. What else is Fran keeping to herself? Their friendship feels false, Fran's concern insincere. And contrary to her intention, Fran's words haven't warned her off. All these links to drugs – the two victims, and now discovering Nico's questions to Fran. Drug addiction and abuse was always close to Nico's heart; she knew something had happened in his past, even though he'd always been reluctant to talk about it.

If anything, she's even more determined to find out what happened to her husband. She's certain now that he's gone. That something he was looking into led to his death. But if that's the case, where's his body?

And, more importantly – who killed him?

Friday

Chapter Eighteen

The day of the county show is bright and sunny, much to Lucy's disgust. There are tractors, and ice-cream vans, and bunting, and tents serving lukewarm beer. She sits on a plastic chair, eating a Magnum for lunch, Moss at her feet.

Fran has tried to call twice already this morning and as her phone rings again, Lucy silences it, incensed. A night's sleep has only maddened her more – as much as she tries to see her friend's point of view, she never wanted to be *protected*. She just wants to know what happened to her husband. She turns her phone off and pushes it into her pocket, turning her attention back to the job in hand.

She's in her police uniform, hastily washed and ironed. Moss is wearing his proper harness, but it seems that doesn't stop well-meaning members of the public from saying hello. A woman in a floral dress bends down to greet the dog.

'He's lovely. What breed is he?'

'A police dog,' Lucy replies gruffly.

The woman is unperturbed. 'But is he a springer or a cocker? He seems too small to be a springer, but not delicate enough for a cocker.'

'He's supposed to be a cocker,' Lucy acquiesces. 'But I guess some other genes got in there somewhere.' The woman strokes Moss again. 'You should ask permission,' Lucy comments. 'Before petting a police dog. Some would take your hand off.'

Lucy points at the dog approaching, and the woman looks up in surprise. The man walking towards them has a black-and-brown German shepherd at heel. The dog is panting, large white teeth on display. 'They call them furry land-sharks for a reason,' Lucy adds, and the woman scuttles away.

The man smiles when he's up close to Lucy. PC Pete Nash, and Dax. 'We're supposed to be building good relationships with the public,' he comments as he sits down on the chair next to her, sprawling his long legs out. The dog winds his way around then settles underneath. 'Not scaring them away.'

Lucy sighs. 'I know. *I know*,' she adds in the face of his prolonged stare. 'At least you have a wolf-beast. I have a cute fluffy one.'

Pete bends down and says hello to Moss. 'They'll be even warier after I've done my demo.'

Dax is what's known as a general purpose dog. Good for tracking suspects overground and – most importantly – bringing them down fast. While your average bad guy will fight the human variety of cop without hesitation, nobody wants to be at the business end of a German shepherd in attack mode.

'We go on in five,' he adds, pointing towards the arena next to them, marked out with brightly coloured tape and hay bales. 'I'll go first with Dax, then hand over to you. You don't even need to do any talking. Sergeant Andrews has the mic – do as he says.'

'I'll do my best,' Lucy smiles.

Pete and Dax leave, and Lucy encourages Moss to his feet as the dog display is announced. Even after all this time, seeing the dogs in action is impressive. Crowds start to move to fill the space around the arena, interested families and younger children, some clutching ice creams and picnic baskets. She sees Pete at the edge, waiting. She's seen him work before; he's a natural.

A voice comes over the loudspeaker. She looks around for the source and spots her sergeant on the far side. She gives a quick wave; he returns it with a thumbs up.

'Good morning, ladies and gentlemen,' he begins. 'Welcome to the Hampshire Police Dog Unit display.' He pauses; he receives an unenthusiastic smattering of applause in return. 'Over the next twenty minutes, you're going to meet two of the best trained dogs in the unit.' Lucy glances to Moss nervously. Maybe on a good day. 'They will take you through a few of the activities they carry out in the field – but before we start, a request. Please don't try this at home. These are highly trained police dogs, and exercises like this will not be safe to do with your pet Labrador, however much you want them to.' A few titters; Lucy sees her sergeant smile in return.

'So, without further ado, let me introduce PC Pete Nash – and Dax.'

Pete marches into the ring, the dog close to his side. Tail up, bouncy trot, looking up at his handler. Dax is an experienced animal; they don't risk unpredictable puppies at events like this one. But even so, he's dangerous, as they're about to witness first-hand.

Pete stands in the centre of the ring, the lead tight. The two of them are impressive – Pete, six feet and wearing his smart black uniform; Dax in a harness, POLICE emblazoned on the side. Dax comes up to his waist: he's a big dog, with jaws that could crush a human arm in seconds. His ears are pricked, tongue panting, ready to go.

'Dax is a five-year-old German shepherd, what we call a general purpose patrol dog, and together we're going to take you through some of the exercises Dax has to do every twelve months, when he's relicensed, so that we're happy and satisfied that he's safe to work on the streets around you.' Andrews pauses, and another man appears. He's dressed in what seems to be an oversized puffer coat. It looks out of place in this heat, but Lucy knows there's a reason he's wearing that.

'The first exercise we're going to see is the standoff, where our criminal – PC Davies over there – will run off.' Davies waves cheerfully. 'A challenge will be made by the handler, the criminal will stop and face the dog, but the dog will not engage.'

At his signal, Davies runs to their left, and Pete holds Dax back. Dax is straining to go, barking loudly, and as soon as Davies stops and turns, the dog is deployed. Dax runs fast towards his quarry, then sits in front, barking wildly. A terrifying sight to even the most hardened criminal; even from here, Lucy can see the German shepherd's sharp teeth, the spittle coming from his gums. But in a second the dog hears Pete's call and returns instantly.

The audience claps. Dax is given a pat and a toy as a reward.

'The next exercise is a straight chase.' He gives a nod to Davies, but Davies hesitates. Andrews gives him a wave. 'Off you trot,' he laughs down the microphone.

Davies snorts in return, then sets off across the arena. Once again, Dax is keen to get going, and the moment he's released, he tears across the grass, grabbing Davies's right arm and twisting his head to and fro, his paws up against their 'criminal's' body for traction.

'And there you are,' Andrews says. 'Nice, firm bite with the full mouth.' Pete calls his dog back. 'And of course, not all offenders are this easy to find. Dax is trained to locate what we call the human scent picture – a combination of pheromones and sweat that any bad guy will give off as they run. And Dax can track this from the ground and in the air, right to where they're hiding. Clever, huh?'

A murmur of appreciation from the audience.

'But, back to the show. Do you want to see Dax in action again, ladies and gentlemen?'

Shouts and whistles.

'I can't hear you. Do you want to see that again?'

This time the cheers are louder. Lucy joins in, caught up in the moment.

'But let's up the ante. This is called a stick attack, a test of courage, where the dog needs to protect his handler.'

Davies starts shouting from the other side, waving a stick and being lairy. Dax wastes no time, charging at him at a sprint and latching onto his arm in mid-air. Davies spins him around, all four feet off the ground, before Pete recalls Dax, laughing, and gives him the toy. Dax chomps gleefully.

'Notice how Dax goes for the side with the stick, effectively de-arming the criminal straight away. One of the reasons why Dax here was chosen for this role is because from an early age he showed a high level of aggression but also the restraint that you'd expect from a GP dog. What we're going to show you now, as a last demonstration, is a display of control around the handler and the criminal.'

Davies moves to stand a distance away from Pete, who directs Dax to lie on the ground. The dog stares up at Pete, his gaze fixed on his handler as he walks across to his colleague.

Dax is barking, but his concentration is fully locked, as Pete and Davies stand together.

'Now, you can see Pete is happy to leave the dog here in the down, and Dax will not break this position, unless one of two situations occur. Either he's called by his handler.' Pete starts doing a pretend body search of Davies. 'Or...'

At that, Davies turns and pretends to attack Pete. The dog doesn't hesitate. He's across the grass in seconds, grabbing the right arm of the puffer jacket and pulling Davies to the ground. Pete struggles to his feet, leaving Davies on the floor, held by the dog.

Dax is quickly called away by Pete and settles instantly back into the down position.

'And you could see there how quickly Dax came to his handler's aid. A useful dog to have around.'

Pete bends and clips a lead on the dog's harness. 'That's all we have time for today. A round of applause for PC Pete Nash, and for Dax.' The cheering is louder for Dax, and Pete waves to the crowd as he leads his dog away.

'Now, I'd like to introduce PC Lucy Halliday, and her dog Moss.'

Nerves bubble in her stomach. She picks up her bag and dog lead with shaking hands and heads into the arena.

'You'll be fine,' Pete whispers as they pass. 'Breathe.'

She walks into the centre of the ring and forces a smile.

Andrews begins. 'Moss is a cocker spaniel, and he is a specialist search dog.' She crouches down to Moss as the claps echo around the field. She takes a deep breath.

'Don't let me down,' she whispers. Moss is sat, waiting, tongue lolling. He knows what's coming next is going to be fun.

'Now, Moss here is trained to detect blood and cadavers.' Andrews pauses. 'That's dead bodies, kids,' he adds with a smile and gets a groan of disgust from the audience. 'But his role is important. Without him, bodies might never be discovered, their killers might never be brought to justice, and families might never find closure. But.' He stops. Lucy doesn't dare look up; she knows her sergeant is grinning. 'Because the chief constable doesn't like us bringing body parts to a county fair, we're going to do an exercise using a tiny drop of blood. And where is this blood from, you may ask? Well – it's provided by the good old NHS. Many donations aren't suitable for clinical use, so some surplus blood comes to us. Although we do expect sweat and tears from our dog handlers, we don't ask for their blood. Usually,' he adds, and chuckles with the full knowledge that training the dogs happens whether the NHS can provide, or not.

'Today,' Andrews goes on, 'Moss is going to show us what he can do. A tiny amount of blood has been placed on a swab in these containers…'

Lucy reaches into her bag and pulls out two small tins, holes drilled in the top. She holds them up so the audience can see.

'Lucy is going to ask Moss to wait, while she places the scent around the arena.'

She unclips his lead; Moss does what he's told and obediently watches while she walks quickly to the far side, dropping one and then the other in the grass.

She walks back to him and, on her command, Moss starts sniffing, darting around the ring, his nose to the ground, tail wagging.

'We can all see here,' Andrews explains, 'how Moss is working up and down in a systematic routine. And if he misses an area, Lucy will pull the dog back and show him another place to search.' Suddenly, Moss freezes, his nose pointing down. 'And Moss will give a passive indication, like he is doing now, to show he has located the blood.' Lucy smiles with relief and rewards him; he moves on, his nose to the ground, swinging to and fro, until he finds the other.

'It's extremely important that Moss gives a passive indication, so the dog doesn't interfere with the find in any way. To protect the dog, but also to preserve any evidence in case a criminal investigation is required. A round of applause for Moss here.'

Moss sits back at her side, and she grins. Maybe this isn't so bad, after all.

'Now, you might be saying, this is easy. Moss can see where Lucy is placing the scent, and she also knows, so she can guide him there. So, let's have another go, but we'll do it blind. In the same way we conduct most of our searches. Can I have a volunteer please?'

The whole audience is silent.

'Don't worry,' Andrews says. 'Dax has gone. We're not going to put the suit on you.'

A smattering of nervous laughter and a few hands go up. Lucy selects a young lad, probably about thirteen, and he gets a round of applause as he comes into the ring.

'What's your name?' she asks.

'Ethan.'

She passes the tins to Ethan.

'Take these,' she says to the boy. 'And plant them somewhere in the audience. I won't look, I promise. But one request. To keep things simple, please don't pass them around. The more hands they touch, the more scent will get everywhere, and Moss won't be in with a chance. Does that make sense?'

Ethan nods.

Lucy takes Moss to the other side and turns her back, giving her dog a pat and blocking his view. Soon she hears Andrews call her name over the loudspeaker.

'Ready?' she shouts. The kid gives her a thumbs up. 'Look, look,' she says to Moss.

This time she holds on to the lead as he heads one way then the other. He finds the first one quickly, the woman laughing as the dog freezes in front of her. Then they're off again, searching the crowd. Lucy's aware of people standing up, craning their necks, watching. It's taking a while, but she has faith in Moss. She trusts her dog; he'll get there.

At last, they make it to the far side of the crowd, and Moss stops in front of a tall man. He is lit from behind in silhouette, and for a moment she fails to recognise him.

She hears the applause from the crowd, and smiles, wincing at the direct sunshine in her eyes. Then she looks up again. Straight into the face of DI Ellis.

At first, she's confused. Why is he wasting his time at a dog demonstration at a county show? And then she realises.

He's not here for Moss. It's for her.

'I'm sorry,' he says, handing the tin back. She takes it numbly. 'I tried to tell the kid not to give it to me, but…'

His voice trails off. She stands in front of him, open-mouthed. She hasn't heard a word he's said.

The audience fade into nothing. The world leaches of colour. She knows Andrews is speaking; people are clapping, but all she hears are her own words.

'You've found him,' she says. 'You found Nico.'

And he nods.

Part Two

Chapter Nineteen

Jack hadn't intended for it to go that way. Informing a devastated wife that her husband is dead in front of an audience isn't exactly best practice.

In the wake of the applause, Jack guides Halliday away to a quiet part of the arena, Moss at her heels. Behind them, the sergeant continues the display without hesitation, used to unpredictability.

Lucy slumps into a plastic chair, her mouth open. 'When did... How... Is he... Was he...'

She's floundering, struggling to form proper sentences. The dog nudges her arm; she rests a trembling hand on his head.

'Was he murdered?' she finishes.

'We'll talk later. Take it easy.'

'No, not later. Now.'

'Lucy—'

'Give me a moment.' She looks up at Jack, eyes unreadable behind her sunglasses. 'Can you get some water? For Moss?'

'Yes... I... Okay.' Jack hesitates, then leaves her, crossing to the closest stall and asking for a bowl and some water. 'For the dog,' he adds, pointing back to Lucy, the spaniel at her feet.

'We don't have tap. You'll have to buy it,' the stallholder says, holding out a bottle of cold spring water and an empty plastic tub. Jack rolls his eyes but agrees, buying two cans of Coke at the same time.

He walks back, pouring the water for the dog and handing Lucy a can.

'Drink that, for the sugar. You're in shock.' Moss sniffs the water and ignores it, curling up in the shade under Lucy's chair. 'You drink out of ponds but turn your nose up at Harrogate Spring?' Jack says.

'He has refined tastes,' Lucy replies with a weak smile. 'Tell me. What happened?'

'Lucy, this can wait. Can I call someone to take you home?'

'I don't want to go home.' She pushes her sunglasses onto her head and fixes him with a stare. 'For nearly two years I've been completely in the dark. Desperate for someone to listen to me, to take me seriously. And now you've found him, and he didn't leave me and…' Her voice breaks; she presses her fingers against her mouth for a moment. 'And he's dead,' she continues, quieter. 'This can't wait any longer. I need to know.'

Jack's resolve crumbles. He grabs a plastic chair and sits down next to Lucy. 'He was to the far west of the search area. You were looking in the right place.'

'Same MO?'

'We don't know anything for definite yet. We found him yesterday afternoon, but it took a while to get him out of the ground. The PM is being done soon.' He glances at his watch. 'As we speak. I wanted to make sure we had enough to identify him before I came to find you.'

'Is Fran doing it?'

'No – conflict of interest. But she'll supervise. She said to tell you she'll look after him.'

Lucy nods slowly. 'When can I see him?'

Jack steels himself. The sun is hot, his shirt sticking to his back. 'He's been there a while, Lucy. At least a year. You know what that means?' She nods slowly. 'That's not how you want to remember your husband.'

'How did you identify him?'

'He's wearing the same clothes as when he disappeared. Same watch. Wedding ring.'

'What's your working theory?'

'I can't talk about the case with you. You know this.'

For the first time, Jack sees a different emotion in her eyes. A flash of anger.

'You wouldn't have found him if it wasn't for me.'

'Drink your Coke,' he replies. She's right, and he looks away – to the crowds, the kids gathering around the man making balloon animals, the farmers grabbing their second bacon sandwich of the day. The jollity and fun jar with the nature of their conversation. A man dead. That's three people now.

'It's my assumption that he was killed not long after he disappeared. And, given where he was found, by the same people. Why, we have no idea. And we don't believe he was killed in the woods like the first victim. He was wearing shoes, and his burial site was closer to the edge of the trees, but further down. A few feet under the surface, so they took their time to properly hide the body.'

'He knew something, Ellis. He found something.'

'We don't know that.'

She gives him a sceptical look. 'What? An investigative journalist gets brutally murdered and you think that's random? Who was the second victim?'

'The investigation is ongoing.'

'Seems to be a lot you don't know.'

He opens his mouth for a sharp retort, but bites it back. She's grieving. He'll let it go – just this once.

'You know how these things work, Lucy. You were a DI. Let me do my job.'

'I can help.'

'You can stay away.'

Before she can reply, a man in black uniform approaches, a large German shepherd at his side.

Lucy smiles at him. 'Sorry to leave you in the lurch, Pete.'

'Not a problem. We got Davies back for another round with Dax. Everything okay?'

'Unexpected news,' Lucy says. 'Pete, this is DI Jack Ellis. From MCIT.'

'Major crime, eh?' he says, but Jack doesn't elaborate. 'Pete Nash. And this is Dax.' Jack shakes his hand but keeps a good distance from the German shepherd. Pete smiles, knowingly. 'Not a fan of dogs?'

'Not a fan of the teeth,' Jack replies.

'He won't bite you.' Pete grins. 'Probably. Don't make any sudden moves.'

Like many handlers, Pete has the build to match his dog. Strong shoulders, wide chest, white teeth. He has an air of nonchalance Jack envies — unbrushed hair, grubby uniform, muddy boots. Bronzed, from working outside in the sunshine. He looks cool and composed, whereas Jack can feel sweat blooming on his forehead, skin burning on his neck.

'Could you take Moss for me?' Lucy says to Pete. 'I need to go with Ellis.'

'No problem.'

'I don't think—' Jack begins.

'You said the PM would be done by now,' Lucy snaps at Jack. 'You'll need me to formally identify the belongings. Right?'

Jack has to concede that, yes, as next of kin, that is a box they need ticked.

'You can meet me at the mortuary,' Jack says. Lucy stands up, ready to go. 'But don't go inside without me. I'm the SIO on this, not you.'

'Right you are,' she says, but Jack notices the disparaging look that passes between her and Pete as she hands him the dog lead.

'Lead the way, guv,' she adds, making her sarcasm clear.

Jack runs a finger around his collar, loosening it from his neck, then crumples his finished Coke can and tosses it into the bin.

'As you wish,' he says, striding across the grass towards the car park.

Chapter Twenty

He's dead. She's known it, deep down, but now she has the confirmation, it feels surreal. Nico's dead. Her husband is *dead*.

She follows Ellis's old Mercedes in her police Mondeo, bumping over the scorched grass of the car park. She knows the way to the mortuary, but she stays behind him – deference, for now. She doesn't cry; she feels she ought to, but her mind has detached. Nothing will come.

She takes roundabouts and junctions automatically as a thousand thoughts run through her head. A body underground for that long will be little more than bone. Maybe hair clinging to a skeleton, some soft tissues; she's witnessed a few over the years. Jack was right on one thing – it's not something she wants to see. The bodies of the dead rotate through her head at night; she doesn't want to add Nico to the parade. She wants to remember his smile, his ridiculous laugh – his eyes closed, his mouth wide with mirth. The way his hair curled at the nape of his neck, how it looked after he'd had a shower, curly and skew-whiff as he towelled it dry. That was the man she loved, not whatever they dug out of the ground.

Parking is difficult and she loses Jack in the multi-storey, only to find him waiting for her outside the mortuary. She wonders why he's here. He could have sent a DC or even a PC from patrol to inform her of Nico's death, yet here's the SIO – as he pompously reminded her – escorting her to a formal identification.

'Ready?' he says. She nods.

They walk in silence down the empty corridors, the smell of bleach and imagined decay cloying and sticky. She takes small breaths through her mouth as they approach the doorway.

'Wait here,' he says, and goes inside. She sees through the flapping double doors to the stainless steel and tiles. For that fraction of a second, she imagines a body on the table, but when Jack gestures her through, the place is empty. Scrubbed down to gleaming silver.

He escorts her to a side room, and that's when her breath hitches. She pauses in the doorway – his clothes in front of her, laid out on a shiny table. She takes a step closer. They're dirty, tatty, but unmistakably his. The worn blue-and-green shirt, soft from years of wear. A grey T-shirt. A pair of faded black jeans. And trainers – navy blue Vans.

How she'd mocked those shoes. *Skater boy*, she'd say, *how old do you think you are?* And he'd ignore her, an indulgent smile on his face as he tied the laces.

'Are they his?' Jack asks.

'Yes,' she replies, although the word doesn't come out. She clears her throat. 'Yes.'

'And this?'

He hands her two evidence bags. The first – an Apple watch. Nothing special – the strap grey and grubby. Could be anyone's. But the second bag is lighter. His wedding ring.

Her hand presses against her mouth. She swallows, then holds it up to the light, looking for the engraving. It had worn in the two years they were married but she can see the lines of the curved writing within.

'It's his,' she confirms.

'What does it say?' Jack asks gently. 'We couldn't make it out.'

'"Will you love me in December",' she replies. She tugs her own wedding ring from her finger and passes it to him. '"As you do in May",' she recites as Jack squints inside. 'Nico loved Kerouac, but I believe the quote was around before Kerouac

used it. Maybe James Joyce, Irish roots?' She shrugs. 'I forget.'
Jack passes her ring back and she slips it on, the platinum fitting
easily into the groove. She hands the evidence bag to Jack. 'I
can have this back at the end?'

He nods. 'I'm sorry for your loss,' he concludes. 'Do you
need a moment?'

'Please.'

She hears his footsteps, then the swing of the double doors.
She regards the rows of fridges on the far side – and the bodies
behind. Nico is here. For the first time in nearly two years, she
is in the same room as her husband.

She walks over and scans the labels. David Carter – the man
they found first. The second just a number – the woman they
haven't yet identified. And here. Here is Nico.

The label says no more than *Halliday* and a six-digit number.
She makes no effort to open it but places her hand, fingers
splayed, against the cold metal. She knows it's not him. In life
he was full of energy. A force to be reckoned with, who believed
that nothing would stop him. Nothing would hurt him.

And yet.

The tears come. Her legs wobble and she sags, placing her
hands over her face as she collapses. Her knees press against
her forehead as she sobs on the cold, tiled floor. She's aware of
the snot, tears, spit soaking into her T-shirt. Aware of the door
opening behind her. She turns, and it's Fran.

Fran sits down and wraps her arms around her. She accepts
her comfort for a moment before she remembers their argument last night. Fran's deceit. She pulls away, sniffing.

'I'm so sorry,' Fran says, handing her a tissue.

Lucy wipes her face, uselessly; Fran takes another, and gently
dabs her cheeks and chin.

'You've seen him?' Lucy asks.

Fran nods. 'You don't want to.'

'I won't. But you'll confirm? For sure?'

'I've already sent samples off. Skin. Hair. It won't take long.
But you saw his clothes, his ring?'

'It's him, I know.' Lucy shrugs, weakly. 'But some part of me will always question until we get the DNA back.'

She tries to stand but her legs feel like rubber. Fran gets up then pulls her to her feet.

'How did he die, Fran?'

'I didn't—'

'You didn't do the PM, I know. But you must have read the report?'

The doors swing again behind them; Ellis pauses in the doorway. Fran gives him an uncertain look.

'She deserves to know, Jack,' Fran says.

His face is stern, and for a moment Lucy thinks he's going to keep it from her. But instead, he nods. 'Fine. But not here.'

—

Fran leads the way to the back room where Lucy's been many times before. A small poky office, with crayoned pictures Blu-tacked to the wall over a meticulously ordered desk. Files line up on shelves behind, along with a row of textbooks tackling subjects from anatomy to the zygomatic bone. Fran sits down at her desk and gestures to Lucy to take the seat next to her. Jack stands against the wall, behind them.

Fran begins. 'How much do you want—'

'All of it.'

Fran glances, warily, over her shoulder. Jack stays silent. 'Because this isn't like a normal murder case, Lucy. This is your husband.'

'I'm aware, but… I need to know.'

'Okay, then.' Fran reaches for a file in her in-tray and opens it. Lucy braces herself for photographs, but Fran only takes out a sheet of typed A4 – the pathologist's report – before closing it again.

'So, as you know, decomposition rates vary depending on a number of factors—'

'Temperature, moisture, method of burial, condition of the body. Yes, I know.'

Fran gives her a look; Lucy mentally resolves to be more patient. 'Clothing, positioning. Even down to the metabolism of the individual,' Fran continues. 'Buried bodies generally decay more slowly, depending on factors such as the depth, the level of moisture and acidity of the soil, but generally speaking, a body buried about a metre underground retains most of its tissue for a year. Soft tissues will be absent by two years. After about five years, the bones will be bare. Nico was closer to the surface than this – and given all the differing factors, we estimate his time of death as between twelve and twenty months. We can't be more precise than that.'

'How did he die, Fran?'

She glances back to Jack, who nods. Fran sighs. 'Even given the levels of decomposition, the pathologist found a substantial amount of injury to the body. Multiple facial fractures, including a broken nose and jaw. Three teeth missing. Fractured humerus, a break consistent with his arm being forced up behind his back. Four broken bones in his left hand. Breaks to...' Fran pauses to count. 'Six of his ribs. And multiple other widespread fractures.'

Lucy swallows. 'He was beaten?'

'Substantially so. Maybe even tortured. Cause of death was a tension pneumothorax causing cardiac arrest,' she explains. 'The pressure in his chest increased to such an extent that the blood flow to his heart stopped.' She pauses. 'I'm sorry, Lucy. Nico was definitely murdered.'

Lucy leans forward, putting her head in her hands. She pushes her fingers into her eyes until she sees stars.

Behind her, Jack says, 'You've uploaded this report?'

'Yes,' Fran replies.

'I need to get back to the station.' Lucy glances up as Jack pushes himself away from the wall. He looks down at her. 'Is there anyone we need to inform of Nico's death?'

She thinks for a moment. 'No. Nico's parents are dead, and he's an only child. His editor, Cal, maybe. But I'll call him.'

'If you're sure?' Lucy nods. 'Do you have a mobile phone for Nico?'

'No,' she says quickly. 'Sorry,' she adds. 'He must have taken it with him. He was on O_2, if that's any help? And we had separate bank accounts, so you should be able to get his finances without a problem.'

Jack agrees. 'I'll be in touch,' he says, and with a final thank you to Fran, he leaves.

Fran places a gentle hand on Lucy's arm. 'Are you okay? Do you need me to come home with you?'

Lucy shrugs her off. 'No, no. I'm fine. Finish up here. It's more important you do everything to catch whoever did this.'

'We will, Lucy.'

Lucy gives her a dubious look. 'After nearly two years? You know as well as I do that all leads will have gone cold. Evidence degraded. CCTV deleted.'

'They've killed three people. There'll be something. We've got scrapings from Nico's fingernails, dried blood on his clothes. His burial works in our favour – the cold and soil may have protected the DNA, and labs can get a result from the tiniest of samples nowadays.' She takes Lucy's hand and squeezes it; Fran feels reassuringly warm. 'And Ellis seems more than up to the job. Have faith.'

Lucy nods and, without another word, gets up and leaves the hospital. She walks back to her car mechanically, concentrating on putting one foot in front of the other, then on driving, collecting Moss. Netley HQ is quiet; Moss is waiting patiently in the kennels and jumps into the back of the car without hesitation.

She doesn't remember driving home, only that when she gets there, she shuts the door behind her and slumps down on the floor of her hallway. The dog senses her mood and curls into her lap, resting his head on her leg. He looks up at her with baleful brown eyes.

'You never knew him, Moss,' Lucy says, stroking his ears. 'But you would have liked him.'

The shock has worn off, leaving her tired and numb. Nico hadn't left of his own free will; he loved her when he died – but that knowledge doesn't assuage the despair and dragging horror that his last moments were spent in pain and fear.

She needs to know who did this.

She pulls her phone out of her pocket and calls Cal.

'It's him, isn't it?' he says straight away. 'There are rumours – that another body's been found. And the dates fit.'

'Off the record, Cal. But yes. It's him.'

There's a long silence, then: 'How?'

'He was murdered. What was he looking into? Come on. You must know something. He must have spoken to someone at the paper, surely?'

'I asked around when he disappeared. No one knew anything.'

'He was tortured, Cal,' Lucy stresses. Emotion licks at the edge of her voice. 'Beaten.' She hears Cal take a sharp breath. 'Ask again.'

'I will.'

He says his goodbyes and hangs up, with the promise he'll be in touch soon. Lucy lets the phone drop out of her hand and lowers her head to Moss's. She's so exhausted she can't move. Never wants to move, now Nico has gone.

And, her tears soaking the spaniel's fur, she stays there, on the floor, as the world continues without her.

Chapter Twenty-One

All heads swivel his way as Jack arrives in the incident room. He takes his time at the board, looking at victim one, David Carter, and the unnamed body of victim two. Carefully, aware of the team watching, he wipes out the words *VICTIM 3* and replaces them with *Nicolas Halliday*.

'I fucking knew it,' Blake crows. 'What did I tell you?'

'A little respect please, Harry,' Jack says gruffly, and Blake flushes. 'I want an update. What have you been doing while I've been gone?' Blake opens his mouth but Jack cuts him off. 'Amrit?'

'DNA results on victim two aren't back, so I've been calling tattoo shops and following up with photos of her ink. No luck so far. There's still a few on the list,' she adds quickly.

'Good. Keep going. Blake, go on then?'

'We got a huge number of calls on the tip line about David Carter. Most of them dull. A few parents, singing his praises about what a wonderful teacher he was. A few detailing his movements – I passed them on to Phil to follow up. And one...' He smiles smugly. 'One from a guy who went to university with him. Says our David had quite the past.'

Jack waits, frustrated by Blake's deliberate pause. He folds his arms across his chest and Blake gets the message.

'Cocaine, marijuana, Es – a regular occurrence most weekends.'

'And when was this?' Jack asks, thinking about the hair follicle with no trace of drugs.

'While he was at uni.'

'So… what? Eleven, twelve years ago? Didn't we all do some dodgy stuff at uni? I know I did.'

'You did, boss?' Amrit says, eyes wide.

Jack pulls himself up abruptly. Those blacked-out nights, blurry mornings. He was another person then. 'Some,' he admits, embarrassed he revealed too much. 'But I stopped, like David Carter.'

'It shows he had links to drugs and dealers?'

'It shows he knew a few dodgy people at uni. But say it is significant, where would you go with it? What would you do next?'

'I'd bring the girlfriend in. Interview her under caution.'

'I've spoken to her already today,' Amrit interrupts. 'About David's movements. She's utterly distraught. And she said again that David wouldn't go near drugs or anything like that. He was too focused on his career.'

'Was she under caution?' Blake fires back. 'Did you push her?'

'No, but—'

The two continue to bicker, as Jack's attention is distracted by a buzz coming from his rucksack. A mobile phone. And not his work one, which is silent in his pocket. He ignores it and waits; the vibrating ceases and his shoulders drop.

'Enough,' Jack says, interrupting Amrit and Blake. 'The hair follicle tests show David Carter wasn't using before his death. And I agree with Amrit, I don't think the girlfriend's hiding anything. Moving on…' Blake tries to protest. 'Moving on,' Jack repeats decisively. 'What did you find out about Carter's movements?' he directs to Lawrence.

'Nothing of significance,' he says reluctantly. 'He went to Waitrose on Sunday. He filled the car up with petrol. He went to the pub with a mate that evening and had two pints. But no sightings after Sunday night and nothing that would point towards a risky lifestyle. And I spoke to the parents – the ones Carter thought were abusing their kid. They had a few choice words to say about our victim, but they were hundreds of miles away at the time. They live in Glasgow now.'

Jack frowns. More dead ends. 'Let's leave Carter, then. It's more important we ID victim two and look into Nicolas Halliday. I've spoken to the victim's wife—'

'Lucy Halliday,' Blake adds, unnecessarily, to DC Gill. 'Was DI, now PC. She was the one I was talking about—'

'Yes, thank you, Blake,' Jack snaps for the second time. 'She's the wife of the deceased, not to mention a serving police officer, so rein it in. At this point she has no further insight into why her husband went missing than what was written in the original misper report, so keep your distance for now.' He picks up a pen and starts to write details on the board. *TOD 12–20 months. COD punctured lung. Tortured. Beaten.* He turns and the team are gawping at the words.

'It's Lucy Halliday's hypothesis that something Nico was investigating got him abducted and killed. We have no evidence to back this up – yet – but I would like to consider it as a theory. Especially, given all victims have links to drugs – David Carter and victim two have clear injection marks, and Nico Halliday had been an addict in his past.' Blake raises his eyebrows with interest; Jack ignores him. 'Phil – please pick up on tracing Nico Halliday's movements around the time of his disappearance. It was the view then that Nico had simply left his wife, so see what CCTV they managed to get at the time and whether it was actually watched.'

'Have we got a mobile phone for him?' Blake asks.

'Nothing, no. But it was on O2, so do all you can to persuade them to part with the details. Get bank statements, track down the witnesses interviewed at the time – if there were any. I'm going to speak to DCI Kane about getting more resource. We can't investigate multiple murders with the four of us. Blake – can you get the new team up to speed when they arrive and co-ordinate the lines of inquiry?'

Blake nods, satisfied as Jack knew he would be. His second-in-command needs to have power. He is his DS, as much as he annoys Jack.

'What about me, boss?' Amrit asks.

'Your priority is to get an ID for victim two. Keep going with the tattoo shops. Chase up the DNA results. If you're lucky we'll get a match, like we did for Carter, and you can stop.'

'Do you think vic two is related to a serving police officer, like Carter?'

'And Nico Halliday was married to a cop,' Blake adds.

'It's one theory.'

'But why?'

'That, I don't know,' Jack replies. 'Crack on, all of you. Keep me up to date.'

He leaves them to it and heads upstairs to see DCI Kane. But before he goes, he picks up his rucksack and pulls out the mobile phone. It's an old one, a small, cheap Nokia. He glances behind him and slips it into the palm of his hand, waiting until he's in the stairwell before clicking onto the voicemail. He stops dead the moment he hears her voice.

Jay, it's me. It's Sophie. I know we said not to call but we need to talk. Please.

The message comes to an abrupt end. He stares at his phone, one foot paused on the step above. He hasn't heard from Sophie in years. Ten years, to be exact.

And without thinking further, he clicks the number to redial. It rings twice, then it's answered, her voice clear and soft.

'It's Jack,' he says. 'It's...' but he can't bring himself to say it. Not here.

'Thank you for calling me back,' she replies. 'And so quickly. I'm sorry for—'

'It's fine. Is it news about—'

'No. No, sorry. Nothing. But... we need to talk. I know we said we wouldn't... but... Face to face.'

'I'm in the middle of something. Work.'

'It's important. I wouldn't have asked if it wasn't. You know that. I'm nearby.'

He doesn't ask how she knows where he is. He glances at his watch. 'Give me a few hours. Four p.m. Meet me at the Waterstones café in the Westquay shopping centre.'

'I'll find it. Four, then.'

She hangs up. He nearly calls back to cancel – he can't do this, not now – but something stops him. If Sophie called, it must be essential. He needs to know. And soon.

Chapter Twenty-Two

Sophie's waiting for Jack when he arrives. He's on time but she's been there a while, a line of mugs and a book half-read in front of her. She looks up and smiles; he points to the coffee counter and she gives him a thumbs up.

He needs the time to compose himself. He'd raced over here, stupidly choosing to walk rather than take the car, and now he's hot as well as flustered.

The meeting with DCI Kane had not gone well. He had headed in prepared, but hadn't expected much pushback: a case like this requires multiple detectives, analysts, civilian adminis-trators. He'd been stunned when his request had been met with blank refusal.

'But, ma'am, if we're to investigate properly—'

'Didn't you hear me, DI Ellis?' she'd snapped. 'I don't know what it was like at the Met but here we're restricted on budgets. Knife crime, sexual assaults, other suspicious deaths. They've all been rolling in while you've been tying up our officers in the woods. You'll have to make do.'

Confused, but reading the writing on the wall, he'd backed off. She'd seemed distracted, busy, barely listening; he'll regroup, try again later. Her only flicker of interest had been when he'd mentioned the new victim was Nicolas Halliday. She'd responded with a quiet, 'Oh, no,' but hadn't asked any more.

He orders a black coffee for Sophie and a mug of tea for himself, picking up a bottle of water at the till as an afterthought. He carries them across to the table and sits down.

Sophie picks up the till receipt from the tray and uses it as a page marker, closing the book.

'Any good?' he asks, pointing to the novel.

'Passes the time. Waiting for you. Murder detective now, I hear?'

'My mum should keep what I tell her to herself.'

'She's proud of you.'

Sophie smiles. She hasn't changed. The same dark eyes, dark hair, curls loose and longer than when he saw her last. She reminds Jack so much of her brother that it makes a hard lump build in his stomach. She tips three sugar packets into her coffee and stirs.

'You remembered,' she says.

'Hard to forget. Coffee that sweet.'

'Like me,' she says, then winces at the awful joke before her face turns serious. 'I'm sorry to call you down here at such short notice...' She hesitates. 'It might be nothing, but we've been getting calls.'

'Still? After all this time?' That's not new. The crazies have hounded Sophie and her family for years.

'Yes. But these were different. These were about you.'

His skin prickles. Adrenaline racing. 'What were they asking?'

'Where you were. What you were doing. We didn't tell them anything, of course, but Jay—'

'Don't call me that.'

She reels at his tone. 'I'm sorry. Jack.' She recovers her composure. 'They weren't who they said they were. They claimed they were journalists, from *The Daily Mail*, but when we googled, we couldn't find their names. And we called. We phoned the paper. They'd never heard of them.'

'So, they're some nutter with a conspiracy theory.'

She averts her eyes, her lips pressed together, her face grave. Jack regrets his tone and reaches out, gently touching two fingers against her closed fist.

'Hey, Sophie,' he says softly. 'I'm sorry. Nobody's called me that in a long time.' She glances up for a second. 'And thank you. For coming down to see me. I must admit, I'm a little relieved.' He forces a smile. 'We've had this for years. It's nothing new.'

'*We've* had this for years?'

'Sorry. You. Give me the names and I'll look into it. Type it into a police database or something.'

She nods and reaches into her bag, taking out a pen and writing the names on the till receipt from the book. She pushes it across to him.

'You've lost your place.'

'It was crap anyway,' she says, but a trace of a smile touches her lips. 'Did you worry it was something else? Me coming down here.' She takes a sip of her coffee, her eyes mischievous. 'That I'd appear with a nine-year-old boy with dark skin, blond hair and grey-blue eyes?'

He snorts. 'The thought did cross my mind.' He pauses. 'So, no?'

'No. Definitely not. You're free to continue your playboy lifestyle.'

'Playboy?' He scoffs. 'Hardly. The only action I see are police chases and digging up dead bodies.'

'That's not so bad.' She laughs, but his phone rings, interrupting them.

He looks at the number. 'I need to take this.'

'Of course.' She starts to gather her belongings, but pauses, looking fondly at him. 'I miss you. We all miss you.'

Jack pauses, his finger hovering over the green button. 'I miss you too.'

And with that, Sophie gives him a quick kiss on the cheek and leaves. He stares after her. Ten years, and in a second the old feelings have come flooding back. That conversation, seeing her. It was too short. He wants more.

He snaps himself out of it, the phone still angrily vibrating in his hand.

He answers it quickly. 'Lucy? What's up?'

'The van,' she says. 'Where's his van?'

'Sorry, what?'

'His fucking van. It went missing the same time as he did. It was a vintage VW camper. I tried to look for it at the time but I was suspended, there wasn't anything I could do. The fact we couldn't find it was one of the reasons everyone assumed he'd left me. But if he's dead in the forest…'

'Then where's his van?' Jack finishes for her.

Chapter Twenty-Three

Jack walks into the incident room at speed, the door hitting the wall behind with a bang. The whole team looks up.

'The van. Nico Halliday had a VW camper van. Where is it?'

He's met with blank faces.

'We need to find it. It went missing when he did – we find that van, chances are we'll find trace from whoever took it.'

'But it'll be long gone,' DC Lawrence says. 'Crushed. Sold for parts…'

'Let's be sure, shall we? Get on to ANPR, traffic cams. Anything from around the time he disappeared. See what records are left.'

'We've not had much luck tracking his movements so far.'

Jack casts him a look as Amrit interrupts. 'DNA results for victim two are in.'

'And?'

'Nothing,' she admits reluctantly. 'No match to anyone on the system. Not even a partial,' she adds, referring to victim one.

'Could still be related to a serving police officer,' Lawrence says. 'Their wife. Adopted. A step-kid. The other two are, after all. Seems a bit of a coincidence.'

'But why?' Jack asks. Nobody answers. The case is cold before it's even begun. They need this ID. They need one solid line of inquiry they can follow.

'We do have Nico Halliday's mobile phone records and bank statements, though,' Lawrence says, cautiously. 'I was going through them when you came in. Digital have already pinged the last known location, although it doesn't help us much – it's Lucy Halliday's house. It makes sense he'd have been there.'

Jack frowns. 'Which house?' Lawrence shows him the address. 'That's her current address. She only moved there six months ago. When was it last on?'

'Er… Oh. On Tuesday.'

'This Tuesday?' Jack exclaims.

'Do you want me to go and see her, boss?' Blake asks.

'No, I'll go.' Jack glances at the clock. It's gone six p.m. now. On a Friday. 'All of you, get off home.' Smiles abound as the team start to shut down their computers. 'Don't be too appreciative,' he adds. 'I'm going to need you back tomorrow. First thing. Our request for extra resource has been turned down. I know, I know,' he says, seeing the whole team about to protest. 'I get it. I'll try again. But for now, we've a lot of ground to cover on these murders and we've only just begun.'

Grumblings but nobody objects. This is the job. The long hours, the stolen weekends. But they must feel the same way as he does – determined to catch whoever did this.

The team wave their goodbyes as Jack retreats to his office. He sits at his desk and patiently makes his way through the updates from the day. The list of tattoo parlours and piercing emporiums that Amrit has been calling, to no avail. The CCTV that's been deleted, traffic cameras that show no trace of Nico Halliday. He considers David Carter, victim one. Their most recent but most mysterious. Vincent Carter is still AWOL, gone to ground, and Jack scans the reports from HR about his conduct over the years. A dedicated copper, steady worker. Not a single complaint or negative report over his entire twenty-something-year career. But he'd lied to the police. Failed to report his missing son. Something doesn't stack up.

He turns his attention to Nico Halliday's phone. The original misper report from Lucy included the statement that, while the van was missing, the phone had been left behind, something she protested he would never do if he'd walked out on her. He's annoyed he didn't remember that earlier. Nico's whole life was on that phone, she'd said, and Jack can imagine the extensive data they'd find if they went through it. Calendar appointments, contacts, emails, photos. He flicks back to the latest mobile phone bill – no calls since October 2021, when he disappeared. No text messages since.

So why had she lied?

Jack sighs and shuts the lid of his laptop. He's in no mood to confront Lucy Halliday now. He's hungry and tired – and the chat with Sophie has rattled him. Who is asking questions about him? And why – after all this time?

Remembering their conversation, he takes the receipt out of his pocket and types the names into both police databases. No hits.

Could be made up. Could be someone without a record. But it's odd.

The old hunted feeling has returned. He likes to be insignificant, unnoticed, and this? This is strange.

Plus, seeing her – after all this time – has brought long-suppressed emotions to the surface. Fear, confusion, but also affection and nostalgia and… love. Yes, maybe even that, he admits to himself. Aspects of his life he can't control – not a feeling he enjoys.

He pushes his laptop into his rucksack and leaves the office, switching lights off and putting used mugs into the kitchen. He takes a last look back before he closes the door. His first week. Five days. Three bodies. A baptism of fire, but a challenge he relishes. Feeling that familiar wave of resolution, he shuts the door, and strides out into the cool summer evening.

Hours have no meaning here. She measures time only by the throbbing in her face, the waves of fear that overwhelm her in the darkness.

At night, she suffocates in the pitch-black; during the day, only the slightest glow can be seen through the layers of newspaper taped over the windows.

At some point her hands were untied, but her shoulders still ache, her wrists burn around the broken skin. She is always cold. She doesn't sleep.

Her nose has solidified into a congealed mess. She can only breathe through her mouth; her eyes have swelled; her nose is definitely broken. Bones crunch in a flood of agony and nausea if she moves too quickly.

But even in her weakened state, she can tell. This house stinks. When Daisy first arrived, there was a pervading smell — of sodden floorboards, damp, rot — but as the days have gone by, something else has taken over. Something so awful it can't be described, which instinctively makes the hairs stand up on her arms and a cold sweat break out across her body.

The man comes back in, his aftershave eye-watering. He stands in the doorway and watches her as she cowers in the far corner.

'Come here,' he says. When she does nothing but shake in fear, he holds out a bottle of water. He places it on the floor in front of him. 'Come here, little one.'

She looks at it. Licks her chapped lips with a parched tongue. The last bottle feels like ages ago. Gone too fast. What choice does she have? she thinks as she shuffles across, barely looking at him, as if direct eye contact will cause him to attack.

When she's closer, he takes one long stride towards her, reaches down and grabs her hands. He pulls her near as if she were no more than a rag doll, so close she can see the spinach from his lunch caught in his teeth.

He pushes his face next to hers. 'You want something?' he says. 'Dull the pain?'

She's confused, but then it becomes clear. She's heard of women, girls. Taken and plied with drugs to become prostitutes. Is that what this is?

She shakes her head.

'Pity.' A meaty hand goes out, grabs at her crotch, then pulls away quickly. She's wet herself. Can't remember when. The shame and disgust, but her saving grace now.

'You dirty bitch,' the man growls. He shoves her away; she falls, heavily.

'Drink your water. You might change your mind.' He points to a corner of the room where a chair lies on its side, lost in shadows. She hadn't noticed it in the never-ending night.

'Others did,' he says, and closes the door.

Once more, she is in darkness. She gropes around for the water bottle, opens it and gulps greedily. Then she forces herself to stop. Who knows how much longer she will be here.

She looks behind to the chair, now lost again in the black. She could pick it up, hit him over the head next time he returns. But who is she kidding? Hunger gnaws at her insides. She's so weak, she can barely stand; she has no chance against her captor.

But she doesn't stop thinking about that chair. The dull stains on the woodwork.

And the people who were here before.

Saturday

Chapter Twenty-Four

Another morning, same wet nose. Lucy wakes with a jolt. Soft light trickles in through the open curtains; she glances at the clock, surprised to see it's seven a.m. Moss sits by her head, looking at her beseechingly. Once again, forgotten. He must be hungry; he needs to go in the garden.

She pulls herself out of bed, noticing with shame that she's still in yesterday's clothes – the uniform she was wearing when she took the dog to the county show. That demonstration was barely twenty-four hours ago but it feels like days, weeks. Her life split into two: Nico missing and Nico dead.

There is no doubt now, no uncertainty. Whatever vestiges of hope existed, they are gone. Time yawns. An emptiness where he once was. The thought that she'll never see him again is surreal; she wishes she believed in heaven, in the reassurance that would provide. Assuming he would have ended up there. Given what she knows about Nico, nothing is certain.

Yesterday, she'd lost track of time, sat crying on her hallway floor. When the storm passed and she'd finally struggled to her feet – her legs numb, her body cold – she'd operated on autopilot and gone for the default. A bottle of basic Spanish plonk. She regrets it now. The cheap white wine has turned to vinegar in her stomach and as she goes downstairs, following Moss into the kitchen, she burps – acidic, dirty – and feels disgusting. She runs her hands through her hair, pulling stray strands back from her face. It feels greasy and – for the first time in days – she's starving.

She feeds Moss, watches him in the garden, then heads for the shower. The hot jets are rejuvenating, and after, she puts on tracksuit bottoms and a T-shirt, throwing a load of laundry into the machine.

She checks her phone. One message: a voicemail from PS Andrews, expressing his sympathies and confirming that her schedule has been transferred. She's on compassionate leave for the next few days.

The empty space annoys her. The end to the uncertainty surrounding Nico's fate has created a void. For years she's wondered where he was. Flip-flopping emotions of anger, regret, worry. They're still here but now she has a focus – finding his killer. His departure wasn't because of something she did or said. Someone took him away from her. She wants to find them and make them pay.

She cooks toast and eggs, chewing on a large lump of cheese while they fry. It's all she has in her fridge. Even the cheese is old, but it does the trick. Restored, she sits at her kitchen table, a new notepad in front of her, and writes down everything she remembers from that time. Anything he said, where he went. And the information she's gathered since.

All together – it's not much. If she was in charge of the murder investigation she would be going down the usual routes of CCTV, forensics from the body and gathering his personal data, but she has to trust Ellis on that.

Frustrated, she heads out to the garden. Spends an hour giving Moss's kennel a well-overdue clean – mop, bucket, disinfectant – the dog watching her from the lawn, basking in the sunshine.

Job done, she picks up her door keys and dog lead. Moss recognises that playtime is here, and leaps around her as she tries to clip the lead onto his collar.

It doesn't take long to walk out of town, and once pavements are replaced by heathland, she lets the dog run free. Moss darts here and there, frantic zigzags, his nose to the ground, inhaling every molecule of scent from deer, horses, pigs – whatever has been passing.

Like Moss, Lucy loves the New Forest. The huge expanse of blue sky, dotted with solitary cotton-wool clouds. A cool breeze whips across the grass, speckled with daisies and butter-cups, stretching to the horizon. She walks quickly, letting the air fill her lungs. It smells of *nothing*. Fresh, cold. It cleanses her.

She makes her way to the enclosure on the far side. A wood, made up of oaks, birch and yew, much like the one where Nico was found. But there are no ghosts here. Moss looks back, checking she is there; she follows her dog, his tail high. Sunlight dapples through the lush leaves, turning the canopy every hue of green.

In the winter, the landscape changes. The greens switch to blues, frost on the heather. Sharper, as spears of sunlight pierce through the gaps in the Douglas fir trees, highlighting the frozen puddles and the ponies with their thick coats.

It feels like a world away.

She keeps moving, her arms swinging, her shoulders back. They walk for miles, losing track of time as Lucy's legs tire. Moss shows no hesitancy, such is the energy of a young spaniel. But he'll sleep later, his brain full of the multitude of smells and scents Lucy can't even imagine.

Her mind is calm, her body restored, as she turns the corner back into her road. And outside her house is a large black Mercedes. Moss pulls as they get closer; Ellis is waiting on her doorstep. He's in a dark grey suit, navy tie and white shirt – his only concession to the warmth of the summer's day is the undone button at the top of his shirt, the loose knot of the tie.

He looks up as they draw closer. He's closed off, expres-sionless. 'Can I come in?' Then he catches himself. 'How are you?'

Moss dances around his legs; Ellis ignores him.

'I'm fine. Well, not fine, but… you know.' Lucy puts her key in the door. 'Have you found his van?'

She ushers him inside, through the hallway to the kitchen; notices him side-eye the dirty plate and frying pan on the hob.

'Not yet,' he replies.

'You're—'

'We're searching CCTV and ANPR, yes. It's under control. I'm here about his phone. Could we have it, please?'

Lucy's surprised by his bluntness. 'His mobile?' she repeats, playing for time.

'Yes. We know you have it.'

She should have guessed they'd ping the number. It was a silly error turning it on, but it had to be done. No point denying it now.

She turns and heads to the spare room.

Jack follows, Moss bringing up the rear, and she goes inside, appraising the pile of boxes labelled, simply, *NICO*.

'This is everything he owned,' she says.

'Everything?'

'Before we got married, Nico was itinerant, almost home-less. He lived out of his van. After that, he accumulated a few bits, but not a lot.' She opens the box closest to her: old records. His tastes were eclectic but classic: Rolling Stones, the Beatles' *White Album*, Bob Dylan, Cat Stevens. Some of these might even be worth a few bob – if she can bear to part with them.

She flicks through then shows him the next box. Books, ranging from political tomes to flimsy paperbacks of *Fight Club* and *Breakfast at Tiffany's* and *On the Road*.

'May I?' Jack asks and she nods. He leans forward and selects one from the pile. It's a copy of *Fear and Loathing in Las Vegas*, littered with Post-it notes and illegible scribbles in the margin. He holds it up to her.

'He used to do that. He had plans to write the British equivalent of the great American novel. One day.' She feels tears threatening at the thought of Nico's unfulfilled ambitions, and takes it from him, dropping it back and resuming her search.

The next few containers are full of clothes, but she moves quickly on, not wanting to lose herself in the familiar shirts and jumpers that may still smell of him. Not now. Maybe not ever. Get lost in those memories and she might never return.

Onwards – to a rattling box. The contents of his desk drawers, the miscellaneous crap he must have kept for a reason.

And his mobile phone. Dumped here, earlier on in the week. Useless.

She holds it out to Jack. He takes an evidence bag from his pocket and she drops it inside.

'Why did you lie?' Ellis asks, fixing her in his stare. His eyes are grey-blue, the colour of arctic ice, of biting winter days. His gaze feels just as inhospitable.

She shrugs, as apathetic as a sulking teenager. 'I offered it to the police when he first went missing but they didn't care,' she begins. 'And now, it's all I have left.'

The excuse sounds pitiful, even to her.

Jack tries to turn it on through the evidence bag. The screen remains blank.

'You'll need to charge it,' she says when he shows her. 'And I haven't any idea of the unlock code.'

'So it wasn't much use to you anyway,' Jack replies. He doesn't wait for an answer. 'We'll get the tech guys onto it,' he finishes. 'Thank you.'

He leaves the spare room, heading for the front door.

'I'll be back in touch soon. When we have news.'

'DI Ellis.' She grabs at his arm. 'Give me something to do. Please. Not in Nico's investigation – I know I have to stay away from that – but on one of the other victims? I need to keep busy, and my skipper has me on leave.'

'Perhaps he's signed you off for a reason,' Jack points out. 'You need time. To grieve.'

'I've had years to grieve. I'm going mad here. Please.' Her voice rises in pitch and volume, desperation getting the better of her. 'I won't give up. You know that. I won't stop.'

He pauses, one hand on the lock, thinking. He turns back.

'Promise you'll do as I ask? Follow orders? Nothing more, nothing less.'

'Promise.'

He stares at her then sighs. 'We're struggling to identify the second victim. DNA has come back a blank. She has a distinctive tattoo on her shoulder and arm – Amrit's been phoning around shops but it's time-consuming, and I need her back on the team. It's boring—'

'I'll do it,' Lucy interrupts. 'Thank you.'

'We'll send you the information.' She notices his gaze flick to her tatty tracksuit bottoms and T-shirt. 'Uniform, please, PC Halliday.'

'Absolutely,' she replies, and he nods a final goodbye.

She watches him leave, battling with her emotions. He's let her work on the case, and that's something. But the phone, the investigation into Nico's death? For the first time she's not keen for Ellis to follow up on the evidence. She's lied. She's withheld information that could be vital to the case. It's only a matter of time before Ellis discovers exactly what.

And that thought chills her to the bone.

Chapter Twenty-Five

Ellis was right. Searching for the artist who tattooed victim two is laborious and boring and thankless.

Within moments of Ellis leaving Lucy's house, DC Amrit Gill emailed her a comprehensive list of Hampshire's tattoo parlours – keen to pass it on.

There are over twenty shops in the city of Southampton alone, not to mention artists operating out of houses or private studios. And Gill had been working outwards – starting with the centre of the city, widening to the suburbs and then to the whole of Hampshire. Some she had ruled out from the nick, telephoning and emailing photos of the tattoo, but she had reached an impasse, reluctant to resort to the more time-consuming job of treading the pavements, crossing them out one by one.

By midday, Lucy had only scrubbed out three, and was starting to regret her offer. The latest tattoo artist – an impressive-looking guy, white vest showing his muscles and ink to perfection – studies the photo clutched in his hand.

'Not my work,' he replies, handing back the image of the woman's arm. 'It's striking, though. Or would have been. She's dead, you say?'

'Yes. Three to eight months ago.'

'Definitely not us,' he confirms. 'We've only been operating since May and this work, well…' He looks across at the photo again. 'See the layers, the way the octopus is bridged to the fish by the seaweed? I've seen people knock out sleeves of this size in days, but my guess would be this took a good few months.'

Lucy thanks him, disappointed, and walks back to her car. She consults the list. There's one more shop a mile or so from here – she resolves to get it done before lunch.

The breeze is cool, the sun bright, so she walks, checking her phone for directions. But the free time does her no favours.

Her thoughts turn to Nico, and the couple of weeks before he disappeared. He'd been distant – as he often was, as he got deeper into an investigation. And she'd been distracted too. A murder case was keeping her busy: a body had been found a month before – a bullet in the centre of his forehead, left for the world to see in the middle of a patch of waste ground. Clearly a gang hit, a professional job and one they had zero leads for. She worked all hours, sometimes falling asleep on the sofa, her laptop open and whirring next to her.

But their marriage was solid. Nico would return, often at the dead of night, sliding into bed, skin cold and stinking of cigarettes, and they'd find solace and connection in touch. In his mouth on hers, his desire and longing more reassuring of his love than any words or affirmation.

Lucy had assumed the summons to her DCI's office was routine. An update or a request for information. But Kane's face on that early October morning was stern. A representative from Professional Standards stood behind her. And the betrayal that unfolded had been more devastating than any affair could have ever been.

Her phone announces her arrival at Sadie's Tattoos and Piercings. The door is open but the counter is deserted; she can hear the buzz of a tattoo gun in the room behind and cautiously makes her way through.

A man is reclined on the chair, his shirt off, and a slender woman is bending over him, instrument in hand. Lucy clears her throat, not wanting to do anything that might make the woman jump.

The man says a few words and the woman turns.

'You can wait out the front,' she says, and switches the gun on again.

'PC Lucy Halliday,' Lucy says, louder, holding out her ID. 'I won't take up much of your time.'

The woman sniffs, annoyed, and turns off the gun, placing it down on the table beside her. She sits up, removing her protective goggles, and for the first time Lucy can see the tattoo she was labouring over. It's a work of art. A snake makes its way up the man's arm, the tail starting at his bicep, then over his shoulder and down his chest, ending with a head of fangs and bright purple eyes. The blue-and-red python is complete, each scale intricately picked out, but the space around it is being filled in with a sophisticated network of thorns and roses and leaves.

'It's beautiful,' Lucy says. 'How long has it taken?'

'Three months so far,' the man says proudly, sitting up so Lucy can see how the flowers continue down his back. 'Another eight weeks before it's finished. This one here should take the credit,' he says, nodding to the woman. 'It's her masterpiece.'

'Helps to have a husband you can experiment on,' the woman replies. She smiles, softening. 'I'm Sadie,' she says, taking her glove off and offering her hand. Lucy shakes it. 'How can I help?'

Lucy takes the photos from her pocket and holds them out to Sadie. Immediately, her face changes.

'You found her?' Sadie says, her voice choked. She takes the photos and studies them closely.

'You know who this is?' Lucy says, trying to keep the jubilance out of her voice. 'What's her name?'

The husband places a comforting hand on Sadie's shoulder; Sadie hands the photos to him and he nods.

'That's Ness. Vanessa Savage,' Sadie replies. She gets up and fetches a binder from the bookcase behind them, selecting a page and handing it to Lucy. A slender, pretty woman smiles out, her shoulder pushed forward towards the camera. 'She came in a few years ago, wanting this octopus. It meant a huge amount to Ness. We were honoured she chose us. Where is she?'

'She's dead,' the husband says, bluntly. Sadie blanches. 'Look at these photos, Sade. She's dead.'

Both faces look expectantly towards Lucy.

'I wish I could share better news. But yes, I'm sorry. We found her body earlier this week.'

'Where?' Sadie asks. 'Was she murdered?'

'Why do you ask that?'

'Just…' Sadie glances to her husband, who nods. 'She'd been through a lot. In her childhood. She wanted the octopus because she said it signified intelligence and resilience. Strength and growth. She didn't give us all the details, but she shared a bit sat in this chair. She was here a while, as you can imagine.'

'What did she tell you?'

'That she grew up in a shit part of town. That her parents were drug dealers, thieves. In and out of prison. But that she was over the worst of it. She said she'd put it behind her. Found a good man. Someone who would look after her. Her very own Scottish hunk, she said.'

Lucy flicks through the binder. In life, the tattoo was rich and vibrant, the purple of the octopus contrasting perfectly with the blue of the water, the detail of the tentacles and suckers sharp.

'She clearly loved the tattoo,' Lucy comments. In these photos Vanessa Savage is full of life. Her face laughing at the camera, pleased with what Sadie had achieved.

'She did. So much she booked to come back. Have a consultation and maybe get something else done.'

Lucy's phone rings in her pocket. She apologises and pulls it out, her heart jumping when she sees the name on the screen.

'I have to answer this, I'm sorry,' she says, and moves to the front of the shop.

'Cal?' she says eagerly.

'Lucy – we have something.' Cal's voice is echoey, as if he's standing in a stairwell, talking in hushed tones. 'I got the team together, everyone who knew and worked with Nico, and let them know what had happened. Off the record,' he adds quickly. 'And one guy, one of our researchers – I knew something was up straight away. He stayed quiet but went bright red, so I cornered him afterwards. He said that Nico had asked him to do something.'

'What? When?'

'About three weeks before he disappeared. Asked him to do some digging, on the quiet. Our researchers know better than that, to work at the bidding of the freelance journos, but this guy had known Nico for years. They went to uni together.'

'And?' Lucy prompts impatiently.

'He won't tell me. Says he made a promise. That Nico made him swear he'd speak to you first.'

'So put him on the phone!'

'He wants to do it in person. Are you free tomorrow? Half-ten? He's heading up north – for a family wedding – but he'll meet us at Waterloo before he goes.'

Lucy agrees and hangs up, puzzled and annoyed. What could be so important that the researcher is refusing to tell his boss? What had Nico got himself into?

Lucy returns to the back room, where Sadie and her husband are whispering. They see Lucy and stop immediately.

'Tell her,' the husband pushes.

Sadie looks uncertain but sighs. 'We were worried when she missed her appointment so we phoned her mobile. A man answered. He had a Scottish accent and he claimed he was her husband, but when we asked to speak to Ness, he refused. Said that she'd changed her mind and didn't have any spare cash. We thought it was odd at the time – Ness had been so excited – but people often have second thoughts about tattoos. We try not to take it personally.'

'But?'

'But now you're saying that she's dead, we're wondering who this man was. I mean, he sounded genuine and we had no reason to doubt him, and even if we had, there's no way we would have called the police.'

'Why not?'

'Well, that's just it. If we'd been worried, if Ness was missing, we would have assumed that he would have contacted you himself.' She pauses, glances to her husband.

'He was one of you,' the man says. 'Ness said her husband was a cop.'

Chapter Twenty-Six

'Vanessa Savage's husband is police?' Jack repeats, Lucy on the other end of the phone.

'That's what they said,' Lucy replies. He can hear traffic as she walks back to her car. 'That can't be a coincidence, right? That all of our victims were related to cops?'

'No,' Jack says thoughtfully. 'Excellent work, thank you. Go home.' Lucy protests, but he cuts her off. 'Go home, Halliday,' he repeats sternly. 'I'll be in touch.'

He hangs up, then turns and writes victim two's name on the board. The team stop what they're doing and look over with interest.

'Thanks to Amrit's diligent groundwork, we now have a name for our second victim. Vanessa Savage. Also known as Ness. And her husband is one of us. Find him. And get me everything about Vanessa.'

Faces turn back to their screens. Frantic typing. Jack doesn't have to wait long.

'Vanessa Savage,' Amrit says. 'Thirty-one. Multiple arrests for minor drug offences. Juvie record is sealed, but she has a conviction for possession of a class B in 2012, served six months for supply the year after. Nothing since she got out. Married to—'

'Mark Savage,' Blake interrupts. 'For the last five years. DS in – and this is interesting – the drug squad.'

Amrit frowns. 'Seems like an odd match.'

'Or maybe a perfect one,' Jack says. 'Did he report her disappearance?' he directs to Lawrence, who shakes his head.

'Nothing with missing persons,' he confirms.

It's too much to be coincidence. 'Track down Mark Savage. Now. And get his inspector in here. I want to know everything about this pair. I'm not messing about this time. Get in touch with PolSA. I want a full search of their house, preferably with a drug dog and a VRD.'

The team are back on the phones immediately, energised by the fresh injection of information.

'Boss,' Lawrence calls, phone against his ear. 'PolSA have a drug dog but no VRD available.'

Jack pauses. 'When can they be ready?'

'Soon. Fifteen hundred hours, if needed.'

'Confirm that. We'll meet them there.' Lawrence goes back to his call; Jack picks up his phone.

'Lucy?' he says, when she answers. 'We need you. We need Moss.'

—

They gather down a side street. A nice part of town – houses with tarmacked driveways, pots of flowering plants providing colour. A neighbourhood unused to police raids. Saturday afternoon and the residential road is quiet, bar a few families with kids and walkers with their dogs. His DCI has confirmed that Mark Savage isn't at work today – hasn't been in since Wednesday, since Vanessa's body was found. Jack suspects he's long gone, that they're too late, but hopefully the house will hold some clues. The warrant has been signed; they are ready to go.

Initial intel tells them the curtains are open but the house is quiet. The risk to the public has been assessed and deemed acceptable. There is no reason for firearms officers but even so, Jack wants to go in hard, efficient, fast.

The two dog handlers wait. Lucy, Moss by her side. And Pete Nash – with a petite brown-and-white spaniel. Pepper, Nash tells him. Trained to find weed, cocaine, heroin. Anything your heart desires. The dogs are eager, Moss looking up in anticipation at Lucy. Pepper twirls on her lead, a ball of energy.

Jack gives the go-ahead over the radio and the uniforms knock, loudly. *Police. Come to the door.* A crash follows the resulting silence, as the red battering ram forces its way through. Jack moves then, striding to the house, the radio next to his ear. He hears the calls of *all clear* as the officers move from room to room, then the final declaration that the house is empty.

No more than expected; but it would have been nice to have been wrong.

The dogs are deployed and go in first, a speculative search. Jack dons a mask and gloves, and follows.

The house is quiet but presents a compelling picture. In contrast to the well-maintained street, it's messy. Filthy, even. The carpet is grey with dirt, a walkway tracked through from the sofa. The kitchen smells of old cooked food; a sink full of washing-up, more stacked on the side. Takeaway containers and pizza boxes burst from the bin, and flies buzz over the greasy cooker. Jack heads upstairs, waiting on the landing where Lucy watches over a sniffing, darting Moss. He peers into the bathroom, screwing up his nose. Brown lino, a line of dirt around the sink. He doesn't want to explore any further and goes back to Lucy.

'Anything?' he asks her.

'Preliminary search, no,' she replies. 'No trace of blood so far. If you want to be sure we'll need a few more dogs. More time.'

'If she was killed here you would have found the blood, right?'

'From a head wound? Probably. Look, look,' she says to the dog, directing him towards the next room, where he sniffs, tail wagging.

'DI Ellis?' Nash calls and Jack turns, heading towards the main bedroom. A large bed takes up the majority of the space, a line of cupboards down one side. The bed is in disarray, the sheets grey, but it's the wardrobe that holds the dog's attention.

The doors are open and Pepper is frozen, nose down, pointing to the bottom. Nash praises the dog and releases her, throwing her a tennis ball, which the spaniel catches happily.

'Down there,' Nash says. 'Clear indication.'

'Any idea what?'

'Let's find out,' Nash says with a grin.

Jack squats down, clearing the shoeboxes and discarded clothes from the bottom of the wardrobe. He taps on the base; the sound comes back hollow. The board comes away easily.

A large space is revealed within. One foot by two, and disappointingly empty.

Nash leans down, with what looks like a large cotton bud in his hand and runs the tip around the space. Jack watches closely as he opens the testing kit and drops the swab inside, shaking it for a moment.

When he stops, the liquid is blue.

'Traces of cocaine,' Nash confirms. 'Without a doubt.'

Jack looks at the hole. 'Could have stored a lot in here. Tens of thousands of pounds' worth.'

'If not more.'

'So where is it?'

Nash shrugs affably. 'Your job, boss,' he says. 'I'll inform PolSA,' he shouts over his shoulder as he beckons his dog away.

Jack thanks him and looks up as Lucy appears in the doorway, Moss at her heel.

'You have drugs?' she asks and he nods. 'Sounds like a dodgy copper to me.'

'Looking that way. And he's gone to ground. Hardly the actions of an innocent man. Blood?'

'Not that we can find in such a quick search. Sorry. What's next?'

'Mark Savage's DCI is waiting for me back at the nick. Hopefully, he'll have some answers. Meanwhile, we'll get the SOCOs in, see what else they can find.' She opens her mouth, looks like she's about to say something, but closes it quickly.

'You're heading home?' Jack says. She nods. 'Lucy?' She turns. 'Thank you.'

She nods again, and leaves. He wishes he had more to tell her. That they'd located the missing van or had the results back from the forensic tests on Nico's clothes. He resolves to chase them up when he gets back to the nick.

DC Amrit Gill joins him in the bedroom. 'Whatever Mark Savage has been doing for the last few months, it doesn't look like he was happy.'

'Indeed,' Jack agrees with a sigh. 'A man with a guilty conscience?'

'Up to his eyeballs.' Amrit looks to her notebook. 'I spoke to the neighbours. They haven't seen Vanessa since February. And when they asked Mark, he said she'd left him. They thought that's why he's looked so awful lately.'

'Did she have a job?'

'Yes.' She flicks the pages again. 'Nail technician, at a salon in town. I called them.'

'Already?'

'I don't hang around, boss.' Her face flushes at her uncharacteristic immodesty and her eyes drop back to her notepad. 'They said she quit, in February again, so it looks like we have a clear point when she went missing, but here's the kicker. She didn't resign. He did.'

'Her husband did?'

'Yeah. Called and then followed up with an email – from his own account. They asked to speak to Vanessa, but he hung up on them. When they tried to call her mobile, it rang out.'

'Weren't they worried?'

'Yes. They thought it might be an abusive relationship but...' She pulls a face. '"We didn't want to interfere."'

'How lovely.'

Jack's phone rings. It's Phil Lawrence.

'You on your way back, boss?' Lawrence asks. 'DCI Perry is here. And he's keen to talk to you.'

'On my way,' Jack confirms, and leaves the empty house of the dead woman and the missing man. No arrests but they're making progress.

Something will fall into place soon, he can feel it.

Chapter Twenty-Seven

DCI Perry is exactly the sort of man Jack has come to expect from officers in charge of drug squads: muscular, wide, with the stance and underbite of a bulldog. He stands, legs apart, waiting motionless until Jack enters the room. But at that point, the man's demeanour changes – a broad smile at Jack's introduction, a double-clasped handshake.

'I knew something was up,' Perry says as they sit down at the table in the middle of the incident room. 'Mark's been on the decline for a while, but he's never not turned up to work. I reported to HR that he'd gone AWOL but they did fuck all. Called his mobile and left a message. Like I hadn't done that already.'

Jack nods in understanding. 'What do you mean – on the decline?'

'Savage was an excellent officer. But about a year ago things started to slip. He was distracted, paperwork late, that sort of thing. He'd been married a few years – to Vanessa – so I wondered whether things were falling apart at home but when I asked, he seemed surprised. Said no, things were great. They were even trying for a baby.'

'What was it?'

'Not a clue. But he got worse – if I could have thought that possible. Started coming in stinking of booze, not showering.'

'When did that start?'

'After Christmas. Winter. So – February? Yes, February.' He smiles with satisfaction, revealing shiny white teeth. 'We'd had that raid by the docks.'

February. When Vanessa Savage went missing. They pause as Lawrence brings them their drinks; Jack thanks him and when he turns back, Perry's deep in thought. He leans towards Jack.

'Between you and I, a lot of what we do in the team is on the down-low. Not, strictly speaking, procedure. The most successful of my officers are the ones who foster the relationships. Who get out there on the streets and listen to the whispers, throw a few tenners here and there. So no, they don't keep records of who they speak to or why. They don't tell me what's going on. But that's okay.' He sits back again and takes a large gulp of his coffee, smacking his lips together with satisfaction. 'What I'm saying, Ellis, is that it's worthwhile because these off-the-record conversations and the shit I know nothing about often come together, and we get huge busts out of it. That raid by the docks I mentioned?' Jack nods, but he's not aware. Wasn't around then. 'That was the result of years' worth of intel, all coming together beautifully. We didn't seize as much as we expected, but it was significant.'

Jack quietly sips his tea. He's not naïve, he knows there are parts of the police force more closely connected to the criminals than they'd like. But they get results. Arrests, charges, convictions. The outcome he needs on this investigation.

'So – DS Mark Savage?' he asks, pulling the DCI back. 'You had no idea his wife had been missing for four months? Since February.'

'Hell, no. Four months you say? That would fit, but Mark's been going downhill for longer than that.'

They both look up as Amrit approaches, a piece of paper clutched in her hand.

'Sorry to disturb you, boss, but…'

'Go on?'

'Results from the tapings from Nico Halliday's clothing came back. Small chips of blue were found. Paint. Lead paint, specifically.'

'But that's not been used since…'

'The Seventies, or thereabouts,' Amrit says. 'It helps to narrow things down. And the lab went back to the clothing from victims one and two.'

'Found on them too?' Amrit nods. 'So we're looking for an old building, possibly disused, probably in a secluded area,' Jack says, thinking out loud. 'I would guess within the vicinity of Gallows Wood, as our kidnappers wouldn't have wanted to transport the victims far, whether dead or alive.'

Perry has been looking behind him, to the map of the woods stuck on the wall, the location of the three victims marked with red pins.

'This the place?' he asks, pointing upwards.

Jack nods. 'Why?'

'Well…' Perry stands up, runs his hand across the map, then places a stubby finger on a road, north of the crime scene. 'This here was the site of a raid, back in… I don't know… maybe 2018? We seized over two kilos of high-purity cocaine. Would have netted over a hundred and sixty grand on the streets once cut and sold.' He looks back to Jack and Amrit. 'I remember it because one of the SOCOs tried to take the police to court. Said that working at that house had caused severe anaemia, and joint and muscle pain. Claimed he never worked again.' He taps his finger on the map. 'Because of the lead paint on the walls.'

Daisy cries silently in the darkness.

She wonders why she is here – money, or for something else? Human trafficking, prostitution. She has heard stories about young girls being abducted for sex. Hooked on drugs then sold to the highest bidder. Foreign countries, broken bodies, rape.

She begs for escape; prays to a God she had long forgotten.

The house creaks and groans; an inanimate force protesting to the violence within. She hears shouts and conversations, most in a language she doesn't understand but some in heavily accented English.

'…She is alive. Yes. You do as we ask…'

'…Find it. Find out…'

'…What do you mean, they know? They are coming…'

That last comment is shouted; for a moment it gives her hope. She is going to be rescued! Her uni friends have reported her missing, she will see her mum soon.

But no.

The mood shifts. Panic. Urgency. Raised voices, the clattering of heavy footsteps on the stairs. Shouts and swear words. The revving of a car engine outside. Mobile ringtones play before they are answered with frantic barks.

The door to her room is opened. She flinches – him again.

'How is your nose?' he asks with a leer.

She doesn't reply, stays cowering in the corner.

He looks at her for a moment, appraising her as one might a disgusting stain or a dog shit on the pavement, then takes his arm out from behind his back. There is something in his hand. A needle, attached to a syringe.

He takes two quick steps towards her.

'No… no, please,' she pleads. Those trafficked girls, the drugged women. Her fate. 'I don't want… I don't…'

He tugs roughly at her body. She resists but he forces her to lie face down and puts heavy knees on her back, her arm wrenched behind her. A sharp prick. And then… nothing.

He has gone. The pain has gone. The room vanishes.

Into a blissful, heavenly, peace.

Chapter Twenty-Eight

The calls go out; the teams assemble. An observation post is set up in a house nearby – a covert team watching the property. Jack wants them to move fast, but efficiently – if this is the place where all their victims have been held, there's a possibility there could be someone on site, but so far the reports back have stated no movement.

'How much do we need to worry about the lead paint?' Jack had asked Perry as they drove to the location. Perry had demanded to come, saying he needed to see some action after a week behind his desk.

'Not at all,' he replied. 'Environmental health went in soon after we did. Did their tests and found that while the paint was deteriorating and the lead might become airborne, the time we were in the property rendered it insignificant. No greater risk than the exhaust we inhale every day, walking along the road.'

'I'm not sure if that's reassuring,' Jack had commented and his colleague had scoffed.

'I'm not worried about lead paint,' the DCI had replied. 'It's the smackheads with knives that bother me.'

They bother Jack too – but given the lack of activity, a house entry team is all they're granted. PCs kitted up to the nines, a sergeant in charge.

Perry has been in the house before so explains the layout to the team. Two floors, all dilapidated and in poor repair. Watch out for needles, for squatters, for junkies protecting their stash. Jack emphasises what's at stake: there could be other victims. Vital evidence. Clear the area and get out.

Forensics are pending. Digital have done a preliminary review of Nico Halliday's mobile phone and have come up blank. No data. 'Possibly wiped, but we might be able to restore it,' the analyst had said with a grin.

PolSA are deploying the full search, so Jack expects the dog team. Sure enough, he spots the unmarked cars on the far left. Lucy is waiting by the open boot, Moss inside.

Lucy looks in his direction but doesn't give any other acknowledgement. The empty phone gives Jack pause. Why had Lucy Halliday been guarding it so closely if there was nothing there? Or had she been the one to erase it?

She shouldn't be here, he thinks. This is potentially where her husband died; her presence could compromise any evidence they find. Coming to Savage's house earlier, that was justified – barely. This is too close for comfort. But he hasn't got time to deal with this now; he'll intercept her before she goes near, once the house entry is complete.

Pete Nash is also standing by – with both dogs this time. Just the threat of sending a toothy dog into a building can get even the toughest guys coming out with their hands up; nobody wants a ninety-pound German shepherd hanging off their arm. And as Jack watches, Nash turns to Lucy and they have a heated exchange. Pete's normally easy-going manner is reduced to jerky arm waving and annoyance. Lucy's sullen, eyes to the ground.

Jack's concerned – they don't want to attract attention. But almost as soon as it began, it's over, Lucy moving around to the opposite side of the car to avoid Nash. Probably the same objections he has; Jack hopes she'll get the hint and leave.

He casts his eye over the search area. It couldn't be more different to the forest where they'd been days before. The summer sun sets behind the large house, casting the rubble and tree stumps into shadow. Used condoms, smashed bottles and tiny canisters of nitrous surround burned-out bonfires. A hang-out for the homeless, for teenagers, for anyone looking to get off their faces, and fast.

It's nasty, treacherous, stinking, where the forest was calm. Nature, undisturbed. A peaceful resting place for the victims, until the police took over.

A voice comes over the radio: the team are ready. Jack makes a silent wish for this raid to give them something concrete and issues the command to go. It's based on weak intel from years ago. A hunch. It's hardly a solid lead, but it's all they have.

He listens down the radio as thumps and bashes echo around the building. Then there's silence.

'Give me an update, sergeant?' Jack barks.

A hiss as the button is pressed, then the sound of retching. 'All clear, boss,' the voice says. 'But you might want to see this.'

Jack frowns at Perry, and the two of them suit up and make their way into the house. Inside it's dark, grey half-light filtering through dirty windows as Jack's feet crunch on broken glass and splintered floorboards. He heads through the hallway and up the creaking stairs, following directions to where the officer in charge is waiting. A few burly policemen pass, clearing out, their expressions haunted.

He reaches the top of the stairs. Torches dance inside a room, but he doesn't need to go in to realise what he's facing – the smell hits him hard. Even behind his mask, the stench is overpowering. Warm, rotten meat. Every instinct wants to turn and go out into the fresh air, but he pushes on.

One officer remains, his hand over his mouth. On seeing Jack, he lifts his torch towards the focus of the disgust.

Jack gags, then puts his gloved hand over his mouth, pushing the mask hard against his face. He takes small gulps of breath then forces himself to look again.

A man hangs from the wooden rafters. Underneath him a chair lies on its side. His hands hang loose; his face is purple and bloated. Almost unrecognisable.

Almost.

'That's Mark Savage,' Perry says, thickly. 'Fuck. He must have been here...'

'A few days,' Jack finishes for him as he appraises the dead body. In the summer heat, exposed to the elements, his rate of decomposition would have been swift. The body has a green tinge, swollen and marbled. Flies buzz, angry at being disturbed from their new home.

'Shit,' Jack says. Then he spots something poking out of his shirt pocket. A centimetre of white.

He calls to a SOCO lurking behind him. 'Can you capture this?' he asks, and photographs are taken, before Jack picks up the chair, rights it, then stands on top. To extract whatever's there, he needs to reach forward, excruciatingly close to the body, the smell septic and sticky. He holds his breath as he gently tugs the piece of paper from its mooring.

He climbs down and places it in the offered evidence bag. He seals it, then holds it to the torchlight.

It's a scrap of paper. A receipt for a restaurant. But scribbled across are three words.

Catch these bastards.

Jack looks up at the putrefying corpse of Mark Savage. He has no doubt that the man killed himself just after his wife's body was found – and that the reasons he did so are related to the case. He chose to die here. It must be significant.

If only he could have stuck around to tell them why.

Chapter Twenty-Nine

'You shouldn't be here.'

'So you said,' Lucy replies, looking away from Pete Nash to the house. Police officers surround it like flies. She bends down to stroke Dax; Pete is circling him around the scrubland, a good distance from the crime scene, trying to get him to do a wee.

'You're involved,' Pete repeats on his second lap. 'You're family to one of the victims. There's a reason you're on leave.'

'You see any other victim recovery dogs around here?' Lucy replies, looking around in an exaggerated manner. 'Anybody else ready to go?'

'Yes, we need more VRDs. Not my point,' Pete snaps.

They stop their bickering as a PolSA heads towards them. 'You can stand the dogs down,' he says once he's close. 'No one in there but a dead body. It belongs to the SOCOs now. I'll call you later if you're needed.' He pauses, glancing back and lowering his voice to a whisper. 'DS Mark Savage, apparently. Hanged himself.'

Lucy and Nash both swivel to the scene. SOCOs are starting to arrive in greater numbers, spirits in the half-light, gathering kit and heading inside.

'Did you know him?' Pete asks Lucy.

'No, but…' The same surname as victim two. Can't be a coincidence. She blinks and shakes her head. 'No,' she repeats. 'Wonder why he killed himself.'

Dax stops his circling and does his business. Pete waits, before loading him back into his car. Pepper sticks her nose out of the crate, sniffing eagerly.

'Sorry, old girl,' Pete says to Pepper then closes the boot. 'I'm off.' He taps Lucy briefly on the arm. 'You should go too.'

'I will,' she says, and gives him what she hopes is a reassuring smile. But the moment his car is out of her eyeline, she shuts the air-conditioned boot on Moss and steps forward, closer to the crime scene.

Pete's right. She should stay away. But the link to victim two – and whatever else that house might hold – is too compelling.

She walks tentatively to the cordon. Ellis must be inside, no sign of Blake – no one to stop her. She's in uniform and shows her badge to the scene guard then signs in. He doesn't give her more than a cursory glance.

She dons the white protective suit and makes her way through the front door, avoiding the crime scene manager. Yellow triangles are already scattered across the hallway. Foot-wear marks. Cigarette butts. Empty bottles. The evidence-gathering alone could take weeks, and even then, only a small proportion will be tested. Unless there's an indication that a particular exhibit holds something relating to the killer, it will languish untouched, forever, in storage.

She can hear Jack talking in a room to her right and swings away. The white suits lend an air of anonymity, but from what she knows about Ellis, he'll spot her. He has a sixth sense, that man.

Moving in the opposite direction to Jack also means that the smell is subsiding. After witnessing the pallor of some she saw leaving the house, she has no wish to get any closer to the stinking dead body.

She turns down a corridor to the left-hand side. This floor has carpeting; faded, old, rendered muck-brown over the years. Tattered, torn curtains hang in the smashed windows like tentacles from a dying ghost; the carpet is saturated with rainwater and squishes softly under her feet. The wallpaper, once blue but now dirtied with smears and streaks, slowly peels away from the crumbling plaster. Lucy keeps her hands close to her sides.

A SOCO emerges from the far room. Spotting her, the woman asks, 'You MCIT?'

Lucy nods and the woman points.

'In there.'

Inside, the room is large, almost completely empty. There is no carpet here, the floors stripped back to bare wood. The window is covered in layers of newspaper, blocking the remaining light from outside; wind whistles through the gaps in the frame, causing the battery-powered floodlight to sway, giving a sinister, drunken ambience. The flickering beam highlights the only furniture – a chair on its side in a corner of the room.

'Do you want to see?' the SOCO asks and Lucy nods again, no idea what she's agreeing to.

The SOCO holds a large light bar. She turns the floodlight off then flicks a switch; the bar bursts into light, throwing out an eerie purple hue. And instantly, Lucy realises what the SOCOs have found.

The room glows. Dots, smudges, pools, smears. Spatters of green-blue highlight skirting boards and door frames. And the chair. The chair lights up like a Christmas tree.

These are the effects of luminol and a black light. That chair had been coated in blood.

This is the room.

'That's enough, thank you,' a male voice says behind her, and the black light turns off. The apparitions disappear; the room is plunged into darkness before the floodlight is put back on and the normal level of squalor returns.

'You're contaminating my crime scene.'

'He was here,' Lucy whispers.

'That's our theory,' Jack replies. She turns now and faces him, expecting a reproach, but he gestures to the door behind him. 'The room with the dead man – that's where we believe victim two was held. We've found items of women's clothing, as well as plastic bin liners similar to the ones her body was wrapped in. But this room…'

'Was where they tortured Nico,' Lucy finishes dully.

'Tortured a lot of people, by the looks of it. Some of the blood in here is fresh, last few days, while other spatters could have been around for years. The DCI of the drug squad is going to ask around but he thinks this is one of the houses used by a local gang.'

'OCG?' Lucy asks. Organised Crime Group. One of the most common reasons for crime in the city. Drugs. Money. Gambling. And all of those lead to violence. In astounding proportions.

'Possibly,' Jack replies. He sighs, loudly. 'We're not going to get anything much today. Go home, Lucy,' he says, in a tone that suggests he's bored of saying it. 'You're not doing yourself any good by being here.'

She looks at the chair. She takes in the scratches on the floor, the faded brown stains she can see now she knows they're there. She can feel his fear, absorbed into the wood. The pain, the hatred, the desperation.

The lump in her throat threatens to choke her and she leaves without another word. She takes the stairs fast, wrestling her white suit off the moment she's free of the cordon, sprinting to her car. She throws herself inside. Gulps lungfuls of cool air.

She could see him. There. Tied to that chair. For how long? Days, weeks? His bones broken, teeth knocked out, face smashed and torn. And for what? Punishment or interrogation, to find out what he knew?

What had Nico discovered?

Lucy's convinced something he was looking into brought him to that house. If Nico found it, then Lucy will too. And she will make those monsters pay.

Sunday

Chapter Thirty

Waterloo station is alive with people, even on a Sunday morning. A live wire, a battery powered by overhead announcements and chatter, and the rattle of trains and wheels on suitcases. For someone who has barely been around any living creatures other than her dog for the past year, the noise physically hurts.

Lucy's early. Unsurprising, given she barely slept; she couldn't stomach breakfast, wondering what this researcher at *The Guardian* might know. She'd walked Moss as the day broke. Watched horses and donkeys graze peacefully at the edge of a pond, wobbly nervous foals at their sides. They'd eyed Moss warily as they passed, but the dog's interest was held only by the scent of deer and rabbits, tracking like he was on rails, nose to the grass.

She'd showered and dressed, leaving Moss in the cool of his kennel. He'll be fine. She envied his day; almost changed her mind and backed out.

But no.

The train had been on time, half-empty. She'd bought a coffee, drunk it quickly, and now she negotiates a path across the concourse, avoiding teenagers and backpackers and toddlers, and takes the escalator to the mezzanine floor. She stops at the closest café and orders more caffeine, sitting at one of the tables that look down into the main station. Being at eye level with the huge clock makes her vertiginous, but it's worth it for the view. To know who is coming and when.

Having seen the room where Nico died hasn't helped. Her imagination fills the gaps. The spatter of blood as a fist hits his face. The crack of his ribs as he is beaten. His final wheeze as his lungs collapse. That's what she remembers of him now. That – and the burning anger threatening to break her.

While she waits, she scribbles in her notebook. Everything she knows; her suspicions; potential lines of inquiry. Old habits die hard, but there's not much she can do. And little she knows for sure.

She checks her watch. They're late. Perhaps the researcher has changed his mind, but no, at a quarter to eleven her phone rings and she answers, directing Cal up the stairs to where she's waiting.

Her eyes flick towards the escalators. Cal – his thatch of unruly grey hair, fast receding into a widow's peak, wearing a tweed jacket and jeans. And with him – a tall, slim man. Shaved head, rimless glasses; Nico never mentioned working with someone he went to university with. Still, there was a lot about Nico she didn't know.

Cal grabs her in a tight hug the moment he sees her. 'Fuck,' he says, when he finally lets her go. 'Fuck.'

Up close, he's aged. Unshaven, now more salt than pepper, his previously angular face has sagged into hollows under his eyes and cheekbones. He introduces Lucy to the researcher.

'Giles Bonner,' he says. Giles looks shy and scared, lacking the confidence normally seen in middle-aged men. He shakes Lucy's hand limply.

'Sit down,' Cal instructs. 'I'll get coffee.'

Giles's fear seems to intensify with Cal gone. He repeatedly interlaces and unlocks his fingers, his eyes flicking to where Cal is ordering the drinks.

'Don't worry,' Lucy says. 'I won't bite.'

Giles utters what Lucy assumes is a laugh; it comes out as a squeak.

'Have you been at *The Guardian* long?' she says, attempting conversation.

'Ten years,' he replies. 'Before that I was an analyst at UCL.'

'Do you enjoy it?'

'It's fine.' He goes back to staring at his fidgeting hands. She can see why Nico never mentioned this guy: he's a shadow, a peripheral player to her extrovert husband. Giles Bonner barely registered in his thoughts.

Lucy accepts the silence and waits. Cal returns. He passes the drinks out; Giles takes two packets of sugar and pours both into his coffee.

'Well?' Lucy says, when she can't bear the wait any longer. 'What did Nico ask you to do?'

The researcher looks nervously from Lucy to Cal, as if preparing himself for a big speech to thousands rather than a casual chat with two.

'Nico came to see me. We'd kept in touch over the years, gone for a coffee every now and again. But this time – must have been a few weeks before he disappeared – he wanted me to do a freedom of information request looking into drug overdose and death rates across hospitals in the UK.'

'Drug deaths?' The conversation Nico had with Fran flashes into Lucy's head. Testing heroin.

'Yeah. And he said not to tell anyone, that this was going to be a secret between us.'

Lucy glances to Cal, who rolls his eyes.

'And? What did you find?'

The researcher leans down and pulls a laptop out of his bag, opening it. 'All the data came through well after Nico had disappeared, but out of curiosity I analysed it.' He turns the laptop around to face Lucy. 'It shows what Nico had suspected, that rates for both overdoses and related deaths are significantly higher in Hampshire than in the rest of the country.'

Cal pulls the laptop around to look at it more closely. His forehead furrows. 'And why couldn't you mention this before?'

'I–I,' he stutters. 'Nico said… He said to keep it to myself. That it was going to be a huge scoop and he didn't want anyone to steal his thunder. I–I honestly thought he was coming back.' Uncomfortably, the man looks like he's going to cry. 'And he said that if I ever needed something, and he wasn't around, to talk to you.' His gaze shifts to Lucy. 'And only you. He wanted you to hear it first. Said that if it went in the papers, it would compromise the criminal investigation.'

'Criminal investigation?' Lucy says, surprised. Normally, nothing was more important to Nico than the story. 'He said that?'

'Yes, that you were a senior detective and you'd know what to do. Is that true?'

Lucy flushes. 'I was,' she mumbles. 'Not anymore. Is that all he asked? It doesn't seem much.'

'It was the only thing I could do. He also wanted me to look into the police records from drug raids across Hampshire constabulary. Get them to share the data of how much was expected versus how much was seized. But they wrote back and said no. That sharing that data would compromise national security and potential future arrests.'

Lucy makes a note then sits back in her seat, puzzled.

'Does that make any sense to you?' Cal asks her.

'He never told me what he was working on. But then…' She remembers the week before he disappeared. The arguments, the fights. They weren't talking about much at all at that time. She picks up her mug, surprised to find the coffee cold. 'What had he told you, Cal?'

'The same – nothing. Although…' He pauses, considering. 'I remember he sent an email about some charity thing he wanted me to get involved with. A fundraiser he was supporting. Wait a sec…'

Lucy waits as he picks up his phone and types.

'Yes, here it is. Drug Matters, the charity's called. You know he had problems in his twenties, heroin overdose and the like, so this was close to his heart. Perhaps he was investigating something related. Have you found his papers? He was chaotic but he always kept extensive records of his sources.'

'No, and that's the weird thing, Cal. His van's missing.'

'That old VW?'

'That's the one. He used to work out of there. Peace and quiet, better for his concentration. At least that's what he said. He probably just liked to smoke and drink undisturbed.' She smiles at the thought. 'But I bet that's where all his notes are.'

'What do the police say?'

'Not much. Have you seen? Nico isn't the only murder they're working on. There's another two.'

'Three murders,' Giles squeaks. He gathers his laptop, shoving it in his bag. 'You didn't tell me it was a multiple-murder case.'

'They're not going to go after you,' Lucy says wearily. 'Why would they kill you?'

'I know too much. I have to go,' he says as he gets up. 'I'll email you the data,' he directs to Cal, glancing over his shoulder as he scuttles away.

'Enjoy the wedding,' Cal calls after him, laughing. 'He's a weird one but excellent at his job. Clearly been watching too many Bourne films.'

'Yeah, and Matt Damon's hiding behind that advertising board, right there,' Lucy replies with a smile, watching as Giles descends the escalator and disappears out of sight.

When she looks back, Cal is giving her a sympathetic look.

'How's life in the dog unit?'

'Quiet. Simple. And that's what I need. Send me the report. I'll pass it along to the SIO. He can try and make sense of it all.'

'I must admit, I'm curious,' Cal says. 'Three people dead. The first guy squeaky clean but related to a cop.'

'That wasn't in the papers.'

'I'm a newspaper editor. I know how to poke around. It's odd, that's all. And Nico looking into all this drug stuff, just before he died.'

Lucy stays quiet. Cal leans forward, his eyes narrowed.

'Come on, Lucy. What do you know?'

'I didn't tell you this—'

'Of course.'

'But the second victim was the wife of a DS in the drug squad. And he's been found dead, in the house where Nico was probably killed.'

Cal blinks with surprise. 'Murdered?'

'Suicide.'

'But in the same house?' Cal says. 'That can't be coincidence.'

'He knew his body would be discovered at some point. He knew he'd bring police in his wake. So why not tell us himself?'

'He was implicated? Didn't want to face the consequences?'

Lucy just shrugs. 'Not my case. No idea.'

'Oh, come on, Lucy! You're as fascinated as I am.'

'I'm not *fascinated*. My husband was murdered because of this.'

'Even more reason.' Cal gets ready to stand. 'Look, I'll do some more digging at my end. See if any of our sources local to Hampshire know anything – for Nico.'

'For Nico. Obviously,' Lucy repeats sarcastically.

'And for the paper.' He squeezes Lucy's shoulder. 'Take care of yourself,' he says and leaves.

Lucy stays in the café. The day is heating up; even in the spacious warehouse of Waterloo station, the air feels uncomfortably close. She runs her finger around the collar of her T-shirt, feeling envious of Moss, probably lying flat on the top of his bed box, in the shade, in his kennel. The thought of her dog is instantly calming, and an image comes to mind. Arriving home, putting on running shoes, and taking Moss out into the fields and the countryside, the peace and quiet. Getting air in her lungs and tiredness in her legs. Anything but the suffocating buzz of the people around her.

She looks across to the departures board. The next train for Southampton is leaving in ten minutes. She hurries down to platform twelve.

Chapter Thirty-One

Jack watches from his car as people swarm the squat. A full team of SOCOs are now here, the crime scene manager expertly commanding them as they cover every inch, gather every sample, photograph every sordid scene. He prays for a finger-print or a skin cell. Anything to get an arrest.

His window is open, but it doesn't bring relief. The midday sun is high and stifling; in the distance Harry Blake chugs water under a scraggly tree, his aviators on, shirtsleeves rolled up above his elbow. Even Jack has abandoned his usual strict dress code and has done the same. The weather is oppressive. Hottest June on record, the Met Office is saying. He hates to think what it's like in the house.

The front door opens and Fran emerges. He gets out of the car and lifts his hand; she sees him and heads over. Behind her the undertaker and their team carry a black body bag to the waiting van.

Fran wipes a hand across her brow and pulls off her crime scene suit, revealing a sweat-stained T-shirt and a pair of shorts.

'What a day,' she sighs, cracking open a water bottle and taking a long swig. 'I'll share all I know. And it's not much. No signs of a struggle, no defensive or offensive wounds. The body shows all the trademark indicators of suffocation. My guess at this point is he kicked the chair out from under himself, resulting in a sudden drop and injury on the neck. Vagal inhibition – and it would have been quick. I need to do the post-mortem, and if you find another contributor of DNA on the rope I'll revisit my opinion, but otherwise...'

'He killed himself,' Jack concludes.

Fran nods grimly. 'In the place his wife was murdered.'

'Damn,' Jack mutters under his breath. Fran leaves him with a reassuring tap on the arm, and he heads towards the CSM, who's staring at a clipboard outside the house. She gives him a wary side-eye as he comes closer.

'You're the new guy,' she says. 'I'll give you the benefit of the doubt, but if you're coming to ask me when I'll have results, we're going to have a problem.'

'I would never dream of doing such a thing,' he says with what he hopes is a beguiling smile. 'Jack Ellis.'

'Rachel Lennon,' she says with an acknowledging nod. Then she sighs and rolls her eyes. 'We'll go as fast as we can. Collection of exhibits in a place this size is going to take time, but we'll transfer them back to the lab as soon as we have them. I'll take the first batch across myself now. You might start seeing results on some of the fingerprints as soon as the next few hours.'

'You have fingerprints?' he says eagerly.

'Some. Blood samples too. But don't get excited. By the looks of it, the whole place has been used as a crack den and squatters' paradise for years. Your nightmare will be distinguishing the murderers and the kidnappers from the rest of the everyday scumbags.'

'Don't I know it,' Jack mutters. 'Want to swap jobs?'

'Hell, no,' she replies. But he gets a smile in return so he must have done something right.

Blake joins him and the CSM's smile fades. She walks away without another word.

'Don't bother with Lennon,' Blake says. 'Ice queen.'

Jack nods, but says nothing, taking a small satisfaction in his victory. 'What do you think is going on, Blake?' he asks. 'What's your theory?'

Blake looks up at Jack in surprise, then back to the house.

'Everyone knows about this place, right? A regular haunt for the homeless.'

'Right…'

'They figure it's been raided once, won't be raided again, so they use it as their base. It's probably always full of unconscious junkies. Who would pay any attention to a corpse in the corner, slowly withering away like Vanessa Savage?'

'And Nico Halliday? I'm guessing he would have made a lot of noise?'

'But who's going to interfere? Throw a few more baggies around and everyone's happy. They're not going to go to the police, because who would believe a smackhead and—'

'Have we checked that? That nobody called 999?'

'No, but—'

'Do it. Run the call logs. And who are you talking about here? Who are these mysterious people throwing drugs around?'

'An OCG, must be. But which one, well…' Blake shrugs apathetically. 'Could be any.'

Jack raises his eyebrows at Blake's nonchalance, but before he has time to reply, his phone rings. He answers it.

'DI Ellis, this is Raj from the digital team. I have Nicolas Halliday's mobile phone here, and… well…'

'I heard already. It's wiped.'

'Well, yes. But…' A chuckle sounds down the line. 'Lucky for us – or you – even if the operating system thinks the data is gone, the phone itself can have information on it. Information we can recover with a specialist program. Everything's here.'

'Everything?' Jack repeats with surprise.

'E-ve-r-y-thing,' he says, elongating the word. 'And pardon my language, DI Ellis, but fucking hell, you're going to want to see this.'

Chapter Thirty-Two

Blake leads the way to the digital department, Jack following into a darkened room lit only with desk lamps. Cables and equipment litter the floor; a potential health and safety hazard with every step.

A man waves from the far end – must be Raj. Sure enough, Halliday's iPhone lies on his desk, a wire connecting it to the computer. Text glows from the monitor; Jack squints but it might as well have been ancient Greek for all he can decipher.

They sit down and Raj flicks displays, alternating between a chat function and photographs.

'Now, the beauty of our software is that it knows how to look for certain file types. Photos, messages – everything stored in a bunch of folders.'

'Including WhatsApp?' Blake asks.

'Not WhatsApp. The end-to-end encryption makes that a bloody nightmare. But everything else.'

Raj seems confident but every now and again he glances at Blake, his forehead furrowing. Jack catches his eye and Raj gives the slightest shake of his head.

Blake is leaning forward, examining the text on the screen, and Jack does the same. It's an exchange between Nico Halliday and someone unknown, their texts made up by nothing but emojis.

Jack turns to Blake. 'Speak to Perry in the drug squad, see if he can shed any light on what all this means.' Blake nods but doesn't move. 'Go now,' he directs and Blake sighs, heading out of the room, leaving Raj and Jack alone.

'Now he's gone, what aren't you telling me?'

'Blake used to report to Lucy Halliday, right?'

'I wasn't aware, but go on?'

'There were rumours. That the reason Lucy was investigated by the PSD was because details from confidential cases kept on popping up in articles written by Nico Halliday.'

'I heard. What's this got to do with Blake?'

'Well, I've been digging around the phone, and there's a lot of stuff here. Personal stuff. So if it's not relevant to the case, it makes sense to keep it between you and I. Lucy doesn't deserve to be gossiped about again. But if it is...'

'I need to see it.'

Raj nods. Jack senses there's something else going on, but he's never been a fan of gossip and lets it go. For now, at least.

Raj points back to the screen. 'First of all, the deletion. We assumed that Nico Halliday wiped it before he disappeared. Either he knew he was in trouble or was about to get into it. But among everything the software recovered was the data for the operating system. And, oddly, it's the latest release. It must have completed an auto-update last time it was turned on and plugged into the mains. And this version only came out on Tuesday. This week.'

Jack's stomach plummets. 'So Lucy Halliday wiped the phone sometime between Tuesday and Saturday morning when I collected it?'

Raj nods grimly. 'And the easiest way of doing that, assuming she didn't have the unlock code, is to enter it ten times in quick succession. It's an option you have to select in set-up but it's common. And the phone would have auto-deleted.'

'Could it have been a mistake?'

'Yes, but...' He flicks screens again and leans back so Jack can see. 'It's more likely she was hiding this.'

Jack cranes forward. It's a video taken from a front door. Two people stand outside a house, their arms wild, clearly angry.

'Where's this footage from?' Jack asks without taking his eyes from the screen.

'The Ring doorbell outside the Hallidays' old house. There are loads of videos downloaded to his phone but this one is twenty-four hours before he disappeared. This could well be the last known sighting of Nico Halliday.'

Jack continues watching, then recoils. He stares, open-mouthed, as a fight breaks out. Violence, inflicted with little hesitation.

'So this means...' Jack begins.

'Looks that way,' Raj replies. 'Poor sod.'

Feet thunder down the room, and Jack looks up to see Amrit hurrying towards them. A piece of paper flutters in her hand.

'Boss, you need to see this,' she says, breathlessly. 'You weren't answering your phone.'

'No reception down here,' Raj says, extending a hand. 'You're new. Raj Johal.'

Amrit ignores him, her attention grabbed by the paused footage on the monitor.

'Is that...?'

'Yes. What is it, Amrit?' Jack asks, then snatches the piece of paper from her hand. As Amrit continues to gawp, he scans the lines of type. It's a report from the lab, detailing the findings from the clothing and nail scrapings of Nicolas Halliday. And as he finishes reading, his gaze slowly shifts back to the video on the screen.

He thinks he's going to be sick, such is his physical reaction to the news. It's not the first time he's been wrong about someone, and it won't be the last, but this feels personal. He had sympathy for her. He gave her the benefit of the doubt, despite her overstepping at every turn. And it's all blown out of the water in a second.

'Get back upstairs,' he says to Amrit. 'We've got work to do. We need to arrest Lucy Halliday.'

Chapter Thirty-Three

Jack wanted to be there. To see the look on Lucy Halliday's face as the officers recited the caution, as her hands were cuffed, as she realised her fate. But all he sees is confusion and fear. He sits a good distance away in his car, the window open. Late afternoon sun still shining, gentle traffic on the road, birds and trees and middle-of-the-range cars on the driveways.

Lucy had run past, oblivious, the dog streaking ahead, her feet thumping the road in her final sprint, only to be met by this.

An arrest for murdering her husband.

She falters at first, looking down in concern for Moss as the lead is unclipped from her waist. Another car draws up alongside Jack's – a standard issue Ford Mondeo. Pete Nash gets out, sees Jack and gives him a brief nod. His face is stern.

Pete steps forward and takes the dog from the uniformed officer. Lucy mutters a few words and it's clear that Nash wants to give more reassurance than the brief reply he offers. Lucy's loaded into the waiting police car; the door is closed. And as they drive away, Lucy stares straight at Jack.

He can't meet her eye.

Pete walks the dog back to the car and opens the boot. He places a bowl on the ground and fills it with water; Moss laps quickly then circles, confused, looking for his owner.

Nash coxes the dog into the boot and shuts the crate. He pauses in front of Jack.

'Do you think she did it?' Nash says.

'The evidence is pointing in that direction.'

'That doesn't answer my question,' Pete replies and shakes his head, his face dark. He slams the boot of his Mondeo and gets in without another word, gunning the engine down the road.

It's not hard to tell Nash's sentiment about the arrest. But what can Jack say, when he feels the same way, deep within his bones.

Chapter Thirty-Four

Lucy's panic hovers at a dull roar. The hum of blood rushing in her ears, the pounding of her heart in her chest. She can't sit still, can't concentrate, can't make out what the officers are saying.

She knows these guys, has seen them around the nick. She stayed silent on the drive to the station and is now guided through the same door at the back that she's been through a thousand times as a police officer escorting her own offender. She is that suspect now. In her husband's murder.

She goes through the usual procedures. Is checked into custody, the sergeant behind the desk the epitome of politeness. She gets a sympathetic smile, a head tilt when she's asked if she has any mental health concerns, whether she has ever considered suicide. She answers no to both, asks for a duty solicitor.

A nod to that. Lucy hopes for a good one but it's a lottery. Not that it matters – what can they do for her now? It was only a matter of time before Ellis asked for the phone; they've obviously recovered the data, or she wouldn't be here. The guilt throbs in her veins like a sickness. It renders her stupid.

She can't think. But she must. She has to get out of this.

She worries about Moss. Asks the custody sergeant where he's gone but gets no reply. She saw Pete Nash at her house; knows that Moss has probably been taken to Netley, to the kennels. He'll be well looked after there but he'll hate it. He'll be bored. He needs to work. *She* needs to work.

The Lycra from her run is stuck with gluey sweat to her skin and she's starting to shiver; she asks for a change of clothes, but the grey tracksuit doesn't help. She's itchy, restless. Freezing cold but burning up. She needs a shower and eyes the tiny sink when she's shown to her cell. She looks up to the camera, blinking red in the corner of the room. She won't be taking her clothes off. Not that indignity, along with everything else. She puts the sweatshirt on and awkwardly removes the T-shirt underneath, doing what she can to dab water under her arms. She splashes handfuls over her face, soaking the front of her sweatshirt and the floor. It's a relief. It wakes her up, pulls her back to the here and now – there is nothing more she can do but sit on the edge of the bed and wait.

–

When the next knock comes, it's her duty solicitor. A pinched-looking man who confirms he knows nothing and can do nothing, but makes indecipherable notes on his iPad anyway. It doesn't matter. She knows what she's going to say.

The two of them are escorted into interview room one. It feels wrong, sitting this side of the table. She asks for a pad of paper and a pen; she fiddles with them while she waits.

The door opens behind her and the last residue of hope fades as she sees who's interviewing her. DS Harry Blake and a younger woman. She introduces herself as DC Amrit Gill and gives her a smile. She's new. Lucy's seen her at crime scenes, another of Jack Ellis's team.

The tapes are inserted into the machine, the recording starts. They make their introductions. And they begin.

Chapter Thirty-Five

Jack watches from the room next-door, the action from the interview duplicated onto the monitor in front of him. The sound is faintly muffled, a distracting slight buzz from the microphone, but Jack is focused on Lucy Halliday's face as Blake repeats the caution. She looks on the edge of tears, but there's something else. Resolution. Anger.

'So, Lucy – do you mind if I call you Lucy?' Blake begins.

Lucy glares. 'Fine.'

'Lucy. Can you tell us about the day your husband was reported missing?'

Jack feels a flare of irritation. The team decided on the interview strategy together and this was not it. Even Amrit can't hide her surprise, glancing sideways at her colleague.

'No comment,' Lucy says, staring pointedly at her solicitor.

'Ms Halliday has already given her misper statement on that subject,' he says.

'Yes, this,' Blake replies, taking a piece of paper out of the file. 'It says that your husband, Nicolas Halliday, went missing on the twelfth of October 2021 – is that correct?'

'He went missing on the eleventh,' Lucy replies. 'I reported it to the police on the twelfth.'

Blake moves on without acknowledging the error. 'And that he was wearing a green-and-blue shirt, black jeans and blue Vans trainers?'

'Yes.'

'This?' Blake pushes a photograph across. It shows a dirty checked shirt, laid out on a silver table.

'If those are the clothes Nico was found in, then yes, I assume so.' She looks to Amrit. 'Where's my dog? Where's Moss? Is he okay?'

Blake ignores her question. 'Did you see your husband on the day of his disappearance?'

Lucy frowns. 'No comment,' she replies and Jack sighs. She's keeping quiet. It's frustrating, but no more than they expected. She's a cop, she knows how these things work. The less you say in interviews, the better for the suspect. It forces the police to show their hand, exactly what Blake's going to do now.

'Because we believe you did. We took scrapings from under Nicolas's fingernails—'

'Nico,' Lucy interrupts. 'Nobody called him Nicolas. He hated it.'

'Nico's fingernails,' Blake says. 'And your DNA was found. Your skin cells.'

'Did you find anyone else's?' Lucy asks.

'How did your DNA get there?'

'No comment.'

'My client was married to the deceased. It's hardly surprising her DNA was on him.'

'No, true,' Blake says with a brief nod to the lawyer. 'But we also tested the shirt. And as well as your husband's blood – copious amounts of your husband's blood – we found someone else's.' He pauses and Lucy stares at him. They've caught her attention.

'Yours,' Blake concludes.

He lets the silence hang. Jack leans forward to the monitor: Lucy's forehead is furrowed.

'Could you tell us how it got there?'

'No comment.'

'There was a lot.' Blake points to the photo of the shirt. 'Large patches, mainly across the front and down one arm. Would you like to share?'

Lucy glares. 'No comment.'

'Like you'd injured yourself badly. Maybe a nosebleed? A split lip?'

'No. Comment.'

Blake glances up to the camera. He knows Jack is watching, wants to convey his satisfaction at how the interview is progressing. *Smug git*, Jack thinks. *You have a long way to go yet*.

His phone rings and Jack looks at the caller: Fran. The pathologist has rung once already this afternoon, left a short but curt message telling him in no uncertain terms not to be so stupid, that Lucy's no killer. Jack ignores the call; he has no wish to receive an earbashing.

Blake takes the next piece of evidence out of the file: a photo of Nico's iPhone.

'You gave this to DI Ellis yesterday morning. Nico's phone.'

'I would have given it to you earlier, but nobody wanted it when he went missing,' Lucy snaps. 'Nobody took his disappearance seriously.'

'We're taking it seriously now. Did you know the phone had been wiped when you gave it to us?'

Lucy sits back, clenches her jaw. 'No comment.'

'It looks like someone entered the wrong unlock code ten times. That erases the phone. Did you know that would happen?'

'No comment.'

'And did you also know that the police have specialist software that can recover a large proportion of the data? Photos, messages. Videos,' he adds pointedly.

A flicker passes Lucy's face. A narrowing of the eyes and a twitch at the corner of her mouth. She knew they'd find it. And she did her utmost to try and stop them.

Lucy looks to her solicitor, but he can't help her. This is it. They have her. Jack leans in, resting his elbows on the desk as he stares at the monitor.

Up to this point Amrit has been silent, but now she takes a laptop out of the bag at her feet and opens it up. She turns it around to face Lucy.

'This is exhibit AG/1. A video downloaded by Nico Halliday from your Ring doorbell at your old house. The one you lived in with your husband. This was the day before Nico went missing.' Blake leans forward and presses play. Jack doesn't need to see; he's watched it far too many times already.

It shows the porch of the house where Lucy and Nico Halliday used to live. Amrit had been out there late this afternoon, had taken photos to confirm it. The front door is bright blue; Lucy goes to unlock it. But as she does so, a hand reaches forward, grabs a fistful of her hair, and pushes her forcefully against the door. It must have hurt but she makes no attempt to resist as Nico Halliday comes into shot, still shoving her face against the wood. The video is silent but the exclamation of surprise is clear. Her fear, her complete submission as Nico presses his mouth close to her ear, his face contorted with anger. After a few words, he releases her, and that's when she retaliates. A sudden burst of rage – slapping, punching, kicking at her husband. His hands go up to protect his face; he flinches. And then he grabs her hands, subduing her. A confident move; he has no doubt he is bigger, stronger. He pushes her into the house.

The whole interview room is hushed as this plays out on the screen. Lucy is watching, but out of the corner of her eye. As if seeing it head-on would be too much to bear.

'What were you arguing about, Lucy?' Blake says.

Jack frowns at his choice of words. It was hardly an argument. More a sustained assault: Nico Halliday the instigator, the more powerful of the two.

Lucy blinks back tears as she stares at Blake.

'No...' she begins, but the word comes out as a croak. She clears her throat. 'No comment.'

Blake raises his eyebrows. He turns the laptop back towards him and clicks, finding the second file.

'This one was taken a few months before Nico disappeared. We didn't expect to find this. It was in the original misper file but never viewed – a hotel receptionist emailed it in when he heard that Nico was missing. Early days,' he says flippantly. 'At that point the team must have assumed Nico had left you and therefore ignored the CCTV, but here it is.'

He turns the laptop around to a frowning Lucy. She's curious about this one, shifting forward to look at the screen.

Again, Jack knows what's on the tape. The inside of a lift. Nico in a tuxedo, Lucy in a light blue halter-neck dress. And the moment the lift doors slide shut, Nico Halliday holds his wife against the mirrored wall by her neck and screams into her face.

Lucy closes the lid of the laptop.

'I don't need to watch it,' she whispers.

'What happened, Lucy?' Amrit asks, her voice soft. 'When was this?'

'The August, before he disappeared. A summer party for his work,' she begins but her face turns hard again. 'You know when, you can see the timestamp.'

'We can also see what Nico did to you,' Amrit continues. 'You can't tell me these were isolated incidents. He was violent. He was a bully.'

'Which has fuck all to do with how he was killed,' Lucy says. She angrily swipes her fingers under her eyes. 'Get back to the point, detectives. Why do you give a shit about domestic abuse?'

'Because that's how he died, isn't it?' Blake takes over again. 'You had enough. His threatening behaviour. Living in fear. We all know about coercive control, how a beaten wife can snap. How one day it all gets too much. Like it did there.'

Blake's pushing her. Jack's not keen but it's getting a reaction. Lucy's tears start again but she's not cowed. She points a finger in Blake's direction.

'You know nothing about this,' she hisses. 'Nothing about our relationship, our marriage.'

'So tell us. Tell us what it was like—'

'Fuck off—'

'How did he die, Lucy?'

'Fuck you.'

'Did you kill him?'

Blake's losing control, straining across the table, spit flecking his lips. Aggression, anger – the wrong stance to take with a victim of domestic violence. And, a switch flipped, Lucy backs away from him, folding her arms across her chest.

'I know what bullying looks like. And I won't take it from you, Blake. You utter piece of shit.'

'Did you kill him?' Blake asks again, and slowly Lucy leans forward, putting her face next to his. Her lip curls.

'No comment,' she says.

Chapter Thirty-Six

'She did it!' Blake shouts once the interview has been concluded and Lucy has been returned to her cell. 'She fucking did it and you know it.'

'We know no such thing,' Jack replies. 'And she was right. You were being a bully. What part of that was the interview strategy we agreed on? We said to go in sympathetic and understanding, not shout in her bloody face.'

'I changed my mind,' Blake blusters. 'I thought this would work better.'

'And did it?'

Blake reluctantly shakes his head. 'I still say she killed him.'

'You didn't even ask about the texts,' Amrit interjects, then blushes as Blake glares.

'Amrit's right,' Jack says before Blake can chastise her. 'We needed to know who she was referring to in those messages and you pissed her off before you could get there.'

Among the data hidden on the phone were a series of one-way messages from Lucy to Nico. Beginning the days after Lucy reported him missing, most were dull – begging him to come home. But a few were more interesting:

He's nothing. It was nothing. A mistake.

I'm sorry. I was drunk. I don't even remember it.

Kane had mentioned rumours of an affair; he wants to know what happened and with whom. But that opportunity has gone.

He faces the rest of the team. 'Judging from her responses so far, it's unlikely Halliday is going to talk. DCI Kane has requested an update so I'm going there, and in the meantime,

I need you all to focus. Nico Halliday isn't our only murder investigation – two other people are dead. Someone needs to follow up with Rachel Lennon, the crime scene manager, and with forensics, and I want the area around the squat scoured – CCTV, traffic cameras, anything from around that site. We came up trumps with CCTV on Nico Halliday, let's see if we can get lucky again.'

He turns before anyone can object and heads up the stairs towards DCI Kane's office. When he gets there, the door is open and she's head down, peering at her phone. He knocks gently.

She jumps, her hand clutched across her chest, then utters an embarrassed laugh.

'Ellis, you're like a bloody ninja. No surprise that your background's in covert ops.'

'Sorry. But you requested an update on Lucy Halliday's arrest? We've completed the preliminary interview.'

'What did she say?'

Jack sits down. He's been updating Kane regularly on the case, as he would with any senior officer, but ever since Jack shared the evidence on Lucy Halliday, she's been more invested than he'd expect. He puts it down to concern for one of her previous officers, knowing Kane went out on a limb to secure the dog posting for Lucy.

'Mainly no comment,' Jack begins. 'Emotion when we showed her the videos. It's clear she didn't want us to find them.'

'I'm not surprised, poor woman. But no admission of guilt?'

'None.' Jack pauses. 'And I have to say, ma'am, I'm not convinced by this angle. Yes, we have evidence of something awful in their relationship, but there's nothing that directly points to murder.'

'She attacked him, it's there on the video.'

'Hardly. She defended herself, that's all. We've got search teams in her house now – both the old one and the new – and they've found nothing so far.'

'They wouldn't, if she killed him in that squat.'

'But why? Our theory is she killed him because she'd had enough, or she was trying to defend herself?' Kane nods. 'So why was there so much of his blood in that squat? Why would she torture him? It's incredibly premeditated.'

'She enticed him out there, knowing it would be empty? And knowing drug dealers hung out there. Maybe she was trying to make it look like someone else did it?'

'So why move and bury the body? Why did she try so hard to find him last week? And what about the other victims?' To Jack, this theory is going from improbable to downright wild. 'We're not possibly implying she killed them too?'

'Of course not. Maybe that's coincidence.' Even Kane has the self-awareness to look embarrassed at this statement. Detectives don't believe in coincidences, least of all ones related to three bloody murders. 'Maybe they're not connected. Oh, I don't know,' she snaps, exasperated. 'You arrested the woman.'

'We arrested her because the evidence showed she'd been lying to us and that was suspicious as hell.'

'You arrested her because we have evidence that shows her being violent to the victim before he was killed. You wanted an explanation – have you got it?'

Jack reluctantly shakes his head.

'So do your job. Get her to talk. And see to it that she's charged,' she finishes, and picks up her phone. He pauses, stunned. Kane looks back to him and glares. 'Thank you, DI Ellis.'

Jack takes his cue and leaves, pausing in the corridor. There's no way that the evidence they've found so far will cut it with the CPS, let alone in a court of law. And he has severe doubts they're going to find any more. Kane's an experienced copper, she must know that.

He turns to head back down and as he does so, his phone rings. It's DC Amrit Gill.

'We need you,' she says. 'Now. It's Lucy Halliday. She's requested a follow-up interview.'

'So interview her,' Jack says, taking the stairs two at a time.

'That's just it, boss,' Amrit concludes. 'She says she'll only talk to you.'

Chapter Thirty-Seven

'Interview with DI Jack Ellis and Lucy Halliday. The time is…' Ellis glances up at the clock. 'Eighteen-fifty-three. I have read you the caution and you have declined legal counsel. Is that correct?'

'Yes,' Lucy replies.

'And I've spoken to Pete Nash. Moss is fine. Been out for a walk this afternoon with him and Dax and Pepper, and is now in kennels. He's promised to take good care of him.'

'Thank you.'

Lucy grips one hand in the other and sits up straight, trying to keep steady. Calmness is an impossibility, but she needs to be still and measured to get this out. Ellis is the only one she trusts. Something about him, even though he's the SIO. He's new, she's hoping the rumours about her haven't tarnished him yet. And Fran likes him – which says a lot.

'You wanted to talk, Lucy,' Ellis says. His voice is steady, soft. Maybe even sympathetic. 'What do you want to tell me?'

She takes a sip from the small plastic beaker of water on the table. When she places it back, her hands are shaking.

'The videos you found, the ones you showed me?' Jack nods. 'Those weren't a one-off. Nico was… a complicated man.' She struggles to find the words to explain; this is the best she can come up with. 'He had a shitty childhood. His mother left when he was young. His father beat him, even hospitalised him a few times. He left home when he was fourteen, found his own way. He was proud of that.'

She pauses. She can feel Jack looking at her but doesn't want to meet his gaze.

'And yes,' she continues. 'He hit me. Usually when he was drinking, and often when we'd been out and I'd said something stupid, or someone had set him off.' Her gaze shifts to the floor. 'Didn't take much. Any excuse.'

'I'm sorry, Lucy.' Jack is completely calm. But his composure is soothing, in contrast to her constant twitching, her hands that won't stay still. She needs Moss, to wind her fingers through his fur. 'When did it start?'

'Later on. When we first met, he wasn't drinking, and things were good. But when he started up again...' She glances up. 'You think I'm an idiot, don't you? Me, a detective. A police officer. I'm trained in compliance and restraint, know how to put someone in a straight armbar. Why didn't I fight back? Defend myself? Better than *that*, I mean. Whatever *that* was on the tape. Why did I stay?'

'I know it's complicated.'

She laughs, a cackle, mocking herself. 'No, that's not it at all. It was simple. I loved him. I didn't want to leave because I knew he'd go under. He'd wind up in that camper van, maybe even go back to drugs. He'd been clean for so long, I didn't want to be the cause of a relapse. And, as it turns out, I'm no different to any other abused woman. Blinkered, deluded. I thought he'd change. I thought I could fix him.'

'And did you?'

'No. He got worse. Before he disappeared, he was drinking all the time. First thing in the morning to last thing at night. But when I tried to talk to him about it, he just said "after".'

'After what?'

'I don't know. He was investigating something and I got the feeling he was making progress. But then... well, you know. He obviously got too close.'

'That's what you think happened to him?'

'Must have been. Because I didn't kill him.' Lucy stops then and looks right into his strange grey-blue eyes. He doesn't flinch, just stares back. 'You have to believe me, Ellis. It wasn't me.'

'How did your blood get on his shirt? Your skin under his nails?'

Lucy takes a long, slow breath in. Her solicitor had advised against telling Ellis any of this. It incriminates her, he said. It backs up their theory. But for the investigation to have any chance of moving on and finding the people who did this, she has to be honest.

'You've heard about Professional Standards? Accusing me of sharing confidential information with Nico?' Jack nods. 'I had my interview with them on the Friday, then we fought. All that weekend. I was furious because one thing I did know was that I hadn't told him any of that shit.'

'You hadn't?'

'No! I took the confidentiality of this job seriously. Always have.'

'Where did Nico say it had come from?'

'He didn't. But he was a resourceful bastard, he'd have got access somehow. And it all ended with...' She waves her hand, helplessly. 'That video you found. I knew that would be on his phone. They downloaded automatically. Nico thought someone was following him, and he'd review them regularly.'

'What happened that day?'

Lucy swallows. 'We had reached an impasse. He said he hadn't done it. I was suspended and, god knows, I wanted to believe him. So we went out for food. But when we got back, I asked him again for the truth and he slammed my head into the door. You saw it, on the video. I tried to fight back. No point. He was bigger than me. Stronger. Just pushed me into the house.'

She says it as impassively as she can, but the thought of it makes her heart rate spike, her breathing quicken. When Nico's rage came on – as it did frequently, in those latter days – the best tactic was to ride it out. To take the punches, the choking, and to submit like a tiny boat on storm-racked seas, until he collapsed, full of self-hatred and remorse.

'I couldn't take it anymore. I turned around and walked out. Got drunk. And when I got back, everything… came out.'

'Everything?'

'Blake,' she spits. 'Fucking Harry Blake. You must know?' Jack looks blank. He hasn't got a clue. 'That Sunday night, as if being suspected of sharing confidential information with my husband wasn't bad enough for my career, I got wasted and ended up sleeping with Blake.'

'DS Blake,' he repeats.

'DC then. An officer in my team. He didn't mention it?' Ellis shakes his head, his jaw tight. 'Of course he didn't. Because then he wouldn't have been allowed to interview me, and that was his moment of glory. His way of demonstrating what a piece of shit I am.'

'I wouldn't have let him anywhere near that interview if I'd known.' Ellis's whole manner has changed, body rigid, eyebrows low. He glances backwards to the camera, high up on the wall, and Lucy realises that Blake is probably watching the exchange. 'How did Nico find out about the affair?'

'It wasn't an affair, it was one night,' Lucy snaps. 'And Nico guessed. The state of me. The fact I hadn't come home. I probably looked so guilty, I might as well have had it written on my forehead. Not that I could remember.'

'You have no memory of what happened?'

'Not a single second. I went out, I got drunk. And eight hours later I woke up in his bed.'

The recollection stops her in her tracks. Opening her eyes, her head blurry, her stomach churning, appalled to be naked, sore and lying next to the slumbering shape of Harry Blake. Someone she'd never flirted with, never even fancied. Blake, who had woken and given her a sickly-sweet smile before she made her excuses.

She's never felt worse. An absolute shit of a person, knowing she'd made the biggest mistake of her life.

Jack's looking at her, mouth agape.

'I got home that Monday morning. Nico and I argued.' She gives a sarcastic laugh. 'If that's what you want to call it.' She starts crying then. Hates herself for it, for being so pathetic, the tears blurring her vision. But she has to get to the end. 'He punched me in the stomach, slapped me around the face. Grabbed me by my hair. It was… It was terrifying. I'd never seen him like that before. And at some point I hit my head on the mantlepiece.' She lifts her fringe, shows him the small pink scar in her hairline. 'Head lacerations, they bleed like nothing else. It was everywhere. In my eyes, in my hair. Down my clothes. It must have transferred to his shirt. He didn't even blink. Pushed me to the floor like I was nothing and walked out.' Tears, snot, dribble drop onto the tabletop. 'I never saw him again.'

Lucy sniffs, then feels a gentle tap on her arm as Jack holds a tissue out to her. She takes it and dabs at her eyes, blows her nose.

'You have to believe me,' she says.

'I do,' he replies.

Chapter Thirty-Eight

Lucy's escorted back to her cell, her shoulders slumped, head down, feet dragging – telling Jack the truth about her marriage has drained her completely.

Before he'd ended the interview, Jack had asked one final question: 'Why didn't you tell us this before?'

'What would have been the point?' she'd replied, looking up at him with reddened eyes. 'By the time I reported him missing, it was a day later. The head lac had stopped bleeding, my hair covered the bruise and the cut. Besides, at that point I thought he'd come back. I didn't want to get him arrested. Days passed, months. Everyone assumed he'd left me. Mentioning a fight would have only reinforced that. And then he turned up dead. If I had told you all of this on Friday, you would have assumed I killed him. Same as you do now.'

Jack's ashamed of that. For being so narrow-minded that he couldn't see further than the wife, even when every instinct told him it was wrong.

Lucy had continued: 'I wiped the phone out of sheer terror – that everyone at the nick would know what Nico had been doing. And think less of him, and less of me.' She'd shrugged, a defeated gesture. 'He was still my husband. I loved him. He had a good side, too.'

Jack plods upstairs to the incident room. Despite the late hour, Blake, Lawrence and Amrit are waiting. Blake shifts nervously from foot to foot, his face the epitome of guilt.

Jack turns to him first. 'You should have told me about your relationship with Lucy Halliday,' he hisses, utilising every last bit of restraint not to shout.

'I assumed Kane had told you,' Harry splutters. 'That you didn't consider it important.'

'Of course it's important. You reported to her. You slept with her. From now on you stay well away from the Nico Halliday investigation.'

'But boss. We don't have enough people as it is.'

'You can work on the other two. On David Carter and Vanessa Savage. But you're not to touch anything to do with Halliday. Do you hear me?' Blake nods, meekly. Jack turns to the rest of them. 'I need total honesty from my team. I need to trust you all. We work so closely together, day in, day out, we have to operate as one. And crap like this – it ends now.'

He faces down Amrit and Lawrence. 'Has either of you got anything you need to share?'

Phil Lawrence's face goes beetroot.

'Phil?'

'I-I-I slept with a hooker. Last month. On a stag do in Amsterdam. And now I'm terrified my wife will find out.'

It comes out in a rush, Lawrence about to burst into tears. Jack blinks in surprise.

'O-kay,' he says slowly. 'You and I will need to talk about that. Does it affect you doing your job now?'

'No, boss.'

'So, carry on. We'll chat soon. Amrit?'

She jolts. 'No, nothing.'

'Good. Go home. All of you. Lucy Halliday isn't a killer – we'll release her first thing once I've had a chance to speak to DCI Kane. We have a lot to do. Get some sleep.'

They do as they're told, packing up their things and leaving the office in silence.

He slumps down in the nearest chair and looks up at the whiteboard. He sighs. Back to square one. The SOCOs are still working their way around the squat; a small team has been deployed to search Lucy Halliday's house, little use that'll be now. His heart goes out to the woman. Demoted, disgraced, destroyed. All because she fell in love with the wrong man.

He remembers the phone calls from Dr Rosetti and takes his mobile out of his pocket, redialling. She answers on the first ring.

'She didn't do it,' Fran snaps. 'This is ridiculous. Let her go.'

'I know. I will.'

Jack's admission silences her immediately.

'Did you know?' he asks. 'That Nico was… violent?'

There's a pause, then a long sigh. 'I didn't know. Not for sure. But we wondered, my husband and I. About a year into their marriage, Lucy changed. She withdrew, spent less time with us. She seemed… I don't know. Insecure. Timid. Especially around him.'

'And you didn't ask her?'

'We did! She said everything was fine. What more could we do?' Jack can hear the strain in Fran's voice, the regret. 'I didn't want to push her. I could only make it clear that, whatever happened, we – Mike and I – would be there for her. And we still saw her and Nico, as much as we could. Kept an eye out.' Another pause. 'She told you, then?'

'She did, yes. We found footage.'

A swear word, whispered. 'Call me the moment you release her,' Fran says. 'And make it soon. Please, Jack?'

'I will.'

Jack hangs up, then leaves Kane a message. He has every intention to take his advice to his team and go home, but once he's in the car, he finds himself taking a detour to Lucy Halliday's house. The crime scene techs are just finishing, loading boxes into their van.

He approaches them, holding out his warrant card by way of introduction. They eye him warily.

'What have you found?' he asks, gesturing to the large plastic box filled with evidence bags.

One nervously looks to the other, who eventually speaks.

'Not a lot. We've taken a few samples and fingerprints from around the house. No visible signs of blood. A hell of a lot of dog hair.'

'Mind if I take a look?'

The crime scene tech nods and Jack cranes forward over the box, working his way through the bags. They'd been instructed to look for anything that might belong to Nico, to get an idea of what he was investigating, maybe even another phone, and anything incriminating belonging to Lucy. It looks like the former has come up blank, but Jack pauses over a bag containing an A5 notepad. He takes it out.

'What's this?'

'We found it in the living room. Thought it might be a diary, but it's more like an investigator's notebook.'

The kind used by detectives to record their decision-making and actions taken in a case. But it's not. Investigator's notebooks are standard issue – this is something else.

'Full of Lucy Halliday's writing,' the tech adds. He holds out a hand to take it but Jack pulls it back.

'Can I keep this?'

'Whatever you want. Sign it out.'

Jack leaves the other evidence with the techs but takes the notebook.

'Anything in their previous house?'

'Even less than here,' the tech replies. 'The new owners have gutted the place. New floors, new wallpaper. New kitchen. If there was evidence, it's gone.'

Jack thanks them and they head off. He taps the notebook thoughtfully against his hand, then gets in his car. But he doesn't get as far as turning on the ignition before curiosity gets the better of him. Grabbing a fresh pair of latex gloves, he opens up the evidence bag.

Chapter Thirty-Nine

Lucy has done her best to settle down for the night. The lights are dimmed, the custody sergeant has made his last round – even the drunk in cell four is quiet. The cell is hot, almost suffocating, but Lucy lies with the light blue blanket over her, her legs tucked to her chest in foetal position.

She hopes that Jack believed her – otherwise all she's done is dug herself a bigger hole. And she'd barely told him a fraction of what life was like with Nico.

When he was sober, he was the man she fell in love with. A ball of energy and affection, sparkling eyes; when his attention was on her, Lucy felt she was the only woman in the world. But when he was drinking, his insecurities would emerge. The self-doubt, the anxiety – all the negative jibes his father had drilled into him with his fists and smacks. And nothing Lucy could say would make them less true. He'd alternate between pushing her away and threatening her if she made steps to leave. He'd pull her around by her hair, pinch her viciously until she cried. He once pushed her face so aggressively against a brick wall that she had road rash down one cheek for weeks. She said she'd fallen when running and her colleagues laughed, called her clumsy. But she'd never been clumsy until she met Nico.

That day, the day he disappeared, had been the worst. She'd betrayed Nico in the most terrible way by sleeping with Blake, a fact she couldn't deny, even though her memory was blank.

She'd returned that morning to a quiet house. Sneaking in, head pounding, stomach churning. Assuming Nico had gone out, or was at least sleeping, she'd headed for the shower, only to find her husband sat at the dining table. He looked up at her with half-closed eyes filled with more hatred than she could ever have imagined.

Blustering, useless denials were followed by hysterical apologies, Lucy retreating fast, her hands already out in front of her, knowing what was coming. Useless, as he slapped her around the face, slammed his fist into her stomach. She folded in two, gasping for breath, but still the assault continued. Yanking at her scalp, pulling her around the room by her hair. Slapping, kicking. Adrenaline, pain, fear. Then her head on the corner of the mantelpiece – a bolt of agony, dizziness, confusion. Blood. So much of it.

She had told Jack the truth. But the worst she'd kept to herself.

Normally, Nico would stop. At broken skin or bloodshed – something would sober him into remorse. But not this time. He was out of control, driven by fury at her betrayal.

She'd pulled herself to her knees. Begged, pleaded, apologised, clawing at his shirt. And he paused. Looked down at her, disgust clear. He lowered his face to hers.

His breath smelled of day-old curry and a fresh intake of spirits. His eyes rolled as he slurred words and profanities, calling her a bitch, a whore, a slag. How could she? How could she betray him? And she took it all, because he was right. He was a wife-beater, an alcoholic, a shit – but she was the dirt on his shoe.

She deserved it all.

That was her lowest moment. He had won. She was nothing. And then he was gone.

She gives in to the self-pity, letting the tears roll down her face, pooling on the thin blue plastic mattress. She doesn't even try to wipe them away as she hears footsteps coming down the corridor. Let the custody sergeant see her cry. It's not like he can think any less of her right now.

But to her surprise, she hears the grate of the door, the creak of the hinges. She looks up and a different figure is silhouetted in the doorway. Tall and slender, not the overweight biscuit-eating sergeant. He takes a step into her cell; she squints against the light, then realises who it is. He holds out an evidence bag; she recognises the contents.

'Tell me about this,' Jack says.

–

Somehow, two cups of tea in flimsy plastic cups appear. It's lukewarm and pale, probably the worst-tasting tea Lucy has ever had, but she holds it tight, taking quick sips, trying to restore some semblance of normality into her body.

Jack holds the notebook, still in its evidence bag. They're sat in the cell, side by side on the uncomfortable mattress. The door is open but they are unsupervised.

'You were trying to work out what Nico was investigating?' Jack says. Head down, he's talking in whispers, too quiet for the cameras.

'My own notes, yes. Everything I knew about what he was doing and whatever I've learned since.' She gives a brief overview of her conversation with Cal and Giles at Waterloo station, stunned when she realises it was only yesterday, that just over thirty-six hours have passed.

'Hampshire have a higher than average rate of drug deaths and overdoses?' Jack repeats, almost thinking out loud. 'Which would indicate a larger quantity of drugs on the street? Is that what Nico inferred?'

'I guess so,' Lucy confirms. 'Mark Savage was drug squad, right?' Jack looks surprised that Lucy knows, but nods. 'And his body was found in the same place where Nico and the other victims were killed. He was trying to tell you something. Has anything else come back from the squat? Forensics?'

'I checked before I came here. Fingerprints from a number of sources, many have records on the PNC but all for low-level offences like dealing and possession. The blood on the floor in that bedroom was Nico's. The rest has yet to be analysed.'

'But there was nobody at the squat when you raided it?'

'What are you saying?'

'Did you ever consider that someone might have tipped them off?'

Lucy looks at him. In the half-light from the doorway, Jack's skin looks sallow as he tilts his head down to his hands. 'Damn it,' he groans. 'Shit.' He looks back up. 'Do you think that's what we've got here? Dirty cops? Mark Savage, I could understand. He was drug squad, and he was involved in that original raid five years ago. But Vince Carter? A custody sergeant?'

'He's only been in custody a month or so,' Lucy replies. 'Before that he was down in stores.'

Jack's head snaps up. He stares at her for a moment.

Lucy hadn't given much thought to what Jack is going through, but for the first time she takes in his crumpled shirt, the messed-up hair, the stubble across his jaw.

'How late is it?' she asks.

He glances at his watch. 'Just past two a.m.' He rubs his hand across his stubble with a scratching noise. 'I need some sleep.'

'You and me both,' Lucy jokes and for a moment they share a weary smile.

'I'll get you out first thing,' Jack confirms. 'Nico's murder has nothing to do with you.'

'Thank you.'

'And I'll make sure Harry Blake keeps his distance.'

'Appreciated.' Lucy's gaze slips to the notebook, as Jack turns it around in his hand. 'There's not much in there that will help you.' She considers it for a second. 'Have you found his van?'

'No. Why?'

'Because if you want to know what Nico was thinking, that's where all his notes will be. When he was investigating something, he'd start out chaotic. Compiling notes, clippings, data. Paper everywhere. I got sick of it in the house, so he worked out of the van. Often just sat on the driveway. And then, eventually, tapping away. Pulling it all together on his laptop.' She smiles. There are some good memories. 'I didn't find any of it. I bet you that's where it'll be.'

Jack jumps to his feet. He strides to the door, then looks back. 'Thank you,' he says, and is gone.

The door stays open for a moment, until the custody sergeant returns and pokes his head around.

'You okay, Lucy?' he asks, sympathetic now. 'Do you want anything?'

'No, I'm good,' she says and he closes the door again. But this time she doesn't feel so claustrophobic. This time she has faith that Jack Ellis is in control.

When Daisy comes around, her head pounds and her body aches. But within a second, she realises she's somewhere new. Her first thoughts: carpet, curtains, no terrible smell. She tentatively moves; she's not restrained. She sits, then jumps in surprise, springing back so she's up against a wall.

There's a man in the room. Sat on a wooden chair, a copy of The Daily Mail clutched in hands the size of saucepans. He regards her impassively.

'You awake. Good. Here.'

He reaches down and holds out a bottle of water. When she flinches, he places it on the floor and rolls it to her with his foot. It's half-full, and so soon after her last sedation, the thought of contamination – poison, drugs – pops into her mind. But her body is so parched that she doesn't think about it for long. She downs the lot in a few long gulps, eyes locked on this man, wary.

He's young. Also broad, but clean-shaven, with long almost-black hair tied back in a ponytail. Ripped jeans, white T-shirt. Even through her busted nose, she can smell old sweat, cheap booze, but he seems more relaxed, less hostile than the man before.

'Where are we?' she asks.

'Safe house.'

'I don't feel that safe.'

He laughs, genuine mirth. 'Sit still, keep quiet. You be fine.'

'What are you doing here?'

'Make sure you behave.' He goes back to his paper, flicking the edges up and retreating behind.

She stares at him, but he doesn't move. Just the quiet sound of humming, remarkably tuneful. The rest of the house is in silence.

'Why am I here?' she asks, tentatively.

The paper lowers an inch. 'Keep quiet.'

'Can I have something to eat?'

'Soon.'

She shares her name with the man, although he must know it already. 'What's yours?' she asks.

She remembers something from a TV programme. A ridiculous show where someone was taken hostage. Talk to them, it had advised. Make them see you as a person rather than a commodity. She thinks it worth a try, but he ignores her.

'Your English is good,' she says. 'Where did you learn?'

He sighs this time and closes the paper, folding it in half, then half again. He drops it under his chair and rests his arms on his knees, regarding her carefully.

'You are chatty,' he says. 'No wonder he bust your nose.' He winces in sympathy. 'Pity. You have pretty face. Before...' He mimes a punch and she recoils.

She's made a mistake, trying to befriend this guy. Not for the first time, she becomes hyper aware of the precarious nature of her situation. She's alone. Dressed only in flimsy summer pyjamas. Locked in a room with a man twice her size. If she screams no one will care.

He leans closer to her. She tucks her knees up to her chest, wraps her arms around them, and tries to push herself tighter against the wall.

But he doesn't attack her. He smiles and holds out his hand.

'I am Tritos,' he says. 'Nice to meet you.'

Monday

Chapter Forty

Jack tosses and turns all night. The duvet too hot, the sheets too sticky. The discussion with Lucy repeats on a loop in his mind the moment he switches off the light.

Dirty cops. The worst, the thing Jack despises above all else. To abuse the position of trust they're placed in as police officers is unthinkable, horrific, yet he knows it goes on.

He just didn't think it would happen here.

Last night he wanted to call the team straight away, get them looking for the van, but something niggled. Whether it was Blake withholding his previous relationship with Lucy Halliday, Lawrence's dalliance with a prostitute or the fact that Amrit refuses to tell them anything at all, Jack's trust in this lot isn't as strong as it needs to be. He had resolved to call HR first thing, do some background on the three, but as the first traces of sunlight trickle in through his curtains and the traffic on the road escalates to a dull hum, he has made no firm decisions.

He gives up on sleep and swings his legs out of bed, sitting on the edge and rubbing his sandpapery eyes. The shower helps, as do clean, ironed clothes. He stands at his kitchen window, watching the birds flutter around the feeder. His own tiny patch of paradise. Blue tits bicker with robins, until a starling disrupts them all. The speckled bird looks black from a distance, but up-close Jack knows it would shimmer with iridescent purples and greens. This one's a male, his feathers almost oily, his beak blue at the base. Jack's favourite – with their assertiveness and their chatter. Odd to envy the personality of a bird.

He grabs his laptop and Lucy's notebook, and heads into the office. It's barely seven a.m. so he's surprised to see Amrit at her desk.

'What are you working on?' he says from the doorway.

She jumps, then gathers herself. 'Reading the door-to-door enquiries from the neighbourhood around the squat. It's as you would expect.'

'Nothing?'

She nods. 'Barely anyone would answer the door, let alone share anything helpful. CCTV's the same – any cameras put up are quickly vandalised. We did get a hit from a fingerprint, though. One found on a syringe at the squat. Comes back to a man called Aron Dushku.' She flicks screens then glances up as Jack reads over her shoulder. 'Looks squeaky clean, bar a conviction for driving when unfit six months ago. Drink. Let off with a fine and a disqualification.'

'And a link to… what's this? Wise Monkeys?'

'It's a who, not a what. An OCG, operate out of South-brook. Down by the docks. They're notorious for keeping themselves out of the system but it looks like Dushku ruined that for himself. Should we get him in?'

'No, not for now, not until we know more. A print on a syringe could just mean drug user. Can you get in touch with DCI Perry? Get him in asap so we can pick his brains. In the meantime, where are we with tracking down Nico Halliday's van?'

'Phil found it on traffic cams a few times before he went missing, but they were all dead ends. Each time he returned to the house.'

'Well, it must be somewhere. Keep looking.'

'Boss.'

He pauses. Can he trust her? DC Amrit Gill was new, like him. Little chance to be corrupted by whatever is going on here. And he needs his team. Police work relies on trust. On the experts around you – the people who have your back. Whether making a tricky arrest or patrolling late at night, working alone in this business will get you in trouble. Maybe even get you killed.

Phil Lawrence has fessed up to his mess with the hooker; Harry Blake has been held to account. Jack knows the worst of his officers now, and they've come out the other side. He makes a decision.

'Amrit? There are a few other things I need you to look into.' She looks up eagerly. 'Could you pull the mobile phone records of both Mark Savage and Vince Carter?'

'Easy, boss.' She starts clicking immediately.

'And start looking through for numbers that seem suspicious. Burner phones, any correlation between the two men. Plus, you need to have a look into the intel for any drug raids – how much was expected, and how much was seized. Going back at least five years.'

Amrit pauses, the scale of what he's asking sinking in.

'And somehow, I don't know how, we need to persuade stores to do a full stocktake. Starting with drugs and cash.'

She looks up, her mouth open.

'But...' she begins.

'That's a lot. I know. Get Raj, down in digital, to help – he seems efficient. And tell Blake and Lawrence. We need this.'

'Why *do* we need this?'

Jack pauses. 'A hunch. Do what you can. Report back to me, and only me. Call DCI Perry first.'

She nods and picks up the phone; inside his office, his own extension rings. He hurries to answer it.

'You let her go?' Kane retorts. 'You let Lucy Halliday go?'

'Sorry, ma'am, but we had nothing—'

'You had forensics and a motive. What more do you need?'

'Forensics that Lucy Halliday more than adequately explained. All we had was a traumatised woman with an abusive husband.'

A face pokes around his door while Jack's talking. DCI Perry. Jack wordlessly waves him in and Perry slumps in the chair in front of the desk, his legs splayed, full of bravado. He places a dirty coffee cup on the wood.

'I thought I made myself more than clear,' Kane continues, 'when I told you to charge the woman.'

'With all due respect, ma'am. We can't charge someone for a crime she didn't commit. We're circling back, regrouping. We'll—'

But Kane has hung up. Jack lowers the phone from his ear with a sigh.

Perry grins, obviously having enjoyed the exchange.

'Settling in well?' he asks. He glances around Jack's sparse office. 'Planning on staying long?'

'As long as I'm needed,' Jack replies vaguely. He picks up a coaster and places it under Perry's mug; there's already a dark mark on the wood.

Perry nods sagely. 'I'm more of an oak tree, me. I set down roots. You need a digger to get me out.' He chortles, finding himself amusing. 'This about those text messages Nico Halliday sent, right? Those bloody emojis?'

'Among other things. What does it mean?'

'It means your victim was buying drugs, that's what it means. It's not an elaborate code – these dealers aren't Bletchley Hill.'

He means Bletchley Park, and Perry's got it backwards, but Jack lets it go.

'An eight ball – that's buying an eighth of an ounce. The rocket ship means your boy was looking for high-potency shit, and the snowflake – can you guess?'

'Cocaine?'

'Got it in one. Nico Halliday started off buying a wee bit of coke, and progressed to asking about H. See this – the brown heart? That's heroin. And the cookie emoji? He's asking about a large batch. Did he get it?'

'No reply,' Jack says. 'That's when the messages stopped.'

Perry raises his eyebrows. 'Pushed them too far, that's my guess, and they got suspicious. You got any idea who it was?'

All the while Perry's been talking, Jack has been studying him closely, but all he can see is a smug man who enjoys his job and the dubious company he keeps. Has he strayed over the line? Jack has no way of telling, but keeps his cards close to his chest.

'Not yet,' Jack replies. 'Any ideas?'

'Could be any number of the OCGs that operate out of the city. We have our eye on a few...' Perry pauses. 'But you're not to go near them, right? I heard about the blood in that squat, and from what I know, that's the least of it.'

'You've not made any arrests?'

'Covert ops have been keeping an eye on a few groups for us, but without direct testimony from eyewitnesses there's nothing they can do. They rule by fear. Nobody wants a jugging—'

'A jugging?'

'Boiling sugar water. Sticky, burns like fuck. You can imagine.'

Jack can, and winces. 'What about the Wise Monkeys?'

Perry's eyes open wide. 'You looking at them, huh? Doesn't surprise me, given the location of that squat. Albanian. So called because of their signature move. Anyone crosses them and they cut out their eyes, slice their tongue down the middle then finish them off with an ice pick in the ear. Nasty bastards. Their dealers keep their eyes shut and their mouths closed.'

'Even the cops?'

Perry's manner turns. No more smiling casual DCI – he sits up straight and eyes Jack from under lowered brows. 'You're new here, so I'll give you the benefit of the doubt. We do our best. Same as everyone else. We don't arrest the low-level soldiers unless we can get our hands on someone at the top. And that takes patience.' He stands up decisively and strides to the door, before he looks back one last time. 'If your murders are related to the Wise Monkeys I suggest you stay away and let the big boys do their stuff. Or the next man tortured, with his blood sprayed across the floor of a dirty squat, might well be you.'

'Is that a threat, DCI Perry?' Jack snaps.

'It's a fucking warning, Ellis. And a direct command. From what I've heard, Nico Halliday had it easy. There are far worse ways to die than from a beating.'

And with that, he walks away, his heavy footsteps thumping through the office.

Jack watches him go. He's met a few dirty cops in his time and they tend to fit a type. Arrogant, narcissistic and generally unpleasant, not attempting to hide the racism and misogyny that run through their veins. Is Perry one of those?

Impossible to tell, but one thing he does know is that he's not giving up yet.

He wonders about Nico Halliday and logs on to check his post-mortem results. Sure enough, there were no traces of drugs in his system when he died, which would indicate that his enquiries about purchasing heroin were more to do with his investigation than to satisfy his own needs.

But as he turns back to his email, a line at the top catches his eye. There, surrounded by mundane spam about canteen menu changes and car parking warnings, is an email from Mark Savage.

The dead cop. The man currently residing in Southampton's finest mortuary, definitely in no fit state to send emails.

Received at five this morning. No subject. He clicks on it, and freezes.

The email contains a photograph. A woman, glancing behind her as she crosses the road. Her handbag is slung over her shoulder, her manner relaxed. It's taken from a distance with a long lens, but Jack knows immediately who the woman is.

Sophie.

And the message is short. *Jason. Stop.*

The comment from Perry may not have been a threat, but it's clear that this is. Primitive instincts kick in – his skin prickles, he's paralysed by fear. Whoever sent this isn't bluffing. With the mention of that one name, Jack is certain. The secret he's kept hidden for decades, the life he ran away from?

They know.

Chapter Forty-One

Ellis is true to his word: before breakfast, before even her first cup of coffee, the cell door is opened and she's out in the cool, summer morning. No further investigation. She's free.

She walks quickly from the police station, before any of her colleagues can spot her, and marches decisively towards the city centre. She stops at a Costa for coffee and a chocolate twist, devouring it in huge hungry bites as she waits for a taxi. One stops; the driver eyes her warily. She must look a state – in the grey tracksuit, clutching her sweaty running gear in a clear plastic bag, her phone shoved in her pocket.

'Rough night?' he asks.

'You could say that.'

He hesitates when she tells him her address, but agrees when she places her Apple Pay against the reader and authorises the first thirty quid upfront. The next thing she knows, she's waking up outside her house, the engine idling.

She wipes the dribble from her chin, pays the taxi, then gets straight into her own car, heading back towards Southampton.

—

Moss is overjoyed to see her, doing twirls in his kennel as she unlocks the door. She can't help laughing as she sits on the concrete and he jumps all over her, his wagging tail making his whole body shake with joy.

'Did you miss me, huh? Did you miss me?' she giggles as he tries to lick her face. He's warm and solid, a reassuring presence, albeit one with zero ability to sit still. Together, they walk back to her car, and he jumps inside the moment the crate is opened. When she turns, Pete Nash is standing a few metres away.

'I'm glad you're here,' he says with a hesitant smile. 'When I spoke to Andrews, I assumed the worst.'

'What? That I'd been charged with murder?' Pete nods. 'What did Andrews say?'

'That someone would be covering your shift. That was it.'

'PC Halliday?'

The two of them turn and Sergeant Andrews is standing behind them. He hasn't fared well in the recent spate of good weather, his nose peeling, face red. He has a white sheen, indicating he may have learned his lesson and donned the sun cream.

'Have you got a moment?' he says.

Pete gives her a quick nod and heads away. She follows her skipper into the building; he gestures for her to go into the empty kitchen, follows and closes the door behind them. Lucy stays standing, while Andrews clicks the kettle on. He fetches two mugs, spoons instant coffee inside.

'I didn't expect to see you here today,' Andrews says at last.

'I wanted to collect Moss. He'll be happier at home with me rather than in kennels, getting bored.'

She's waiting for the inevitable – for Andrews to tell her she's suspended, that Moss will be reassigned. She swallows, forcing tears back – after everything that's happened, she can't face losing her dog, too.

Her boss makes the coffee, handing her a mug. His face is grave.

'That sounds like the best plan,' he replies.

She blinks. 'Sorry, Sarge?'

'That Moss stays with you. You can brush up on your training, run some drills. Keep both of you fresh.'

'I–I'm still on the job?' Lucy stutters.

'We all know it's bullshit, Halliday,' Andrews says. 'You didn't kill your husband and I'm not about to lose one of my best handlers on the whim of some pumped-up Major Crime suit.'

Lucy doesn't tell him that it was Jack who let her go; she keeps quiet, taking the first compliment she's received since she arrived at the unit.

'But I think it's only right that I keep you off shift. Give you a chance to catch your breath. Let the gossip die down. Let's call it extended compassionate leave. Or maybe I'll just forget to rota you.'

His kindness brings her to tears. She chokes a thank you, then sips at her coffee. He raises his mug in a quick salute.

'I'll be in touch,' he says, and departs.

She stays in the kitchen for a moment, listening to the murmured conversation of coppers in the car park, the bark of the dogs, a PolSA briefing next-door. It calms her. Ever since she started with the dog unit nearly eighteen months ago, she's felt like an outsider. Her appointment was seen as favouritism, box-ticking. Bypassing better coppers who had failed for years to get into the unit.

She'd been one of those, too. Early into her career. She'd applied many times before her move to MCIT, but had always been turned down. Feedback of 'too erratic', 'immature', 'not able to handle the rigours of the job'. That last one smacked of discrimination in the years when being a woman was justification alone.

In the end she'd given up and made a move to Major Crime, where her determination and bloody-mindedness had served her well. She'd treated her team much like her canine companions – reward the behaviour you want repeated, find what motivates them, give clear instructions. Humans aren't complicated, even if they think they are. She forgot about the rejections, pushing dog handling to the back of her mind.

But now, with Andrews's kindness and Nash's friendship, she finally feels she's home. She understands the language – gentle nods, overt emotion reserved solely for a good track or tricky find. Where swear words equal affection – and where the dogs always, without exception, come first.

She finishes her coffee, rinses her mug in the sink, then heads home: a shower and bed the only plans in her future.

–

Moss wakes her. She'd fallen asleep on the sofa, the spaniel tucked happily in the crook of her arm, but now she opens her eyes and the dog is standing on the rug, his ears raised. He looks at her for a split second then runs out into the hall.

The knock comes again. Two quick thuds. Moss gives a gentle woof then sprints to the doorway, looking at her accusingly. She's slowly getting up, putting a jumper over her T-shirt. The dog leaps and whines with excitement by the front door.

She knows who it is. She can tell by his outline – that tall, slightly stooped shadow of dark grey. It's a different suit to yesterday; he's back to his usual precision and straight edges.

'Sorry to disturb you,' Jack says. 'But…'

Lucy runs her hands through her hair, aware it's dried at odd angles while she's been sleeping. She gathers it up and ties it into a ponytail.

'But what? Are you here to arrest me again?'

'No, I… Can I come in?'

She moves out of the way, giving an exaggerated sweep of her arms into the house. Moss blocks his way, dancing around his ankles until, at last, he bends down and gives the dog a stroke.

'That's it now. You're his friend for life.'

Jack gives her a small smile. 'He'd be the first,' he says as he follows Lucy into the kitchen.

'Jack Ellis made a joke,' she says. 'Things must be getting bad.'

But he doesn't reply, just sits down at the table and pulls her notebook out of his rucksack. He hands it to her and she accepts it, wary.

214

'I think you were onto something,' Jack says. 'You and Nico.'

Lucy frowns. She takes a chair next to him. 'In what way?'

'I think there's someone dirty on the job.' Jack gets up, walks quickly to her kettle and fills it under the tap. 'David Carter, Vanessa Savage. Nico. They were all related to serving coppers at the nick, right? Coffee?'

Lucy baulks at his familiarity in her house but welcomes the caffeine. 'Two sugars. Cupboard next to you. And yes, okay?'

'Excluding Nico for now: Vincent Carter was assigned to stores. Mark Savage used to work for the drug squad. What do those departments have in common?'

'Access to narcotics. Carter and Savage were dirty cops?'

'No, I think they were threatened into being dirty cops. You do as we say or we kill your loved ones.'

Lucy blinks, surprised, as Jack pours the water into the mugs and opens the fridge. 'You don't have any milk,' he says.

'I haven't had time to go to the shops. I was too busy being wrongfully arrested,' she says, pointedly.

He closes the fridge and places the black coffee in front of her, sitting opposite.

'Nico had been texting someone to buy cocaine and heroin,' Jack continues. 'But no, he wasn't on them again,' he adds quickly, pre-empting Lucy's question. 'I think he was trying to get to the OCG behind it all. We did some digging. Looked at the intel into drug raids over the last few years – what little information we could find – and there's a pattern. Every time, the records show they seize substantially less than they were expecting. And who is the common factor on each of the raids?'

'Mark Savage,' Lucy says and Jack nods. 'He was stealing drugs from the raids before it was properly logged?'

'That's my assumption. We found a hidey-hole in a wardrobe in the Savages' house. Empty, but the lab confirms that the trace found inside links to batches of cocaine and heroin distributed by a particular OCG.'

'He stole the drugs, passed them to the OCG and they sold them on? So why is his wife dead if Savage was doing as they asked? Did he stop?'

'That's my guess,' Jack confirms. 'Same with Vince Carter. His move to custody began a week before his son was kidnapped. I spoke to HR – Carter requested that move—'

'Trying to take himself out of the equation?'

'Maybe. Then on the Tuesday, the day after his son was taken, he asked to transfer back. But it was turned down.'

'They killed his son because he wasn't useful anymore?'

'It certainly sends a message,' Jack finishes.

'It's a pity Mark Savage can't help,' Lucy adds grimly. 'Are we sure he killed himself?'

'The only skin cells and DNA on Mark Savage or that rope were his own. So yes, we have to assume so. And no sign of Vince Carter, before you ask.'

Jack's phone rings and he jumps, spilling coffee on the table. He quickly pulls it out of his pocket, looks at the number. 'I need to get this, sorry.'

He stands up and walks out of the room. Moss's eyes follow. She rubs the soft fur on her dog's head thoughtfully; finds the hard nub of a burr behind his ear and gently teases it out. Lucy echoes her dog's suspicion – she remembers Jack's iPhone from before, and what he's holding isn't it. This phone is cheap, old. She strains to listen to his conversation but he's turned away from her, back stooped.

If anything, he looks worse today than last night. Sure, the neat, brusque façade has been restored, but the shadows under his eyes are smeared on, like bruises, his forehead locked in a perpetual frown. And showing up here, out of the blue? It's odd.

He comes back into the room, the old mobile phone already secreted away, out of sight.

'Why are you here, Ellis?' Lucy asks. 'Haven't you got a team for this?'

'What's your view on them?'

'You want to know if they're trustworthy? I'm not fond of Blake, you know that, but away from the personal, he's always been a decent detective. A lazy sod, but clever. I've worked with Phil Lawrence before, and he was steady but sound. And DC Amrit Gill's new, right?'

He nods. 'And my theory? Does it make sense?'

'It does,' Lucy agrees. 'But what do you do with it now? I assume you've been through the finances and residences of all the victims, including Vince Carter?'

He nods. 'Ongoing. But so far, nothing.'

'And the squat?'

'There's too much. The budget won't cover testing everything – where do we even start? What would you do?'

The question surprises her. 'If I was a DI, you mean? If I was the SIO?'

'Yes.'

She stops for a moment, considering Ellis's motives. In the past, male colleagues have asked for her opinion, only to go on and suggest it themselves, taking the glory. Jack seems to be genuinely interested.

'I'd focus on the squat,' Lucy says, giving Ellis the benefit of the doubt. 'That's the intersection of the murder cases. We know all three victims were there – and that was where two of them died – so it stands to reason that their killer left something behind. That and the digital footprint. Mobile phones – our own personal surveillance devices. Go through all the old phone records, something will correlate.'

'On it. We've found a few burners. Already disconnected.'

'But one won't be. That's all you need.'

He nods, but before he can add anything, his phone rings. The iPhone, confirming Lucy's suspicions. 'Amrit?' he says.

He listens for a moment, then his eyes lock on Lucy. 'Wait a sec, I'll put you on speaker.' He places the phone on the table and presses a button. 'Amrit, you're on with Lucy Halliday.'

'Halliday?' Amrit squeaks in surprise.

'Yes.' Jack gives Lucy a conspiratorial eye roll. 'Repeat what you said to me.'

'Okay. We haven't found the camper van but we did find a direct debit in Nico's bank statements. To a company called RCJ Holdings. Two hundred quid a month.'

'Any idea?' Jack says to Lucy and she shakes her head, puzzled.

'We kept our bank accounts separate,' she says. 'Even after we got married. Guess there was enough money to cover whatever this was all this time.'

Amrit continues: 'Made no sense to me, until I searched. Turns out RCJ Holdings run a variety of different businesses, but one rents out office space. And, more specifically, car parking and garages.'

'So it hadn't been nicked when he was abducted,' Jack says. 'Get on to them. Find out what they were renting to Nico.'

'I did that. They refused to tell me anything without a warrant. Said they'd only speak to next of kin and...'

'And she's sat right here,' Lucy replies.

'Send us the details. Excellent work, Amrit.'

He hangs up and turns to Lucy. 'Did you know Nico was renting a garage?'

'Not a clue. But then Nico was often out doing who knows what. Renting a garage would have been the least of my worries.'

A beep, and an email from Amrit.

'You trust her?' Lucy says, gesturing towards the phone as Jack writes the number down.

'As you said, she started just before I did. Came from Manchester. Out of all of them, she has the least connections.'

'Or maybe she came down to Hants constabulary for a reason.'

Jack gives her a long stare. 'Let's assume not. Or we really are screwed.' He pushes the piece of paper across to Lucy. 'Call them.'

Lucy types in the number; a bored-sounding woman answers. She asks Lucy the bare minimum of security questions, then gives a monotone, 'How can I help?'

'I need to know the address of the garage my husband rents.'

There's a long pause, a rustle of paper. Lucy meets Jack's eye; he's motionless, waiting, while she can barely sit still.

The woman clears her throat. 'Winterbourne Gardens. Mill-brook. You'll want the row behind the block of flats.' She pauses. '16A.'

Chapter Forty-Two

There was no way Jack could refuse when Lucy asked to come with him. He could have done without the dog, but Moss was reluctant to be parted from Lucy again and swiftly darted out the front door, waiting next to the boot of her VW estate. He accepts defeat and climbs in the passenger side.

'Have you always lived in Southampton?' Jack asks once they're on their way.

'Mostly,' she replies, eyes on the road. 'When I applied to the police, they had vacancies here, so this is where I ended up. Saw no reason to move.'

'No family somewhere else? Where do your parents live?'

'Only my dad now. And he lives in Newcastle. With his new family. He lost interest in me once his new wife came along. I have two little half-brothers I've only met once.'

She says it matter-of-factly but Jack senses bitterness lurking under the surface. 'And how did you meet Nico?'

She snorts. 'Because of this bloody van. He was sleeping rough on an industrial estate, same time as a man was attacked walking home nearby. Nico was the prime suspect until he gave his alibi – a woman he'd picked up at the pub had been with him all night.'

'Classy.' Jack checks his phone. 'Left at the roundabout. Then right.'

'That was Nico for you. He was perfectly lovely, good-looking in a dishevelled sort of way, and we got chatting. Turns out police and journalists have a lot in common. Same perverted sense of wanting to do good, expose the truth and get justice.'

She says this last sentence somewhat mocking, and Jack wonders how strongly she believes that now. 'I'd see him around, catch sight of his van here and there. Sometimes he'd make me a coffee, sometimes we'd talk. One thing led to another. He stopped picking up women in the pub. He moved in. We got married.' She shrugs. 'Not the world's greatest love story but we were happy.' She stops and he glances over. Her face is like stone. 'Until we weren't,' she finishes.

'Would you have left him?' Jack asks. 'If he hadn't died?'

'Probably not. Because I was that stupid. *Am* that stupid,' she corrects herself. 'He would have probably left me for sleeping with Blake, that's how fucked-up our relationship was. Anyway,' she says, mock-brightly. 'What about you? Where were you before you were here?'

He feels her eyes glance across to him; he stares resolutely forward. 'All over the place,' he replies, as blandly as he can. 'Did my initial training up north, then moved around. Met before here.'

'Covert ops, the rumour says.'

'Rumours are never correct.'

'But is this one? Left here?' she adds, gesturing to the T-junction.

'Yes. Then straight on at the roundabout.' He ignores the other question.

She continues regardless. 'Is there is a Mrs Jack Ellis you left behind?'

'No.'

'Or a mister, pardon my assumptions.'

'Also, no.'

Jack doesn't offer any more and Lucy rides the pause. But Jack's used to it, he can stand a bit of silence, especially when it comes to his personal life.

Jack's been on edge since the moment he read that email, the photograph of Sophie attached. The relief when his phone had finally rung, her name on the screen, had been temporary.

'Are you okay?' he'd asked immediately. 'Where are you?'

'I'm at home,' Sophie replied. 'Why the panic?'

'Someone's been following you. You could be in danger.' Jack explained the murders, the email, the threat.

'I told you someone had called. And you've had death threats before.'

'Not like this one. This was directed at you.'

'So why don't you report it? Get one of your colleagues to look out for me?' Her voice had turned bitter and he'd winced, knowing what was to come. 'Because you don't want to draw attention to your double life,' she continued. Her tone was half-mocking, half-angry. Well-trodden ground, worn to hard mud and dust. 'You tell them about me and the whole thing comes out. I'm assuming you haven't stopped investigating these murders?'

'No,' Jack admitted reluctantly.

'So, in order of priority, it's me at the bottom, then your... past or whatever we like to call it, then this case. Right?'

All the glow he experienced seeing her on Friday had gone. 'It's not as simple as that.'

'It is, *Jack*.' She said his name bitterly. 'It always has been. Thank you for the courtesy of the heads-up. Now you're free to carry on doing what you enjoy.' And with that, she hung up.

Now, in the car, a different woman has also given up talking to him.

'You don't give much away, do you, Ellis?' Lucy says, with resignation. She pulls up in front of a row of garages. 'I think this is it.'

The garage is one in a long line, belonging to the block of flats in front of them. A few are freshly painted, well maintained. One is open, a man sawing on a work bench, a line of two-by-fours next to him.

The last ten garages are dilapidated, all owned by RCJ Holdings, Jack assumes, the numbers faded and hard to make out. Jack counts down the line and the two of them stop in front of a metal door. Moss watches them from the open car boot, tongue lolling.

'You need to be the one to break in,' Jack says. 'He was your husband. If I do it, it's unlawful entry.'

Lucy appraises the garage door for a moment, then turns her attention to the man on their left. He pauses, as Lucy heads over. They talk for a moment, then the man goes into his garage, returning with a heavy black crowbar. Lucy nods her approval and carries it back to Jack.

'Men with garages always have useful tools,' she says with a grin.

Slowly, with purpose, she places the prongs of the crowbar either side of the small silver lock in the centre of the door. It's old and cheap, letting out little more than a disgruntled crack as Lucy pops it off.

Free of the lock, the door comes clear with a screech and a grind, rising up on its runners and revealing exactly what they've been searching for.

The 1986 VW camper van.

Chapter Forty-Three

Lucy runs a hand tenderly over the metal of the old van. Two years in a damp garage hasn't done it any favours – patches of rust infest the rims of the wheels; mould frosts the windows. She tries the door handle, unsurprised to find it unlocked. Nico was always lax about security, claiming he had nothing to steal – he'd rather someone had a good rummage than smash a window. She pulls the side door open.

Overhead, a light flickers into life. As she climbs into the van, she glances back at Jack; he's put gloves on and is walking slowly around the outside, looking for who knows what.

She's still not sure what to make of him. He knows almost her entire repertoire of dirty embarrassing secrets, yet he's private to the point of rudeness. That phone call; the way he's working with her, here, completely outside police protocol. But what choice does she have? She wants to get justice for Nico, and Jack Ellis is the only one listening.

She ignores Ellis and starts the search. It's a small space, it won't take long. There are a few clothes stored in the top cupboards; teabags, coffee granules, sugar in the tiny kitchen. She sits at the table, taking it all in. The stale air somehow holds the smell of him – that mixture of toothpaste, two-day-old clothes, deodorant hastily applied – and a rush of nostalgia and sadness hits. Early days, hanging out in this ridiculous van, converting the seats into a bed and lying on the lumpy mattress under blankets and duvets, staring into each other's eyes. Things were much simpler then – when had it all changed?

'Anything?' Jack calls, pulling her back to the job in hand.

'Not yet,' she replies, casting an analytical eye around the space. Nico's own private man-cave. She'd expected to see a mess: scribbles on scraps, stacks of newspapers. Notes compiled haphazardly, distilling his research until he committed it to the digital page. Yet there was nothing.

And then she looks down, between her legs. When the bed is put away, the blankets are stored in the bench seats. She gets up and pulls at the lid – and here it all is. Interview transcripts, reports, letters. Piles of Nico's thoughts, all shoved roughly into the hole. She grabs handfuls, lumping it in messy stacks on the table. And, in the middle of it all – Nico's laptop.

It's a clunky old thing. An Apple Mac, daubed with stickers – some faded almost to nothing, others layered on top of the old. Souvenirs from tourist attractions lie side by side with political symbols – a rainbow Thank You NHS, Vote Remain, a Greenpeace logo. She rests it on the table and opens the lid. It asks for a password.

Jack looks over her shoulder. 'Any idea?'

'None.'

'We could give it to digital. See if they can get in?'

'And then what? It disappears? Like Vince Carter? As fast as all the witnesses from that empty squat?'

Jack hesitates.

'Besides, this isn't a crime scene. We have no evidence to say he was killed here, or that any of this is related to his murder. This is nothing more than the property of my deceased husband. So it belongs to me.'

After a beat, Jack nods. 'But I want to see what's on it.'

'Deal.'

They find a few old shopping bags and load the papers inside. Lucy can tell Jack is unhappy about this breach of procedure, but it's hard for him to complain when her involvement alone is enough to raise eyebrows at the top.

Once the contents of the bench seat are in the bags, they load them into the back seat of Lucy's estate. Lucy returns to the garage, taking one last look at the VW camper. Nico's pride and joy; a complete piece of shit.

'I'll be back soon, old boy,' she whispers to the van, then pulls the door closed with a grind of metal.

'One condition,' Jack says when she gets back to the car. 'We go through this at mine. No dog. And I keep a record of every single thing.'

'Yes, but Moss comes too.'

'For crying out loud,' he mutters. 'Fine.'

They get in and head back towards Lucy's so Jack can collect his car. But as she drives, she glances towards her new reluctant colleague. Jack Ellis's face is passive, almost completely without expression. What's going on behind that mask?

The private phone calls, the second mobile. A past he won't share, and now all this talk of dirty cops, at the same time as he arrives on the scene. He's been by her side throughout this investigation, but there's something about him she doesn't yet trust. Despite Moss's fondness for his new best friend.

These notes, this laptop – this is Nico's final investigation. His life's work, the thing that could have killed him. So she'll stick with Jack Ellis, until she knows more.

Chapter Forty-Four

They drive back to Jack's house in separate cars. He doesn't want her there, but where else can they go? He can't work through all of this at Lucy's house, in the mess and chaos and mud and dog hair. To think, he needs calm and ordered surroundings. With good teabags, and milk.

The dog is part of the package. Moss rushes inside the moment Jack opens the door, sniffing and huffing, his tail wagging with excitement.

'What happens if he gives an indication?' Jack asks, attempting to defuse the awkwardness.

'Then you have some explaining to do, young man,' Lucy jokes. She walks in. 'Have you lived here long?' she asks. She's checking out the place, hardly subtle.

'A few weeks. It's rented.'

'It's so *tidy*.' She drapes her jacket over the back of a kitchen chair. He picks it up and hangs it next to his in the hallway.

'I don't own much. I move around a lot.'

'Right,' she says. 'Do you have a bowl? For Moss. He needs water.'

Jack fetches a cereal bowl from the cupboard, silently resolving to boil-wash it after. Or throw it away; the thought makes his stomach turn. While he puts the kettle on, he watches the spaniel, who has started licking the side of a kitchen cabinet.

'Can you stop him?' Jack asks with a wince. 'Coffee? Tea?'

'Coffee, please.' Lucy gently moves the dog away with her foot, only for Moss to carry on further down. 'Just milk.'

Jack tries to block out the dog, making the drinks and carrying them over. Meanwhile, Lucy has retrieved the bags and placed them on the table. She stares at them, hands on hips.

'Do you think the answers are in here?' he asks.

'I think so. I mean…' She glances at him; he senses her hesitancy. 'Nico was brilliant. When he went down a rabbit hole – as he had before he went missing – he always found something. It was remarkable how these incredible insights came from this… chaos. But his process worked. He used to tell me to trust my instincts. Mine weren't always on key,' she adds, ruefully. 'His were spot on.'

She peers into the top of one of the bags, and Jack takes in the jumble of paper and scribbles.

'Although,' Lucy says with a reluctant smile, 'it would have been nice if he were better organised.'

—

Three hours later, that wish has become more prescient. It soon became clear that Nico's paperwork wouldn't fit on the dining table, so they have decamped to the floor of Jack's living room.

Circumstances aren't ideal.

Moss sniffs at the edges, then, growing bored of the old stuffy paper, transfers his attention to Jack, now changed into jeans and his favourite *Jurassic Park* T-shirt, sitting cross-legged on the floor. He pokes a cold nose in his ear, then circles, trying to land his black fuzzy rump in Jack's lap.

'Oh, come on,' he grumbles, as he attempts to push the spaniel away. 'Control your dog.'

'He likes you.'

Moss settles for proximity, lying down next to him with a grunt. He looks up with brown reproachful eyes.

'Stop it,' Jack mutters, as Lucy withholds a snort of laughter.

He picks up a pile of seemingly random newspaper clippings, filtering through. Without Nico there, it is impossible to know why some of these items had been kept, but with others, there are definite themes.

For the most part, they're stories about drug busts and murders. Reading between the lines, the work of organised gangs around the city. There are highlighted sections – what was seized, the officers commended for their work. DS Mark Savage is one of them, another an officer called Gareth Collins. Had Nico suspected Savage, even then?

Jack adds the names to his own notebook, then selects another piece of paper. Written at the top are biroed capitals: *WHAT?? HOW???* Jack reads on. It's a clipping from *The Daily Mail*, the date 3 March 2019. It's about a consignment of drugs – cocaine, heroin, marijuana – totalling almost a million on the street, all of which was stolen on the way to being destroyed.

'Here, Lucy?' he says, holding it out to her. 'Do you remember this?'

She reaches over from where she's sat on his sofa, her feet tucked under her, reading a pile of printouts from what seems to be microfiche. She takes it and skim-reads.

'Vaguely,' she replies. 'There was a fuss at the time. Armed robbery, right? The press called it the fluke of the decade, saying that those holding it up got away with the motherlode.'

'Nico didn't seem to think it was down to luck. Look at what he's highlighted.'

'...*Expecting cash or jewellery...*' Lucy reads. 'And he's put a question mark next to it.' She looks at Jack. 'Was he saying they'd been tipped off?'

'Did he think there was someone dirty on the inside from the beginning?'

'Maybe.' Lucy gives him a smug smile and indicates with a tilt of her head. Jack realises what she's noticed: without thinking, his hand has been resting on the spaniel's head, massaging his silky ears. Moss, who was previously fast asleep, opens an eye as Jack takes his hand away. He pushes his head back against Jack's arm. *Carry on*, he's saying.

'Told you,' Lucy says. 'He likes you. What's so wrong with dogs anyway?'

'They're so... uncontrollable. They do what they like.'

'And what's wrong with that?'

'I like things my way. Clean, tidy, ordered. I don't see the attraction in something so demanding. I need my freedom.' Jack gets a disbelieving look from Lucy; a head tilt that reminds him of Moss. 'What then? Why are they so necessary?'

'Assuming we're not talking about working dogs?' Jack nods. 'They're company. Unconditional love. And they know who needs it the most,' Lucy finishes with a raised eyebrow at the dog at Jack's side.

'Bloody hell,' Jack mutters again, and gives a reproachful poke to Moss, who finally accepts defeat and joins Lucy on the sofa.

'Can he not?' Jack says.

'I can't tell him not to go on sofas, it goes against his training.' Jack gives her a questioning look. 'He needs to search everywhere. Nothing is out of bounds.'

'He's not bloody working now,' Jack grumbles as the dog lies down comfortably next to Lucy. He opens his mouth to protest again but doesn't bother. This can be a lesson in not being such a neurotic arsehole, he tells himself. Lucy places one hand in Moss's fur and goes back to her reading.

Jack pushes his hands above his head and stretches, straightening out his spine. His phone buzzes next to him. A call from the team. Up to now they've been quietly working unsupervised, more than enough lines of inquiry to keep them busy, but he takes the call from Amrit, putting it on speaker. Lucy lifts her head with interest.

'Boss, where are you?' she says in a half-whisper. 'Blake's pissed you've left us alone.'

'He'll get over it. What do you have for us?'

'Bank records from Mark Savage have come back. Large amounts of cash being paid in over the last three years. Nothing huge, but enough to raise eyebrows.'

'Payment for services rendered?'

'I assume so, yes. Nothing from Vincent Carter's accounts but he could have been sensible and kept it away from the bank. And taken it with him when he ran.'

Lucy agrees. 'Old school,' she mouths to Jack with a nod.

'And you were right about the stocktake from stores,' Amrit continues. 'It's ongoing, but there are already substantial differences between what should be there and what actually is. Large quantities of cash, seized cocaine, drugs. All missing.'

'Any idea where it went?'

'No, and as soon as those on high got a sniff of what was going on, they locked it down tight. There needs to be a full investigation, going through what was signed out, when and by whom. It's going to take months. Vince Carter is in the frame, big time.'

'Thanks, Amrit.' He glances up at the clock, surprised to see it's so late. 'Go home. Tell the others.'

They fall back into silence, although, as Jack is realising, Lucy can never be quiet. She hums, tuts, mumbles to Moss. He tries his hardest to ignore her, filtering through another batch of paper. Leaflets this time, sandwiched inside one other. Drug addiction charities: Turning Point, Change Grow Live, Drug Matters, Action on Addiction. Personal interest or professional? Hard to tell. He discards them and pulls a pile of printouts from the mess.

They seem to be reports, including dates and locations, sorted by codes. He recognises a few – they're used for recording crimes in the Record Management System. And then another: a screenshot from the Police National Computer.

He looks over at Lucy. She's chewing on the end of a pen, her other hand absentmindedly stroking the dog. She seems... if not happy, maybe content. This has the potential to derail that.

'Lucy?' he says.

She looks over, her eyebrows raised. He holds the pieces of paper out to her. 'I'm sorry.'

She looks at them and her face darkens.

'So he was,' she says. 'That bastard.' She flicks through them. 'That sneaky so-and-so.' She pauses, deep in thought. 'I'd seen him do it: watch passers-by as they tapped in entry codes, PIN numbers, the lot. It was second nature to him – he'd repeat them back to me, a smug grin on his face. He always said that people are too naïve. I just never thought he was referring to me.'

'Did you often work at home?'

'All the time. I trusted him. He knew how important my job was to me. So when Professional Standards started investigating, I swore blind Nico wouldn't have stolen my password. And I hadn't told him. He maintained he'd got the information from another source.' She rustles the pages angrily. 'Apparently not. Lying bastard.'

And then, with a grunt of anger, she forcefully throws the pages across the room. They flutter gracefully to the ground, where they settle on a pile of documentation. Jack's not sure what to say.

'Are you hungry?' he asks. But apparently, that's the right thing, as she looks to him with a smile.

'Curry?' she replies. 'I could murder a bhuna.'

Chapter Forty-Five

Jack's easy to talk to; Lucy's surprised. Sure, he's uptight, bristling whenever Moss gets on the sofa or sniffs something he shouldn't, or generally behaves like a dog, but he knows it. He gives her a look when the curry arrives and she heads towards the living room.

'Fuck, no,' he says.

'You said fuck!' Lucy replies.

'Only language you understand, Halliday. And don't let that dog eat off your plate, it'll make you sick.'

Lucy fetches a portion of Moss's food from the car, and the dog inhales his dinner while they distribute great dollops of lamb bhuna, saag aloo and vegetable dhansak between them. He's a vegetarian, but thankfully not so clean-living he doesn't drink. She takes the offer of a beer gratefully.

'Nico was definitely onto something,' Jack says, knife and fork in hand. 'The links to the crime gangs, corruption within the force.' He frowns at Lucy. 'You're feral,' he says. She's using the naan bread to shovel curry, her mouth close to the plate. Moss has decamped under the table; she passes him a piece of naan with a triumphant grin.

'Do you think Mark Savage and Vince Carter were the only dirty cops?' Lucy asks with her mouth full.

'Why would they be? The OCG know this is a plan that works. And it can only be more effective now we've found their victims, and the cops know they're true to their word – they'll harm their nearest and dearest if they don't do what they want.'

'But who?'

'Isn't that the question.' Jack gets up and goes to the living room, returning with the notebook he's been scribbling in all night. He flicks through, then hands the open page to Lucy.

She runs her eye down the list of names. 'All of these?' she says, surprised.

'Stop talking with your mouth full. And no, not necessarily. These were the ones Nico highlighted in the newspaper articles. Do you recognise any?'

Lucy scans the list again. 'I know Gareth Collins. I went through training with him, but I never would have thought...' She trails off. She doubts everything now. 'They've certainly got someone on the inside. The missing exhibits from stores, the consignment of drugs going AWOL on the way to being destroyed, the skimming after drug busts?'

'And I went through the spreadsheets that Nico printed from the PNC and RMS. He ran a report containing all arrests due to drug charges and cross-referenced them with records on the PNC. And the only people charged were members of rival gangs to the Wise Monkeys.'

Lucy stares at him, agog. 'Wise Monkeys. Is that the OCG we're looking at?'

'Yes. Why?'

'The gang hit – the murder I was investigating before Nico went missing? We always suspected that was connected to the Wise Monkeys, some guy called Dushku, but could never prove it. Didn't have enough evidence to get a warrant, and without a warrant we couldn't get evidence. Chicken and egg. So nothing came of it. Trail went cold, I was suspended.' She pauses, loading up another piece of naan. 'How come nobody's spotted this before?'

'Nobody's been looking. As long as prosecutions have been at their normal level, which they have, nobody cares.'

'Fucking hell.'

They descend into silence, finishing off the meal. What they've found, what they suspect, it's overwhelming. It's been going on for years, undetected. And it took Jack's arrival for it to be noticed.

Lucy finds this house, and the man who lives within it, fascinating. The dinosaur T-shirt is nerdy, almost endearing. The house — show-home pristine. The only photograph on display is one of two small boys standing together, yellowed with age. Emboldened by her one beer, Lucy stands and picks it up.

'Who's this?' she asks. She squints at the shot: one of the boys is dark, fuller of face, his arm around the blond, skinnier, taller child. 'Is this you?'

Jack glances across. A look of something — annoyance, anger? — flashes in his eyes as he snatches the photo from her. He rubs the bottom of his T-shirt across the glass then puts it in a cupboard, closing the door decisively. 'That was me, yes,' he replies. He starts picking up the empty containers, stacking them into one another.

'Who's the other kid?'

'Best friend.'

'How old are you there? About eleven, twelve?'

'Eleven,' he says. He gets up and dumps the containers in the bin.

'Where is he—'

'Leave it, please.'

He says it quietly, his back to Lucy, but his shoulders are slumped, his chest heaving.

She backtracks quickly. 'I'm sorry. I didn't mean to—'

'It's fine. Drop it.'

He turns away from her and carries on tidying up, loading the dishwasher, wiping down kitchen surfaces that haven't even had the chance to get dirty. Moss follows him and attempts to lick the inside of the dishwasher; Jack doesn't notice.

The silence hangs like fog. Lucy sucks on the inside of her cheek, regretting the casual way she mentioned it. She tries to think of something to restore the easy conversation, but before she can, Jack speaks.

'Why did you join the police force?'

Jack turns, leaning against a kitchen worktop and folding his arms across his chest. Lucy feels like she's being interrogated, but answers anyway.

'I was a restless kid. Couldn't sit still, always wanted to be doing something. I was out drinking one night, too young, but somehow got chatting to a copper in the city centre.' She glances up at Jack; he's watching her, that half-glare on his face. Lucy continues. 'She started telling me about the job. How it's different every night, different people, different situations. Sometimes dangerous, but never boring.' Lucy marvels: how far she's come from those strange days on response and patrol. 'And she was right. I could be freezing cold, starving, desperate for a wee, but those shifts passed in a flash.'

Lucy leaves out the parts about wanting to join the dog unit, even then. A part of her still wants to impress him; he doesn't need more evidence of her failure.

She continues: 'And eventually, I moved to MCIT, worked my way up from there.' She feels her cheeks flush, knowing she's right back where she started. But not quite. She reaches down and gives Moss's silky coat a stroke. 'What about you?'

Jack takes a long breath in. 'I wanted to make a difference. Right some wrongs.'

'What wrongs?'

Jack carries on as if he hasn't heard. 'You do the job well, it makes a huge impact on someone's life. But make a mistake...' He stops, pulling at his nose, his eyes closed.

Lucy's determined to avoid the silence again. 'I know what you mean. I feel like that more than ever with dog handling. I see the guys go out with the general purpose dogs. They make things better, immediately. They track the bad guy, catch them. Put them in jail. It's instant gratification. But for Moss and me? The crime has already been committed. The most we can do is bring closure to those left behind. It's bittersweet, when Moss is successful – someone's future that will never happen.'

'But that's huge,' Jack says, softly. 'The not knowing. It's torture.' Then he clears his throat. 'Why do you only have one dog? I've noticed most handlers have two, or if they only have one it's a GPD.'

'I should have a GPD. I had one. A dog called Finn. He was magnificent – we did all our training together, licensed, passed out. And then on the first call-out, he jumped a fence and something went wrong with his hips. Congenital, they said.' She shrugs, trying to minimise that familiar disappointment. 'So he was rehomed, to live his best life on someone's sofa, and I was left with nothing. Again,' she adds bitterly. 'No dog available, no training courses scheduled until this summer. They had me in the kennels, cleaning out. Walking the dogs, laying the tracks, making tea. All the shit jobs.' She catches Jack's eye; he's watching her intently. 'I think they hoped I'd quit but I'm too stubborn. That taste of being a dog handler – it was the best. I hung on in there. In the end Andrews wanted his men on the street, not fucking around being a kennel bitch, and there was a VRD course available. There's always a shortage of VRDs so he put me on that – and there was Moss.' She smiles. 'He's been with me for a year now. And it's still just the two of us.' She lowers her face to the dog and fusses his ears. 'Isn't it, Mossy?'

The dog, hearing his name, pushes up from under the table, resting his front paws on her leg. 'Anyway,' she says, embarrassed at her oversharing. 'What about you? What brings you here?'

'There was a vacancy. I applied.' Jack walks to the fridge and takes out another beer, screwing the cap off. 'Do you want one?'

'I didn't mean to Hampshire. I meant to MCIT. And no, I shouldn't. Thank you. I have the car.'

'You could stay.'

Lucy thinks she's misheard – Jack says it so quickly, his head in the fridge – if it wasn't for Jack's sudden stillness, his hesitation. But he can't possibly mean… like that? The two of them, together? Surely not.

'I should be heading home,' she gabbles. She gets up, and Jack shuts the fridge. It has the unfortunate result that they're now standing next to each other. Too close. She looks up into his flushed, embarrassed face.

'Yes, you should—'

'I owe you for dinner—'

'You're fine. Go. I mean… I don't mean…' He takes a quick breath in. 'I didn't mean you should stay… not like that. I meant – I have a spare room.'

'Oh. Well. Er… no.' She backs away, almost tripping over Moss. 'I'll go home. Now. But thank you. For dinner. I'll call. Tomorrow.'

And, stammering, she grabs her bag and rushes out to the hallway, opening the door and ushering Moss into the boot. As she reverses out of his drive, she looks back. He's standing at the front door, half-lit in shadow. And as she watches, he slowly closes it, his head tilted to the floor.

She drives away feeling the flush of shame. Ellis is an attractive man, tall, single. And she hasn't had sex in nearly two years. So, yes – for a fraction of a second – she considered it. Until he made it perfectly clear that wasn't what he had in mind.

She had seen the disgust – written all over his face. It's embarrassing. Rejection, out of nowhere. For doing nothing more than help him with the case. Humiliation turns to anger. Who does Jack Ellis think he is? Bad-tempered weirdo. Who is he to judge? Snub her? But deep down, the old insecurities surface. Look at the mess she lives in, the state of her life. He probably thinks she's a right piece of shit.

And he'd be right, the voice in her head tells her. He'd be right.

Tuesday

Chapter Forty-Six

Jack uttered it without thought, like a normal person, a gesture of friendship. But the moment the words left his mouth, and he took in the gaping silence, he heard it anew. He wanted to take it all back. And only succeeded in making it worse.

Lucy left at the speed of light, Moss at her heels, and he couldn't blame her. He'd practically propositioned the poor woman. A grieving widow. This is why he shuns friendship, keeps his mouth shut. The awkwardness he spreads, like a virus.

It's been a strange week. New job, three murders. Seeing Sophie for the first time in years. And meeting Lucy Halliday, with her mess and bluster and unguarded honesty. Lucy is the only olive branch he's received for a long time, although maybe he's misinterpreted that. Maybe she just wants her husband's murder solved, and he's the albatross she has to tolerate.

With the flush of his foolishness, he'd taken himself off to bed, leaving the mess of Nico Halliday's investigation lying in piles on his living room floor. He has no dog to disturb them. No one.

He'd slept. A strange, blurred slumber, where disembodied faces danced. Sophie. Lucy. Theo.

Theo.

He was talking, but Jack couldn't make out the words. He chased him, begged, but he was too far away. Always too far.

So when he wakes to a cacophony of sound, he believes himself to be dreaming. A banging on his door. His phone

239

ringing. A mish-mash of voices, shouting, clamouring to be heard from the street outside.

He blinks. Awake. Definitely awake. His phone stops, then starts again. He picks it up: DCI Kane.

'You're answering,' she says. 'Good. Are you at home?'

He glances at the clock: six-fifteen. 'I've just woken up.'

'You might want to check the papers. Go online. Do you have your laptop?'

'Yes.'

'You can work from there. PSD want to speak to you. They'll be in touch. Don't come in,' she finishes, and abruptly hangs up.

He stares at the phone for a moment: The noise continues downstairs: the doorbell, the knocking, the commotion in the road. It feels... familiar, and a rope knots in his belly. Without getting out of bed, he googles *Jack Ellis* – a headline leaps off the screen.

CHILD MURDER SUSPECT NOW TOP MURDER COP

'Shit,' he mutters and clicks through link after link, his name in bold. *The Daily Mail, The Times, The Guardian*, all spouting a variation of the same, some even using the photograph that sits in his kitchen. The one Lucy had asked about last night. His past, the truth he has done so well to hide, has caught up with him.

And everyone knows.

They know everything.

–

Jack shuts his curtains, ignores the knocking on the door. He retreats back to bed, pulling the duvet over his head. He stays there for a while, furtively glancing at his phone until he starts to feel ridiculous – a grown man hiding under the covers in his boxer shorts.

'Stop being so pathetic,' he mutters. He is no child now. No more the defenceless victim, left unprotected at the whim of the UK's media. He's a forty-year-old man. Six feet, two inches tall. A detective inspector.

Get a fucking grip.

He pulls on tracksuit bottoms and the T-shirt that smells of last night's curry. He heads downstairs. The baying hyenas sense his movement behind the glass and the clamour reaches a new crescendo, but he ignores it, walking to the kitchen at the back of the house. He boils the kettle, fidgets, makes a mug of strong builder's tea, then carries it into the living room where the curtains have been closed since last night. He opens his laptop and sees a report from the lab. The forensics from the squat, but when he reads it, the scientific jargon won't make sense. Words are dancing, laughing at his lack of concentration. He looks away, stares at the mess of documentation and newspaper clippings littering his living-room carpet.

He can't do this now. He can't.

His skin crawls; he jitters, unable to sit still. Every part of him screams to get away, but he's trapped. A rat in a cage. A prisoner of his own personal war.

He goes back into the kitchen and paces, putting his hands over his ears in an attempt to block out the commotion outside. The shouts of his name – both names – the clatter of his letter box as business cards are dropped through.

'Speak to us, Jack. Tell us your side of the story.'

'Where's Theo?'

'What happened that day?'

'Don't you feel bad? For Sophie and his family?'

Sophie. Shit, Sophie.

He grabs for his old Nokia, switching it on. The voicemail icon flashes up but he ignores it, dialling Sophie's number. She answers immediately.

'I'm so sorry,' she says. 'I promise they didn't get anything from me.'

'I know they didn't. It's not your fault, Soph. Are they making your life hell?'

'They'll get bored. They always do. They're asking the same questions, spouting the same theories. Mum's okay, I'm with her now. I'm worried about you.'

He's soothed by her concern. 'Don't be. I'm fine.'

'Is anyone with you? Are you at work?'

'No. And no. My boss told me not to come in.'

'Shit, Jay. Tell me where you are. I'll come over. As soon as I can. I—'

'No, don't.' The use of his old name is cold water to the face. It's too easy for him to get caught up in her, to pretend that they're the same people they were ten years ago, when the vultures at the door are a dose of reality. A reminder that nothing has changed about their situation.

'I'll be fine, I promise. Look after yourself and your mum, Soph.' His voice cracks. 'I'm so sorry this is happening again,' he manages before he hangs up.

Slowly, he slumps into a kitchen chair. He puts his arms on the cold wood of the table and lowers his head onto them. All that he's worked for, the life he's built – gone in a second. He could cry, but he's spent. Tired, worn out, defeated. He can't run anymore.

The voices outside fade, reporters growing bored. But then he hears another noise. The French doors to his garden sliding open behind him. The click of nails on tiles, paws on his leg; a cold nose pushes itself against his face.

He lifts his head, lowers a hand to greet the spaniel and looks behind him.

Lucy is standing in the open doorway.

'I thought you could use some company,' she says.

Chapter Forty-Seven

'It's not what they're saying,' Jack exclaims, once Lucy is inside. 'It didn't happen like that.'

'It never is,' she replies. 'Can I make you tea?'

'Oh, hell, no,' Jack says, remembering the last few weak offerings she's made. He gets up, gesturing for her to take a seat. 'Coffee?' She nods. He asks the question he's been dreading. 'How did you find out? It must be all around the nick?'

'Not there. Although, yes, I'm sure it is,' she admits with a wince. 'Nothing coppers like more than a good bit of gossip, and I expect you're it today. But I saw it online. I look every morning. Habit. In case Nico showed up.'

'And instead you got me. And a cold case.'

He brings her a coffee and tries to read her. Why is she here? Curiosity, or friendship? She seems sincere.

But she detects his suspicion, because she says, 'I know what it's like.' She points vaguely to his front door. 'When that happens.'

Jack nods. 'I'm sorry you had to go through it all.'

'It's okay. I got this one out of the whole mess.'

Moss senses he's being discussed and opens his eyes, getting up and resting his jowls on Jack's leg. Jack strokes his head, rubbing behind his ears.

'He's good stress-release,' Lucy says. 'Not just because he's a small black fluffy teddy bear, but he's an old soul. He knows when I'm sad. He understands. And he loves without question. That's the beauty of dogs. They don't judge. All Moss needs is love, and to be by my side every moment of the day.'

'Not much then,' Jack says with a smile.

'I can cope with the dog hair and the mud, if I get to spend all day playing with this one. That's how he sees searching. It's a game for him. Hide-and-seek. I've always had a natural affinity with dogs. You put the time in, you're calm and consistent, and you get results. The dogs are successful and their confidence grows. And that feeling when your dog gets the scent? The rush. In that moment you're one.'

Jack sees the attraction now. The simplicity. You get a call-out. You show up with your dog. You get the job done. There is none of the politics of his rank, the complexity of forensics, making sense of it all, persuading the CPS. For Lucy and Moss, it's simply following the trail.

'Don't you get lonely?' he asks.

'I've always been a bit of a recluse. And it's a nomadic life, solitary. As a dog handler, I spend a lot of time outside on my own but that's no hardship if you like dogs. Besides, I'm not by myself. I have this one. I hang out all day with my best friend, and I get paid for it. I have more freedom than your average copper on the street, driving around with my partner. What could be better?'

Moss pushes his head between her legs and she lowers her face to his, looking into his eyes.

'When they love you, they'll never leave you. Loyal to a fault.'

For the first time, Jack envies Lucy. Her job, her relationship with Moss. The purity of their partnership.

'It's not what they say,' Jack repeats.

'What did happen?'

Jack looks back to his tea, staring into the brown murk. 'I was never a murder suspect, and I certainly didn't kill him. I was eleven.' He looks back up, meeting Lucy's sympathetic gaze. 'I would never have killed my best friend.'

Chapter Forty-Eight

Jack's been silent for nearly thirty years, but when he starts talking, it's like a dam has burst.

'Theo was my best friend,' he begins. 'We met on the first day of school and something between us clicked. We were so different in many ways. My family were well off – I was an only child and cripplingly shy. Theo had three brothers and sisters, and his family was… Well. They didn't have much money. I was this skinny white kid, and Theo was short and dark and strong, and wouldn't shut up.' He glances to Lucy; she's listening intently. 'But we both liked dinosaurs.' He shrugs. 'Friendships have been built on a lot less.'

Jack remembers Theo – a ball of energy, always talking, as if his brain was on fire and he had to get it all out. He ran everywhere, flat-footed thumps slapping down school corridors. Jack followed in his wake, a pale ghost, drinking in the adoration that Theo offered. Neither was popular at school. Theo was too loud, too boisterous, too… everything, while nobody noticed Jack. They went everywhere together.

Jack's parents weren't keen on Theo – this mixed-race kid from the poor part of town – but as it seemed to Jack that they weren't keen on children, full stop, he paid no heed.

The world was simpler then. Parents didn't worry about paedophiles or serial killers. Theo and Jack roamed the streets on their bikes, buying sweets from the corner shop with their pooled pocket money, eating them, sticky-fingered, in the woods on the far side of town. They'd build dens, dream about staying up all night, with midnight feasts and ghost stories. They fought imaginary dinosaurs, wolves, dragons. Monsters with sharp teeth that could be vanquished with sticks and stones.

But in the end, a different kind of monster came for Theo.

It had been a Saturday, much like any other. July, and the start of a stifling summer, days after school had broken up, so nobody cared about homework. Nobody cared about anything really, except the suffocating heat and the wish for a breeze, or an ice cream, or one solitary rain cloud. The adults complained, but the boys loved it, solely for the freedom from T-shirts, and socks, or even shoes. The two of them ran feral in the forest, the trees providing respite from the sun. Their hands were tacky from ice pops, their tongues blue, their bare feet filthy.

Jack doesn't remember now what they talked about, what game they played. Days rolled into one. They had nothing to worry about, except being home for dinner. The one ritual his mother enforced – a formal sit-down affair. Jack had eaten at Theo's many a time. Delicious curries, bobotie, chakalaka, creamy pap. Strange words for delicious flavours that Jack gobbled with relish, but Theo had never been invited back to Jack's. Family only, Jack's mum said, her lips pursed tight. Even then, Jack knew something about racism, albeit as a concept he didn't fully understand.

It wasn't until late that night, when the policeman showed up at Jack's door, pulling him from his bed, that Jack realised something had happened to Theo.

At first the police were gentle, sitting opposite Jack on the plastic-covered sofa at his house, refusing offers of tea and coffee. Shadows darkened under their eyes, and frustration grew as visible as the damp patches under their arms as Jack repeated himself, over and over. He didn't know when he left. He assumed Theo went straight home. He didn't know, he didn't know, he didn't know.

The next morning, he was tired and confused. He changed his story. His grief-stricken eleven-year-old mind started forming blanks, empty spaces where the memories should have been.

And then the witness was found, and Jack was interviewed under caution. At the police station. An appropriate adult present, although what that nameless, faceless person did for him he was never sure.

'Did they think you'd killed him?' Lucy asks.

'I assume so,' Jack replies. 'This was 1994, not that long after the murder of Jamie Bulger. Everyone knew kids could do horrible things, and there was me, this little white rich boy, and Theo, the poor mixed-race kid. The papers claimed institutional racism, that the police hadn't charged me because I was white and Theo was black, but looking back, they had no evidence. A witness, saying she saw us together, burying something, but that could have been anything. We were always digging holes, making dens.'

'And they never found him?'

'Never.'

'Where do you think he went?'

Jack sighs. 'I wish I knew. I've been over so many possibilities over the years. That he was abducted. Abused. Murdered. That he made it home and someone in his family killed him.' He shakes his head. 'No, I never believed that. Not that family. Mine, maybe.' He laughs, bitterly. 'But not his. I think someone took him. And if that's the case, we may never find him. Not now. Not thirty years later.'

'They never charged you?'

'Didn't even arrest me. But according to the papers, I was the prime suspect. Theo's family never believed that, but in the eyes of the public I was guilty. My face was on every paper. My family had to move away. Even that didn't work. Someone would always find us, and the graffiti, the dog shit through the door – it would start again. In the end we changed our names. And I became Jack Ellis.'

For Jack, it had been a shedding of the skin. A goodbye to Jason Kent. A new start and a relief, of sorts. But his parents never forgave him. It was their shame. Even though they never said it out loud, even though he was eleven and hadn't done anything wrong, they blamed him for this new uncomfortable life. Hiding. Pretending.

'What's with the phone?' Lucy asks. She gestures towards Jack's old Nokia. 'Who has that number?'

He picks it up, turns it tenderly over in his hand. 'Sophie. Theo's sister. Two years older. We kept in contact after I moved away. Wrote letters, you know, childish stuff. I went off the rails at university. Drink, drugs, the lot. Completely out of control. We lost touch. And then, when we were in our twenties, we bumped into each other and… one thing led to another.'

Lucy raises her eyebrows. 'That must have been… complicated?'

Jack gives a quick laugh. 'You have no idea. She didn't blame me for Theo's disappearance, but her family never gave up hope. And seeing me? It was painful for them. It reminded them of what they'd lost.'

'How long were you together?'

'Five years.'

Lucy lets out a long whistle. 'That's marriage material.'

'Could have been.' He shrugs, feeling useless. 'But the crossover between my old life and new was tricky. I was paranoid. Didn't want anyone to catch on about Theo and the accusations. It was just as my career was taking off. I felt like I had to choose and…'

'Your career came first.'

It hadn't felt like that at the time, but Lucy stating it in such stark terms makes Jack realise that's what happened. No wonder Sophie hadn't spoken to him in years. Even the different phones marked the line between old and new. A separation.

The knocking distracts them; Lucy looks towards the door.

'How did they find you? Why now?'

'That, I don't understand. I've been Jack Ellis for nearly thirty years, and my name was changed legally, by deed poll. It's public record. We weren't under witness protection. Any reporter could have looked me up, if they'd bothered. But they never did. Yet somehow, this morning, every newspaper in the country knows my name.'

Lucy's thoughtful for a moment, then takes her phone out of her pocket. She places it on the table in front of them and pulls up a number. *Cal Watson.*

It rings for a moment, then a deep voice, with a cockney accent, answers.

'Lucy, I haven't used anything you told me, I promise.'

'I know, Cal. Listen. I have Jack Ellis here.'

There's a sharp intake of breath. 'Jason Kent.'

'I was,' Jack says.

'Calvin Watson. From *The Guardian*. Nice to speak to you.'

Lucy interrupts. 'Cal, we need to know where you got the information from. Who tipped you off?'

There's a long pause. 'Lucy, you know I can't reveal my sources.'

'That's bollocks and you know it. We're not going to arrest anyone. But don't you think that it's odd that just as we're getting closer to finding Nico's killer, this happens? That the SIO on the murder investigation is discredited?'

'And I got a threat yesterday,' Jack adds. 'Someone telling me to back off.'

Lucy looks at him sharply. 'You did?' Jack nods. She turns back to the phone. 'Please? For Nico?'

'That's low, Lucy. You know I'd do anything for Nico.'

'So tell us.'

Another pause, and a sigh. 'You didn't hear it from me, not that I know much. We all got an email last night. From a guy called Mark Savage. Who, as you know, is very dead right now. So it got our attention. All it said was to look into DI Jack Ellis with respect to a kid called Jason Kent.'

'And you did,' Lucy states.

'Yes. And it checked out. And I'm sorry, but it was too big not to run with.'

'Didn't you think it would detract from what's important?' Lucy snaps. 'From finding the people who killed Nico?'

'I pushed it to the middle pages. I did my best.'

'You did your—' Lucy almost shouts, but Jack places his hand gently on her arm and shakes his head.

'That's exactly it,' Jack says. 'They want us distracted. They want me to run away and hide. We found Nico's van yesterday,' he explains to Cal. 'And all his research. They must know. They're worried.'

'What did you find?' the disembodied voice says from the phone.

But Jack ignores him. He sits back, squaring his shoulders. 'I did nothing wrong in 1994, and I'm doing nothing wrong now. I passed all my security checks when I joined the police force, and I worked my way up fair and square. DCI Kane may not want me to come in, but I'm not going to be bullied by these people. I let the events all those years ago change my life then. I won't let it happen again.'

Jack's determined. Restored by Lucy being here, and their conversation. She gives him a slow nod, then reaches for the phone.

'Thank you, Cal. We'll be in—'

'No, wait,' Cal says. Lucy pauses, her finger hovering over the red button. 'Kane? You say you work for DCI Kane? Emily Kane?'

Jack's gaze swivels to the phone.

'Yes. Why?'

'Because I did some digging. Like you asked me to, Luce. And something about that drug charity caught my eye. Drug Matters? The one Nico wanted me to get involved with?'

Something sparks, and Jack jumps up, rushing into the living room and scrabbling around in the mess. He finds what he's looking for and brings it back, showing it to Lucy.

'There was a leaflet for the charity in Nico's research,' he tells Cal. 'Among some others.'

'Yeah, it wasn't for personal reasons, as I assumed. Nico had put in a freedom of information request. Asking for details of their financial records and their trustees. They denied access to their finances, but they came back with a full list of names of people on their board. Mark Savage was one—'

'Our dead man?'

'And another was Emily Kane.'

Jack and Lucy turn to each other in confusion. Her mouth is open.

'It could be perfectly innocent,' Lucy says. 'They might not have known each other. Savage could have been involved because of his wife. And maybe Emily…'

'Maybe nothing,' Cal interjects. 'Nico suspected that charity of something dodgy. You need to get on to your fraud division. See what they can find out. You know Mark Savage was up to his neck in it. Emily Kane must be too. It can't be coincidence.'

And that's when something flashes into Jack's mind. The report, the forensic report from this morning. He'd seen something. Information he hadn't taken in at the time because of his addled state.

As Lucy hangs up the phone to Cal with a quick goodbye, Jack rushes to fetch his laptop, banging it onto the table and pulling up the document. He scans it quickly, Lucy peering over his shoulder, curious.

'There,' he says, decisively, pointing to the screen. 'Definitely not coincidence.'

Lucy reads the sentence, then locks eyes with Jack.

Blood sample taken at location 34C (bedroom 1) – no direct match. 50% familial match to Kane, Emily.

'A sample of blood found at the squat comes from someone related to Kane,' Jack states. And Lucy says the next thing that comes into Jack's mind.

'Fuck.'

Chapter Forty-Nine

'Eyes front, face blank,' Lucy whispers to Jack as they get out of the car. 'Yes, they are probably talking about you, but fuck 'em.'

He stares at her for a moment, astonished, as if she's read his mind. He squares his shoulders and pulls himself to his full height.

Lucy had waited while he had a shower, shaved, put on a suit. Battle armour, when all she has is a small black spaniel and a scruffy uniform. But they work in the same way, emotional support for tough times.

They'd left through the kitchen door, out through the back gate and into Lucy's car. They drove in silence to the nick. Lucy questioned not involving Professional Standards. It's their job, to investigate bent coppers, but Jack was resolute.

'We have no idea how far this spreads,' he had said. 'Or how long it's been going on. They investigated you. Kane says they want to speak to me. Do you trust them?'

No, she doesn't. But they don't have much. Blood at a crime scene and Kane linked with a drug charity. While she drove, Jack called DC Gill – as he expected, she was already at work.

He didn't let her speak for long, before he started barking instructions.

'I need you to search every single mobile phone record we have on file from the investigation. For this number.' He recited Kane's mobile. 'Do it now. Call me back.'

Lucy didn't know what Amrit said in reply.

Now, in the empty car park, she phones. Jack puts her on speaker.

'Boss, you were right,' Amrit says, her voice echoing around the concrete. 'That number pops up numerous times. Once calling Mark Savage on Wednesday…'

'After we found his wife,' Lucy hisses. 'She must have known who it was.' Jack nods.

'…And once to one of the now-disconnected burner phones. Late Saturday afternoon.'

'Just before the raid on the squat,' Jack concludes.

'Who is this, boss? Do you want me to request an authority for their full records?'

'No, hold fire for now.'

'Are you coming in?'

'I'm already here,' Jack says and hangs up. He looks at Lucy. 'Kane warned them we were coming. That's why there was nobody at the squat.'

Lucy nods. It's not much.

But it's enough.

Leaving Moss in the back of her Mondeo – he's used to waiting, he'll have a nap – they leave the car park and start walking through the nick. Steady speed. Side by side. Conversation pauses as they pass, eyes follow. Whispers, open mouths. They keep going.

Lucy glances up to Jack; apart from a slight flush to his cheeks and the tension in his jaw, it's impossible to tell what's going on in his head. Nothing good, she assumes.

They take the lift to the third floor.

'You okay?' Lucy asks as it ascends.

He continues looking straight ahead. 'Fine. You?'

'Tip-top,' she replies.

They're about to arrest his boss. The insanity of that.

They reach the doorway and pause. Kane's PA is absent; the door is ajar. Inside they can't hear anything but a quiet sniffing.

Jack pushes the door open and strides into the room, Lucy following. He stops in front of Kane's desk; she looks up slowly.

Her eyes are red-rimmed, her face blotchy. Lucy has never seen her like this. In all the time Lucy's known Emily Kane, she's been steely, focused, driven. Disappointed and angry, but never weak and upset. Lucy expected protests, anger, refusal. Maybe even threats to have them fired. But Emily's reaction confounds her.

Kane lifts her eyes, defeated. She nods slowly, with acceptance. And then she presses one finger against her lips.

Lucy looks up to Jack and he glances at her, as confused as she is, as Kane picks up a pen and writes something on the pad in front of her. She turns it around and pushes it towards them.

They're listening, it says.

Kane looks up with desperate eyes, switching her gaze from Jack to Lucy and back again. Lucy slowly tilts her head to one side, raising her eyebrows. *And?*

Kane stands up and comes out from behind her desk. She points through her open doorway and starts walking. They follow.

Down the empty corridor, to the disabled toilet at the far end. Lucy feels Jack's glance, knows what he's thinking: if this is a play, it's an odd one.

The three of them go into the toilet, Kane last. She closes the door behind them and locks it. It's compact, but there's space to move; an unpleasant smell of lemon-scented chemicals pervades. It's clean, at least.

Lucy debates whether Kane might be suffering from delusions, paranoia, schizophrenia – and if that's the case, she has no desire to be locked in a confined space with her. But how much damage can a five-foot-five woman in a business suit do? She doesn't seem to be concealing any weapons.

Kane reaches across and sets a tap running. Only then does she speak.

'I knew you'd find me,' she says.

'Emily, start talking,' Jack replies, sternly. 'Now. And you're under caution. You do not have to say anything—'

'They have my office bugged. They know everything. They hear everything.'

'Who?' Lucy asks. 'Tell us what's going on and we can help you. We can end this. We know there are dirty cops, we know it's connected to the Wise Monkeys, and they killed Vanessa Savage and David Carter and...' Her throat constricts as tears threaten. 'And tortured Nico,' she manages. 'Did you know?' she says. 'Did you know?'

Kane gives a quick succession of nods in reply. Then her face collapses and she starts to cry. 'I'm sorry. I'm so sorry,' she burbles through an avalanche of tears and snot. 'I didn't know what they'd do. I didn't realise they'd kill them.'

'Who?' Jack pushes.

'I don't know. You have to believe me,' she pleads. 'I honestly don't know. They send me messages from burner phones. They tell me what to do and when, what information they need. It was easy at the start. A few reports, a bit of information here and there.' She's gabbling now, words spilling like vomit from her dribbling lips. 'And in exchange they got me promoted. Pay rises. A word in the right person's ear, I don't know. But then they wanted more.'

'Mark Savage was in on it.'

'Yes. There was this charity...'

'Drug Matters.'

'You know? Of course, you know. It's a front, have you worked that out? Money laundering for the OCG. What better place to clean the cash – donations in, donations out. They needed respectable faces on the board. Mark and I, plus one of their accountants. Savage was their main man inside. At least, in the beginning. He knew what was going down and when. He could skim drugs, cash off the top, store it until the coast was clear. He recruited Vince Carter. Controlled everything that happened in the nick. There was nothing I could do to stop it.'

'So why did they take his wife? Why kill her?'

'I don't know. I don't!' she pleads. 'Maybe he got a conscience, maybe it was a power play and someone else wanted in.'

'Maybe that person was you?' Jack interrupts. 'You called him. Told him his wife was dead.'

She hangs her head. 'Yes.'

'What did he say?'

'Nothing. He started crying and hung up. Next thing I know, you'd found his body in the squat. I knew it was starting to go wrong.'

'Tell me about Nico,' Lucy says.

All this time and they're so close. To getting to the end of this. To knowing who was behind her husband's death.

Kane stays silent.

'Tell me,' Lucy growls.

Kane looks at Lucy, her eyes pleading. 'They knew there was a reporter out there digging. That he had something on them. So I told them who you were. Where you lived.'

Lucy's skin turns cold. 'You led them to Nico.'

'I'm sorry. I didn't know they'd kill him.'

'What the fuck did you think they would do?' Lucy shouts, overcome by fury. 'Take him out for dinner?'

Kane shakes her head, crying.

'They tortured him! Left him to die!'

Lucy feels a gentle hand on her arm but she pulls away from Jack.

'Emily Kane, you are under arrest for conspiracy to murder,' Lucy roars. She reaches for Kane, twists her arm behind her in a painful lock. 'You do not have to say anything—'

'Don't. Please don't.' Emily tries to pull away from Lucy and grabs at Jack's arm with her free hand, practically hanging off it. 'If you arrest me, I'm no use to them. They'll kill her.'

256

Lucy remembers the blood in the squat. The familial match.

'Who?' she asks, fearing the worst.

'My daughter,' Kane replies, then collapses in a heap in the middle of the tiled floor. 'They have my daughter.'

Part Three

Chapter Fifty

Lucy and Jack stare at each other, as their boss cries on the bathroom floor. A thousand thoughts run through Lucy's head. This woman contributed to her husband's death. A senior detective in their constabulary is corrupt. And most importantly: a girl has been kidnapped. They all know how that will end – they have the bodies in the woods to prove it.

'You have to help,' Kane pleads. 'You have to find her.'

Lucy swallows back the hatred and the contempt. She crouches down to her level.

'When did she go missing? What's her name?'

'Daisy. She's only nineteen. Someone called me Wednesday morning. They took her Tuesday night. A week ago. She's been with them a week, oh God…' She dissolves into sobs again.

Lucy grits her teeth, her sympathy wearing thin. But the fact is that Kane's daughter, like David Carter and Vanessa Savage before her, is innocent. And, assuming she's still alive, she knows nothing about the mess her mother has got her into.

Nico was a jaded journalist. He'd spent his life risking his own personal safety in search of a story. He never expected to die for it, but he always knew what he was doing.

She glances at Jack. His brow is lowered, shoulders hunched, thinking. He wants to catch these guys as much as she does.

Lucy rips a length of toilet roll from the wall and holds it out to her former boss.

'Pull yourself together,' Lucy says. 'For Daisy's sake. Start talking.'

The sound of her daughter's name has the desired effect. Kane looks at Lucy with swollen eyes, then takes the tissue and dabs at her face.

'Someone new contacted me,' she explains in halting, whispered breaths, 'after you had spoken to Vince Carter. They didn't like you,' she directs to Jack. 'They weren't happy, wanted me to give them updates. Do all I could to interfere with the investigation. And if I didn't then Daisy would die.

'They told me to call the university. To explain there had been a family bereavement and Daisy had to leave at short notice. But they're going to kill her, aren't they?' Kane looks at them, desperately. 'Please help me. Help her.'

'Have you heard from them lately?' Jack asks calmly. 'Seen proof of life?'

Kane shakes her head quickly, her lips pressed together. Lucy glances to Jack but he stays expressionless.

'Ask them to provide that. Next time they call.'

Kane starts crying again, tears streaming. 'She's dead already, isn't she?'

'We have to assume she's not. Make sure they have a reason to keep her alive. Make yourself useful. Stay calm,' Jack adds, and Kane sniffs, trying to pull herself together. 'Tell us anything you know. Quickly. How do you know your office is bugged?'

'They told me.'

'How?'

'Text message. Always different numbers. They share information that they could only know from listening in to my office. Conversations I've had, evidence we've recovered. They wanted to know if we were getting closer to the house where Nico and Vanessa Savage were killed. Told me to warn them if we were going in.' Kane holds out her mobile phone. 'I've been making a note of all the numbers they call me from. But they go out of service almost as soon as they're used.'

'Show me?' Jack instructs. With trembling fingers, Kane pulls up a page on her Notes app. Jack takes the phone from her and presses a few buttons, and soon they hear the whoosh of an email being sent. 'What else?'

'That's it. That's all I know.' Kane is desperate again. 'Don't you think I'd have done my own investigation if I could? I have nothing. That's why I hired you.'

'Me?' Jack repeats.

'I was in too deep and I knew it, even before they took Daisy. I needed someone to stop them. So I hired you. Everything I heard indicated you were unpopular. That you kept to yourself. Didn't have much of a life.' Lucy glances up at Jack, who's blanched at the description. 'But that you were good and you got the job done. I needed someone with no ties to Hampshire. That couldn't be corrupted. You had the cleanest record of anyone I've ever interviewed.'

'You knew about my past,' Jack says.

'They didn't like that I'd taken you on. Must have done some digging of their own. Told me to use it if I needed to keep you in line.'

'And what about me?' Lucy says. 'Why did you try so hard to keep me in the force?'

'Because I felt awful. It was my fault your husband had...'

'Been murdered,' Lucy finishes, bitterly.

Kane's gaze drops to the floor. 'Yes. And I knew you were a good detective. Even out of MCIT you wouldn't let his disappearance lie. However bad it would be for me, I wanted you to find a resolution.' Kane looks up at Jack and Lucy. 'You have to find my daughter and put an end to all of this. Please.'

'Why did you do it?' Lucy asks, ignoring her plea. 'Just tell me that. You're a police officer, a detective. Your job is to catch the bad guys, not go into business with them.'

'I know, I know,' Kane replies. 'But it started small. Almost unnoticeable. I was a DC and we'd arrested this guy for murder. He'd killed his girlfriend, cut and dried, and we were searching his house. And someone... They screwed up. A piece of evidence went missing. The knife – the murder weapon. It wasn't for long, about half an hour or so, but it meant the chain of custody was broken. His lawyer would have had a field day so I… I… I falsified the records. Nobody suspected, nobody noticed, but somehow, they knew what I'd done. And didn't hesitate to let me know – the texts started, always anonymous, always different numbers. Then they got more specific – who they wanted me to arrest. Where I'd find the evidence. All against their rivals, of course.' She looks up into Lucy's eyes, mascara scoring her cheeks with dripping black lines. 'I was getting convictions; my DCI was happy. I got promoted. What could be the harm?'

'People died,' Lucy hisses. 'My husband died. They have your daughter.'

Jack pulls Lucy to the side of the bathroom as Kane starts crying again.

'Leave her be,' he says. 'We have her now. She won't get away with it.'

'We need to arrest her.'

'No! No, you can't!' Kane pleads, scrabbling to her feet. 'Then they'll kill Daisy.'

Jack looks at Lucy, gravely. 'She's right. As much as I hate to say it. Once they know that Kane's no use to them, they'll kill her.'

'Fuck's sake,' Lucy growls. She turns to Kane. 'You need to tell Jack everything you know. Every detail. Leave it to him. And if you do anything that jeopardises this investigation – if you try to run – I will kill you myself. Got it?'

Kane nods.

Lucy looks at Jack. His face is stern and she knows what he's thinking. Over a week on from the first victim showing up in Gallows Wood, and they have nothing concrete.

They need firm, conclusive evidence. And a way to find Daisy Kane. But what?

What the hell are they going to do?

Chapter Fifty-One

While Kane's been talking, the facts of the case have been whirring in Jack's head. They have links to an organised crime group and three dirty cops – but of those one is dead and the other, Vince Carter, is still in the wind. A crime scene with more exhibits than they can process. Missing cash and drugs. A list of mobile phone numbers, all burners, which are now probably disconnected. One name linked to fingerprints from the squat. Not forgetting Nico Halliday's piles of newspaper clippings, plus his laptop they can't get into.

None of it is proof.

None of it will help to find Daisy Kane.

He realises both Kane and Lucy are looking at him. Waiting for a way forward. He needs to make sense of it all, and fast.

'Go to your office,' he says to Kane. 'Keep your head down. Your first priority is to get proof that Daisy is alive.'

'And then?'

'And then do your job. Act like nothing is happening. I'm going back to work; I'm not hiding anymore.'

'You'll need to make a statement to the press,' Kane says.

The thought makes Jack want to curl up and hide, but he's had enough. Theo's disappearance was never his fault, yet he's been the one taking the blame for nearly thirty years.

'Whatever,' he says to Kane. 'Set it up.'

'What about me?' Lucy asks.

'I'm going to need your help,' he replies. 'But the official line is that you're on compassionate leave.'

He says it flippantly but realises that, for her, it should be true. What she's been through, what she's *still* going through – there's no way she should be anywhere near this investigation. But what can he do? He needs someone close by he can talk to. Someone he can trust. 'Is that okay?' he finishes, gently.

Halliday nods.

'We'll be in touch,' Jack says. And with that, he unlocks the door to the bathroom.

They stand in the corridor and watch as DCI Emily Kane heads back to her office, head bowed. Once she's out of sight, Lucy turns to him.

'You don't have a clue, do you?' she says.

'Not a scooby,' Jack replies.

–

Lucy's first priority lies with Moss. And the car park is as good a place as any to regroup. Moss is napping when they get down there, but treats Jack as his long-lost friend the moment he's allowed out of the boot, his entire behind wiggling in time with his tail. Jack crouches down and allows the dog to shove his cold nose in his face, while Lucy laughs.

'Get in the front,' she says. 'We need to make some calls.'

The first to Raj Johal down in digital.

'I have a list of mobile phone numbers,' Jack says. 'I need you to run every single one. Last known locations, numbers called, whether they're still in service. Has DC Gill been in touch with the ones we had before?'

'She has, much to my joy,' Raj says with no hint of sarcasm, his voice echoing from the loudspeaker. 'I've been through the entire repertoire of mobile phone bills from your victims, traced every single one. Sad to say, I've come up empty. Was desperate to put a smile on that lovely lady's face.'

'Nothing?'

'Nope. All burner phones – and there were a lot of them – are disconnected. All other numbers have been checked and came up clean.'

'Pity. Do what you can with these new ones. And Emily Kane is going to give you permission to access her own mobile account.'

There's a long pause. 'DCI Kane?'

'Yes. Do it. But report directly back to me. Check every number. And I have a laptop.'

'A laptop? Whose?'

Jack glances to Lucy. She's sat in the driver's seat; Moss is perched on her lap, panting, ears up. She nods, then presses her face into Moss's fur.

'Nico Halliday's. I need you to break in. I'll bring it down shortly.'

'No problem. I'm here all day,' Raj confirms and hangs up.

Jack turns to Lucy. 'Nothing,' he says. 'Except a new crush in the making.'

'What now?'

'Now we contact covert ops.'

Lucy stares at him. He knows what she's thinking. He's run it through his head a thousand times and this is the only conclusion he's come to.

'We can't find this girl by ourselves. We need negotiators, a full surveillance unit, multiple observation points watching the OCG, and specialist firearms teams when the time comes.'

'But what if someone's compromised? They'll kill her.'

'I know,' Jack says, dully. 'But what option do we have?'

Lucy stays silent; he knows she's in agreement.

'We'll continue our own investigation into the murders. And maybe we'll make headway before they do.'

Lucy thinks for a moment, then nods slowly.

'How can I help?' she asks.

'Who do you trust? Who can we definitely rule out?'

'Fran,' Lucy says without hesitation.

'Go and see her. Find out what she can do for us. Can she chase up the lab? I suspect if I phone Rachel Lennon again, she'll block me, but Fran might have more luck.'

'Will do. And have fun with the vultures.'

'Huh?'

'The press?'

Jack shakes his head in disbelief; with everything going on, his own personal nightmare had completely slipped his mind.

'I'll be fine.'

Lucy gives him a long look. Then she reaches behind her and pulls Nico's laptop from the back seat. She passes it to him solemnly. 'Good luck,' she says, then gets out of the car to load Moss into the boot. Jack does the same, watching and waiting as she drives off, the laptop tucked under his arm.

A tiger kidnap is tricky for your average bad guy to pull off – trusting that the act of capturing someone's nearest and dearest will convince them to commit a crime. They're difficult for the police at the best of times; the balance of risk for the victim, catching the kidnappers in time. And the fact that there's someone listening, feeding information to the other side, makes it damn near impossible.

But they need to find Daisy Kane. And fast.

Chapter Fifty-Two

Within the hour, the team arrives. An army of plain-clothes detectives, technicians and analysts, bringing computers and laptops and equipment. Jack wonders where this lot were a week ago, when they had murders to solve.

The man in charge introduces himself to Jack.

'DCI Craig Dawson,' he says, offering a bone-crushing handshake. 'Covert ops.' He's bulky, with an angular face, hollows beneath his cheekbones – the look of someone who does CrossFit, with the arrogance to match. 'I'll be handling this operation.'

Jack starts to protest. 'I'm the SIO—'

'And you still are, Ellis. Don't you worry. But this one's a bit over your paygrade, wouldn't you agree?'

His patronising tone grates.

'Leave this one to us. We know these guys, we've been watching them for a while. Haven't you got enough on your plate?' he says, gesturing to the whiteboard. 'And rumour has it, a little personal matter to deal with.' He places a hand on Jack's shoulder and steers him to the side. 'We know about the inside man. Emily filled us in. Awful business,' he says, as if he were talking about a change in canteen menu rather than corrupt cops. 'We'll be the picture of discretion. We'll set up a green room next-door. You won't even know we're there. And we'll have Daisy home, safe and sound, before you know it. Just keep out of our way.'

And with a firm pat on Jack's shoulder, he leaves, his battalion following.

'Shit,' Jack mutters. He regrets his decision to involve them, but what else could he have done? Protocol dictates this is what happens, and they clearly have the resources at their disposal.

He turns back to his own team, surprised to find all three pairs of eyes fixed on him.

'I'll explain in a sec,' Jack says. 'Now, tell me where we are on these murders.'

'Boss... we thought... Aren't you...?' Blake stutters.

Jack pulls up a chair into the middle of the group. He'd barely had a chance to speak to the team before covert ops arrived, and now Harry Blake, Phil Lawrence and Amrit Gill – the only people Jack has – have questions.

'We've got three murders to solve,' he says. 'I'm not going to sit at home while there's work to do. I assume you've read the papers? Seen the news?' The three glance nervously to each other. 'Is this going to be a problem? What do you want to know?'

'What happened to that kid?' Lawrence blurts out.

'I have no idea. I wish I knew.' And Jack explains everything about Theo for the second time that morning. Strangely, it's getting easier. Those damn therapists were correct – the more he talks about the events all those years ago, the better it feels. Like a three-ton weight is slowly being lifted from his chest.

'Any further questions?' he concludes. The three of them shake their heads. 'Good. Because there's been a development on the case.'

Their expressions graduate from surprise to shock as he tells them about Kane, her connection to the OCG, and her missing daughter.

'So they're...' Blake looks towards the clatter in the corridor.

'Here to find Daisy, yes. We'll do our job, they'll do theirs. Okay?'

The team nod.

'Then, we have work to do.'

Lines of inquiry are discussed. While they wait for forensics, Amrit offers to take Nico's laptop down to Raj in digital and find out how he's getting on with the mobile numbers – obviously, the crush is fast becoming two-way. Blake, subdued after the Lucy Halliday debacle, is even offering to go back to the CCTV and traffic cameras, in an attempt to find how the bodies were moved from the squat to Gallows Wood. And Lawrence disappears to IT to look into how someone might have emailed from Mark Savage's account.

Jack heads to his office. He closes the door; he needs to think, to regroup. They have little to go on for the murders. And he needs to have faith that the bull-in-a-china-shop, DCI Dawson, knows what he's doing. But something in the back of his mind niggles. Nobody knew about Vince Carter and Mark Savage – for years. And – if Kane's instinct is correct – there's someone else out there, pulling the strings, who's taken over from Savage.

They have one lead – a fingerprint found on a syringe at the squat that connects them to Aron Dushku. A notorious member of the Wise Monkeys. He knows it's not enough to prove involvement but he remembers his conversation with Lucy last night – her waste-ground murder in 2021, the investigation that came to nothing. Another payoff that might work. Assuming the OCG are the ones holding Daisy, Jack might be able to attract their attention, drawing it away from their captive.

Kick up some dust. Create a distraction.

As crazy as it feels, it just might work.

Chapter Fifty-Three

Lucy's conflicted feelings about Fran remain as she drives to Fran's house, calling her on hands-free. Her best friend's deliberate failure to tell her about Nico's question still niggles, like a splinter under her skin. But her gut tells her that, however annoying Fran's omission was, she can trust her. On this, if nothing else.

The first two attempts ring out; Fran answers the third.

'You ignore me for days, don't return my call when you're released and now you phone? I have a dead body on the table, Lucy. What is it?'

'It's an emergency. I need to speak to you.'

Fran's exasperated but agrees to meet Lucy at her house in half an hour. Moss is glad to be out of the back of the car and runs laps of Fran's lawn. Lucy sits on the grass and he joins her, panting hot doggy breath into her face.

'Are you crazy?' she says to him in a silly voice. 'Are you a crazy boy?'

He pauses his panting to look at her, his jowls caught in his teeth, his fur askew. It rather proves Lucy's point. She puts her arm around him and gives him a pat; he slumps down to her side, tipping over to his back for a tummy rub.

It's not long before Fran arrives; Lucy holds on to Moss's collar while she parks up.

'Do you know how worried I've been?' Fran gasps as she rushes over. 'I've barely slept. How are you?'

Lucy gets to her feet, feeling awkward around her friend. There's still tension, resentment – from her side, at least – but now is not the time to get into it again.

'I'm fine,' she manages. 'And I'm sorry. Things have been... strange.'

'I know. I heard. A bit, anyway. What's up? I'm glad you called but I haven't got long. I've left my technician prepping the next.'

'Suspicious death?'

'Heart attack is my guess.' The two of them walk to the front door, Moss dashing inside once Fran has opened it.

Fran wordlessly begins to make coffee and puts a bowl of water on the floor for Moss, while Lucy explains the situation as best she can. Fran pauses, the teaspoon hovering over the mugs, when Lucy gets to the bit about Daisy Kane.

'He's called in covert ops?' she says, when Lucy has finished. Fran joins her at the dining table, putting her coffee in front of her.

'What choice did we have?'

'What if one of them is your dirty cop? And tells the OCG what you're up to? They'll kill her. Same as they did to Carter and Savage. These are dangerous people. Look what they did to Nico.'

There's no answer to that. Fran plunges into silence. Then she looks up at Lucy.

'What do you want me to do?'

'Anything you can. Use your contacts at the lab. They keep on telling Jack that they're caught up in a backlog but someone there must be able to help.'

'I know Rachel...' Fran says thoughtfully. 'She might be able to get things moving.'

'Thank you. Jack just needs something to point them in the right direction. Then they can get them to talk.'

'Who says they know anything? You said Kane's as much in the dark as you are.'

'Kane's just a soldier on the ground. If someone was at that squat, they'll be a man on the inside. Same if they own one of the burners. They're the ones we need.'

Lucy's phone rings; she pulls it out of her pocket and answers it. Jack talks without pause, Lucy listening intently.

'You think…' she says once he stops for breath.

'I know,' Jack replies.

'You hope. I'll ask Fran.'

Lucy hangs up and looks to her friend. 'That was Jack,' she begins.

'Jack now, is it? You two have got close.' Fran gives her a cheeky wink, teasing Lucy as she has always done, but today it feels forced.

'Not like that,' Lucy replies tersely. 'But he needs a favour.' And she explains his plan.

'Fine,' Fran says. 'I'll do what I can.'

They both stand and make their way out, Fran back to the mortuary, Lucy heading home. But before Fran gets into her car, she turns to Lucy, worry etched across her face. 'I'm not…' she begins. 'I'm not in danger, am I?'

Lucy pauses. 'No more than I am,' she offers.

Fran laughs uncomfortably. 'You owe me one.'

'I think this makes us even,' Lucy replies.

Chapter Fifty-Four

'In 1994, my best friend, Theo Nkosi, disappeared. I was eleven.'

Slow. Calm, Jack tells himself. He's standing outside the police station, a sea of journalists in front of him. Cameras flash; lenses focus on him and him alone. He places his shaking hands flat against the polished wood of the podium; when he lifts them, a perfect print of sweat remains. He takes a long breath. He continues.

'I was the last person to see Theo alive. And while it's true I was interviewed by the police, I was never a person of interest in the case.'

'Why did you change your name?' a voice shouts from the front.

'I changed my name from Jason Kent to Jack Ellis after my family and I were continually targeted and persecuted in a sustained campaign by members of the press. We found it was impossible to live our lives and were forced to go into hiding.' He can feel the anger trickling back. *Rein it in*, he thinks. *Slow. Calm*. 'Vettings for my appointment as a police officer have always been full and above board. My name change was legal and a matter of public record. The events of my childhood have no bearing on the crimes I have investigated in the past, nor the ones I investigate today.'

'Are you staying on as SIO on the Gallows Wood murders?'

'Yes.'

'We hear you have a suspect in custody?'

'I will update you on the investigation in due course. Thank you for your time. No further questions.'

Jack turns quickly and walks inside, shouts hurled like weapons at his departing back. He stretches his hand out; he's been gripping the edge of the podium so tightly that his fingers ache.

'Good job,' the publicist says next to him. 'Now, if we could check the press release—'

'Nothing else,' he says. 'I've said all I'm going to. I have a murder suspect to interview.'

And he walks away. Down to the interview room, where the accused is waiting. Amrit Gill meets him in the corridor and hands him a file.

'You were right,' she says. He pauses for a moment, reading the report within. He grins. A self-satisfied smile, the first since this case began.

'Interview room one,' Amrit says.

'Lead the way,' Jack replies.

—

Aron Dushku is broad-shouldered, with a shaved head, a full beard and a generous tuft of chest hair poking out the top of his white T-shirt. His aftershave is so strong that it makes Jack's eyes water. He looks at Jack and Amrit with utter contempt when they sit in front of him.

He came without protest when the uniforms showed up at his door. He held his hands out for the cuffs, answered the questions in custody politely and said nothing superfluous, except to give the name and number of his solicitor. Jack appraises them both, as Amrit does the caution.

The lawyer, Anthony Bolton-French, is wearing an expensive three-piece suit, silk tie and pocket square, iPad resting on the table, screen black. His hair is side-parted and slicked to the right; even his skin looks expensive, the sort of photoshopped complexion that only regular peels and moisturising can achieve. Both have their arms folded across their chests. They state their names when asked.

Once the formalities are complete, Jack rests his hands on the beige folder and smiles. He lets the silence hang.

The solicitor lets out a pronounced sigh.

'I suggest you start by explaining why my client is here,' Bolton-French says. 'Who are you claiming he's murdered? You have declined to share anything in disclosure.'

'Since you asked so nicely.' Jack opens the beige folder and pushes a photograph of a fingerprint across the table. 'This print – of your client's right-hand thumb – was found at a residence on Saturday. A house where, we have concluded, at least two people were murdered.'

The solicitor picks the photograph up between his thumb and forefinger, gives it a cursory glance, then drops it back on the table.

'And may I assume that this house is the one your constabulary raided on Randall Road?'

'That's correct. Would your client like to offer any insight into why he was there?'

Dushku leans over and whispers in his solicitor's ear; Bolton-French nods.

'It is drug den,' Dushku says, his English heavily accented. 'My friend, he shoots up there. I go to get him home.'

'And what's your friend's name?' Jack asks, trying hard to keep the derision out of his voice.

'No comment.'

'My client doesn't want to risk getting his friend into trouble.' A smarmy smirk from the lawyer. 'I'm sure you understand.'

Jack gives a sarcastic smile back, his lips pressed together, then shifts his attention back to Dushku.

'This print was on a syringe. One that contained traces of ketamine. A strong painkiller which, when given in sufficient doses, acts as an anaesthetic. Can you explain that?'

A flicker of doubt crosses Dushku's features. 'No comment.'

'Could you tell us when you were there? And who else you saw?'

'No comment.'

'Anyone who can corroborate your story?'

'No comment.'

'Must have stunk, considering there was a dead body in one of the bedrooms. Did you notice that?'

Dushku taps his nose with a finger. 'No smell. Nothing. Too much coke,' he finishes with a sneer.

'Is this your only evidence, DI Ellis? Are you so desperate to get an arrest to detract from your own problems that this is the best you can do?' The lawyer stands up, gesturing for Dushku to do the same. 'If this is the case then you can release my client now—'

'Sit down!' Jack barks. Next to him, Amrit jumps. The lawyer's expression turns dark. 'You are under arrest. You will leave when I say so.' He pulls another photograph out of the file and slaps it on the table in front of Dushku. He reacts to this one. No more amusement: his eyes narrow, his jaw clenches. Under the T-shirt, his sizeable biceps tighten.

It's a shot of a man, face up, a dark-red hole in the middle of his forehead. Eyes glassy, skin white. Dead.

'This is Vratislav Bosko. A Slovakian national found shot – some may say executed – by a nine-mil bullet, in September 2021. A murder that has, so far, gone unsolved. Whoever shot him made two mistakes. Firstly, they left the bullet in his skull, so we could recover it. And secondly, they got arrested for drink-driving six months ago, so we could get their fingerprints on file. When we arrested you on suspicion of the murder of Nico Halliday, we searched your house. And we found a nine-millimetre Glock – illegal, I might add – that ballistics have matched to the bullet. It is your gun. It is covered in your fingerprints. You are now also arrested on suspicion of the murder of Vratislav Bosko,' Jack says. He repeats the caution, then leans forward. So close he can smell the bitter tang of old beer sweating out of this man's pores.

'Perhaps you might like to explain all of that, Aron?' he finishes.

Dushku looks to his solicitor; Bolton-French stares at the photograph then back at his client, his mouth opening and closing like a goldfish in its death throes. But before anyone can answer, there's a loud bang on the door.

Jack looks over in annoyance. 'Interview paused, sixteen-twenty.'

He shuffles the photographs back into his file and gets up, Amrit following. He opens the door and DCI Perry is standing there. Jack closes it, but not before Perry cranes his head around and looks inside.

'You have,' Perry blurts out. 'You've got fucking Aron Dushku in there. A little bird told me you'd arrested him but I thought, "No, he couldn't have. Especially after I warned him." But there he is. Are you mad?'

'We have the gun used in a shooting in 2021,' Jack replies, as calmly as he can. 'Found at his house, covered in his finger-prints. It's murder, fair and square.'

'It's got nothing to do with you, that's what it is. DCI Dawson and his team are working their balls off up there to get Daisy Kane back—'

'How do you know about Daisy?'

'Joint task-force, you idiot. NCA, covert ops and drug squad. We've been trying for years to get this gang. And not some foot soldier, some gun for hire like Dushku, but the big man at the top. We want his brother, Roan. And you come along and wreck it all in a week.' Perry pauses. 'But it might be salvageable. Let him go.'

'I will not.'

'You bloody well will. I've already spoken to my bosses, and Dawson, and we're in agreement. You are to let him go, now, and you're not to go anywhere near the Wise Monkeys again.'

279

'I—'

'I outrank you, Ellis. So does Dawson. Do it. Or it's insub-ordination and we'll fucking suspend you.'

With that, Perry turns on his heel and stomps down the corridor. Anger surges, tremors of rage vibrating around Jack's body. Is Perry their inside man? Jack suspects Kane won't be any help; those on high will have spoken to her. Disobey orders and he'll get nowhere. With all the press attention, he's on shaky ground already.

Amrit is waiting, looking up at him. He turns to her.

'You heard the man,' Jack says.

'But—'

'Let him go.'

And with that, he stalks back up the stairs to his office.

He needs to calm down, to gather the pieces of this shattered investigation back together. But when he gets there, Raj is waiting. The analyst looks like Jack feels, anguish written all over his face.

'What?' Jack says. 'Please tell me you have good news.'

'I-I'm sorry,' Raj stutters. 'No. The laptop. It was wiped.'

'Wiped? How? Who? But you can get it back, right?'

'I don't know who. And no. They booted it up in recovery mode, then used Disk Utility to erase the whole hard drive. It's all gone.'

Jack utters a growl of frustration. 'Anything from the mobile numbers?'

'No. Yes. One.'

'One?'

'All unidentified burners have been taken out of service. Except one.' Jack feels a flare of optimism. Misplaced, as Raj continues. 'But it's switched off and I can't turn it on remotely.'

'What was its last known location?'

Raj turns and starts walking quickly away. Jack assumes he's supposed to follow and the two of them hurry out, down the stairs to the digital office. Once at his desk, Raj starts to type, his fingers moving like lightning across the keys. He clicks his mouse a few times and waits.

'Here,' Raj says triumphantly. Then his face falls. 'Oh, fuck,' he whispers.

Jack looks at his screen, then back to Raj. 'Don't tell anyone, you hear me,' he says. Raj nods quickly. 'This stays within our team. No one else.'

Raj nods again, but a look of fear flashes across his face. Because the little blue dot confirms what Jack's known all along.

The last known location of the burner phone was within this building.

Chapter Fifty-Five

Lucy can't settle; she can't think straight. To give herself something to do, she takes Moss out for a long walk across the forest, striding out down path after path, enjoying the ache in her thighs, the sweat running down her back. There's no reception out here – she's tempting fate.

Sure enough, when she gets back to the car, she has a voicemail from Fran.

'Damn it,' she mutters. She opens the back crate for Moss, who jumps inside as she returns the call. 'That was quick,' she says once her friend answers.

'Yes, well…' There's a hesitancy in her voice that Lucy doesn't like. 'It's not good news. The samples taken from the squat? They've gone missing.'

'What do you mean – missing?'

'Gone. Vanished. The crime scene manager called. She was crying. Somehow, between the crime scene and the lab, the second batch were taken. She escorted the first lot herself, but the second…'

'Aren't there controls in place to prevent that? Security? I–I don't know,' Lucy says, disbelieving. 'Can they go back to take new samples?'

'No, they've released the crime scene. Anything could have happened between now and then. They're investigating, Lucy. They are. But…'

'The chain of evidence has been broken. They're inadmissible. Even if they do recover them, they're useless.'

There's a long pause. 'Yes.'

'Does Jack know?'

'Rachel's spoken to him.'

'At the nick?'

'I think he was at home. I'm sorry. I have to go.'

Lucy manages a thank you before she hangs up. She's in a car park to the side of one of the main roads. It's a 40-mph limit – to protect the horses and cattle – but as she watches, a white BMW passes, going at speed. It kicks up dust and exhaust; she yells a profanity after it, a target for her anger and frustration.

Moss is patiently watching from the back, panting in the heat. She feels wretched for him, and pours water from a bottle into the dog bowl and puts it inside. He laps, messy and thirsty, then stops and looks at her. His ears are up, his eyebrows raised quizzically. She puts her hands either side of his head and strokes down his body, not minding the slobber that gets onto her hands and arms.

'Shit, Moss,' she says. 'What are we going to do?'

She looks at her phone. Nothing from Jack. She would have thought she'd be the first person he called when he found out the news from the lab – aren't they partners on this? And why is he at home? Why isn't he working every hour on the case?

She brings up his number and calls him. It rings out. She debates leaving a voicemail but his snub makes her feel foolish. Maybe she overestimated him – and their new friendship.

Moss has settled into the back of the car, so she throws the remaining water away, then closes the crate. She knows where he lives. He can't ignore her.

–

The journalists have left Jack's street; only a few lonely crisp packets and cigarette butts remain. But Jack doesn't answer the bell on the first ring. Nor the second. Only when she thumps her fist on the wood, dialling his mobile at the same time, does she see his shadow appear behind the glass.

'Enough, Lucy,' he growls, once the door is open. 'I can hear you.'

'Why aren't you at work?' She pushes past him into the house. 'Don't you have a job to do?'

'No, since you ask.' He's in his work shirt, but the collar is open, his usual smart tie and jacket discarded. He pads through to his living room in his socks and slumps on the sofa. Moss doesn't hesitate to join him, jumping up and lying at his side. No comment from Jack; he rests his hand on the dog's back.

'Have you been suspended?' Lucy asks. Then a thought occurs to her. 'Is Daisy Kane dead?'

'No. And no. At least, not as far as I'm aware. But covert ops have taken over. Some DCI called Dawson.'

'I know him,' Lucy says. 'Good, but an arsehole.'

'I can confirm the second point. I'll keep my fingers crossed for the first.'

'So why aren't you working the murders? Following up on the mobile phone numbers, Nico's laptop?'

His gaze drops to the dog. He works Moss's fur in circles.

'It's been wiped,' he mutters.

Lucy can't believe what she's hearing. 'Wiped? How? When?'

'I don't know. It's the same story as the samples from the squat. At some point someone got to it and ran a hard reset. Everything's gone. I've been warned away from the OCG, the forensics have disappeared and all of Nico's work has been deleted. Someone is faster than us. Better than us. We have nothing.'

'What about the mobile numbers?'

'There's one that's not been discontinued. But the phone's off, and Raj can't turn it on.'

'But he can monitor it, right?'

'For how long?' Jack looks up at her, exhausted. 'On the off chance this person turns it on and we can trace its location? It's hardly the basis for a thorough investigation.'

'But can't you… You must…'

Lucy thinks about everything Jack has already done. And nothing has been helpful.

'What are you saying? That Nico's killer is going to get away with it?' Hot, bitter tears sting in her eyes. 'All this? For nothing?'

'I'm sorry, Lucy. I've let you down.'

'You know what? You're damn right. You have. I was told you were a hotshot. This ace detective from the big city, here to solve murders. And I believed you.' Lucy rains words down on Jack, her anger propelling them, like grenades. In the back of her mind, she knows that it's not Jack's fault, that he's been put in an impossible situation, but she's so caught up in her rage that she doesn't care. He is here, right in front of her. And she takes it all out on him.

'I told you everything. I put my faith in you. But you are so caught up in your own personal mess that you're useless. How could I have been so wrong?'

She turns on her heel and marches out of the room. But when she gets to the front door, she realises that her dog isn't behind her. She turns back; Moss is sat next to Jack, looking at her accusingly.

'Come on, Moss,' she shouts. Only then does the dog jump from the sofa and follow.

She slams the door behind her and stalks back to her car, Moss trailing behind. She opens the boot, but for the first time he won't get in.

'Moss, please,' she half-begs, half-sobs. He looks back to the house. 'Moss. In. Now.'

He finally does as he's told, and she shuts the boot, gets into the front seat. Her disappointment, her frustration and anger – it's physical. A tensing of her muscles, a bitterness in her mouth.

She'd been wrong about Jack.

She was wrong to hope.

Chapter Fifty-Six

Lucy is right – Jack is a disappointment. To himself, to her, to the police force. To all the victims he's let down.

They have nothing.

Whatever evidence they've managed to collect on this case has been destroyed or lost. By whom, Jack has no idea. The OCG have their fingers in every part of the force – whether manipulated by money, or blackmail, or personal gain. They have the upper hand.

After Rachel Lennon had called and told him about the lost forensic samples, he had simply summoned the team together and told them to go home. DCI Dawson and his covert ops team can deal with the kidnap; he is allowed nowhere near. It is impossible to investigate a murder when his every angle has been taken out from under him.

His team departed. He'd done the same. He'd been contemplating turning to the age-old cure for misery – alcohol and ultra-processed food – when Lucy had turned up and vocalised every one of the thoughts he knows to be true about himself.

Barely a few minutes pass before his doorbell rings again. Lucy, returning for a second go? Or maybe the journalists, back with more questions. But the person he sees on his doorstep comes as a welcome relief.

'Sophie.' A mass of feelings, all confusing. 'How do you know where I live?'

'Your mum told me.'

'She shouldn't have—'

'Jack, enough.' Sophie's voice is stern. 'I needed to see you. To check that you're okay.'

She's wearing a simple white T-shirt, blue jeans and trainers. She gives a self-conscious smile, and all Jack wants to do is hug her and never let go.

'Come in,' he says.

They're awkward around each other. He's conscious of all his limbs, what to do with them. How nice she smells, when he has a full workday embedded on his skin.

'How are you—'

'Do you want a drink—'

Their questions clash. They stop and smile.

'I was worried about you. I saw you on the news.'

He winces. 'Hardly my finest hour.'

'How's the case?'

'Awful.'

He can't summon any enthusiasm or cheer; he feels bad that she's come all this way and he's a miserable bastard.

'I'm sorry, Sophie. For everything.' She tilts her head, questioning. 'For how things ended between us. It was my fault. I couldn't give you what you needed and that was a mistake. I know that now. I was...'

'Scared,' she finishes. He nods. 'I get that. What you and your family went through—'

'What *you* went through,' he interrupts. 'Losing Theo.'

'It was a bad time. It still is. But you have no reason to apologise. I took comfort from being with you. You knew Theo. You loved him, as I did.'

'I loved you.'

He blurts it without thinking, instantly regretting it as she stares, frozen. Then she steps forward, takes his face gently in both hands and kisses him. And the last ten years melt away to nothing.

Two days — two long drawn-out days — but conditions have marginally improved for Daisy.

Tritos is the only person she sees, although occasionally the front door slams. Food arrives — pre-packed sandwiches and bottles of water. They eat together in silence, Tritos chewing slowly. She has a blanket now. Has been given a change of clothes.

He seems happy with his lot, her new companion. Not once does he complain about his posting here, watching her. He reads the paper, scrolls on his phone. Escorts her to the toilet, waiting outside. She tries to persuade him into conversation: she's learned he has a family, but they're not in the UK. He likes cheese and pickle sandwiches, hates tuna. He thinks England is cold.

The rest of the house, as much as she can see, is unremarkable. Minimalist, cheap, simple decor. A bathroom that needs updating. Men's toiletries in the cabinet.

There is nothing she can use to defend herself. Not even an aerosol. She figures her best chance is somehow getting hold of his mobile phone, but as yet, he's been careful. She certainly can't extract it from him by force — he's twice her size, and after being cooped up all this time, she's sapped of energy.

In the early days she had faith in her mum, but now she wonders. Why hasn't a senior detective in the murder team managed to get her released? Is she dead? Is she here as well? Daisy can only imagine, her mind turning in circles, until the fear and worry and tears leave her trembling with exhaustion.

Night falls, and Tritos leaves. Daisy tries to sleep.

A noise wakes her. A key being turned in the lock. She looks up and the door opens. Tritos, but the easy manner has gone. He's tense, hands in fists, body tight.

'We go,' he says.

'Where?'

'Now.'

She instinctively knows this isn't good. Her feet scrabble on the carpet; she pushes back, trying to force her body into the furthest corner. He stomps into the room, grabs her ankle with a firm hand and pulls.

She tries to stop it and scrabbles at his arms, kicking out, but she is weakened. As pathetic as a kitten in the face of this man.

'It will be easier if you don't fight,' he says. 'Better this way.'

He hauls her to her feet, tugs her hands behind her back and wraps tape around her wrists. The hood back on her head. The fear is all-encompassing; her legs won't obey; she collapses into a heap. But any protest is useless: he picks her up and slings her over his shoulder, a mere inconvenience.

Out of the house – cold air, traffic. The pop of the boot of a car, the smell of diesel as she's dumped inside.

'Please,' she tries again, little more than a squeak. She summons all her strength. 'Please.'

The hood is pulled from her head. She spits her hair out of her mouth.

'Don't do this,' she says.

Tritos stares at her. She thinks his eyes soften for a moment, but he reaches up and closes the boot.

The engine starts; the car throws her around in the tiny space, head bumping the sides, her stomach churning, until they come to a stop.

She strains to listen. Nothing, until the engine turns off and she hears the crunch of heavy tread on gravel.

The boot opens; she squints up, dazzled by the light, until the hood is placed back on her head.

But before everything went dark again, she saw something. Something new in his hand that made her stomach flip with fear.

She is certain now.

She is going to die.

A baseball bat. He was holding a baseball bat.

Chapter Fifty-Seven

Lucy can't sleep. She's haunted by the case, by what she said to Jack. She's been in his shoes, done his job. She knows how relentless the pressure can be.

But she's also angry. A burning fury, almost painful in her gut. It makes her stomach churn, her muscles contract. How can these bastards kill all those people, torture and murder her husband, and get away with it?

She lies in bed, staring at the ceiling in the darkness. Lines of inquiry rotate like a Rolodex through her head. Everything she would have done as SIO. Appeals to the public, ANPR, CCTV, traffic cameras, door-to-door enquiries. Forensics, bank accounts, witnesses, mobile phone data. She pauses on that last one. The only thing they do have – a mobile number. Unregistered, but still in service.

It takes one mistake. One cigarette butt left at a scene, one footprint, one image on a camera. Maybe this is theirs. If only the mobile phone could be turned on. But how?

Lucy must have fallen asleep because when she wakes, early sunlight is trickling through the closed curtains. And with the arrival of the new dawn, a thought occurs to her. It's a thunderbolt, a dazzling ray of sunshine through a rain cloud.

She doesn't move, doesn't want to risk anything dislodging it from her consciousness. She frowns, rolls it around in her brain. An ethereal thought, a spectre.

But it's not a surreal dream; this could work. There are still samples in play – that first batch brought back from the squat.

And the burner phones. They may be disconnected now, but the last known locations can be traced.

She grabs her phone to call Jack.

Wednesday

Chapter Fifty-Eight

'That's not possible,' Kane says.

Jack and Lucy are sitting in her office. Strain is clear on her face, lines scored into her forehead and around her eyes.

The lack of sleep has taken its toll on all of them. Kane's skin is almost grey, strands of hair escaping from her normally pristine bun. Her shirt is crumpled, her back bent. Lucy's uniform is dishevelled, grubby, but then Jack doesn't think he's ever seen her looking clean and smart.

Moss lies under Lucy's chair, for once silent and still.

Jack had one, maybe two hours' sleep before Lucy called. But he's never felt more alive.

He remembers last night. Sophie's smile, as she undid the buttons on his shirt, as she kissed him, as he led her upstairs to the bedroom. The years have only changed her for the better. A softness to her body, and a confidence. An attitude as she kissed him, straddled him. Reached forward and placed his hands on her hips.

After, they talked, laughed. Nothing serious, nothing to dull the mood. She told him stories about her life now, her job as a secondary school teacher – her pupils, perceptive and funny. He shared the ridiculous and the absurd from police life. There is no shortage of those.

And they slept. His body curled around hers, legs entwined, skin on skin. Until Lucy phoned.

He'd listened, confused, as she explained. Then he was out of bed in a flash, grabbing for his clothes.

'I have to go,' he'd said.

Sophie watched him sleepily, eyes half-closed. 'It's fine.'

He leaned forward to kiss her, and she gave him a slow smile. One he felt from the inside out. Something he knew he'd need to sustain him in the coming hours.

Now, he clarifies again for Kane: 'The lab double-checked the samples found at the squat. The results are unequivocal.'

'And there's no reason for the print to have got there by other means?'

'Only Lucy and I went into the squat that day. And we were both wearing full PPE. No, that evidence demonstrates a clear link to the OCG. We need to make this arrest.'

Kane stays silent. Jack feels Lucy's glance – willing Kane to say yes. Jack can see Kane's considering it, but this is also her last chance to back out. She agrees to this, and a series of actions are put into place that might get her daughter killed.

Assuming she's still alive.

'If we make this arrest,' Lucy says, taking over, 'then we can carry out a full search. Look for any other phones – and with them, the numbers of any other burners that might be in play.'

Kane's chin wobbles. She looks from Jack to Lucy, then back. Jack mouths the word, *Please*.

Kane shakes her head and Jack thinks it's all over, they'll have to find another way, until she says, 'Yes.'

'Yes?' Jack repeats, hardly able to believe what he's hearing.

'Do it,' Kane says.

–

Jack can feel Lucy's eyes on him as they rush out of the office, Moss at their heels. There's no time to waste. Jack pauses outside the incident room. He turns to her.

'You'd better be right,' he says.

'I am.'

'This has to work.'

'It will.'

Jack pushes the door handle down and they step inside.

Jack's surprised at how different he feels today. He is no longer cowed and beaten – his resolve has grown. There is always a way. He will track down whoever's behind these murders, and this, what he's about to do now, is just the beginning.

'Morning, boss,' Harry Blake says, looking up from his desk. Phil Lawrence emerges from the kitchen, two cups of coffee in his hand.

Jack looks for the fear. For apprehension. And he finds it in the face of his most promising detective constable. The newest recruit. The woman with no background, who nobody had met until a couple of weeks ago.

'DC Amrit Gill,' he says, stepping forward. The cuffs are already in his hand. 'I am arresting you on suspicion of murder.'

Chapter Fifty-Nine

Amrit stammers and protests, her eyes wide and panicked as Jack finishes the caution. In the doorway of the kitchen, Lawrence splashes coffee onto the floor in surprise; Blake gets to his feet, shifting forward then back, paralysed by indecision.

'Murder...' Amrit stutters, her voice rising. 'I didn't... I wouldn't...'

'I'll escort you down to custody now,' Jack says and, with a quick glance back to Lucy, he whisks her out of the door.

In the excitement, Moss has been twirling on his lead and now Lucy focuses him with a quick command. He sits by her side, looking up.

'This is ridiculous,' Blake is saying to Lawrence, who shakes his head, repeating, 'I wouldn't ever have thought...' over and over again.

'What's the evidence?' Blake directs to Lucy. 'And what do you have to do with it? You're a dog handler.'

'You need all hands on deck,' Lucy replies. 'And we'll find out soon enough.' She pauses. 'Don't you trust your DI?'

'Of course,' Blake replies, quickly. 'But... Amrit? How?'

She ignores him and starts to leave, following in Jack's footsteps, but Moss has frozen, his nose pointed into the doorway of the office. She spots the bacon sandwich on Blake's desk.

'Now is not the time, Moss,' she says, and pulls him away. He comes reluctantly, looking back as they go. She pulls her phone out of her pocket and dials.

'Raj? Anything?'

'Nothing,' comes the reply. 'I'm watching.'

She hangs up. 'Phase two,' she mutters under her breath.

Booking Amrit Gill into custody takes time, a luxury they do not have. Lucy's phone stays resolutely silent, but at last, Amrit has been processed and escorted straight to interview room one.

Lucy knows the set-up and heads to the adjoining room, turning the monitor on. She sits down; the screen displays the feed from next-door, divided into three different views – Jack's face, Amrit Gill and an overview of the whole room.

Jack has finished the caution.

'And you've turned down all offers of legal advice.'

'Yes, I mean… I've done nothing wrong. And I don't want you to think… I'm not… I'm not hiding anything.' Amrit is rushed and confused; her feet tap in semaphore under the table.

'Good.' Jack smiles. 'I'm glad you know how this works, because it's going to make life easy for us today. Tell us what happened, Amrit. Tell us how you started working for the OCG, what you've been doing for them, and you'll be out and in a nice comfortable solitary cell before you know it.'

The door opens behind Lucy; she scowls as Lawrence and Blake come into the room.

'You shouldn't be here,' Blake repeats.

'Nor should you.'

'This is our case. We've been working on this from the beginning. And why is this bloody dog here?'

'Environmental training,' Lucy says. 'The more places working dogs get exposed to, the better.'

'Fuck's sake,' Blake mutters, as Moss sniffs at his feet. 'Keep him under control, will you?'

Blake and Lawrence pull chairs up to Lucy's left and descend into silence as Amrit starts gabbling.

'I demand to know what you have on me,' she says, her voice quivering. 'What are the grounds for arrest?'

'Fair enough,' Jack says, smoothly. 'Let's talk evidence. The squat on Randall Road. Did you go there on Saturday?'

'You know I didn't.'

'So how come this—' He pushes a photograph of a finger-print across the table. 'Was found there?'

'But... but we lost the exhibits.'

'Not everything,' Jack says. 'The original samples, the ones taken to the lab personally by Rachel Lennon – some of those were processed. As you know, we found the print of Aron Dushku, and last night we asked Rachel to run a few more. And she found yours.' He taps a finger on the photo. 'What do you have to say about that, Amrit?'

Moss stirs at Lucy's feet as the door opens behind them. Lucy turns; she recognises the guy from the squat – he was there with Jack. DCI Penny, or Perry, or something. Drug squad. With him is the massive bulk of DCI Dawson. Professional curiosity, she assumes. The arrest of a police officer was bound to create waves.

The two of them greet Blake and Lawrence; both ignore Lucy.

She reciprocates, continues watching the interview.

'I... I...' Amrit's mouth is opening and closing gormlessly. 'You're setting me up. The OCG is setting me up.'

Jack heaves an exaggerated sigh. 'Really? That's the best you can do? Try harder, Amrit.'

Calm down, mate, Lucy thinks. *Don't enjoy yourself too much.*

'In the meantime,' Jack continues, 'let's talk about what's happening now. Licensed Search Officers are exploring your desk. Going through your bag and your car. Pulling your house apart, inch by inch.'

'My house?' she squeaks. 'You'll find nothing.'

'You know full well what we're going to find, Amrit. A mobile phone. Maybe even a few, if we're lucky.'

'I only have one phone.'

'That's yours, maybe, yes. But I believe you have a few burners at your disposal. Ones you use for making calls to members of the Wise Monkeys.'

'You have nothing. I know you don't. Raj told me. All those phones are disconnected.'

'Yes, but we ran their last known locations. And one of them came back to your house. How do you explain that?'

Amrit falls silent.

'Are we getting close now? Where is that mobile? Or maybe you have a new one. Because soon we're going to find that phone, and when we do, we'll have a record of every single number on the SIM card.' Jack spells this out slowly. 'Every. Single. Number. And what's the bet that one of those will connect to the OCG? You'll all be screwed. You know how it works. Using those phones, we'll build a web. Mini surveillance devices, wonderful things. Everywhere you go, every ping off a cell tower. Every call you make, every internet search, every text. All we need is one to start from.' Jack points a finger at Amrit. 'And you're that one.'

While Jack's been talking, Lucy's sensed something different about Moss. Body language works both ways. If she's stressed or worried she can transmit that through the lead to Moss. And an anxious dog is an ineffective one. But today, the tension is flowing the other way.

She looks down; Moss is frozen in a perfect indication, but before she can work out his focus, he looks up at her.

'Show me,' she says to the dog, but it's too late.

Behind them the door opens, a shaft of light breaching the gloom. Lucy glances around the faces left in the room and feels her stomach lurch in horror. Moss indicated in the incident room. She should have known then.

Always, always trust your dog.

Someone with blood on their clothes was in this room.

The person they are looking for – he was closer than they could have ever imagined. And he's gone.

Without thinking, she stands up and follows. Down the corridor, through the double doors, out into the car park.

And then there's a gun in her face.

Chapter Sixty

Her vision narrows to a razor-sharp focus on the slim barrel, barely moving. It's all she can see; all she can think.

There's a gun in my face.

Then a noise makes her breath falter in her chest. A click as the gun is cocked.

'Put your hands up.'

Lucy does as she's told, dropping Moss's lead in the process. The dog hesitates, confused.

'Couldn't keep your nose out, could you?' He doesn't wait for an answer, but backs up to his car, grabbing something shiny and black from the front seat. Cuffs.

'Get on your knees and lace your hands behind your head.'

Lucy hesitates. There's barely six feet between them. She could run but she doesn't fancy her chances with the gun. She could attempt to get it off him, but he's much bigger than her. Either way, she's going to end up shot.

As dangerous as he is, a part of her is defiant. This is the man behind her husband's torture, behind the murder of countless other people. And she's fucking furious.

She turns to face him. This man who disgusts her, who makes her stomach turn every time she's near him.

He ruined her marriage and killed her husband.

'Fuck you, Harry,' she says. 'Fuck you.'

—

The blow – hard around the face, causing her teeth to chatter, her head to spin – tells her exactly what Blake thinks of her non-compliance. She drops to the concrete, gravel digging painfully into her knees. Her hands are wrenched behind her back, cold metal fastened tightly around her wrists.

It's the second time this week, but the fear is different.

When she was arrested, she knew what would happen next. Due process, a lawyer, interviews. The legal dance she knows like the back of her hand. But this? With him? This could be the end.

She remembers now, Moss lying down in the incident room. An indication she ignored, at her peril. She looks to where Moss is pacing, confused, at the back of the car park. His ears are raised, waiting for a command. She wills her dog to leave, wants anything other than for him to get hurt. But Moss won't go. He circles closer and Blake kicks out. Moss nimbly jumps away.

'Leave him alone,' Lucy shouts. Blake laughs and pushes the gun to Lucy's skull, the metal hard against her forehead.

'I should kill you here,' he growls.

'Why don't you?'

He doesn't reply, but pulls her hands up, forcing her painfully to her feet, and pushes her, stumbling, to the passenger side of his car.

'Get in.'

She does as she's told, her hands uncomfortably behind her. The passenger door slams and he climbs in next to her. He's sweating in the summer heat, and as he closes his driver's door, she can smell the pungent body odour, fear oozing out of his pores. This is not a man in control. Blake is scared. And that's a bad sign.

He reaches into his jacket pocket and pulls out a small, cheap mobile. Her breath hitches as he presses a button. The screen flashes into life, a blue haze in the darkness of the car park.

'You have the phone,' she gasps.

'I know what you're thinking,' he says. He puts it back in his pocket and starts the engine. 'You're hoping they're going to trace it and find you?'

She replies with a glare; he takes her face between his fore-finger and thumb, squeezing her cheeks painfully. The gun is still in his other hand, pointing at her stomach.

'They won't have time.'

He puts the car in gear and drives out of the car park. They're in the middle of a police station, cops all around them, but she doesn't dare try anything, won't take the risk. Scream now, and she gets shot. She has no doubt he means to use the gun; he has killed before, what difference would she make?

And another part of her – the stupid, insolent, self-destructive side – wants the answers.

It was her husband he tortured. Her husband he killed. Despite the fear eating away in the pit of her stomach, her anger swells.

'Why did you do it?' she says. 'What do you want?'

'What do I want?' He laughs for a moment, a hollow, awkward cackle. 'What all of us want! I was fed up of coming last. Never being promoted. Never having any money. And then, do you know what? I wasn't so useless anymore. You must know how it starts?'

He takes his eyes off the road for a moment, glancing at Lucy. She shakes her head.

'A little bit here. A small something there. But the moment you take that first bribe, or you skim that first hundred off the top, you're theirs. They see you. They know that. And they hold your career in the palm of their hand.'

'So, give yourself up. Tell us everything.'

'You fucking idiot,' he spits. 'How simple you make it sound. Do you know what they'd do to me, if I grassed? Worse than they did to Carter, worse than Vanessa Savage. Even worse than your poor pathetic husband.'

That burn of fury kicks back in Lucy's stomach. Her hatred for this man.

'You killed them,' she says.

'David Carter and Vanessa Savage, yes. I knew that if I left them with the gang then things would be considerably worse.

302

They were mercy killings. Pump them full of the good stuff and a quick whack around the skull. Short and sweet. You saw what happened to Nico? That was nothing. He was lucky he died from a few broken ribs. They would have carried on. Pulling out his teeth. Cutting off his fingers, one by one, for the fun of it. There wouldn't have been anything left to dig up. That will be me,' he stresses. 'I wanted this. I'm in charge – their contact on the inside. I tell them what's going on and get handsomely rewarded in return.' He puffs his chest. Lucy can't believe that he's proud of what he's done. 'Mark Savage was sensible. Killing himself. I told the gang that his conviction was wavering, and they snatched Vanessa to keep him in line. I took over. Once she was dead, he knew that was it.'

'We could—'

'Protect me?' He snorts. 'Don't give me that shit. They'll find me. Same as they'll get to Amrit Gill, soon enough. They have their secrets. I didn't know about her. She must have been sent to watch me, report back. No, this is the only way out. Our only way.'

Lucy's fear escalates. Harry Blake is desperate, veering between logic and mania. He believes in Amrit's involvement with the OCG, has taken every word of her arrest as truth. He's twitchy; half-crying, half-hysterical. A man on the edge. As they speed ever further from the police station, Blake's driving erratic, she considers her options. She could leap over and try to get him off the road. Distract him so they crash, take her chance. But she doesn't have a seatbelt on, and he does.

No, her best bet lies with that mobile phone. It's on, as is hers, safely tucked into her pocket. She wills a silent message to Jack. *Please, follow me. Please.* Hoping that their head start isn't too much.

'Things could have been so different,' Blake continues, almost wistful now. 'Between you and me. I'm sad we've ended up here.'

'So let me go,' Lucy pleads. 'You don't need me.'

'That's where you're wrong. I've always needed you. I've always wanted you.'

I've always wanted you. The words repeat in Lucy's head, echoing through her subconscious.

She hasn't been this close to Harry Blake since that night. When they slept together. She's deliberately kept her distance but now, in this confined space, it's impossible to ignore the smell of him. The sweat, his aftershave. A faint recollection intrudes. Bewilderment as he forced his mouth onto hers, as she pushed him away, too weak, too muddled. Too drunk. A body on top, so heavy she could hardly breathe.

I've always wanted you. Hot words breathed into her ear as he held her down.

As he raped her.

She recoils, pressing her body against the passenger-side door, as far away from him as she can go. She starts to shake uncontrollably, crying as more memories propel their way to the surface. The cold air hitting her naked skin as he tugged her clothes from her body. Confusion, fear, embarrassment. Pain.

'You raped me,' she whispers.

Harry jumps, glances at her with narrowed eyes. 'I did no such thing. You wanted me.'

'I told you no. I tried to push you off.'

'You didn't know what you were saying. You were drunk, you silly slut. You spent all evening ranting about your husband, it was clear what you were after. You wanted to make him jealous, and I was only too happy to oblige.'

'You… you…' Lucy's dumbfounded by his arrogance. He doesn't care what he did to her, or Nico, or Vanessa Savage or David Carter.

A wave of bile races up from Lucy's stomach as she realises. Harry Blake is a dangerous man. He has no remorse, no love, no empathy. He didn't murder for money or mercy. It was power, pure and simple. He killed them because he could and he wanted to.

And she's going to be next.

Chapter Sixty-One

Jack ends the interview with Amrit Gill sobbing into her hands; he has to give it to her, she's a bloody talented actress. She knows what's going on, she knows how to make it stop, but her stubbornness and pride will take it through to the end.

He needs a break; he's exhausted. The last few days are starting to take a toll. He hopes, wishing with every cell of his body, that this gamble has paid off.

He heads upstairs to the incident room but he stops as a small black blur barrels past him in the corridor. Moss. The dog twirls a few times in concentric circles, making frantic whimpering noises. He trails a lead, attached to his harness.

Jack looks into the incident room, confused. He calls, 'Lucy?' but there's no reply. The dog is still spinning, so Jack picks up the end of the lead, pulling his phone out of his pocket. He tries Lucy's number. It rings out.

He dials another contact. This time it's answered.

'I was about to call,' Raj says.

'The mobile?'

'It's moving. It's been switched on, and it's moving.'

'Where?'

'It started at the nick, and now it's travelling, fast. Must be in a car.'

A thought occurs to Jack, something that makes him nauseous. 'Can you track Lucy Halliday's phone?' Jack recites the number and there's an excruciating pause.

Then, 'Same direction, same place.'

Jack starts walking, then breaks into a run to get to the car park, holding Moss's lead. The spaniel runs in front, tugging hard. His thoughts race. Concern for Lucy, guilt for what they've done, but also the beginning of a plan. He needs speed. He needs sirens.

He spots Pete Nash on the far side of the car park, the boot of his vehicle open.

He shouts as he approaches. 'Get in the car. Now. You're driving.'

Nash pauses, but the sight of Jack out of breath, trailing a frantic Moss, is enough to get his attention.

Nash opens the spare crate and Moss obediently jumps in. 'What's going on? Why have you got Moss? Where's Lucy?'

'I'll explain once we're on the move,' Jack replies.

Nash slams the boot; the two men run around, throwing themselves inside.

Jack consults his phone, where Raj is sending him regular updates.

'Head towards the New Forest, down the Totton bypass.'

'Roger that.' Nash puts his foot down, flips the blues and twos on, the covert lights bursting into life. 'Now talk.'

'It was Lucy's idea.' Jack hangs on to the car door as Nash throws him to and fro, dodging the traffic. 'Raj in digital had been through the mobile phone records from all our victims, including Mark Savage, Vince Carter and Kane—'

'Kane? DCI Emily Kane? She's involved?'

'Her daughter's been kidnapped.'

'Fuck,' Nash mutters, and makes a hard left down the Totton bypass.

Jack consults his phone. 'A35,' he says. 'Every burner had already been disconnected. Except one.'

'One?'

'Someone who had repeatedly phoned Kane. Someone dodgy.' Jack has to shout to be heard over the noise of the sirens. 'But it was turned off, and we couldn't switch it on remotely.'

'But I heard you'd arrested someone. DC Gill, the grapevine said—'

'Amrit was a set-up. She was in on it. Ready and waiting to be arrested. We knew it was someone inside this nick and we wanted every opportunity for them to hear that we were closing in. We were hoping that by threatening Amrit, whoever owns the phone would get nervous and turn it on.'

'They might have destroyed it.'

'That was a risk we had to take. But it looks like it worked. We're following it now.'

'I assumed we were following Lucy,' Nash says.

'We are. We're following them both.'

Nash glances quickly to Jack. 'How do you know…'

'It's not her.'

'How can you be so sure? Her husband was investigating this OCG and the dirty cops. And he wound up dead. Who better to…'

Jack glares at him and he shuts up, but Nash has a point. Jack trusted Lucy without a second thought – how does he know she's not the one on the inside? But no. Her reactions have been too real. And this was *her* idea.

'There's no way,' he says to Nash.

They're on the A35, and Jack knows instinctively where they're heading. He checks Raj's updates. The latest: *They've stopped. SW corner of Gallows Wood.*

Raj sends a screenshot, a small blue pin showing the location. Then a final message.

Both the unknown phone and Lucy's mobile have gone dead.

Jack silences the sirens. He gives directions to Nash.

'If it's not Lucy, then…' Nash says, slowing the car.

'Then someone has her. Someone has taken Lucy to the place her husband was buried.'

'But who?' Nash asks, his face slack-jawed with worry. And without waiting for an answer, he adds, 'We'll find her. She's going to be okay.'

'She will,' Jack replies with more certainty than he feels. His stomach burns with regret.

The actions he put into place have gone horribly wrong. And Lucy's the one who's going to pay the price.

Chapter Sixty-Two

At first Lucy has no idea where they're going. And then she realises. Gallows Wood. Where it all began.

'Please…' she croaks, the fear making her mouth dry.

But he ignores her. They stop at the entrance, Blake pulling up the car and getting out. The woods are cool; the trees protect them from the midday sun as Blake tugs Lucy out of the car then grabs the cuffs, pulling them painfully up behind her back.

'Walk,' Blake commands, pushing her forward.

He still has the gun; she can feel hard metal in the small of her back as they stumble down the path into the depths of the woods. She prays for a dog walker, a jogger, but they won't be out at this time, in this heat.

Blake starts talking again. Mutters, fractions of sentences, almost to himself.

'I was something. For once in my life, I was important. I knew who could be helpful, who could be swayed. Vince Carter, he needed persuasion. Hard cash, that was his weakness. A gambling habit he couldn't keep in check. And then he wanted out.' Blake laughs again. It sounds wet; Lucy wonders if he's crying. 'There is no out. Not once you know their secrets.'

'What about Nico?' She has to know.

'You told me, can you believe that? When you were drunk. The two of you had argued and you were ranting about some case he was working on. The Dushkus – they knew some journalist was digging. I put two and two together. Kane told them your address. Job done.'

Job done. Her husband killed, discussed as casually as if he were no more than an annoying errand.

'And Daisy?' she chokes through her tears.

'Dead. Or should be by now. I told them last night that covert ops were on their tail.'

Lucy's legs go weak. So many dead. For nothing. Her foot catches and she trips, but Blake pulls her upright, her arms wrenched in their sockets. She lets out a yelp. He pushes her on.

'And Carter, what an idiot. We threatened his son. But he still requested a move to custody. He asked to be transferred, can you believe he'd be so stupid? Thought that if he wasn't any use then they'd leave him alone. Doesn't work like that. If you have no purpose, you're disposable. Simple. That's me. Now. Worthless.'

'But why here?' she asks, desperate to distract him, to keep him talking. 'Why these woods?'

'You don't remember, do you? These woods are infamous in police circles. A hazing ritual. Among the probies. They'd pick on the new guys, take them out here. Get them drunk and leave them to find their own way home. But here's the kicker – they'd tie them up first, blindfolded. Gag them. Except one year, a kid puked. Nearly choked on his own vomit.'

Lucy gasps. She turns, staring at Blake. 'That was you.'

He shoves her forward, the gun in the small of her back. 'Nobody helped. Nobody saved me. They simply took the gag out of my mouth and left me there. Half-dead. Barely conscious.' He pauses for a moment, glancing around the woodland. 'Fond memories,' he says, bitterly. 'Why not create some more?'

He pulls Lucy to a stop; she turns, confused. And then, as she watches, he takes his phone out of his pocket, places it on the hard ground and smashes it to pieces with his heel.

'Now yours.'

'I don't—'

The slap catches her by surprise; his open hand hitting her so hard that she can taste blood where her cheek knocks her teeth. Her tongue explores the pain.

'Where is your phone?' he hisses.

'My pocket,' she says through her tears.

He gropes down her trousers, finds her phone and destroys it.

'Now walk.'

'You knew the phones were on. Why did you…?'

'I want them to find us,' he says. 'I don't want to lie here for days, as animals and insects eat me.' He makes a disgusted retch. 'Wind up like Mark Savage. A rotting corpse. No, thank you. Faster,' he commands, pushing her forward.

'You're going to kill yourself,' she says. She's starting to shake, her body going into shock. He's going to shoot himself, out here, and take her with him. There's no way Jack can find them in time. Not now the phones are gone. There's too much ground to cover. Too many paths.

'Soon. You first.' And Blake pushes her hard. She trips, and without her hands to cushion her fall, she lands painfully on the ground, face down. Mud in her mouth, grit between her teeth.

He hauls her over so she's lying on her back, her hands behind. He stands above her, looking down.

His eyes are wide and wild, his cheeks stained with dirt and tears. He looks insane. A man with nothing left to lose.

She tries to scrabble back, her legs kicking out in the dirt, but it's too easy for Blake to stop her. He bends down, resting his knees on her thighs, his elbows on her shoulders, the gun still in his right hand.

He reaches forward, grabbing her face tight with his left. She tries to move her head but she feels his fingers dig into her cheeks, his nails in her skin. His face is so close to hers, she can smell his rotting breath.

'Shall we try for a second go? Maybe it'll be more fun if you're awake.'

His words have hardly sunk in before her body reacts. He's fumbling for the belt of her trousers, and that slight release of pressure is the only encouragement she needs. Her body arches, anger and fear driving her knee upwards. He lets out a strangled cry, his hands cupping his groin. And it's enough.

He falls off her, yowling and groaning, legs tucked up to his middle. The gun has gone, tumbled out of his hand, out of sight. She rolls away. Somehow, gets to her feet. And she runs.

Her hands are cuffed behind her. It's awkward, but adrenaline and instinct drive her forward. She waits for the gunshot, but instead hears a scream of anger. Heavy footsteps on leaves. And then agony at the back of her head as he catches hold of her ponytail.

She flies backwards, tugged to the ground by her hair. She falls hard, and fists rain down onto her face, accompanied by his feverish screams. Pain. Skin against bone. A crunch. A crack. Her hands restrained; she can't protect herself. She's defenceless, absorbing the blows from a man who can't be stopped.

She sees Nico. His crooked grin, his smile, his laughter. She sees her dog. Soft brown eyes, the tilt of his head, the lift of his ears.

Her consciousness drifts as Blake hollers with fury and regret.

Blood. Dirt. Leaves.

Where it all began.

Chapter Sixty-Three

Jack wants helicopters and a forest full of armed coppers, but as they arrive next to Blake's car, he realises they have all they need.

In the back of the vehicle, Dax is spinning, letting out a volley of fast excited yelps. Nash looks at Jack, sternly.

'Stay behind us,' he says. 'I want that scene sterile.'

'You can find them?'

DC Lawrence has phoned – told them who is missing. The fact that their inside man is Harry Blake is a hard rock in Jack's gut. They knew it was someone within the nick, but never imagined it would be so close to home. Jack's worked alongside him for over a week. Blake knew every fact of the case; had done everything in his power to interfere with the investigation. But Lucy's plan has worked, and the knowledge that that may well be her downfall is nausea-inducing.

Nash glances into the back, where Dax is squeaking. 'It's hot, dry. No breeze. Not ideal conditions for tracking. But it's grass, mud. And it hasn't been long. If there's a trail, Dax will find it. Just give us the nod.'

Jack doesn't hesitate. 'Find them.'

Nash is out of the car in a flash; a hatch is lowered behind Jack and before he can move, a ninety-pound German shepherd leaps past his right ear and out of the driver's door. Nash has his harness on and a line attached in seconds, and the command, 'Dax, where is he?' is given.

At first the dog pauses, pushing his nose to the ground then lifting it, sniffing. He's looking for human scent, for that smell of scared, sweaty man. Perfect for a dog's sensitive nose.

Jack notices a change in the German shepherd's body language, similar to one he has seen from Moss. Dax stops and huffs at the ground, almost hoovering the scent.

Moss himself is sat in his half of the boot. Without his handler, he's quiet – he recognises this is not his job. This is Dax's.

And Dax is off. With a swish of black-brown tail, he's belting into the woods, leaning into the harness, with Nash hanging on behind. But it's hard going, the line getting caught in branches and undergrowth. After a few paces, Nash calls the dog back, and releases him from the lead. The dog doesn't hesitate in picking the scent back up, ears back, tail down, galloping at full pelt.

Jack tries to keep up, but his suit and smart shoes are no match for the difficult terrain of the woodland. And – if he's being honest – nor is his fitness. But he keeps moving, listening for the sound of a large dog crashing through the undergrowth, for the muttered curses coming from Pete Nash as he sprints in his dog's wake.

And then he hears it, to his left. The unmistakable flurry of barking from a German shepherd having the time of his life. Jack sprints, stumbling and slipping, and sees Harry Blake standing over a prostrate figure – Lucy! – his fists raised. He's paused, facing down a snarling police dog: Dax with teeth bared, spit and drool flying as he lets out a volley of barks.

'Don't move,' Nash bellows. 'Or I'll send the dog.'

Blake looks to Lucy, then at Dax. He must know, Jack thinks. He must know he's beaten.

But for some reason, he turns and starts running. The dog's barking increases tenfold, looking back at Nash: *Let me go, let me at him.* Nash shouts a second warning after the fleeing Blake – 'Stop! Or I'll send the dog!' – then releases Dax.

The dog almost flies. In one swift bound he's on Blake, forty-two sharp, white teeth clamping around his right arm. Blake lets out a squeal and goes down hard, the dog attached, but he's flailing, raining down blows on Dax's head.

'Lie still. Stop fighting my dog!' Nash shouts.

'Get him off me!'

'Stop fighting my dog!'

And then he does. Blake lies motionless – and with one sharp command, the dog is recalled, but stays close, focused and growling quietly.

'See to Lucy,' Nash shouts as Jack approaches. 'We have him. He's not going anywhere.'

Jack does as he's told. And for a moment, he's paralysed with shock.

She's lying motionless on the forest floor. Her face is a mess of blood, her hair matted, her eyes closed. He drops down to his knees next to her. Nash is on his radio, calling in their position and asking for backup, for an ambulance.

Her eyelids flicker.

'Help is on its way, Lucy,' Jack says. 'Hang in there.'

She opens her eyes a fraction. 'You got him?'

'We did. Or Dax did.'

'I hope he bit the fucker's arm off.'

Jack glances across to where Blake is clutching his arm and wailing. Dax looks on, calmer and panting now the show's over. To Jack, the dog looks like he's laughing.

'I think he had a good chomp.'

'Good for Dax.' She locks eyes with Jack. She talks through mangled lips. 'Where's my dog?'

'Moss is fine. He's in the car. Waiting for you.'

'Good,' she says. She shifts position, wincing, and he realises her hands are cuffed behind her back.

'Can I…?' he says, and gently rolls her over. Nash tosses him a cuff key and he unlocks them, tenderly helping Lucy to straighten out her arms. She rests them next to her and groans quietly. But she looks like she's relaxing, soothed by his presence.

'Told you it would work,' she mumbles.

And Jack has to agree that she's right.

The noise is terrifying. Crashing, shouting, thumping feet in heavy boots. Tritos is on his feet in seconds but there is nothing he can do before the door is smashed open and large men barrel inside.

Their faces are obscured by masks; they are carrying huge black guns. Daisy cowers in fear as one crouches in front of her. He removes the mask and smiles.

In her terror she hadn't noticed the white lettering across their chests, their cries of 'POLICE' as they stormed the building. She only knew that these were more men. More men that could hurt her, could kill her. Tritos had warned her about them after he'd carried her out of the car boot. To this place. Yet another house, where she was locked up, told to be quiet. Because people were coming to kill her.

But these are not those men. The armed officer introduces himself. Tells her she's going to be safe, that she's going home.

'I want my mum,' Daisy manages through her tears.

'She's waiting for you outside.'

Tritos is led away in cuffs. He doesn't struggle, stays silent as he's read a caution. But he manages one look back. Their eyes meet and he smiles.

Daisy's offered a bottle. She takes it gratefully and swigs at the cold, clean water as a blanket is put around her shoulders.

'Can you walk?' the officer asks. She nods.

She's helped to her feet, a strong arm holding her upright as she wobbles, one foot in front of the other, out of the door.

She blinks in the bright sunlight outside, a sea of faces watching. She sees an ambulance, paramedics in green rushing forward to help. A tall, slim man in a smart grey suit smiles broadly as she emerges. A detective, she assumes, a radio in his hand.

And then – the one person, the only person she wants to see. Her mum runs towards her and grabs her in a tight embrace. Daisy relaxes, wraps her arms around her mother's waist and squeezes tightly. They stay that way for a moment, both crying, until her mum releases her and takes her face tenderly in her hands.

'Oh, Daisy. Look at you. What's this? Blood? You're hurt.' Her mum kisses her cheeks repeatedly.

'I'm fine. I'll be fine.' Despite herself, Daisy laughs as her mum tries to rub some of the grime away with a tissue then gives up and gives her another hug.

'I want to go home,' Daisy says into her chest.

She feels someone walk up beside them and her mum pulls away. The man touches her mother gently on the shoulder.

'Emily, we need to go,' the man says.

He's huge, broad-chested with bulging muscles under his black T-shirt. Daisy senses her mother doesn't like him.

'Please, Dawson. Give me a moment,' her mother says.

'Five minutes,' the man replies, but waits, taking one step back.

Her mum looks into her eyes. Her face is serious, on the edge of tears again. Daisy has a horrible feeling. That this is not the happy ending she wants.

'Listen, Daisy,' her mum begins. Her voice cracks, tears spill. 'I'm so, so sorry. But there is something you need to know.'

Thursday

Chapter Sixty-Four

Twenty-four hours of observation. A whole day in which Lucy tried to convince the doctors that despite her battered and swollen face the best place for her was at home and not in hospital where monitors beeped and people groaned, and nobody – least of all her – got any sleep. She wants to be home, in her own bed, with her dog.

At last, her wish is granted. The nurse arrives with a prescription for painkillers and a warning to take it easy.

'Bed rest,' the woman says, sternly, in a lilting Irish accent. 'You need to heal.'

'I need to walk my dog.'

'You will be doing no such thing. You have a broken nose, two black eyes, a split lip and all number of nasty bruises. Have you seen yourself, young lady?'

She has. It's not good. One eye is barely open through the swelling, a mass of purple and black and red. Delicate stitches bisect a cut on her forehead. Breathing through her nose is impossible; everything is either numb or throbbing.

She submits with a nod.

'Could someone call me a taxi?'

The nurse looks behind her, down the ward, then back to Lucy. 'We assumed it wasn't necessary. A nice young police officer is here to drive you.' She leans forward, conspiratorially. 'And what a looker he is too,' she finishes with a wink.

Confused, Lucy peers behind the nurse. Jack is the first person that springs to mind, but he must be busy with Harry Blake and the investigation. Sure enough, it's not Ellis that's sheepishly standing, waiting.

The nurse leaves Lucy and speaks briefly to the man as she passes. He's in uniform, with the scruffy look standard of all police dog handlers.

'Well, well,' she says. 'Pete Nash. What are you doing here?'

'A little birdie told me you were being discharged today.' He appraises her face with a wince. 'That looks painful.'

'It is.' She swings her legs out of bed and looks down at her socked feet. The effort of bending makes her woozy. 'Could you help me put my trainers on?'

Fran has been in briefly to visit, bringing a change of clothes and pyjamas. Nash crouches on the floor, undoing the laces on her Converse and gently taking her foot.

'I wanted to thank you,' Lucy says. 'You and Dax. For finding me so quickly.'

Nash looks up. 'All Dax. I was just the dope on the end of the rope.'

'Well, give him a juicy steak on me. I hate to think what… What he might have done.'

Any recollection of what happened in the woods still makes Lucy shiver. She's always thought of herself as unstoppable, able to disarm a suspect within moments with a figure-four leglock or a gooseneck restraint. But in those woods, she was weak. Cuffed and defenceless.

'I will,' Nash replies. 'He'll love you forever.'

Nash smiles and for a moment, looking into his deep brown eyes, that fear melts away. The nurse is right: he really is hot.

'How's Moss?' she asks.

'He's with me. Having a lovely time with Pepper. So no rush to take him home. I know he's a handful.'

'He is,' Lucy replies, feeling a wave of relief that her dog is safe and happy.

Shoes done, Lucy attempts to stand up; she wobbles and Nash rushes to help her. 'I'm fine,' she protests, but she appreciates his solid stance as he offers his arm.

'Let's take it slowly.'

He shoulders her bag and they walk together towards the exit. Lucy finds herself gaining strength with every step towards freedom.

'I was going to ask you, before all this happened...' Nash begins. He seems hesitant. Unlike him. 'You've worked wonders with Moss on his training. I was hoping you'd show me a few tips for Pepper.'

Lucy looks up, astonished. 'The great Pete Nash, asking me for advice?'

He grins. 'Don't tease. Dax and I – we're sorted. But specialist search dogs are new to me. And then, maybe...' That lack of confidence again. Lucy's curious. 'Maybe we could go for a drink, after.'

Lucy can't stop her smile, despite the pain it creates. 'I'd like that, yes.'

'Good.'

Lucy senses him stand straighter; the old Nash is back. 'Tell me the gossip,' she says, before the silence gets awkward. They're in the car park now and Lucy relishes the sun on her face after the artificial lights inside the hospital. 'What's going on with Blake?'

'DCI Perry interviewed him yesterday. He lawyered up, some posh city lad, double-barrelled surname, you know the type. On payroll from the OCG, I'm guessing. They didn't get any more than "no comment".'

'That was expected.'

'Yes, but rumour has it that Blake has got more to say. Requested Ellis specifically. And no solicitor this time.' He glances at his watch. 'Should be about now.'

The familiar buzz resurfaces. The thrill of the chase. 'What are we waiting for, then?'

'Lucy, you've just been released from hospital. We can't possibly—'

'We bloody can.' She stops in her tracks and Nash must see the resolution in her one good eye. He sighs.

'Come on, then,' he says, opening the car door. 'But I'll be getting you a chair.'

Chapter Sixty-Five

Here they are. Jack faces Blake for the first time since the woods – now alone in interview room one.

Blake glances nervously up to the cameras, then to the whirring tape.

'Who's listening?'

Jack shrugs, nonchalantly. 'Who are you afraid of, Harry?'

Blake glares. 'You would be scared too, if you had any sense. You were lucky all they did was threaten.'

'Who?'

Blake shakes his head furiously. 'No, that's not how this is going to work. I need something in return. I need to be safe.'

Jack sits back. He knew this was coming.

The request came in twenty-two hours into Blake's time in custody. Jack had been watching the interviews – interest coupled with boredom. Debating an extension to the period of detention but knowing that the solicitor wasn't going to let Blake give anything away. They had all they needed. They'd charge him, let the courts decide.

As it was, the custody clock had a delayed start because of Blake's trip to hospital. His protestations of police brutality and savage dogs met with eye rolls and barely concealed amusement.

But as the threat of a prison cell loomed closer, Blake obviously had second thoughts.

'Tell us what you know,' Jack says now. 'And we'll determine what it's worth.'

'No way. Witness protection. Confirm that first.'

Jack almost laughs. 'You have nothing to bargain with here. We have you. Your second phone number is all over the victims' phone records. Daisy Kane is safe and well – found thanks to a location pinged from a burner phone. A number taken from the intact SIM card you tried to destroy. You couldn't even get that right.

'We have the baseball bat – recovered from the same place where we found Daisy. Your prints are all over it, as well as blood from both Vanessa Savage and David Carter. The gun you had on you – that's been connected to a number of crimes around the city, all linked to the OCG. And…' Jack sits forward, ready to play his trump card. 'Vincent Carter has handed himself in. When he heard we had you in custody, he headed straight here. He's told us all about you and Mark Savage. How it was Mark at the beginning, then you taking over in February. How you threatened him, personally. Passing on the instructions from the OCG. Where to take the drugs and the cash he took from stores. He kept a record, can you believe that? Meticulous, even when he was breaking the law. What was taken and when.' Jack pauses. 'So what can you offer us?'

'I'll give you the OCG. The Wise Monkeys. Aron and Roan Dushku. I'll tell you everything.'

Blake is sweating. A fine sheen across his forehead, damp patches under his arms. He's signing his death warrant, but without protection he won't last a moment in the main residence of a prison.

'We can offer you the VP wing—'

'I want more than VP!' Blake shouts. 'I want seg.'

Full segregation – essentially solitary. The VP wing, for vulnerable prisoners – the sex offenders, the paedophiles – would be too much of a risk. Being an ex-cop, let alone one who's ratted on an OCG, is enough to render him a target.

Jack gives the impression he's thinking about it. He's spoken to DCI Dawson already; they knew they'd come to this.

'Fine,' Jack says after a moment. 'Talk.'

He tells Jack everything. How he communicated with the OCG, his contacts. Times, places, names. Drugs, cash, the money made on the street. His contact in IT, who gave him access to Mark Savage's email account, who wiped the laptop. The safe houses, the squats. Jack imagines DCI Dawson watching on the monitor, putting plans in place to raid every single one.

'Dushku wanted me to prove myself,' Blake's saying. 'To show I had the guts to do what was needed to take Savage out of play. I wanted to be their inside man. The one they needed.'

'This was all about power?' Jack says. 'Being in charge?'

Blake leans across the table. 'I was important,' he says. 'I was somebody. And I fucking loved it. Savage thought his wife was alive, and while we had her, he'd do whatever I wanted. The reality was she was dead within twenty-four hours of being dragged into that squat.'

'You killed Vanessa?'

'I did her a mercy. Those men, they were animals—'

'And you're any better?' Jack spits.

He's been calm up to now, but he's read Lucy's statement. That Blake raped her when he was an officer in her team. He can't stop the rage coursing in his muscles, making them tense and twitch.

'I'm no Aron Dushku,' Blake replies. 'Or his brother. I was at the squat when they brought Nico Halliday in. Early days, but I heard them. Laughing, jeering, as they kicked the shit out of him. Two hours with them and he was barely conscious, a fucked-up mess. I was with him as he died. Recognised me – could tell I was police, although he knew I couldn't save him. He was lucky it ended when it did.'

'They punctured his lung! He died in pain and fear, and all you did was stand by and watch. You should have called the police. An ambulance. You were a detective!'

'So what?' Blake sneers. 'We do this job and we get nothing. The public hate us. We get paid fuck all. Look at you. You drive a ten-year-old shitheap with broken air conditioning. No family. No friends. I wanted more. I had more.'

'And where has that got you now?'

Blake's right, but from where Jack's sitting, he'd rather have his own life. On dark nights, the loneliness eats at him from the inside, but he enjoys his job. And if that means some days his only pleasure comes from drinking a cup of tea as the sun comes up, watching the starlings flutter around his feeder, then so be it.

He gets to his feet. Blake looks up at him, astonished.

'I have more to say,' Blake protests. 'We can talk. We can make a deal.'

'What?' Jack snaps. 'What else could be so important?'

'Nico Halliday. He told me something as he died. Something you want to hear.'

Jack exhales slowly, controlling his annoyance. It's another pathetic attempt to get attention but he'd be stupid not to hear him out.

Jack sits back down at the table. 'Go on, then. This better be good.'

'He was dying. Gasping for breath. I couldn't make it all out—'

'Get on with it, Blake.'

'He mentioned Lucy. Said that she needed to know. What happened to her sister.'

She doesn't have a sister, Jack's brain spits back, remembering his conversation with Lucy in the car on the way to find Nico's camper van. Instead, he says, 'You're sure he said sister?'

'He was adamant.'

'And what did happen to her?'

'Nico didn't say. But it obviously bothered him. Enough that he had to tell me, even though that put him through a huge

326

amount of pain. It's important, right? You can do something for me now? Please?'

'All you've told me is that a dying man – a man *you* had a part in killing – was delirious and thinking about his wife. It's hardly a momentous revelation.' Jack reaches down to the tape. 'Interview concluded, fifteen thirty-three.' And he switches it off.

He walks out of the interview room, Blake protesting behind him as he closes the door decisively. He's surprised to find Lucy in the corridor.

'Oh, shit. Your face,' he says without thinking. She barely looks like herself, swollen and distorted. But he's relieved to see her up and about, when she looked so awful yesterday.

'Yeah, I know,' she says, dismissing him.

'How much of that did you hear?'

'Most of it. I left when he started talking about Nico. I couldn't bear it. Imagining Nico there... so scared...'

Her shoulders sag and he gently touches her arm. 'I'm sorry,' he says, but his mind is whirring. Lucy didn't hear the end of the interview: Blake disclosing Nico's final words. He'd played it down in front of Blake but what he said niggles. Was it the ranting of a confused dying man or was there something in it? Does Lucy have a sister she's not aware of? And if so, what did Nico know?

Before he can come to any conclusions, Lucy interrupts his thoughts. 'Don't agree to what he wants. Blake. Don't give in.'

'He'd go into seg anyway, Lucy. We're not granting him any special favours.'

'But... But he can't win.'

Jack guides her to the edge of the corridor, sitting her down on a chair. He crouches in front of her.

'He's not going to win. He's confessed to three murders, as well as being a key player in organised crime. Any judge will come down on him like a ton of bricks – he won't come out in his lifetime.'

She bows her head. He's exhausted, but Lucy has the pain of her injuries and the grief for her husband as well as the events of the past week. He can't pile any more on top of that. Not today. He reaches up, and gently squeezes her arm; she lifts her head and looks at him, a half-squint out of her one good eye.

'Go home, Lucy,' he says, softly. 'Go to bed.'

She nods, once, slowly. 'Yes,' she replies. 'I think I will.'

Chapter Sixty-Six

Pete Nash had driven Lucy home, walked her to her door. She reluctantly agreed for him to keep Moss – as much as she wants the comfort from her dog, she is in no fit state to keep a high-energy spaniel exercised and entertained.

She barely made it up the stairs before she collapsed into her bed, pulling the duvet over her and falling into a long, deep sleep.

When she wakes, the world has dimmed and her face throbs. Her curtains are open and she peers out to the darkened sky, listening to the cars below and the chatter of people in their gardens, enjoying the beautiful June weather. But also another noise – from inside her house. The clatter of plates being put away, a hum under someone's breath, footsteps up the stairs.

Her bedroom door opens; the triangle of light widens to show a figure.

'Fran?'

'You're awake! How are you feeling?' Fran's voice is artificially light.

'Awful. How did you get in?'

'You gave me a spare key, remember? Wait, I'll get you some painkillers.'

Lucy heaves herself to a sitting position, closing her eyes for a moment to let the dizziness subside. Fran reappears – a box in one hand and a glass of water in the other.

'Here, let me.'

With Fran's help, Lucy gets settled against the pillows and gratefully downs the drugs.

'What are you doing here?' she mumbles, trying to avoid opening her mouth and splitting the cut on her lip. She reaches a tentative hand to her face and probes gently, receiving a cacophony of stings and aches for her trouble.

'Leave it alone,' Fran scolds. 'I thought you could do with some looking after.'

Lucy starts to protest, but she's stuck. She can't phone her father – all the way up in Newcastle – not that he would come. If she called, he'd merely share a lecture on the dangers of Lucy working in the 'man's world' of policing. But nor does she have the strength to look after herself.

And she's hated being so distant from Fran this past week, hated their argument.

As if reading her mind, Fran says, 'I'm sorry I didn't believe you about Nico. I should have supported you. Should have told you what he'd asked me.'

'You didn't know,' Lucy mutters, feeling tears threaten. 'You were only trying to protect me.'

'I was. But that's no excuse. Will you forgive me?'

'Of course.' Lucy tries her best to smile. 'But only if you keep the painkillers coming.'

'Every four hours. No more, no less. I'll stay here with you, I promise.'

The thought of Fran being there brings her sudden relief. She leans back and half-closes her eyes. 'What about Mike and the kids?'

Fran scoffs. 'They'll be fine. Do you want something to eat?'

'Not yet. I would like some company, though.'

'Done.' Fran scoots onto the other side of the bed, lying back on the pillows with a sigh. 'Jack called. He asked after you. He's a good bloke.' She gives Lucy a sneaky side-eye.

'He is. And no. There isn't.'

'I didn't say a word!'

'You thought it.' Lucy pauses. 'Nash asked me out.'

'Pete Nash?' Fran turns so she's facing Lucy, a grin plastered across her face. 'What did you say? Sod Mike – I would.'

Lucy smiles, despite herself. 'I said yes. But Fran, is that awful? Nico's barely a week out of the ground. We haven't even had his funeral.'

'He's been missing for nearly two years. And I hate to say it, but your relationship was hardly perfect.'

'I loved him.'

'I know you did.' Fran reaches over and takes her hand, giving it a motherly pat. 'Take your time. Do whatever feels right. But… Pete Nash.' Fran gives a low whistle.

'I know, right?'

'Would the dogs watch?' Fran says, then peals with laughter.

'Fuck off!' But the thought of shagging Nash makes her face flush and stirs something in her she hasn't felt for a long time. Fran is creased in hysterics and maybe it's the painkillers, or maybe it's the fact they've found Nico and have his killer behind bars, but Lucy can't help giggling. As much as it makes her face hurt.

And there's that flare of optimism again. A peculiar glow. Sat in bed, in her own house, as the night fades to darkness, laughing with her best friend about shagging a hot guy.

This is new. It's normal. And Lucy likes it.

Chapter Sixty-Seven

Harry Blake paces the cell. The walls close in, suffocating, but at least he is alone. Nobody can get to him here.

He feels every set of eyes on him. By talking to Ellis he has signed his own death warrant, but at least here he is in with a chance; in the main residential there was no knowing what would happen. Razor blades, smuggled shanks, faeces in his food.

His solicitor says that with a sympathetic judge he might avoid a whole life tariff and be out in thirty. The thought alone makes his heart pound. Year after year, in this cell. How will he survive?

There's a bang on the door, a fist thumped against metal.

'It's time,' the guard shouts.

He has a specially allocated slot. Alone. He grabs his towel and soap, waits for the door to be unlocked, then follows the guard down to the shower block.

He's embarrassed as he strips off, quickly discarding his grey tracksuit and boxers, hunched and cowering under the guard's gaze.

'Can't you at least turn around?' he snaps.

The guard rolls his eyes. 'Suit yourself,' he says, and folds his arms across his chest, turning his back to Harry.

Harry presses the shower on; the water is lukewarm but it's good to be clean. He can pretend his life is normal. That he's at home and it's polished ceramic under his feet, rather than verrucas and skin cells and someone else's pubes. He turns his face to the shower, closing his eyes and running his hands through his hair.

At first, it's a sharp ache. A stitch, maybe, as if he's been running. He takes a sudden breath and the pain flares; he gulps air; he looks down to the hole in his side. Blue tiles, water and soapsuds tinged red.

Hot breath whispers on his neck. 'You thought you could hide,' the voice hisses. 'You thought we couldn't get to you. You were wrong.'

'Please,' Harry tries, but he has no oxygen in his lungs as a red-hot jab pierces his back. He loses strength, he drops to his knees. He tries to shout for help but the only person he can see is the guard, solid shoulders facing away from Harry.

The tiles are cold, slippery. His legs fold under him. A face looms in his eyeline. Blurred. Nameless, shapeless. His eyes slowly focus. Something held close. A knife. Glinting in the overhead lights.

'See no evil, speak no evil, hear no evil,' the voice says. The blade looms over his right eye; rough fingers prise his lid open.

Harry pleads that his murder will be quick.

But in death, like in life, his prayers remain unanswered.

One Week Later

Thursday

Epilogue

Lucy slowly replaces her mobile in her pocket, face down. She keeps her hand there for a moment, thinking. She knew this day would come, and now it has, she wonders if she wants it.

At last, she can see the end.

She is free.

She is sat on a wooden bench in Hythe, overlooking Southampton Water. The Isle of Wight ferry cruises past in the distance; next to her, seagulls perch, a respectful distance away, eyeing her lunch. She has bought chips, soaked in salt and vinegar and ketchup, and walked along to the promenade, here. In the last week her face has healed – she has two functioning eyes; bruises have turned to dirty green and yellow – but she still gets looks of curiosity and kindness and pity. None of which she wants.

Moss is back with her. He rests at her feet, in the shade of the bench, occasionally looking up, hopeful. She repays his patience with a chip; he gobbles it in a nanosecond.

She tries not to think about the phone call, and silently makes resolutions about the things she is sure about. The boxes, at home. Tonight, she will empty those. Unpack properly. She will go to the supermarket. Buy bread, and eggs, and milk. Invite Fran and Mike around for dinner, to make up for those blurry days and nights when Fran made soup, brought painkillers and watched endless hours of *The Last of Us*, debating the merits of Pedro Pascal.

She hears footsteps and turns. Jack Ellis, walking towards her. Black jacket, white shirt, light blue tie; as he gets closer, he straightens the knot. She smiles at that; always so proper. Even in twenty-five-degree heat. His only concession to the weather is his sunglasses. He takes them off now, resting them in his hair.

'You learning how to surf?' he says, gesturing to her colourful shorts, T-shirt and flip-flops.

'You been to a funeral?'

'How's the face?'

Lucy reaches up gingerly. 'Healing,' she replies. 'But could have been worse, if it hadn't been for you.'

'Nash and Dax. Not me.'

'How did you find me today?'

'Fran. Can I join you?'

It feels like bad news, his tone flat. She squints up at him and nods. He sits down, removing his jacket and loosening his tie.

'What's happened?'

'It's Harry Blake.' He pauses, long enough for her to realise. 'He's dead.'

'Murdered. Someone got to him. In the showers. Cut out his eye, split his tongue. Then pushed the knife through his ear into his brain.'

Lucy winces. 'The Wise Monkeys.'

'Looks that way. But I spoke to the CPS. His testimony stands. His interview was recorded, and they're happy it wasn't taken under duress. It's enough. We've already arrested both Aron Dushku and his brother. And added the charge of that waste-ground murder in 2021 to the list. There will be more. Perry and Dawson are confident they can take down the whole group.'

The news doesn't feel as Lucy expected. It's retribution, justice, but someone will take their place. More gangs, more drugs. The everlasting cycle. But it's something.

'I'm pleased. Thank you. You'll give the exclusive to Cal?'

Jack smiles. 'He's already been in touch.'

'What happened to Kane?' she asks. 'And Daisy?'

'Daisy's fine. Physically, anyway. Dehydration, hunger. She's out of hospital. Dawson says that if it wasn't for the guy that was looking after her, she would have been killed. He smuggled her out just at the right time. Hid her. Kept her safe.'

'Why?'

'We might never know. Maybe he liked her. Maybe he was sick of what the gang were doing. Who can say. He's in custody and not talking, but the main thing is she's fine.' He stops and frowns. 'Or as fine as she can be with her mother in prison. Kane's admitted to perverting the course of justice and participating in activities of an organised crime group.'

'Not conspiracy to murder?'

'The CPS considered it too hard to prove. She maintains she didn't know what was going to happen to Nico.'

'That's bollocks and you know it.'

'But we have no evidence otherwise. This is enough. Her life is over.'

'And how are the team? How is Amrit after her fake arrest?'

Jack laughs. 'She's fine. Enjoying her brief period of notoriety. It's helped her come out of her shell, I think. She's been talking about why she moved down from Manchester. Bad break-up, apparently. And Phil... He's separated from his wife, but hopefully he'll be okay.'

Then he pauses. He's bashful; it's obvious he has more to share.

'Spit it out,' she says.

'I was pulled in to speak to the chief constable today. With Kane gone, and... well...'

'They've appointed you detective chief inspector.'

Jack nods, almost embarrassed.

'Congratulations. You'll take it?'

'I think so. Only temporary, at the moment. But hopefully they'll make it permanent.'

'They should. The constabulary needs you. Capable hands. Someone they can trust.'

'That's what they said. But… look… I have no team. With Blake gone, I need to recruit. I want you to come back.'

'Back? To MCIT?'

'I'll reinstate you. DS at first, but it won't take long for you to get back up to DI. Your old rank. Your old job. You're a brilliant murder detective, this case is proof. Don't you miss it?'

Lucy frowns, looking out to the water and the city of Southampton on the other side. She's restless, been cooped up in the house for too long. 'Can we walk?'

The two of them stand and start towards the old pier. There's a fresh wind blowing, but the sun is bright. Lucy walks quickly, Moss pulling ahead. He darts this way and that, following the smells on the seagull-shit spattered boardwalk, Jack keeping up with long steps. Before long, he has discarded his tie and rolled up his shirtsleeves, his jacket draped over his arm. They walk in silence; Lucy lets the quiet soothe her.

For almost two years, all she's wished for is resolution on Nico's death, and to return to her old job. But now it's here, she's unsure.

'What happened with Sophie?' she asks.

Jack looks at her quickly.

'I saw her. Assumed it was, anyway. A woman came to your house the other week. As I left. You seemed… familiar.'

'Can't keep anything from you,' he mutters. Then, 'It's nothing.'

'It didn't look like nothing.'

He thinks for a moment; Lucy waits, hoping he'll open up again. After a moment he gives a long sigh.

'It was just like old times.'

Lucy glances up with a cheeky grin. He rolls his eyes. 'Yes, that. And we've been in touch since, but…' He trails off. 'The problems are still there. I'm here when Theo isn't. I was the last person to see him alive. There was always a weight. Of expectation. That I might remember something important and they could find Theo. I was a constant failure to my parents. I can't live with being a failure to her, too.'

He shrugs, feigning indifference, but Lucy can tell there's sadness and disappointment – a whole lot of mess wrapped up in that relationship. She knows what that's like.

'I felt that way with Nico. That everything that was happening was so fundamentally wrong, I would never be able to put it right. I'm not saying Sophie was abusive,' she adds quickly. 'But the way she makes you feel. That damage. It's not healthy.'

'It's not her fault.'

'Do you think you'll ever find out what happened to Theo?'

'No.' Jack says it quickly. A long-held belief, one contemplated at length. 'Not now.' He glances down to Lucy. 'It's been nearly thirty years. How many misper investigations do you know resolved after that time?' He doesn't wait for an answer. 'None. The case is cold. No one's looking. Our only hope is that whoever took him confesses, maybe on their deathbed. Or a house is demolished and his body is found.'

'He might be alive?' Lucy suggests, warily.

'He's not.'

Jack says it with such force and bitterness that Lucy lets it go. They've reached the pier now and they walk on worn, grey boards, the names of the dead and the noted stamped into the planks. To their right, the funny little narrow-gauge train chunters past, delivering the few passengers to the ferry at the end. Lucy lets Moss walk on a loose lead. He trots happily beside her, occasionally rushing at the gulls for the sheer fun of it, his ears flapping. The birds launch into the air with disgusted shrieks; Lucy relishes the smell of salt and seaweed, and the suncream mixing with the sweat on her skin.

She thinks about Theo. She endured the uncertainty of Nico's disappearance for almost two years – what must it be like for thirty? And a curiosity twitches. Forensics have advanced in that time. Suspects arrested, DNA on file. What might they have found then that could answer the question now?

But she senses the conversation is over.

She reaches into her bag and pulls out a book. It's a copy of *On the Road* by Jack Kerouac. She hands it to Jack.

'It was always his favourite. He carried it everywhere.' She reaches across and pulls out a piece of paper. A bookmark? Or just somewhere it was kept. It has a list of times and places.

'AA meetings,' she explains. 'And the number on the bottom? That's the helpline for Respect – for domestic abuse perpetrators.'

He stops and looks at her. 'He was trying to get help?'

'I don't know for sure. I'd like to think so. That some part of him knew what he was doing was wrong and wanted to stop.' Her voice chokes. 'That some part of him loved me.'

'He wanted to love you, Lucy. He just didn't know how.'

She swallows. 'Maybe.' And then she blurts it out. The news she's been so hesitant to share. 'I had a phone call. A moment before you showed up.' She feels Jack glance at her. 'From my skipper. He says they've found a general purpose dog for me. A German shepherd. Called Iggy.'

Just saying his name makes a bubble of excitement grow in her stomach. 'There's no guarantees,' she continues. 'We could start training and he could be unsuitable for any number of reasons. Too sociable, no nose for scent, too aggressive, no bite. But...'

'But he could be perfect,' Jack finishes. She nods. 'And if you take him, that secures your position with the dog unit?'

'Yes. Thirteen weeks of training and that'll be me, done. A two-dog man. Or woman. A proper police dog handler.'

Jack stops. He watches the seagulls. One particularly massive bird has purloined a crisp from a discarded packet and is fighting with another to keep possession. Fluttering wings, annoyed squawks. Jack takes a step towards them and they stop, watching him with beady eyes.

'Do you know why I like birds?' he says. 'Why I like watching them?'

Lucy resists the urge to make a joke. 'No?'

'Because of the dinosaurs.' He points at the seagull. 'That's 150 million years' worth of evolution, right there. Evolved from a group of meat-eaters, called theropods. You look into those eyes and you see the dinosaurs.'

Lucy's struggling to see what Jack's getting at.

'Dinosaurs were the first thing that bonded Theo and me. And small boys – the ones that get the opportunity to grow up – they don't change.' He picks up an errant stone from his feet and hurls it over the railings into the waves. 'We're taught to push away the things we love for more grown-up concerns. I chase different predators now, but I try not to forget where it all began. With Theo.'

He turns to Lucy for the first time. 'We all change, Lucy. We evolve. Dinosaurs become seagulls. Small boys become murder detectives. The you who married Nico, who allowed herself to be treated… like that. You're not her anymore.' He points to Moss, who's panting. 'And for better or for worse, you love that. That disgusting animal.'

Moss recognises he's being talked about and bounds up to Jack, placing mucky paws on his smart trousers. But for the first time, Jack doesn't push him away. Just bends down and ruffles his ears.

'Your family,' he says, without looking at her. 'Your dad. He lives in Newcastle, right?'

Lucy's puzzled as to where this is going, but replies, 'Yes. With my half-brothers.'

'And your mum? Any other siblings?'

'Gone. And no, why?'

'Me neither.' He pauses. 'I always wanted a brother. Theo was the closest thing I had to that.'

She senses he has something else to say but he shakes his head, more to himself than her.

'You seem happy,' he says.

'I am.' And to her surprise, she realises that's true.

Jack smiles. 'You've evolved. I know it, Moss knows it. Phone me tonight if you want the job.' He starts walking, then looks back. 'I won't be expecting your call.'

Lucy watches him stride away. When she first met him, she would have never expected he could have led her here. Jack Ellis. That uptight, closed-off, stick-up-the-arse detective.

Her friend.

She crouches down to her dog's level and rumples his ears. Moss pushes his head against her hand, eyes half-closed, enjoying the love. She laughs; her anxiety lifts.

Moss doesn't ask for much. Food, his kennel, a tennis ball. And a job he loves. A game, not even work to Moss. If she takes this job, she will spend her day playing. Getting soaked in the rain. Being pulled through brambles, puddles, up hills, across concrete. Following her dogs.

And giving closure to victims. With Moss, she will bring the bodies home. And with Iggy, she'll be catching the perpetrators mere hours after the crime has been committed. What could be better than that?

Still watching Moss, she takes her phone out of her pocket. She dials.

'Sarge,' she says, the moment he answers. 'I'll take that dog.'

Acknowledgements

In 2021, a year after my mum was diagnosed with breast cancer for the second time, I decided to get a dog. Mum was a key facilitator in this decision, even placing an ad in a local newsagent and passing on a call from someone who had an eight-week-old black cocker-sprocker spaniel going spare in a recent litter. Who can say no to that? And so Max arrived.

Max was a puppy that didn't sleep, didn't stop, howled, whined, chewed, and generally turned my life on its head. And Mum was at the end of the phone with guidance and reassurance every step of the way. She was right, as she usually was: that crazy spaniel grew up into a lovely dog. Still insane, still an absolute dick, but a loyal and affectionate companion – my fluffy black shadow. With a want to sniff, and find, everything. (Sorry, rabbits…)

Of course, Max became Moss, and my mum would have got such a kick out of reading him (and Dax) on the page. My only hope is I've done her proud.

–

First off, a huge thank you must go to Paul Sainsbury. Before I embarked on this book, I knew nothing about police dog handling, and books and YouTube videos can only get you so far. Paul has generously taken the time to tell me all about his chosen profession; I am in awe of the work he and his colleagues do, and I will be forever grateful.

Paul is far from being the only expert to help me on this book. Thank you, as ever, to PC Dan Roberts and Charlie

Roberts, for their help on day-to-day policing; to Dr Matt Evans for red-penning my hideous attempts at medical terminology; to Paul Shutler for help with the PolSA scenes; and to Susan Scarr for everything pharmaceutical.

As always, all mistakes, deliberate or otherwise, are mine and mine alone.

Now to the publishing side.

Thank you to the amazing team at Canelo Crime – to Louise Cullen, Katy Loftus, Alicia Pountney, Nicola Piggott, Iain Millar and Kate Shepherd. This is my sixth book with Canelo, and I have loved every minute.

Thank you to my magnificent agent, Ed Wilson, for getting excited when I pitched a book about police dog handlers, and to Anna Dawson, Hélène Butler and the rest of the team at Johnson and Alcock.

Thank you to Miranda Ward for the structural edits, Daniela Nava for the copyedit (and gifs!), and to Vicki Vrint for the proofread. The book is massively improved as a result of your diligence and eagle-eyes.

Thank you to all of the Criminal Minds group for keeping me company on many a lonely writing day at my desk. So, to Dom, Barry, Jo, Rachael, Heather, Tim, Fliss, Niki, Victoria, Kate, Barry, Simon, Adam, Elle, Polly, Clare, Liz, Rob and Susie – pincers up, my friends.

Last but not least, thank you to my family: to Chris and Ben, Dad, Susan and Jon, and Tom and Mel.

And, of course, thank you to Max. Who is unaware of all this fuss and is currently fast asleep, in his normal spot, by my side.

© CANELOCRIME

Do you love crime fiction and are always on the lookout for brilliant authors?

Canelo Crime is home to some of the most exciting novels around. Thousands of readers are already enjoying our compulsive stories. Are you ready to find your new favourite writer?

Find out more and sign up to our newsletter at canelocrime.com